The Choice Between Safe and Brave

A Teapot Cottage Novel (#6)

by

Annie Cook

www.Anniecookwriter.com

About The Author

www.anniecookwriter.com

Annie Cook is a writer of women's contemporary fiction, and literary fiction. This is her sixth novel in the Teapot Cottage Series. She has also written a number of 'filler' novels as stand-alone works that link by adding different dimensions to some of the characters in the TC series. Annie is also a podcaster and guide to women who want to tell their own stories. She is originally from New Zealand but divides her time between the UK and her home in Southern Italy.

www.Anniecookwriter.com

Other Novels by Annie Cook:

THE TEAPOT COTTAGE SERIES

No Small Change (#1)
The Power of Notes and Spells (#2)
When It's Meant to Happen (#3)
Ruin Reins and Redemption (#4)
The Stuff You Fail to Notice (#5)

~ * ~

A Moral Swerve
Thicker Than Water

~ * ~

*This book is dedicated to my beautiful
friend and mentor, Annah Stretton.*

*As a hugely successful woman on every level,
you taught me that my limitations were never as
big as I once believed them to be,
and you encouraged me to be
braver than I'd ever been before.
Thank you.*

Acknowledgements

Books come to life when ideas start forming, and are transferred to written words, then supplemented with researched information that makes the narrative realistic and relevant to the reader. Several people have supported my work with this novel. Huge thanks go to:

Kerry Purvis, my biggest champion, best friend, and husband of 28 years; I would have died of dehydration, starvation, and sleep deprivation, if you weren't here during all the times when I got so busy that I literally forgot my own human needs. I couldn't do any of the stuff I do without your support.

Barbara Schiavulli, War Journalist and Writer, and winner of numerous national and international awards; beautiful lady, thank you for sharing some of your story with me, and inspiring me to write 'Tezzie Bostock' to be as brave and fearless as you are yourself. You have such courage, grit, and determination, to bring the plight of war-torn people and places to the world's attention. It is a wonderful thing, that you do.

Fiona Powley, Leadership Coach and Facilitator at Bristol Child Free Women, for the loveliest, candid conversation about the different challenges (and sometimes painful prejudices) faced by women of all ages who have elected not to have children. You gave me plenty to think and write about!

Sarah Day at One Day Film Productions, thank you for telling me about your own personal 'bootstrap' journey to become a videographer. You inspired me to make it possible for one of my characters to do the same.

Colin Fraser at Swoop Antarctica; you shared some lovely little gold nuggets that have helped me bring 'Chris Darcy's' long-held dream to life. His journey to the ice and its extreme peaks will be even richer, because of it.

The gorgeous shiny diamonds in my life; Yvonne Raymond, Katherine McDiarmid, Dawn Walter, Keren Cook, Laura Toop, Jean and Trevor Jones, and Heather Barrie; thank you for your unfailing support, frontline cheering and promoting.

Aisha Jamil, my Graphic Designer; for the cover of this book, which I do think is the loveliest yet!

Gwen Morrison and the team at PublishNation; thanks for all the work you so calmly and professionally do, in making this book accessible.

To my fans and readers across the world; thank you so very, very much for being in my corner. It's all done especially for you, with as much heart, vision and inspiration as I can muster, so I hope you'll all enjoy it.

Chapter One

Chris abruptly stopped his van about a hundred yards up the driveway to Ravensdown Farm, and switched off the engine. He sat behind the wheel, staring almost blankly at Teapot Cottage. It looked the same as he remembered, from when he and Daisy had come here last year. The carefully cultivated potted yellow rose bushes that flanked its wide front door were bigger now, at least a couple of feet taller. It was early spring again, and they were probably a month away at best, from blooming. The buds were evident, but he'd be gone again well before they opened.

During their previous visit, every time they'd come back from a walk or a drive down to the town, one of them had always remarked how Teapot Cottage seemed to be smiling, and inviting them back. It was an incredibly welcoming little house; a lovely, gentle place to stay. For the entire fortnight they'd stayed here, it had been all either of them could ever do, to tear themselves away from the sumptuous window seats that offered the most stunning view of Torley Valley, through the multi-paned living room windows. They'd sit for hours, just drinking it in.

The cottage was a far cry from their poky little rented flat in Derby. The view from the living room window of that just showed the opposite neighbour's unkempt, half-dead lawn, complete with an abandoned, gently rusting tricycle in the front left corner. With its missing rear right wheel, it looked lopsided and forlorn. Daisy always said the tenants probably left it there hoping the scrap metal merchants, who routinely cruised their housing estate on the lookout for opportune finds, would take it. Chris suspected they'd already checked it out and decided it wasn't worth the effort. Even scrappies had limits to what they'd drag away.

And here he was, once again contemplating Teapot Cottage's welcoming frontage, only this time without Daisy. Never again would he come here with Daisy, in fact never again would he do anything at *all*, with Daisy. She was gone, and he only had himself to blame.

He lapsed into deep thought again, as he so often did, these days. Was he even doing the right thing by coming back here? Was this particularly poignant part of his self-appointed pilgrimage a step too far? Should he be putting himself through this? They'd been ridiculously happy on holiday here last year, in this beautiful space, well off the beaten tourist track. They'd relished the chance to breathe, sleep, eat, walk and simply be together, with no outside pressures crowding in.

They'd both been so busy in the months before they'd taken that break. Chris had been working more than fifty hours a week in his job as an electrician, and Daisy was an overstretched care worker, wiping bums and mopping dribble for a living.

She'd loved her job though, even when the gruelling shiftwork hours occasionally got her down. She'd adored every single one of the people she cared for at Poppies Nursing Home, a dedicated facility exclusively for ex-military people and their partners. She seldom said no to an extra shift, because they were always so short-handed. She'd often work to the point where she was on her knees with exhaustion, but then the phone would ring, and they'd want her back in, and she'd somehow find the energy to keep going. There was no off-button with Daisy, when it came to work. She kept going and going and going, like the Duracell bunny.

That's what he'd called her. Duracell Daisy, or Dee-Dee for short, and every time he did, she would laugh.

Tears pricked his eyes now and he blinked hard, as the memories came rushing back in a wave he couldn't stop. It was tougher than he'd expected, to be here without her. A growing part of him wanted to throw the van into reverse and hightail it back down to the main road, drive away as fast as he could, and never look back.

But that wasn't what he'd promised himself. From the moment Daisy left his life, he'd vowed to revisit every happy place they'd ever been together, from the church they'd planned to get married in, with its cool, serene interior and its gorgeous carved statues and plinths, to the Greek Island they'd picked for their honeymoon.

He'd gone to Lemnos on his own, done the scuba diving and the water-skiing Daisy had set her heart on trying, and he'd stayed in the resort's honeymoon suite by himself, shrugging off the odd looks he'd got from management when he'd shown up on his own, insisting on still having that room. When the reasons for it somehow became apparent (he didn't know how, since he hadn't offered an explanation himself) their bemusement had turned to reverent support. They never said a word about the circumstances, but they couldn't do enough for him. They even laid on a limousine, at their own expense, to take him back to the airport when it was time for him to go.

Chris' pilgrimages had taken him to all sorts of places, and they'd dragged him through every emotion along the way. The list of locations was surprisingly long. Kitsch cafes, where he and Daisy had laughed at the decor and fed one another cake from their own forks. Watching the wonky Christmas lights getting switched on in town. Train trips to the seaside. Terrifying roller-coaster rides that had made Daisy shriek with fear and joy at the same time as Chris was trying not to heave his guts up. He'd been back and done all of it. He'd watched reruns of the movies they'd laughed and cried at together, and he'd got Misty, the Cocker Spaniel puppy she always said she wanted when they'd finally manage to get themselves out of their poky rented flat and into a decent house.

'Puppy first, and maybe a couple of kittens too, so they can all grow up together,' Daisy had declared. 'I want a coffee-coloured cocker spaniel puppy, and I want to call her Misty. At *least* two cats, called Crackle and Pop – but wait – maybe we'll have to have three, because it's *Snap,* Crackle and Pop, isn't it? The slogan, I mean? So, three then…'

When she'd announced all that, he'd promised her they wouldn't be in the flat for much longer; that they'd buy a house with a decent garden, where she could grow the rockery herb garden she'd dreamed about, where a puppy could run and tumble. He wasn't much of a cat fan himself, but he supposed they could have a couple, if Daisy really wanted them.

But then she'd gone on to mention the 'b' word, as part of her dream for their future, and Chris's stomach had lurched.

He'd always been ambivalent about babies. He liked kids, but he hadn't had a happy upbringing, and he couldn't imagine himself as a father. Admittedly it wouldn't have been hard for him to be a better one than his *own* father had turned out to be (Jack Darcy had been a terrible role model to Chris and his sister Suzanne) but his big passion was extreme mountaineering – and he didn't want to give it up. It carried big risks, in spite of the care he always took, and having kids might compromise how he felt about it.

He was deeply afraid, that such a big change in his life might mean he'd have to turn his back on the biggest passion and fulfilment he'd ever had. He couldn't imagine anything coming close to how it felt to climb a mountain, and stand at the top with the wind in his hair and the majesty of the earth's terrain spread out below him. That intoxicating, overwhelming thrill was as much a part of his DNA as the colour of his hair and skin. It was his lifeblood, pure and simple.

The issue of children had been a tough talk to initiate, but he'd needed to be honest with Daisy. They needed to agree, or at least find a way to compromise, on 'the big stuff' like that – *before* they went ahead and tied the knot. It was something they should have talked about even before they'd got engaged, but they'd felt one another to be their destiny, and it simply hadn't come up. He'd proposed, she'd said yes, and somehow an unspoken assumption had lodged itself; that the 'big stuff' would all fall into place.

Chris knew that to be a bit naïve; that it wouldn't be fair to either of them, to have gone ahead with the marriage without being fully aware of what they both expected for the future. Too many couples did that; they got together without discussing really big issues like personal beliefs, desires, and visions, and whether or not to have children. He didn't want Daisy to end up feeling trapped in a situation she hadn't wanted, but he didn't want that for himself either. He'd seen too many couples fall apart because of wrong assumptions that had ultimately felt like betrayals, because they hadn't been discussed when they should have been.

He'd explained that he didn't want to give up climbing, and he'd reminded her that it took up a lot of his leisure time. She already knew all that, and how much he loved it. She'd already more or less signed up for it when she moved in with him. She didn't want him to give up his passion, but she did want to have at least one child.

They'd discussed their fears and expectations at great length. After they had both thrown their perspectives into the mix, he had eventually decided that if Daisy really wanted to have a baby, he'd go along with it. Her happiness meant everything to him. It was a compromise he decided he was willing to make, albeit with a great deal of fear in his heart.

Daisy had fully understood his reluctance. In what had turned out to be a very big, critical conversation, she came to an important conclusion too. If kids happened, they happened, and if they didn't – if it wasn't on the cards for them – she would find a way of living with it too. She did want kids, but she wasn't the kind of woman who'd end up going crazy if she didn't have them. Daisy Darcy, as she was going to be, would have been happy, no matter what life did or didn't throw at her. She was the quintessential optimist; always focussed on the best of everything. It was just the way she was made.

Chris had considered himself lucky, that she felt that way. If he'd landed with a woman who'd been hell-bent on having a family, he'd have bailed pretty early. Daisy knew that, and because they both reached the conclusion that nothing else in the world mattered more to either of them than each other, they decided they would cope well enough with whatever life did or didn't give them.

Ten months on, from when his life had blown apart and every last dream had been shattered, Chris was still trying to honour the relationship he'd had with Daisy in all the ways he could. He'd done pretty much everything on his list. Coming back here had been one of the last things, and he'd been pleased to be assured that Teapot Cottage did allow dogs, so he could bring Misty with him.

The puppy was wagging her tail now, and making little yippy noises, eager to get out of the van after all these hours, and have a good run around. She could see the fields and was longing to get out to them. Chris reached over, undid the seatbelt harness that held her safe, pulled her to him and snuggled her into his neck. 'Want to stretch your legs, girl? Me too!'

He started the van again and put it into gear, and they slowly made their way to Teapot Cottage. He knew the landlady, Mrs Raven, had put the key under the left rose pot for him but instead of going straight into the house he let Misty have a run around the frontage first. She squatted for a wee, and Chris realised his back was aching and he needed a bathroom stop himself. He let the puppy run full pelt in her silly circles for a couple of minutes then decided to get her indoors. At five months, she was house-trained now although Chris was still leaving newspaper laid out by the back door at night, in case she ever got caught short. He picked her up now, and cuddled her close, and let her nuzzle his neck. They already had a close bond.

Inside, the fire was set, and ready to light, just like last time he was here. He dragged the bags from the back seat of his van and brought them into the house. One had Misty's paraphernalia in it, and the other was his backpack. He hadn't brought much, only underwear and socks, a few t-shirts, and jumpers, one decent shirt, a couple of pairs of jeans and basic toiletries. He was only here for two weeks, if he could even manage that much time. He didn't know yet if staying a full fortnight would help or be unbearable, but only time would tell. The pilgrimages he'd made in Daisy's name had been many and varied, but always with the view to honouring her at her happiest times, in her reality and in her dreams. He could leave early, if it all became too much, but he'd stick it out if he could. It was really all he could do for her now.

In the kitchen, a welcome note sat propped against a bottle of wine on the table. It said there were a few provisions in the fridge, and reminded him about the Farmer's Market in the town, the following morning. He bit his lip, at the memory of that market, and Daisy trying on a silly-looking bubble-gum-pink felt hat with a feather sticking out of the darker pink band, at the side. 'What do you think?' she'd asked him, pulling a cross-eyed face. He'd shaken his head and said no, but Daisy had bought it anyway.

Was that really a whole year ago?

Chris checked the fridge and found Mrs Raven's 'Welcome Pack' of half a dozen free range eggs, a packet of bacon, a dish of tomatoes, a loaf of home-made bread, a small pack each of butter and cheese, a bottle of milk and a bag of ground coffee for the plunger. So that was breakfast sorted, and he figured he could go to the Farmer's Market in the morning, to get a few more things.

He filled the whistling kettle from the kitchen sink and set it on the Aga to boil. A cup of tea felt like a good idea while Misty busied herself with sniffing around and checking out her surroundings. With his tea made, he settled into one of the windows seats and looked out and down into Torley Valley, feeling the most peculiar sense of having come home. It *wasn't* home, and he'd been anxious about how it would feel to come here again. But, from the minute he'd walked through the door, he'd felt like the cottage was embracing him somehow, and holding him close to its heart.

That was weird. He wasn't normally given to such expressions of 'woo-ness' but there was no denying that being here now felt more right than anything else had for the past ten months.

As he sipped his tea, Chris contemplated the future as far as he could see it, which wasn't very far, but he knew he probably wouldn't be able to envisage much, until his pilgrimages were over.

After this visit, there was only one big thing left on his list. It was the most important thing of all, as the one that would finally bring his and Daisy's journey to its full circle and hopefully restore the most vital piece of his own lost soul. Everything else that he'd done was all building up to that final thing. But every time he thought about it, his stomach churned. His thinking simply stalled and wouldn't let him go there.

For ten long months, every fibre of his being had railed against it, but sitting here now, in the gentle peace of Teapot Cottage, he knew he could no longer avoid the inevitable. The final piece of the puzzle, that he'd felt so driven to complete, was pressing at him now.

At some point in the near future, he needed to go back to the mountain.

How do I do that, Daise? How do I go back to the place you never wanted to go at all, that I so selfishly talked you into, because I thought you 'should' have wanted to do what I do, and fall in love with it too? Being in love with me should have been enough. Why did I think it wasn't? Why did I push for more?

Chris felt his stomach go into freefall again, like it did every time he thought about Daisy losing her life on Mulhacén. He wondered when, or if, he would ever get to a place where he could think of her without feeling like the earth was shifting beneath him, that he was falling from a plane without a parachute but never hitting the ground. So many times, he longed for the impact of crashing to the earth, and dying in a shattered heap, just to be free of the torment. As hard as he prayed for it, it never came. Somehow, every time, the sensation would fade again before the mercy of the crash kicked in, condemning him to the endless, savage merry-go-round of emotions he constantly struggled and failed to control.

The impact on his work, of Daisy's untimely and random death, had been huge. Only after three full months of unpaid compassionate leave could he face returning to work. Malcolm, his boss, had been wonderful; understanding and supportive to a fault. But the man had limits to what he could carry, and push had finally come to shove. He'd given the ultimatum they'd both been dreading, and Chris had dragged himself back to his job, to avoid losing it altogether. He hadn't been ready, couldn't imagine *ever* being ready to step back into a world where Daisy would never be again, where he was expected to behave 'normally' and 'get on with his life.'

He was coping, but only just. On some level, he knew he'd eventually be able to live life again like he used to. He just couldn't imagine when it would be, or how his future would look and feel. It probably wouldn't come before he went back to Mulhacén. That much, he *did* know.

A light knock at the back door pulled him out of his thoughts, and he realised that his cup of tea had gone cold in his hands as he'd sat here. Misty, who'd been dozing on a cushion in the other window seat, was awake again and yapping excitedly at the back door, so Chris went to open it. Standing there, as he'd half expected, was his landlady for the fortnight, Adrienne Raven. She smiled generously at him.

'Mr Darcy – can I call you Chris? Welcome back! It's so nice to see you again.'

She bent down and picked up the squirming Misty. 'And who is this delicious little darling?'

Chris gave her a small smile. 'This is Miss Misty Daisy Darcy. She's five months old and has the energy of ten horses.'

Mrs Raven grinned. 'I'll bet she does! She's so adorable, I could eat her!' As Misty licked her face, she laughed out loud. 'Stop it, you little minx! I'll have no lipstick left!'

'One thing you need to know about Misty, Mrs Raven, is that she has no respect for anybody's face. She'll bite your nose if you let her, and lick *all* your makeup off. She's as mad as a box of frogs.'

Mrs Raven set Misty down and laughed again as the spaniel proceeded to run around in circles at her ankles.

'I can see that! But she's totally charming! You know this cottage had a dog very similar to Misty, a few years ago. The owners I bought it from had a cocker like her. His name was Sid. They were Aussies, and they had a close family bereavement, so they all emigrated back there and took Sid and their cat Mittens with them. Siddy and I were great friends. I missed him a lot, after he went.'

She looked around the kitchen, a faint smile playing around her lips. 'Is everything alright in here? Anything else you need? I've stacked plenty of firewood by the back door, for you to feed the fire. You'll need to have it going at night, I think. It might be officially spring, but it's still a bit nippy in the evenings. The central heating works fine, of course, but a fire is cosier on cold nights.'

Chris suddenly remembered his manners. 'Will you stay for a cup of tea, Mrs Raven?'

She nodded gratefully. 'Oh, that's kind of you. Yes, thanks, a very quick one would be lovely. I've been chasing my tail all day, with one thing and another. A two-minute tea break will probably do me good, as long as I'm not intruding.'

She sat at the dining table while Chris refilled the kettle and set it onto the Aga hotplate. Neither spoke as he was preparing the tea. Mrs Raven occupied herself by playing with Misty, who clearly adored her and was dragging her toys one by one out of the bag on the floor and presenting them in turn, hoping to engage her new friend in a proper game of throw and fetch.

Chris put the cups and the now-filled teapot and the bottle of milk on the table. 'I'm sorry, I don't have any biscuits. I don't really do them.'

Mrs Raven waved her hand, to indicate that it didn't matter, then she looked at the two cups and frowned at him slightly. 'Are you here by yourself, Chris? Forgive me if I'm overstepping the mark in asking, but I assumed you'd be here with your fiancée again; Daisy, wasn't it?'

Chris pressed his lips together, unsure of what to say. A few seconds' awkward silence prevailed, and Mrs Raven then blushed bright red.

'Oh, God! I've put my foot in it, haven't I? I'm so sorry. It's none of my business, is it? I just assumed...' she trailed off, clearly embarrassed, and confused. Chris decided to put her out of her misery.

'Daisy died, Mrs Raven,' he said quietly. 'A mountaineering accident in the Spanish Sierra Nevada, ten months ago. It's ok, you probably wouldn't have known,' he hastened to add, as her face crumpled in distress.

'Well, I mean, it was on the news and everything, but I don't suppose the names would have rung a bell for you even if you'd seen it. We were on a group trip. There were nine of us, and three guides. It was Daisy's first climb. She was in a group of three climbers roped to a guide, and the last person in her line lost their footing and fell. Somehow, the rope snapped. The guide and all three climbers plunged to their deaths.'

Saying it in such a nutshell way, so concise and matter-of-fact, left Chris feeling like he'd somehow minimised into virtually nothing the most cataclysmic event of his whole life to date. It felt like the worst kind of betrayal of Daisy, to tell someone else who barely knew her, what had happened to her, in such short stark terms. It was everything *but* short and stark, this life-changing devastation he was still reeling from; one that was threatening to define his whole life going forward if he couldn't work out how to prevent it.

Daisy's catastrophic death deserved more sentences, but he found himself unable to find them. He didn't know if he'd ever manage to fully transcend the shock, the guilt, and the rage he felt towards himself, for having put his fiancée in that terrible position where she'd ended up losing her life. It kept hitting him hard, in so many ways, at times when he least expected it to; like now. It was always so difficult, telling people who didn't know.

Mrs Raven had tears in her eyes, although they hadn't fallen. Chris was glad about that. His own grief was hard enough to grapple with. He wasn't sure how he could possibly offer comfort or solace to someone else, especially a virtual stranger.

'Oh, Chris! How unimaginably awful! I can't even *begin* to understand what you must be going through. I'm so sorry! My God. Daisy was the loveliest woman. I remember her sitting on the lawn here, at the side of the house. Her red hair was blowing backwards, and she was laughing at the chickens running around her. She looked so pretty, in her a floral top and jeans, but she had bare feet, in spite of the awful cold, and I remember thinking at the time that she'd probably end up catching her death if she didn't put some shoes on!'

As soon as the words were out of her mouth, Mrs Raven flushed beet red again. She was instantly mortified and trying to cover her face with her hands. Now her tears *were* falling. 'Oh, bloody hell! Me and my big mouth. I didn't mean... I'm *so* sorry. I'm about as subtle as a brick sometimes. Forgive me, please?'

Despite himself, Chris found himself smirking. It wasn't a funny comment at all, but the fact that she was so flustered by it did tickle him a bit. He understood, in that moment, how hard it must have been for *anyone* to offer condolences to him at the worst time of his life. He appreciated that despite her faux pas, Mrs Raven had tried to offer him a lovely memory of Daisy. He decided to take that with gratitude, instead of umbrage. He shook his head briefly and gave her a small smile.

'Please don't cry, Mrs Raven. It's okay, and I do mean that. You don't have to be sorry about what you've said. Daisy would have found it funny, actually. She loved it when people put their foot in it. She always thought it was hilarious, especially if their attempts at recovery somehow made things worse. Wherever she is now, I'd like to think she'd be giggling at you. And you're right. She *was* lovely. She was the best. Thank you for that image of her on the lawn. I get a lot of comfort from things like that, people remembering her so nicely. Sharing it, you know?'

Mrs Raven nodded, wiping her eyes with the back of her hand. 'I do. I think it's important to have as many good memories as possible and, speaking from my own experience, I don't think they have to be really big, significant ones. The small ones, the innocuous and random ones, they mean just as much.'

Chris stared into his cup, and swallowed hard. 'They do. You're so right, about that. I have so many little ones. Shiny little gems, if you want to call them something. Her waking up and rubbing the sleep out of her eyes. The look on her face one time, when she blew up a balloon too much and it exploded. How much she treasured a horrible little ornament one of her old ladies at the care home left her in their will. I've still got the damned thing,' he said, half to himself. He looked up.

'I haven't been able to clear all her stuff yet. It's all still in boxes, in storage. I packed everything up, you know, after the funeral and everything. I couldn't live in our flat anymore, but it doesn't feel right to get rid of her things. Not yet.'

'When the right time comes, you'll know. Until it does, it's ok to keep everything as it is,' Mrs Raven said gently. Chris nodded.

'Some say it's a bit macabre, holding onto a dead person's stuff, like you can't move on, or something.'

Mrs Raven shook her head. 'No, I don't think that's always true. Everyone has to recover from a deep wound at their own pace, Chris. Grief is different for everyone. There's no prescribed formula, or road map; you feel what you feel and do what you do, or not, until it feels right to do something else.' She pulled her bottom lip with her finger and thumb, as she thought, before continuing.

'You can't allow anyone else to tell you what your experience should be, and you really can't compare it with anyone else's. This terrible hole that's been left in your life is something you have to deal with and figure out how to close in your own way, in your own time. Maybe don't be in a rush to try and figure everything out. That kind of pressure doesn't help.'

She was right, about all of it. He knew that, and he realised that it was actually quite nice to talk about Daisy with someone who didn't really know her or have a vested interest in getting him 'over it.' He didn't want to be rescued or pitied, or anything else, especially not by well-meaning friends and family who imagined they knew what he was going through.

The truth was that nobody did, and here was a wise, gentle woman who wasn't pretending, who was telling him that it was okay to be in his own reality and feel his own anguish. She wasn't prompting him to talk, or recommending counselling, or a new adventure, or anything else so many others had suggested, to pull him through the grief. She was just sitting here, having a cup of tea with him, without passing judgement or offering an insensitive, unwanted opinion.

Almost involuntarily, Chris began to talk. 'She didn't want to be there. She wasn't a winter person at all. I'm the mountaineer. She always said she'd take the beach over the mountains any day. I pushed her to take that trip with me, because she always seemed so interested in the climbs I'd done. I've been climbing since I was a kid,' he explained.

'I started going with one of my dad's workmates and his brother, when I was about twelve years old. They taught me how to climb; small peaks at first, and then bigger ones as my passion for it grew. Before I met Daisy, I used to live as cheaply as I had to, so I could save up all my wages and go off climbing somewhere. I've done Ben Nevis of course, but also Kilimanjaro and Kenya, a few decent peaks in the States and Australia, and handful of glaciers. I've had a dream for many years now, of going to Antarctica to do Vinson Massif, and one day having what it takes to do K2. Daisy used to get me talking about it all for hours, helping me to relive my past adventures and dream about new ones.'

Mrs Raven listened intently, as Chris went on to describe how raptly Daisy herself would listen to his mountaineering stories and ask questions about the people he'd climbed with and the things he'd felt and seen. His voice caught in his throat, as he talked of how she had always made a point of making coffee-table photo albums of his different climbs. She always insisted on pulling them off the computer because she said (quite rightly, he suspected) that he'd probably never look at them again if they just stayed stored there. She painstakingly put them into lovely leather-bound albums and would then bring them out and show everyone who came to visit. She couldn't have been prouder of him, and she never passed up a chance to make that clear to anyone who'd look and listen.

'She got it, you know? The reasons why I do it? She really understood that climbing a mountain is about so much more than just the conquest itself. The test, and the validation, of your own personal stamina and strength. Feeling yourself getting better and better, with every climbing experience How much more connected you feel, way up there, to the greater universe. How much further you might go, on the next peak.' Chris laughed, self-consciously.

'There's something truly spiritual, about getting to the top of a mountain. Some would probably say it's getting as close to God as humanly possible. For me, it's something less quantifiable than that, and I can't explain it to anyone. But I didn't have to, to her. She just got it.'

He looked up to find Mrs Raven smiling gently at him. He took a deep breath. 'I think, in fact I *know*, that I mistook her willingness to listen and understand, and relive those climbs with me, as a desire to do the real thing herself. I booked the trip to the Sierras without even asking her. It was meant to be a surprise.'

He shrugged, embarrassed. 'I was so sure she'd love it, and then want to keep going with me. She was fit, and strong, and I thought she'd smash it and then be hungry for more.'

He swallowed the all-too familiar lump that was forming in his throat and ploughed on. 'I was selfish, and I ignored her when she said it wasn't her thing. She even told me straight, when I sprung it on her, that she wasn't keen. She was tactful about it, but she did make it clear. I just chose not to listen! I more or less railroaded her into going with me. I think she only came to keep the peace.'

'And you feel the accident was your fault, because you insisted that she go with you.'

It was more of a statement than a question, and Chris nodded. Finally, someone who got it, but *didn't* fall over themselves to try and make him feel better about it. That was a welcome change.

'Yep. Got it in one. If I'd listened to her, she wouldn't have been there, and she wouldn't have died.' He drained his cup. 'Anyway, I'm sure you didn't come here to listen to my wretched tale of woe. I must say, it's nice coming back here, even under these circumstances. It was almost like coming home, walking in here and finding everything the same as it was last time. This place felt amazingly welcoming last time, when we weren't even upset about anything. It feels like a real refuge, right now.'

Mrs Raven nodded and glanced around her cottage, the pride in it clearly showing in her face. 'Yes, it's a very special little place. There's a soft, gentle energy here. It's nurturing, isn't it? Many people who've come here have told me they've felt that. It's all to do with healing vibrations and frequencies that the earth has, some of which are more concentrated in specific places. The cottage does tend to attract people who need time and space, for various reasons. I suspect you've been drawn back here to properly grieve, and come to terms with things. It's a soft, healing space, so I hope it works its magic on you a little.'

She laughed, quietly. 'I know that all sounds a bit bonkers but believe me it's true. Most people who come here in turmoil really *do* end up feeling a lot better about their lives when they leave. I did myself, initially, and it's happened enough times with other people for me to believe there's something to it all. My stepdaughter Feen is something of an expert on these things. She could probably explain it a lot better, if you wanted to know more about it.'

Chris went on to explain a little about his pilgrimages for Daisy, including acquiring Misty. 'Coming back here is one of the last things on the list. I hope she'd enjoy me honouring her memory like this, you know, going back to the places where we were happy together. She loved this place. We both did. And the dog, of course, that's a huge thing for me.'

'I'm sure she would appreciate what you're doing in her memory, Chris. What's it like for *you,* though, to be doing all this?'

Well, that was an interesting question, and as he was considering how to respond to it, Chris suddenly realised that nobody else, in all these long months, had asked him that. It hadn't occurred to even *one* of the people who knew he was doing his pilgrimages for Daisy, to ask him if it was helping or not.

None of his friends had asked him. Even his best mate Marcus hadn't, and it occurred to him now for the first time, that neither had any of Daisy's own family. They'd more or less left him to it. Generously, he thought they probably all assumed that he knew what he was doing. They were right about that, at least. He *did* know, but he hadn't been prepared for how torn apart some of those revisits had made him feel, or how much he was dreading the final, most important one, of going back to Mulhacén; the mountain that had claimed Daisy's life.

'The truth? Some of it is lovely, some of it is absolutely brutal, but it's all really poignant, and somehow so *final*, like I know that each place, or each event I sign off, it's the end. Going back again, another time, would feel wrong, almost pathetic, like hanging on when I shouldn't. I dunno,' he shrugged. 'It's kind of hard to explain.'

'No, I understand it, I think. These pilgrimages, this journey, it's a process for you, of saying goodbye in a way that feels right, and because saying a heartfelt goodbye to someone who's died really is a final act. You don't get to say it again. So, revisiting anywhere again, after saying such an important goodbye… well, that probably would feel wrong. I get it.'

Chris decided, after looking into Mrs Raven's pensive face, that she probably actually did. He was grateful that his bumbling, inept description of what he was attempting to do had been so well understood.

She rose to leave. 'Thank you for the tea, Chris. If there's anything you need – anything at all – please don't hesitate to pop up to the house and ask.' As she put her hand on the back door handle, she turned back to him.

'For what it's worth, I think what you're doing in Daisy's memory is lovely. I hope you find the peace you deserve within it all, and as for this gorgeous little bundle, Miss Misty Daisy Darcy, what sweeter thing could come out of all this, than you two having one another to love and cherish?'

Chris smiled at her gratefully. 'Thanks Mrs Raven, it's been great talking to you, and I hope I haven't dragged you down.'

She shook her head emphatically. 'No, you haven't. Not at all. Quite the opposite. You inspire me, actually, but I do think you need to start calling me Adie, now that I know so much more about you. I'll see you around, Chris. Oh, and don't worry too much if you see a tiny woman with very long dark hair, ferreting around in the hedgerows and the back garden, looking for plants, herbs, and stuff. It'll be my step-daughter Feen. She may or may not come and say hello to you.'

'Yeah, Daisy and I met Feen briefly last year, Adie, so I'll know who she is if I see her. Thanks for the sensitive ear. I appreciate it. See you soon.'

After Adie left him, Chris made himself another cup of tea and went back to the window seat. He'd turned into a real 'tea-belly' since he'd met Daisy. She could drink tea for England, and she'd got him into the habit. He used to be a big coffee drinker and, to be fair, he did still relish his mid-morning pot of good strong brew at the weekend. Maybe he'd start to drink more of it again now. Nobody could berate you for doing the things you loved, could they, especially if it wasn't hurting anyone else? Daisy had never told him off for drinking coffee, and she would never have made anything of it if he'd carried on. She didn't really care, but she never drank it herself and it somehow always seemed easier to have a pot of tea with her instead. He wondered what else he might have unconsciously moved away from, in his desire to be more closely aligned with her.

He didn't eat as many chips anymore, that was one thing, although it did mean that whenever they sat on the seafront wall with a tray of fish and chips, he enjoyed them so much more. Daisy knew that. They never had chips at home with anything, even oven ones, but whenever they were out, she was usually keen to get them, and *always* when they'd gone to the seaside! It became something of a treat especially reserved for those times, obligatory in fact, and together they'd savour the salty taste of them, even as the sea wind tried to whip them out of their hands. Daisy would shout and laugh with glee, and she'd turn to face him, usually with a smudge of tomato sauce across her mouth that made her smile seem ten miles wide. He loved to kiss her then, and all the way home on the train, tasting the salt and sauce, and feeling her smile as he pressed his lips to hers.

Yeah, chips. Maybe it's time I went back to enjoying some of my own little 'loves' again.

He recalled that there'd been a chippy in the town, last time they were here. It was called Cat's Fish, and it was run by a smiley woman who treated every customer like an old friend. He hoped it was still there. Fish and chips for dinner would be just the ticket tonight, and he could take Misty for a walk down to the town, to get them. She needed a decent leg-stretch. He checked his watch and was amazed to find it was almost a quarter to six.

Where had the afternoon gone? The last time he'd checked his watch, on the motorway somewhere around the turnoff for Milnthorpe, it had been one o'clock. He must've been sitting here for some time before Adie Raven had shown up. But then, he recalled, it had been like this when he and Daisy had been here before. Somehow the cottage quietly ran away with time, and as gently as it seemed to go, they'd always been amazed and left wondering where the day had gone.

By the time he'd put his jacket on and got Misty all harnessed up and ready for their walk, the sun was already setting. The days were lengthening now, as spring got underway, but even on the sunny days the light was still gone by half-past six.

He grabbed the handy little torch that was hanging on a hook by the front door, figuring he'd probably need it for the walk back up. The last thing he wanted was to slip or go off the path in the dark.

He picked up a jute shopping bag that was also hanging up behind the front door. He wasn't sure whether he'd need it or not, but it was better to have it than not. He slung it across his left shoulder and checked that he had his wallet. Last time he'd been here, he'd gone into the town one day without it, and hadn't realised until after he and Daisy had had their lunch in a café. The owner of the café had been surprisingly blasé about him coming back to pay later. She'd trusted him and waved away his embarrassment, and he hadn't forgotten that. The café would be closed now, but he thought he might stop by there in the next day or two, to see if the same woman still ran the place. He couldn't remember her name but maybe she'd still remember him.

He stepped out with Misty, into the night air, to find that Adie had been right. It was nippy now, and he decided he'd light the fire as soon as he got back.

Misty was enjoying the opportunity to run across the fields. As soon as they were over the stile, Chris let her off the lead, and she ran around like a mad thing. The amount of energy she had was extraordinary. Some days, mostly the ones when his grief had him sucker-punched and breathless, just watching her was exhausting. As they started heading down the fell, he called her back, and he was pleased when she came straight away. She was a fast little learner, and his early anxieties about letting her off the lead and not being able to get her to come back to him had proved unfounded.

Misty adored him, and happily did whatever he told her. Their training sessions were always a lot of fun, although Chris had learned the hard way not to leave boots and shoes within her reach. She'd so far managed to destroy two pairs of very expensive trainers and had made a good start on one of his leather moccasin slippers that had been a Christmas gift from Daisy a couple of years ago. It now had a hole the size of a thumbnail in it. He'd rescued it just in time! His specialist G-Tech mountaineering boots, at a thousand pounds a pair, were very safely locked away, away from gnawing little teeth. It would have broken Chris' heart if Misty had got hold of those.

It suddenly occurred to him that he hadn't felt properly hungry for many months, but he was starving right now, and very much looking forward to his fish and chips.

Chapter Two

As she took off her boots at the front door and placed them upside down on the ornate wrought iron boot-stand just inside, Adie's heart felt heavy. Chris Darcy's pain was unimaginable.

Her own experience with bereavement had been minimal. Aside from the death of her own parents, at a more-or-less 'acceptable' time in life, she hadn't had to deal with anything as devastating as what her latest tenant at Teapot Cottage was going through.

Her mind drifted back, to how she'd felt when she'd found her husband Mark in the barn, unconscious and bleeding heavily after falling through the rotten mezzanine floor. They hadn't been married then, hadn't even talked about their feelings, in fact. But Adie was never going to forget the icy cold finger of fear that had scored her spine, at the thought that he might not survive. If he hadn't, if he'd died with their love still unspoken, how could she have borne it? She shook her head, in an attempt to clear it, then decided that no, it was okay to acknowledge the horror of that time, especially if it helped her to appreciate more fully what poor Chris Darcy was feeling, in his grief.

In the kitchen, she set the kettle on the Aga and made a pot of tea. Mark was still out in the barn, changing the oil in some piece of machinery or other, and it was well past their normal tea-break time. He'd be finished for the day in less than an hour, and coming in to get cleaned up for dinner, but she decided to take him an unexpected cup of tea anyway, and she'd throw in a kiss or two as well. Sometimes, the rush of love she felt for him overcame her.

They had found one another later in life, and this was a second marriage for them both. Mark had been widowed, and Adie had been in the throes of a painful marriage breakdown when she'd arrived at Ravensdown to house-sit for the people who owned Teapot Cottage at the time. Neither she nor Mark had been looking for romance when they'd literally banged into one another twice on the same day, in Torley town. Love had snuck up completely unannounced, and it was all the more delightful for that. It had caught them both by accident, a fact they often laughed about.

A less likely pair you'd have struggled to find – the suburban, middle-class, 'ladies-lunching' homemaker and the rough and ready working-class farmer. But it hadn't taken them long to discover that they had a lot more in common than either would have imagined. Adie never let a single day go by without giving thanks to the great universal plan that had brought her and Mark together. She simply couldn't contemplate how she'd cope if she lost him now.

She'd struggled, many times, to understand why life could be so brutal, but this situation had to be one of the worst. Last year when Chris and Daisy had come here, they were a young couple in love; engaged to be married, with every possible good thing to look forward to. They'd had their whole lives, and endless opportunity, ahead of them. But now, just a year later, poor Daisy was dead, and Chris Darcy's dreams were in tatters. Not only that; he was also haunted by the notion that he'd been responsible for her death.

The fact that it had been a tragic accident did nothing to assuage his guilt at having pressed her into going on the climb with him in the first place. It could just as easily have been him, on that rope line, or anyone else in the group. The fact that it had been Daisy was just a breathtakingly cruel twist of fate that nobody could have predicted, except maybe the person who checked (or maybe *didn't* check?) that the all-important, life-sustaining rope was in top condition.

Adie had no knowledge of climbing, other than what she'd heard in conversation with tenants who'd come to do a little hiking, 'scrambling,' or low-level climbing in the area.

She was anything but an expert, and had never so much as tied a rope-knot in her life, but she did know that a climbing rope wouldn't just snap without warning. That would only happen under extreme stress. The rope should have been robust enough to do what it was designed to do and carry the weight of the people it was meant to protect.

Surely, it had to have been faulty? There must have been a stress on it somewhere, and someone should be held accountable for failing to see that, not that it mattered much now. Chris might ultimately get justice for Daisy, in the form of someone taking responsibility, but it probably wouldn't happen. Even if it did, that lovely young woman was still gone, and always would be. No amount of justice could ever bring her back.

There was no getting away from the fact that if Daisy hadn't gone on that trip, she probably *would* still be alive today. Poor Chris: accident or not, it was a hell of a thing to come to terms with. Adie hoped with all her heart that he'd one day be able to find some peace within himself, but she suspected it would be a long time coming.

She prepared two mugs of tea and put a chocolate-cherry muffin on a plate. They were one of Mark's favourites. Anything with chocolate in it always got a big thumbs-up from him. She thought she might pop a couple of the muffins down to Chris too, sometime before dinner. She'd just pop them on the kitchen windowsill of Teapot Cottage, in a plastic container, so he'd easily see them. She wanted to be kind, but also give him his own space if that was what he wanted. He would seek her out if he wanted to chat, now that she'd told him he could.

Mark was surprised to see her as she walked into the barn with her tray. He beamed at her and grabbed an already-grubby rag to wipe his filthy hands on. 'Ay, 'ello, lass! To what do I owe this random visit? Yer do know I'm almost done fer't day, don't yer?' He looked at his watch and frowned.

His broad Lancashire accent always made her smile. To anyone who didn't know him, he sounded crude and uneducated, but those who did knew he was a shrewd, astute businessman, with plenty of pragmatism and insight. He also had a heart of gold and would lay down his life for his family. He was the most 'real' person Adie had ever met, and while his Northern humour and funny way of talking occasionally had her running to catch up with his thoughts and feelings, she wouldn't trade a single thing about him. He was truly adorable.

She set her tray down on the one clear corner of his workbench and put her arms around him. She buried her face in his neck and smelled a peculiar mixture of shower gel, manliness, and engine oil. She inhaled deeply. It was wonderful.

Mark chuckled and hugged her tight. 'Well, if it's a roll in't hay yer after, yer don't have ter bribe me wi' a chocolate muffin! A simple nudge an' a wink'd do, lass.' He stepped back and held her at arm's length, scrutinising her face. 'A'reet, love? Wassup wi' yer?'

Adie sighed and pulled a face. She told him about Chris Darcy, and what had happened to his fiancée. 'I dunno, Mark. Life is so cruel sometimes. I guess I just wanted to remind you how loved you are, and how I can't imagine life without you.'

Mark grinned at her. 'Well, yer soppy sod, you'd 'ave 'ouse an't farm, and money in't bank, and life as a merry widda. Things could be a lot worse!'

In spite of her sadness, Adie snorted with laughter. 'Merry widow? You better not go *anywhere*, Mr Raven. Not for a very long time yet!'

'An' I don't plan to. But things 'appen Adie, you know they do.' Mark's face grew serious. 'Look at poor lad down at cottage! Life's full o' nasty twists and turns, an' we've no way o' predictin' any of it. An' it's tragic, what's 'appened, but you can't carry't world on yer shoulders, lass. I feel for 'im, o' course I do. But it's 'is pain to work through. Don't make it yer own.'

She knew he was right, but it was hard not to be sad about young Daisy's life being snuffed out with no warning. The young woman was around the same age as her own daughter Teresa, and Mark's daughter Feen. Daisy had been so pretty, so cheerful and smiley, so excited about life. The tragedy of her dying the way she did was almost incomprehensible.

Most of the tenants who came to Teapot Cottage were simply here to enjoy the Lake District and have a lovely break, but there were a fair number who turned up that did appear to be at some kind of crossroads. Many had experienced a terrible loss, of one kind or another. Feen believed that Teapot Cottage (and Ravensdown Farm too, to some extent) had a unique magnetic attraction for people seeking solace of some kind, and that people were often unwittingly 'drawn' here, to start their healing process. She'd explained it as well as she could, and Adie believed her, to some extent, but she was still trying to grasp the true reality of the cottage's ability to offer healing energy to people in need.

Whatever the real reason people turned up at 'Teapot' one fact was certainly true; most who came here suffering with trauma left with a greater sense of resolve. Adie had experienced it herself when she'd originally come as a house-sitter. She'd been utterly distraught; almost deranged, in the middle of an unexpectedly difficult menopause, and trying to deal with a bitter marriage break-up and the exposure of enough family secrets to keep a novelist in full-time work for a decade.

It had been the worst time of her life, but somehow Teapot Cottage had healed her, in a way she couldn't describe. Staying there had been like balm to a gaping wound, and she'd been able to weave back together the frayed and broken threads of her life, and create something more profound and meaningful than she'd once ever thought possible.

Meeting and falling in love with Mark Raven had been the icing on the cake, but even without that, Adie would have walked away from Teapot Cottage a thousand times stronger than she'd been when she first arrived. She'd been lucky enough to not have to leave at all, but to buy the wonderful little house, instead! She hoped with all her heart that Chris Darcy would be able to shed some of his torment this week, within its gentle walls.

'Teresa is arriving tonight,' she reminded Mark, 'but we don't have to get her from Carlisle station as planned. She's driving up. Her flatmate Lucy has gone to California for a fortnight, and Teresa has the use of her car. That's going to make life a lot easier for all of us, I think, if she wants to go anywhere.'

Mark nodded and smiled broadly. Adie knew that he shared a very special bond with his stepdaughter. Teresa had been away backpacking in Australia when Adie had met Mark, so she hadn't actually met him until their wedding, but the two had hit it off. Adie thought it was largely down to Mark's experience with raising his own daughter alone and having to be both mum and dad. He knew how to relate to young women in a way that most men his age really didn't.

Even Teresa's own father didn't understand her as well as Mark did. Bryan Bostock had been perpetually baffled by his daughter, especially throughout her adolescence, and he'd behaved very badly towards his entire family during and after the breakup of his and Adie's marriage. Among the various things that had come out in the wash, during that turbulent time, was the fact that he'd been having an affair for six years prior to that. Teresa was still very upset with him over that, and a few other things besides. They didn't talk much, anymore.

But Mark been a powerful source of support in helping her to pick up the pieces of a failed romance. While she'd been away travelling for a couple of years, Teresa had met a guy called Ross Barker, from Australia's Northern Territories, who she'd truly thought was 'the one.' Romance had quickly blossomed, and Ross had flown over to London to be with her, after she'd come home again. For a while it was all very blissful but, over time, they both realised that living in the same space, month after month under rainy London skies, was a far cry from the balmy beach days and starry summer nights that had fuelled the holiday romance that had kicked it all off.

As it turned out, their views and expectations of life had been fundamentally very different. When Ross abruptly disappeared back to Australia with no warning whatsoever, it became clear that the relationship was never going to have a future. Teresa had been shattered.

Mark had stepped into the breech and offered her a lot of support and wisdom, and she had confided in him far more than she'd done with anyone else, including her own parents. She'd expressed no desire to talk to Adie, and her father was the last man on earth she would go to for advice.

A few years had elapsed now, and a lot of dust had settled, since Bryan Bostock had conducted his long-standing affair right under his wife and children's noses and lied through his teeth to them every day for the entire time. The damage had been terrible, and irreparable, and his behaviour still stung the kids. Adie had long since got over it and moved on, but Teresa and her brother Matty had difficult relationships with Bryan now, and getting onto an even footing with him again still seemed like a long way off. It was sad and frustrating, but it was something they all had to try and figure out for themselves, as best they could. Adie knew that Teresa wouldn't confide in her father in a million years, but she'd been disappointed that she hadn't wanted to talk to her either, about her broken heart. She was thankful for Teresa's willingness to talk to the wise and pragmatic Mark.

Exactly what had been said between the two was still unknown to her and probably always would be. Her husband was never going to betray a confidence, and Adie knew better than to ask him to, but she was grateful that whatever had been shared between him and Teresa had kick-started the healing process. She still wasn't dating, at least not with anyone she was prepared to talk about, but Adie was philosophical about that too. If and when someone special did come on the scene, she and Mark would eventually be allowed to know.

Teresa was arriving tonight for two weeks. She'd just finished a long-term temping position in London and was still unsure if she wanted another one. She had been in the city for a long time now, and had made some good friends there, but she was still very ambivalent about staying. She was tired of temping, but she had to keep doing it until she could finish saving for the cinematography equipment she wanted, to establish a career as a freelance film maker. She needed the right qualifications and training, which she was working towards, but she also needed her own film-making rig, in order to be taken seriously, and none of that came cheap. The cost of the equipment she wanted ran to many thousands of pounds.

It no longer seemed likely that she'd ever want to do anything directly with her Economics degree, after travelling had opened her eyes to so much. Adie suspected that whatever Teresa ended up doing, it would not involve being stuck behind a desk, tucked away in a forgotten corner of an office block or university somewhere.

She reflected back now, to when Teresa had been a teenager. The father of one of her friends had lent her a little video camera, for a weekend away with her friends. He was an indie film-maker, and he thought she might be interested in giving it a go. He'd seen something in her that nobody else had. As he'd predicted, she'd become quite interested in making films. They were short ones, but from what Adie had seen, they seemed pretty good.

Her friend's dad had looked at what she'd 'shot,' and thought the same thing. He told her she had a good eye, and it had spurred her on to keep stretching herself and pushing her boundaries. Adie and Bryan had given her a good video camera for her sixteenth birthday, and it had always been one her favourite and most-used possessions. It was getting pretty old now, in fact Adie wondered if might actually be obsolete. Maybe it was time for an upgrade.

'Making movies' had only ever been a hobby for Teresa but she'd taken a travelling 'gap' year, between graduating, and deciding on her first career move. It had in fact run to almost *two* years, but it had turned out to be a great move. As the saying went, 'travel broadens the mind,' and Teresa had seen that there were wider horizons to explore. She'd ultimately decided she wanted to create films about them.

Her great passion was factual filming; taking footage of people in different real-life situations, and her time away had opened her eyes to how wide the spectrum of life was and how much of what existed within it could and 'probably should' be shown to the world– in her humble opinion!

Her experiences had been extraordinary. In just a few months, she'd gone from staying in a multi-million-dollar beach-fronted home in Coffs Harbour that belonged to the parents of a friend she'd met on her travels, to sleeping in a basic tent near Ayr's Rock, fending off snakes and scorpions, and observing the different tribal elements of Aboriginal life. Across the world, she'd seen no end of extremes, from the ghettos of New York to the bling-encrusted high-rise apartments of the same city's affluent areas. She'd gone from gazing wistfully at the iconic and stupendously expensive Burj Al Arab hotel in Dubai, to witnessing the scarcely believable, desperate slums of Bangkok.

The effect of seeing the worst had been profound. Her outrage rang in Adie's ears, whenever she recalled it.

'Mum, it was wretched! It really was! Bangkok is home to billionaires but, in the slums, there were children shitting in the streets because they had no toilets! Some of them wouldn't even know what a toilet was! How can people in the world who live in luxury turn a blind eye to others who live in such squalor? In the same damn city, Mum! It's completely unacceptable! Isn't there a moral responsibility *somewhere?* What chance will those poor kids ever have, for a better life?'

Teresa had gone on to say how fortunate she now believed herself to have been, having grown up with a high degree of comfort, and getting a good education. 'We never had to go without food, did we Mum? We never had to go without clothes, or holidays, or anything? I remember that tantrum I had when I was fourteen, after you and Dad forced me to choose between a pair of ice skates and a hard-hat for Pony Club, because you said I couldn't have both. What a *brat* I was!

'I know it doesn't help the poor to be one of them, and I don't have to feel guilty about my own great start in life, compared with the lives of so many destitute people I met abroad. I mean, life is what it is for us all, isn't it? But maybe I can make it better in some meaningful way for those who have nothing; you know, draw more attention to their situation in some way? I think that's what I'd like to do, Mum.'

Teresa had become passionate about highlighting the plight of the disadvantaged. She had a goal to eventually go back to some of the places she'd been to, and make short films; showcase-documentaries that highlighted the ridiculous levels of inequality in the so-called civilized world. Bangkok was high on her list.

'Nobody should be living in the dirt, in poverty, in the twenty-first century, Mum!'

It was something she said quite often. She felt compelled to do something – *anything* – to change it.

'And don't get me started on food mountains, and failures of distribution!' That was another soapbox she was always quick to leap onto. Adie never knew whether to laugh or cry, at her daughter's passion. But Teresa's outrage was energy – and she wanted to use it in a good way. Who, in all conscience, could stand in the way of that?

Adie had no doubt that if her daughter set her mind to something, she would find a way to achieve it. But it was hard not to worry about her ability to reach her goals while living in a big city like London, with its exorbitant cost of living. When Adie and Bryan had 'downsized' their big family home to a more modest one, before their marriage had ended, they'd given the kids a decent chunk of their 'inheritance' early, by offering them some start-up money. Matty had used his to get a mortgage on a flat, which he'd then sold to raise the deposit for a house when he got married, but Teresa had spent most of her payout on her travels. Thankfully, she'd wisely put a little aside to come back to, but she'd gone on to use a fair portion of it to pay for her online MA degree in Film and Television. She'd put the rest into a pension plan. It all meant she was starting from scratch, existing on a weekly wage, with no financial backstop.

It was hard to make ends meet in a city where the cost of living was insane, let alone save for anything in particular, but Adie understood why Teresa half-wanted to stay in London. She had a lot more opportunities there than she'd have anywhere else; to meet the 'right' people who could help her establish her career. She also made decent hourly rate doing temporary admin work; far more than she'd make anywhere else. Apparently, after weighing up all the pros and cons, she'd decided that living in London was still the best economic situation, for her to save enough to get the equipment she needed.

Adie appreciated her daughter's refusal to change her circumstances. Quietly, and proudly, she knew Teresa was slowly but surely figuring everything out. She *was* managing to save a little, and still even have the odd city break when time and bargain-basement prices collided. She was also managing to pick up a few important pieces of good quality second-hand equipment. Being involved with a few film and camera clubs, meant that she sometimes got the chance to buy someone else's cast offs when they upgraded their stuff.

As she'd explained to Adie; 'I'd rather have 'used' quality than brand new rubbish, because quality stands the test of time, and I want stuff that will last. Buying shitty, mass-produced, 'new' equipment on the budget I have is simply false economy. It would break in no time, and I'd be back to square one!'

Teresa Bostock was starting to form an idea of where she wanted to go, and what she needed to do and have, to get there. She would ultimately go on to do something magnificent with the passion and commitment she was capable of. The right opportunity would come when it was good and ready, and *she* would be ready when it did. Adie was certain of that.

Back in the kitchen, she checked her phone, and was pleased to see a text from Teresa, with an ETA of around now! She quickly started organising dinner. All her family loved her zucchini and salmon lasagne, so she'd already made a huge dish of it, earlier in the day. She slid it into the oven now, along with a couple of home-made foil-wrapped garlic baguettes, and quickly threw a green salad together, to go with it.

It wasn't long before she heard a car door slam, then the sound of two voices. Mark had finished work for the day, in time to coincide with Teresa's arrival.

When they came into the kitchen, she had her arm flung casually across Mark's shoulders and he was trying to walk, while thus restrained, and carry two large bags. He rolled his eyes at Adie, in mock exasperation. 'Jus' call me Neddy, bloody pack 'orse. Thought she were only comin' fer a fortnight. Looks like she's 'ere for six months!"

Teresa gave him a playful shove and almost knocked him over. He set the bags down and looked at her levelly. 'Any more o' that, an' you'll be haulin' the buggers upstairs yer bloody self.' He sat down heavily at the table, as Adie set the teapot down. Teresa sat also, and Adie noted how tired she looked.

It'll be good for her to have a break. She's been working her socks off, but she doesn't have much choice if she wants to keep living in London.

She planned to pamper her daughter, cook all her favourite foods, hike up to the tor with her to see the view of Torley Valley, and maybe drive her into Carlisle for a mooch around the shops. Maybe she'd treat her to a few new items of clothing too, since she knew there was never much left in Teresa's monthly budget for treating herself. There was a lovely spa over towards the city, at the Beeches Hotel. Maybe they could have a full girly day of shopping and spa, and Adie could invite her friends Peg, Sheila, and Trudie too.

Trudie had a nice boutique in Torley Town. GladRagz tended to cater for more mature women, but it did have a few nice things for younger ones too. Teresa's tastes were still leaning towards late-teen fashion. She had yet to find her own style but maybe Trudie could help, if Teresa wanted guidance, either in her own shop or when they went to Carlisle.

Resolving to make a few calls to try to arrange something, Adie batted away Mark's mischievous recount to her daughter, about trying to get her mother in the hay for some 'hanky-panky.'

They'd done the 'roll in the hay' only once, mostly for a laugh and to be able to say they'd actually done it, but after spending several hours trying to get the terrible stuff out of her hair and clothes, she'd put the experience in the 'been-there-done-that' basket and wasn't keen for a repeat performance. It had taken her a split second to discover that hay was distinctly uncomfortable, and downright prickly, to certain sensitive parts of the female anatomy!

She said as much to Teresa who clearly didn't know whether to laugh or cry, and merely said; 'Ugh, Mum! You can't even let your kids *think* about you having sex, let alone describe it to them! TMI, thank you very much!'

Mark looked baffled. 'TMI, what the bloody 'ell's that when it's at 'ome?'

Adie laughed, in spite of herself. 'Too much information, I think that is, and it probably was! Sorry darling. Dinner's about half an hour away, so have a choc-cherry muffin in the meantime – and I don't want to hear anything at all while you're here, about watching your weight, thank you very much. You are far too thin. It's not healthy.'

'Yeah, well, I've been starving myself, because I know I'll be the size of a house by the time I leave here. Call it advanced preparation for being fed until I explode.'

How lovely it is to have her here. It's the first time she's stayed for more than a couple of nights. I really will spoil her. Maybe she won't want to go back to London.

'By the way, darling, Feen and Gavin and the kids are here too. I forgot to mention that when you called to say you were coming.'

'Oh, cool! I wondered whose lovely new white and gold Porsche Cayenne that was, parked in the driveway. It'll be good to see them. Are you sure I'm not in the way? I know I've crashed in without much warning, and you already have a houseful.'

Mark snorted. 'O' course yer not in't way, lass! Yer family, and God knows we've plenty o' bloody room! Yer could stay 'ere for a week an' not even be noticed.'

'You could have had Teapot Cottage, if it wasn't already booked,' Adie piped up.

'That's okay, Mum. I'm happy to be here in the house with you all.'

'Also, I'm having a coffee morning here on Friday next week. I think you've already met a few of the people who are coming. It's always fun, with plenty of cake of course, so just be warned that I'll have a kitchen full of people between ten and twelve. You can join us or do your own thing; it's up to you.'

Teresa rolled her eyes. 'I guess there's no way of avoiding cake around here, is there? I may as well give in gracefully. Count me in.'

Adie smirked fondly at her daughter and husband, as they sat there contentedly at her kitchen table, slurping their tea. Few things in life were better than having your cherished family around you, even if it was only for a short time. She longed for the day when they'd all be here again at the same time. It never happened often enough because everyone had so many other commitments.

For Adie, having her birthday on Christmas Eve was mostly just downright inconvenient, but at least it meant that the kids had less of a reason to wriggle out of spending the festive season with her. Every second year they did exactly that, but this was the family's 'off-year.' Ruth, Gina, and their daughter Chiara would be going to Gina's family in Southern Italy for

Christmas, and Matty, Marie, Milly and Sophie would be spending it with Marie's parents, Babatunde and Joanne. Adie knew how tricky a balance it was, to try and keep everyone happy, especially when grandchildren were involved! At least Feen, Gavin and the kids would be here this year, and so would Teresa. That was good enough. There was no point in wishing her life away.

The annual Christmas night party would go ahead as usual too, at Ravensdown, and that was always huge fun. It was where she'd properly met Mark! As a tradition started many years earlier, by his first wife Beth, the Ravensdown Christmas party was always well attended by friends in the area. Many were farmers who didn't often get a chance to see one another, or get scrubbed up for a nice night out. It was an important social event in the Torley region and, as a bolt-on to her own birthday, and with the nostalgia of it being where she'd first really noticed her now-husband, Adie was more than happy to carry on with the tradition.

It helped a lot that her sister-in-law Sheila Shalloe, and her close friend, café owner Peg Tripper, commandeered the catering with an almost military precision, and organised everything like clockwork. All Adie ever had to do was decorate the house for Christmas, set up the Secret Santa sack just inside the front door, make her kitchen available, and contribute something herself, to the 'pot-luck' element of the dinner. Everyone who came brought something delicious for the table, and the result was a feast fit for kings. Mark bankrolled the alcohol every year, along with most of the food that Sheila and Peg made, and with every guest contributing some food and drink too, the party was always a roaring success.

She sat back down now, to indulge a cup of tea and a muffin. It would be nice to just relax for half an hour, and enjoy the fact that Teresa had finally landed.

Chapter Three

Packing things that were still on their coat hangers made good sense, Teresa thought to herself as she heaved the first of her two big bags onto the bed. You could simply lift everything out and transfer it directly onto the rails in the wardrobe, and the job of unpacking would be done in just a few minutes. Her mum offered plenty of coat hangers of course, but Teresa was all for convenience and keeping things simple.

She tossed her bras, knickers, and socks into the top drawer of the bedside cabinet, stacked her jeans and jumpers in the drawers below that, and lined her boots and shoes up along the wall behind the bedroom door. Then she reverently placed her camera bag, containing her Sony Alpha 7 III, on the top of the chest, and made sure it was sitting safe. The camera had been a recent purchase, and she was still getting to grips with how it worked. It had cost a lot of money, even second-hand. It was the most she had ever spent on any single tangible thing for herself *ever*, and she was still slightly paranoid about it coming to some unforeseen or inexplicable harm.

She threw herself onto the bed. She still couldn't really believe she'd come here, way up to the tail end of 'Northern Beyond,' but hightailing it home to her mother at short notice was the only response she could come up with, at the news her friend Helen, over in Australia, had dropped on her.

Ross Barker, the erstwhile love of her life, had just got engaged. Apparently, the wedding date was already set for next year. Even while her stomach was still in free-fall, Teresa had done what Helen had begged her *not* to do, and checked out his social media pages. She'd found them full of pictures of the blissed-out, newly-engaged couple; Ross and Rosie, all sickeningly smiley and loved-up to the nines. One of the photos had brought tears to Teresa's eyes, and split her heart in half again; a blonde, buxom woman, unfairly pretty, and showing off a truly spectacular pink diamond ring.

But it *would* be spectacular, wouldn't it? There had to be *some* perks, didn't there, to Ross being a diamond mine boss in Western Australia? What else would his 'intended' be sporting, other than a ridiculously beautiful, shiny pink rock from the Argyle diamond mine?

Knowing Ross, she figured he'd probably dug it out of the earth himself. She pictured him storming out of the mine, like Indiana Jones or something, triumphantly holding aloft the diamond of the century to mad cheers from his colleagues.

The beauty of the diamond itself was enough to drown her in grief again, but she couldn't stop the avalanche of tears that followed, when she'd read the caption beneath the photo.

'One of the last-ever pinkies out of Argyle! I've been holding onto this little rock for years, just waiting for the right finger! Finally found it ... #Rosie'

Teresa knew, in her heart, that the gorgeous rose-coloured rock could never have been her diamond. She and Ross would never have made it. They were, in the end, too different. But Ross had ended their relationship with no warning, and headed home to sun-drenched, tropical Darwin, leaving London and its leaden skies behind. He hadn't even talked to her about it. He'd just slunk away, like a thief in the night, after planning his 'exit' behind her back and leaving a cowardly note on the nightstand.

That had been cruel enough, but it was nothing, compared to the knowledge that he'd had that diamond squirreled safely away for all the time they'd been dating, knowing he was waiting for 'the right finger.' Clearly, he'd *never* thought hers was that finger. Discovering that had been even more devastating than the way he had left her.

The long months of heady happiness, dancing to the incredible, earthy sound of didgeridoos beneath the outback stars, with open fires and the most stupendous sunsets the region could offer as a backdrop. Sleeping in open-top tents in the Kakadu National Park. Diving among the manta-rays and turtles in the crystal-clear waters of the Northern Territories. Making love on tucked-away beaches with the sound of crashing surf in their ears. It was all incredibly lovely, the stuff of dreams in fact, but it hadn't counted for enough, in the end.

It was a very long way from the reality of living in the sombre greyness of a London winter, with Ross feeling frustrated and fed up with bar work and having no idea what else he wanted to do. There wasn't much call for diamond mine engineers in London, and the reality of paying the rent every month on low wages, coping with the cold and relentless rain, and living with her flatmate Lucy because they couldn't afford a place of their own in the city, all took a heavy toll too.

She'd known he wasn't as happy as he'd expected to be, but she had no idea that he was planning to leave, or that he'd end up doing it in such a chicken-shit way.

She'd left for work, one Monday morning, when he'd still been in bed. She'd expected to see him at Toot's, the bar at the corner of their road, on her way home that night. She always called in there for a quick drink, whenever he was working. But he hadn't been there, and when she'd asked one of his colleagues where he was, he'd shaken his head at her, puzzled.

'He left, Tezzie. Handed his notice in a week ago. Saturday night was his last shift. Don't tell me you didn't know?'

She *hadn't* known, and when she'd got home to the flat, she'd found Ross' note, sitting on top of an empty chest of drawers.

'It's not you, it's me.' That was the first sentence. There was only one other; 'I'm sorry Tezzie, but I can't do this.'

She'd tried to call him, but he hadn't answered his phone. She'd guessed he was either on his way to the airport, or already on a flight bound for home.

She struggled mightily, to get her head around the callousness of what Ross had done. Just the previous day, they'd had a lazy Sunday morning, before heading to Goddards, nearby, for one of their famous traditional pie and mash lunches. Then they'd gone to the National Maritime Museum for the afternoon. Lucy had cooked Sunday dinner for them all, and they'd binge-watched a series on Netflix. In all that time, Ross had behaved 'normally,' without a single hint that he was going to bolt for the horizon a day later. It was beyond incredible to Teresa, that *anybody* could do something that cold, cruel and selfish. She'd sat on the edge of their bed, trying to get her mind to comprehend what had happened. She'd been too stunned, to even think 'coward.'

Lucy had come home from work then, and switched the radio on, which was always the first thing she ever did when she walked through the door. The radio always came on, even before her coat and shoes came off.

The song that was playing was Pearl Jam's Wreckage, and Eddie Vedder was singing about combing through the wreckage of a failed relationship, raking through its the ashes, drowning in the yesterdays, and being powerless to make someone stay who wanted to leave. Teresa had listened to the words of the song, powerless herself, as her world quietly crumbled.

And that was what she was left to do – comb through the wreckage of her hopes and dreams, to a beautiful but desperately painful song that became her personal anthem.

She'd immediately canned her temp job, saying she had a family bereavement, and she'd lain in bed for almost a full week before she could get up. Lucy, who'd been furious, and raging, and calling Ross all the names under the sun, had cried with her. She'd held her, cooked for her, and drank with her on many a night, while she combed and fell and crawled through the most terrible, painful wreckage.

She hadn't known it was possible to cry as much as she did, for that first few weeks. She hadn't known how much it would hurt, even just to keep breathing. She played the Pearl Jam song, over and over, a thousand times, as her yesterdays with Ross slowly drowned.

He had never called, never emailed, never explained. He'd never responded to any of her attempts to contact him. His abandonment had felt like a death. The suddenness of it, and the *brutality* of having planned and done it, left her breathless and bereft for a long time. There were no words to describe that wreckage, and no actions that could have stopped her from falling through it.

Teresa's mother had been superficially sympathetic and supportive, in the aftermath of her life falling apart, but she'd been fairly quick to gloss over it and imply that it was nothing more significant than a failed holiday romance. Adie expected Teresa to have recovered a little quicker than she had. She hadn't understood that it had been so much more than just a flash in a holiday pan. Teresa had given her whole heart away to someone who had slashed it to pieces without a word or a backward glance.

It was Mark, her stepdad, who had hauled her through the worst of that wreckage. He had listened, while she'd poured her heart out with the kind of anguish she once hadn't even known she was capable of feeling. He'd never judged or said a single word that hadn't helped her. He somehow knew when to listen, and when to speak, and what to say when he did. He was the strongest rock imaginable. She'd been torn apart, and how ironic it was, that a man she hadn't known well at all had enabled her to find her strength again to start putting the shattered pieces of herself back together.

Teresa adored Mark. He was a man without a scrap of finesse, but everyone knew where they stood with him. There had to be more men like that in the world; men who didn't cheat for more than half a decade and lie to their families about it, like her own father had, and men like Ross, who couldn't commit, or at least man-up and be honest about their feelings before their cowardice destroyed someone else's world. An honest, authentic man without a hidden agenda; that shouldn't be too much to ask for, should it?

Even now, after all this time, Teresa still couldn't imagine ever giving her heart like that again. Mark had tried to reassure her that there would be a time when she'd feel ready to 'get back in the saddle,' and he'd used his own experience as an example. He'd told her how he'd been resigned to widowhood after Feen's mum had died, until Adie had come along and unwittingly picked away at the lock that had his heart firmly squirreled away behind it.

'If a gnarly old bugger like me can fall in love again, lass, after summat like bein' widdered, anyone can! Yer young, and yer beautiful, and yer'll find love again. 'Appen it'll be when yer not lookin' for it, but one day some lucky bloke'll waltz into yer life and turn it upside down, an' you'll turn *'im* upside down, and that'll be that.'

He'd told her to focus on herself for a while, and what her career goals were. 'Concentrate on gettin' to where yer want to be, jobwise, and let the rest 'appen when it's good an' ready, lass. Time's its own master.'

Teresa was grateful for his perspective, and his advice, but she couldn't imagine feeling about another man the way she'd felt about Ross. That was still too big a stretch. She couldn't trust anyone else; she couldn't even trust herself to *try* with anyone else, and she had no idea when or if that would change.

The latest news, that Ross was getting married, had thrown her back into the turmoil she'd clawed her way out of. She still wasn't really over him – not yet – but she had got hold of herself a little more quickly than last time. She wasn't a sobbing mass of hysteria, but the feeling of desolation was back in full force. She now just felt hollow inside, and kind of 'scraped-out,' for want of a better term. It felt like there was a *hole* inside her now, that she didn't know how to fill.

A little time out, here with her mum and Mark, might make all the difference. Lying here now, in this lovely guest room, she was glad she'd given in to her overwhelming need to come here to Ravensdown. It was time for serious change, and she didn't know what or how she was going to get things onto a new footing, but she knew it had to happen. For reasons she couldn't fully understand, this felt like the only place where she might be able to do it.

*   *   *   *   *

It was always really nice to see Feen. Even though she lived in London too with her husband and their twins, for at least half of the year, she and Teresa hadn't made a habit of keeping in touch. It wasn't that they actively avoided it, but Feen and Gavin were in Mayfair, which was one of the poshest parts of the inner city, and Teresa was south of the river, further out in the more 'hip and trendy' Greenwich. Ten miles or so wasn't much, but in London it could take an hour or more to cross the city by car. The tube was an option, of course, but they all led very different lives and were always busy, so there never seemed to be much time to even get in touch for a natter, let alone plan to meet up anywhere.

But Feen was here now, and Teresa was looking forward to a catch-up with her quirky and interesting stepsister. Although she knew she had little chance of understanding most of went on in Feen's ethereal, strange little head, she liked her, nonetheless.

Her husband was lovely too, not to mention drop-dead gorgeous. Gavin Black (or Gavin Raven-Black as he was now known) was a genuinely nice guy, wildly creative, and filthy rich to boot, but not in the least affected by it. He was down to earth and grounded, and Teresa guessed it was a good counterbalance to Feen's somewhat 'airy-fairy' approach to life. He also seemed to be a pretty good husband and father. He adored his wife and twins; they were everything to him, and it gave Teresa a wistful pang, to wonder whether she would ever be lucky enough to have a man like Gavin in her own life.

Ross Barker had been a different kind of guy altogether. He didn't have a creative bone in his body. He was an engineer, and almost nerdy with it, and he'd been sweet and charming enough, in his own way. But what you saw was pretty much what you got, and apart from the unpleasant discovery that he'd kept a ridiculously beautiful rose diamond under wraps for a very long time while he waited for 'the right girl,' he'd been fairly predictable – until he'd left, of course, which Teresa hadn't predicted at all. It really underscored the point that however well you think you know someone; they can always turn around and surprise you in a way that could leave you scarred for life.

It was hard sometimes, to be happy for people who were all 'loved-up,' when you'd been abandoned and left hanging out to dry. It was hard not to feel at least a little resentment towards those who had everything you wanted, and actually thought you *had*, until it all fell apart. Teresa wasn't the jealous type, and she certainly didn't begrudge Feen's happiness with her husband and children, but seeing someone so content was a keen reminder of her own shattered hopes and dreams.

She wouldn't have traded places with Feen – at least not as far as the children went. Marriage had always been vaguely on her radar, for some time in the future, but having kids was never going to be an option. It wasn't that she didn't *like* them; she just didn't want to *have* any – and that was not a new thing. She'd always felt that way and, if she was honest with herself now, she had to admit that it may have been a deal-breaker anyway, for her and Ross' relationship. They'd never talked seriously about stuff like that. Teresa had mentioned, almost in passing, that she didn't want to have any children, and he'd said he was cool about it. But that conversation had been fairly superficial. He might've changed his mind when he realised that she'd meant what she'd said.

Seeing his nauseating Instagram posts, with a woman who looked like she'd happily have a football team, was a big plate of food for thought.

Maybe we never talked about it because he never had any intention of making a life with me. What was I, then? A temporary distraction until Miss Right rocked up?

It was a hard thing to accept, that she'd merely been a stop-gap, but she wasn't the first woman to have acted as a temporary distraction for a man who had his sights set on something 'better,' and she wouldn't be the last. People used other people like that all the time, didn't they? She recalled a conversation, years ago, when a friend had been talking about a boy her friend was seeing. 'He isn't Mr Right for Me, but he's Mr Right for Now.'

She understood that sometimes it was about not wanting to feel lonely, or like some sad social misfit within your group. Back then, there was a lot of pressure to conform; to have a boyfriend or girlfriend. Nobody wanted to be the 'oddball' who couldn't get one. Everyone lived in a perpetual state of fear, about being the 'gooseberry' everyone else felt sorry for, or eventually froze out of the social circle because they no longer fitted into the emerging 'couples' scene. Having a partner was expected, so you did it, even if it *was* just a Miss or Mr Right for Now.

She'd simply been that, to Ross. As the old saying went; 'if you can't be with the one you love, love the one you're with.' Ross' feelings for her might have been real, but they clearly weren't the kind that could go the distance. He'd realised that, and while it wasn't his fault that he felt that way, he'd chosen to be a coward about it.

That was what upset her the most. He'd left her feeling like she wasn't worthy of an explanation. If he couldn't love her, that was one thing, but she deserved to be respected for the love she'd given him. She didn't deserve to be left wondering if any of it had mattered to him, or whether he'd ever meant a single thing he'd said.

Teresa had started becoming aware of something else now too. The realisation that she'd never have a marriage with Ross had pushed her towards reevaluating her future. A 'shift' was starting to occur within her. She couldn't describe it, other than to say that a few intrinsic dynamics were changing, and it felt as if she was being pulled in a very different direction from dwelling on love and a failed relationship.

She wasn't sure if that was merely a symptom of a broken heart, and the need to find some way to recover, but she suspected it ran a little deeper than that. In the days since Ross had announced his engagement, she had felt herself tilting in a slightly different direction. It was hard to describe, in fact she probably couldn't, if anyone had asked her to try. She didn't know exactly what to do about it, either. Annoyingly, the unquantifiable restlessness that she'd always felt, before she started travelling, was back and more profound than it had ever been, but she had gained enough wisdom to know that the answer wasn't to pick up her backpack and go off into the sunset again.

Something had very quietly and almost imperceptibly tilted on its axis, and it had exposed a very real need to commit to something solid. She had no idea what it might be, but it wasn't going to be another relationship – at least not yet.

Perhaps, rather than continuing to do what she'd always done and keep everything to herself (and drive herself slowly mad in the process), she could articulate her thoughts and get some different perspectives on them. Sometimes, when left to your own devices, you really couldn't see the wood for the trees.

Maybe I'll figure a few things out while I'm here. I can talk to Mum, and to Mark, and maybe even to Feen, about how I'm feeling. Maybe they can help me make sense of where I'm at in my crazy, mixed-up head.

She had definitely reached a crossroads; there was no denying that. She and most of her friends were heading into their late twenties now, and starting to make the big life commitments, like establishing careers, getting engaged or married (or at least cohabiting), buying houses and having kids. Her own brother Matty had settled down very quickly after meeting the love of his life. He now had a wife, a solid job, a fairly hefty mortgage and two little daughters. His life had changed beyond all recognition, in the blink of an eye, but he was happier than he'd ever been.

Teresa just had work out what would make *her* happy, and start working to achieve it. Goals were important, and right now, she didn't have one. She had a few ideas, but that's all they were – half-formed notions in her head about what she might like to do. The need to find something a little more fulfilling than the endless merry-go-round of temping jobs in London was starting to chip away at her. It seemed that even if she wanted to stay in a place of self-wallowing, her own thoughts weren't going let her.

Later that evening, as she was making a pot of tea, Feen wandered into the kitchen. 'Hello, you! Ah, tea! I'd love a cup if there's one going spare? Gavin's just popped out to take my friend Josie's daughter Nelle home. We've had her for the day, after they all went to Bubblegum this morning. It's a nursery in town. It's only for a couple of hours, but it's an important part of socialisation and pre-education for them. They all love it. Alder and Willow have gone along for the ride with their dad because we couldn't set them to gettle. It means I might just have a free pass for an hour while he has a brew with Josie's husband Tony. D'you nancy a fatter?'

'Yeah, that would be great. I'm on my own tonight. Mum and Mark have gone into the town to have a drink with Bob and Sheila. It was prearranged, and they asked me if I wanted to go, but I just want to chill, really, after the drive up here from London. It's the longest I've been behind the wheel for. Not exactly a killer, but far enough, right?'

Feen giggled. 'Right, and I heard you arrive, before. I'm sorry I didn't come and say hello, but I was working next door, and up to my neck in resin, at the time. Don't ask,' she added. 'It's all to do with the jewellery I make for your sister's wife Gina and her clothing brand GinGio, and for my own website. I have a workshop here, where I make quite a bit of my stuff. Adie brought our dinner up on trays tonight, because we were too busy to stop, bless her.'

She pulled a face. 'Being here isn't a holiday, like a lot of people think. Life doesn't change just because we change location. But sometimes I really need this place, if you know what I mean?'

'I do! London is crazy, isn't it? I'm thinking about getting out, to be honest. Not sure yet what my plans are, but let's just say I won't be upset if they *don't* involve the need to stay in London. People tend to either love or hate the place, don't they? But I'm actually quite ambivalent about it. I suppose that makes me a bit of an oddity.'

Feen shook her head. 'Not at all! I think you'd be surprised at how many people seel the fame as you and me. If I didn't have my home here, to come back to, it might be a stifferent dory. I think there's a lot to be said for knowing you've got somewhere else to go, if it all becomes too much, and sometimes it really does – for me, anyway.'

Teresa nodded. She remembered now, about Feen's natural use of Spoonerism, transposing the consonants on a pair of words or within a phrase. Being in a conversation with her was always interesting, and sometimes a little bamboozling. Occasionally, it could be hilarious. But it was never boring.

Teresa was curious about her life. 'You got married and had kids pretty quickly, didn't you? My brother Matty did that too, and he's as happy as you could ever imagine. Oops!

He's *your* brother too, isn't he? Stepbrother, anyway. Sorry, I keep forgetting that! Tell me, are *you* happy, Feen?

Feen nodded, without hesitation. 'I am. I do wish I had a little more time, you know, for myself, and for the things I like to do. I sometimes feel we're on a bit of a whamster heel, but we're only as frantic as we allow life to make us. Whenever I find my stair handing on end, I usually don't have to go further than the mirror, to find the cause. Aside from that, I think life is pretty good and, as I say, this place is a fig bactor in that.' She gestured with her hand, around the kitchen and at the back garden.

Then she fixed her gaze contemplatively on Teresa. 'What about you? I know you could be happier. You've had your heart broken, haven't you?'

Teresa felt her cheeks flush. Had her mother said something about her predicament to Feen? She didn't want to feel that she'd been the topic of discussion between other members of her family! *Surely, that wouldn't have happened?*

Feen smiled, gently, and shook her head. 'Don't worry, nobody has been talking about you. I just pick up on things sometimes, as you might remember.'

'Right. Yeah, I kind of was aware, but we've never really talked, have we, about your weirdness? No offence, you know? But you are kind of weird, to me – in a nice way, I mean. Don't get me wrong.'

Her stepsister giggled. 'Oh, stop digging! No offence taken, truly! Trust me, I've been called a lot worse than weird. And it's true. I'm probably *desperately* strange, to some people! But I can't help it. Certain psychic gifts have been passed down through my maternal lamily fine, from my great grandmother to my Anny Gralice, then to Mum, and down to me. And I'm pretty sure my daughter Willow is heading down the pame sath. We can't avoid who we are, as much as we might want to. It is what it is, I'm afraid. We are what we are; the witches of the North.'

'Is your grandmother still alive?'

'Anny Gralice? Yes, she is, although I really wish she wasn't, to be honest. She's completely addled with dementia, bless her. She's in a hare comb in Keswick. It's heartbreaking that she doesn't remember me anymore because she was always my link to the other realm. Mum didn't use her gift. I think she wanted to avoid it. She was never comfortable with it, from what I remember, and from things that Daddy's told me. But Anny Gralice was my rolid sock and guide for my whole life, until she got sick. I don't think she has long left, to be fair.'

'I'm so sorry.'

'Oh, don't be! I miss her badly, but I'll be glad when she goes; for her dignity and for the fact that once she shuffles off the cortal moil I will again have the link with her that I always had, because in the spirit world she will be whole again.'

Teresa couldn't get her head around that, but it probably wouldn't have helped to have said so. She needn't have wondered how to bridge any awkward gaps in conversation, however, because Feen piped up again.

'I know you're at a purning toint in your life. Please trust me when I tell you that your relationship had to end. It was inevitable because it wouldn't have survived the direction your life is about to take. He wasn't the might ran for you, who would support the really big change that's coming. Its hutal to brear that, I'm sure, and I'm sorry if it hurts, because the last thing I want is for you to be hurt any more. Please believe that. But you are going to have a big life, Teresa. A *very* big life indeed, and he was not the man to be on that journey with you. He wouldn't be able to hack it, no matter how much you'd have wanted him to.'

Teresa felt a quick, cold tingle as it slid the length of her spine. She stared at Feen. 'What makes you say that? What can you see?'

Feen sighed, gently, and frowned. 'Let's just say that the man who *can* hack the way your life will go is still on his way to you. But he *is* on his way, and he is a man who won't want to live 'conventionally' either. You will end up very happy, my lovely, but in a very different way than what you always imagined.'

'Wow! That's a lot. A lot for you to say, and a lot for me to take on board.'

'It probably sounds like that, but you don't have to worry about it. In fact, you really shouldn't, because it's all going to be amazing. All you have to do is let things unfold and accept the opportunities that show themselves. 'You're on a very pecial spath, Teresa. You have a destiny, at the end of a dream you haven't yet fully formed in your own head, but the loss of your relationship is – albeit painfully – part of the necessary 'clearing' you need to go through, to be ready for what's next.'

She giggled lightly, before carrying on. 'You might also find that certain friends won't ay in your storbit either, through their choice or yours. That is inevitable too, I'm afraid, but it helps if you can look at it as inappropriate people leaving, that make room for more compatible ones to come in. So, don't be afraid! Stand tall. You're going where you are supposed to go, with the tribe you're supposed to go with, and it will be an amazing life. I'm excited for you.'

'Gosh! Well, I don't really know what to say to all that! It's a lot, too! But do *you* feel you've ended up where you were supposed to, Feen?'

'Yes, I do. I think we *all* end up where we're supposed to, if we allow ourselves to be guided by a universe that really does have our est binterests at heart! Sometimes it doesn't feel like that, especially when things are going horribly wrong and it feels like we're being torn apart, but pusting the trocess invariably takes us to a place that's usually better than where we thought we wanted to go.'

'I don't want children, Feen. I know that's a very big statement, and I hope that as a mother yourself you won't condemn me for it. I know we're *all* supposed to be mothers as well as everything else, aren't we? But the truth is that I've never wanted to have kids, and I do wonder if maybe my relationship would have foundered anyway, on that basis. We never talked about it seriously, because I just assumed we had a future, and we'd get to all that stuff in good time. Clearly, he wasn't on the same page about that but, either way, I think it might have made a difference.'

'Well, I think you might be right about that. And it's perfectly fine to not want to have kids, by the way. We *don't* all have to be mothers, Teresa! It's the worst irony that some women who *are* mothers shouldn't be, and they make a jerrible tob of it. Then, at the other end of the spectrum, there's the women who can't have kids who would make wonderful mothers! I have a friend who went through so much, trying to have them. She got there in the end, but it wasn't without *years* of anguish first, and she almost lost her marriage in the process. Procreation is a very personal thing. Nobody has the jight to rudge anyone else for whatever choice they make.'

Teresa sighed. 'I'm dreading telling Mum. I think she'll be really upset.'

'No, I think she might surprise you, on that. Adie's pretty easy-going. I'm sure she'll respect your decision, and support whatever choices you make, if she understands that they feel like the right ones for you.'

'It's funny that you talk about friends dropping off. Some of mine have been quite dismissive, and condescending,' Teresa admitted. 'I really wish I hadn't told them now; some of them, anyway. Their reactions have been a bit patronising or critical, and I've even doubted myself at times, because of that. Not *fundamentally.* I'm pretty solid on my decision, deep down, but I do sometimes wonder if I'm being selfish, in not having kids as part of my life plan. Some people have hinted that it is.'

'Unfortunately, most people judge by their own experiences or desires. It's short-sighted of them, and it can feel really jean and mudgy, but if they can't respect your choice, it's their problem, not yours! And I do think it's part of the atural nevolution you're going through. Getting clear about what you do and don't want is a really big part of establishing your path and feeling comfortable about it.' Feen shook her head a little, and frowned.

'You can't listen to everybody else, Teresa. They're not living your life, so they don't get to judge it or try to influence it – certainly not over something as big as whether or not you have children! Its *yourself* you have to be true to, and you *can* trust yourself. It's vital that you do, going forward.'

Teresa drained her cup. 'Thanks, Feen. My head feels so stuffed full of everything, right now. Grief, worry, sadness, anxiety about the future…' She trailed off, not knowing how to explain herself better. But Feen's smile was kind. She did understand. It was reassuring, that at least someone in her family understood exactly what she was trying to grapple with.

'You'll be just fine. Sometimes, when you're not sure about what you really want, it helps to get honest and clear about what you *don't* want. That does go some way to establishing your pathway. And, with your decision around the kid thing, you've already made a powerful start, in faping your own shuture.'

Feen looked up as the front door opened and closed. 'That's Gavin. Is there enough tea in the pot for him? I can make him some upstairs, if not.'

'Well, I'm going to have some more, so let's all have a fresh pot.'

'Sit down, Teresa. Let me make this one.'

Gavin came in, and Teresa was startled once again, at how good looking he was. One of the nicest things about him was that he didn't seem to have a scrap of conceit. Feen waved the teapot at him, and he grinned.

'Perfect, thanks. The twins are asleep in the car. I figured it was ok to sleave them noring for a few minutes.'

Teresa liked his deep, Home Counties accent that seemed slightly at odds with his rock-musician persona. He pulled a hair tie off his right wrist and pulled his long dark wavy hair back, and dragged it into a scruffy ponytail. Then he turned his attention to Teresa.

'How are you enjoying Ravensdown? It's pretty cool here, isn't it? I tend to get quite creative when I'm here. Feen says it has something to do with the ley line that runs under the place. I don't profess to fully understand this whole thing about vibrational energy, but I'm doing what she says and being open to it. If it means I get witloads of shirk done, I'll take it.' His startling green eyes twinkled, as he grinned at Feen.

She rolled her eyes at him in return. 'Well, if I've explained it once, I've done it tixty simes. And I know that you *do* understand fully, and that you are messing with me which, I might remind you, is never a good idea. So, you can quit it, right now, or you might find an eye of newt or a toe of toad in your tea.'

Gavin winked at Teresa. 'Don't tell me you've let her make the tea! We might all be glass-eyed and barking at the moon by midnight!'

Teresa laughed. This was the first time she'd really had the chance to spend time with her stepsister and her husband. They were a nice couple. The fact that Gavin was prone to a little bit of Spoonerism too was quietly hilarious. They seemed perfect together, and bounced well off one another with their funny banter. She tried to ignore the little pang of wistfulness that washed over her.

Feen seems pretty sure that my life has a big direction, and that things will turn out well. She mentioned a man coming into my life, and everything coming together. Maybe, one day, I'll be as happy as they are.

Chapter Four

The town was pretty much as Chris remembered it, with the big old pub, The Bull & Royal, at the foot of the walkway. He and Daisy had gone in there a few times. It was a nice pub, and the food was good. As he walked around the front of it, he saw the familiar sign; 'Dog and Muddy-Boot Friendly.' A food menu sat propped in the window, and fish and chips were on it. Since the pub welcomed dogs, it suddenly seemed like a better idea to have dinner here, instead of buying a takeaway that would probably be stone cold by the time he'd walked back up the hill with it.

It was six o'clock and the bar was already quite full, with the after-work crowd mostly finishing their second or third happy-hour pint, but most of the tables designated for diners were still empty. He noted that a couple were reserved. He asked the bartender, who introduced himself as Nick, to reserve one for him too, for half an hour's time. He figured it would give him time to pop across to the town's little supermarket, grab a couple of things, and be back before the rest got taken.

Nick told him that dogs were only allowed in the bar. They couldn't come into the dining area but, apparently, there was a 'puppy crèche' out the back; a side room where local diners could leave their dogs to play together (provided they got along) while they ate in the dining room. It was mostly set up for regular locals, Nick said, because of the knowledge of their dogs' vaccination status and temperaments. But, since Misty was so small and young, and clearly well cared-for, he thought perhaps she might be allowed in. He offered Chris the chance to see straight away if she would be, so he could go and do his shopping in peace. Chris was grateful. No other dogs were currently in there, so Misty would have the exclusive attention of the Bull and Royal's landlords' daughter Cassie, whose job it was on Friday and Saturday nights to watch the dogs, ensure they were happy, and to nip any bad behaviour in the bud.

What a great idea, Chris concluded. Only in a local village pub, where most of its punters were regulars, would you ever have something as helpful and sweet as a puppy crèche! He followed Nick through to a mid-sized room at the back of the restaurant with French doors leading to a small patch of grass out the back. It was fenced off from a bigger area that served as the pub's beer garden. He was introduced to Cassie, who seemed to be about thirteen years old. She immediately bent down and picked up Misty, who proceeded to lick her face like it was covered in gravy.

'Aw! She's so gorgeous! She'll be absolutely fine in here, won't you girl?' Cassie reached up onto a nearby shelf and pulled down a jar of small, bone-shaped biscuits. 'Is it ok if I give her a treat?' Chris nodded, smiling, and watched with a grin as Misty joyfully crunched the little bone. Cassie asked him if she had any socialisation issues, and he shook his head.

All around the edges of the tiled floor there were bean bags of different sizes, chew-toys, balls, a few soft teddy-type toys, and plenty of bowls of fresh water. A large rolled-up rug was propped in one corner of the room, against a stack of chairs and a few collapsible card tables. Chris assumed the room doubled up as club-rooms for various groups throughout the week.

'I guess she has all her vaccinations, and stuff?' Cassie's question brought him back into focus.

'Oh, yes of course, although I don't have the papers with me. D'you need them? I can call my vet if you like, although I dunno if anyone will still be there now that it's past six o'clock. I do have the emailed appointment confirmation on my phone, if that helps? I can also show you the bank transaction for the payment, if you want to see that too.'

He showed Cassie the email from his vet, confirming the appointment time when he'd taken Misty for her shots, a couple of months earlier. 'Normally we'd want to see the actual certificates, but that's good enough. I trust you. No-one else is booked in tonight anyway, and you don't seem the type that would put anyone's dog at risk, especially not your own. Misty will be fine.'

'What's the cost for the service? I presume you'll want cash.'

'Yes please, it's just two pounds, if that's ok? You pay when you collect her.'

Chris nearly laughed. Two pounds? It seemed like such a paltry amount, but there again, Cassie was young, definitely still at school, so this was probably just pocket money to her. If she had a few dogs in, it would still add up to a bit for her to spend on make-up, and burger-dates with her friends. He decided he'd check on Misty after he got back from the supermarket. If she was ok, and happy enough, he'd leave her in there while he had his dinner.

The supermarket was busy. He found a few essentials, and one or two treats, and splashed out on a bottle of Penderyn whisky, which was his favourite, and which he was astonished to find in a tiny supermarket in a place like Torley. It was the only bottle left on the shelf, and it really did seem wrong to leave it there.

A woman ahead of him at the checkout had a fully laden trolley but, when she saw that Chris only had a handful of things, she gave him a wink and kindly let him go in front of her.

That never happened in Derby! Most times, when he was queuing with a small number of items, most shoppers with more did everything they could to avoid eye contact, making sure they didn't have to feel shamed by not letting him in, or compromise their own precious time by doing so. Even the checkout operator here greeted him as if she knew him. She asked him if he'd found everything he was looking for, and when he said that he had, she smiled gently and nodded, seeming genuinely glad. Her name badge said her name was Ginny.

'Thanks, Ginny,' he said as he was leaving. She rewarded him with a beaming smile.

That was all most people wanted, wasn't it? To be acknowledged, and treated as 'somebody'? He'd learned, a long time ago, that validating someone by calling them by name often meant their jobs didn't seem so thankless.

As he made his way back to the Bull and Royal's rear entrance, his eye was drawn to the little dress shop where Daisy had bought a summer dress last year. It was called GladRagz boutique, and Chris remembered how helpful the woman had been who ran the place. He wondered if she still owned it. Maybe tomorrow he'd wander by, before or after the market, and see if he recognised whoever might be behind the counter. It was another place where Daisy had been happy, trying on clothes, and treating herself to something nice, at the start of the new season.

'This dress is fab, Chris! I'll wear this all summer, and probably the next one too!' she'd said gleefully, as she'd twirled about in it. Chris swallowed down the lump in his throat, remembering. Little did they know at the time that there'd be no 'next summer' for Daisy. That little strappy sundress was now packed up with the rest of her things in one of a dozen boxes, waiting for him to decide what to do with it all.

Chris had wondered if he should just give Daisy's stuff to her parents to deal with, but somehow that didn't feel right. If they'd *offered* to take it off his hands, to relieve him of that burden, he would have accepted, but it didn't feel appropriate to ask them. Besides, Daisy's belongings were legally all his, now.

They'd made mirror wills; Daisy had insisted. That hadn't felt particularly appropriate either, at the time they'd done it. Chris thought it was something they would eventually get around to doing once they'd got married, and bought their own home, but as they were so young, still renting, and neither of them had any significant assets, he hadn't seen much point in making wills. They had nothing of note to leave to one another, at the time. But Daisy had been adamant.

'You just never know what might happen, Chris! The future can change in an instant. What if we forget to do it later, when we do have assets, or even kids? If either one of us died, would the other one left behind have to fight for our home, or something? What if you died on some mountain, somewhere? Wouldn't you want me to be financially okay, after something like that? We should get private life insurance policies too, I think. Call it peace of mind, or even an anti-jinx! If we do all this, it means nothing bad will happen.'

How brutally, cruelly ironic, for her to have said that.

The worst of the irony was, that he was now glad they *had* made wills, leaving whatever they might have to one another. The travel insurance that he'd arranged for them both, for their fateful trip, had paid out a hefty sum on Daisy's policy. It had in fact been one of the highest single payouts the insurers had ever made. Her private life insurance policy had paid out handsomely too.

Without her will, any member of her family could have come along and tried to claim that money, or any of her other belongings. Chris had been the beneficiary of her insurance payouts, and the assumption from her family seemed to be that he'd be the one to decide what to do with all her stuff as well. Not one of them had asked for anything at all. Daisy had an engraved gold locket that her parents had given her for her twenty-first birthday, but they hadn't even asked for that back! Chris intended to return it to her mother, at some point, when he felt ready.

Daisy's body had been repatriated, and for a couple of months after the funeral, her parents had kept in fairly regular touch with him, to see how he was doing. They'd been divorced, and both had remarried. Daisy said they'd never been a super-close, touchy-feel family, so he supposed it was probably par for the course that they'd keep their distance. But he realised now that he would have appreciated a *bit* more connection with them. After all, he and Daisy hadn't just been dating! They'd been engaged to be married, with a wedding and a honeymoon all planned, and that was a whole lot more significant. Chris felt it *should* have been, at least, but her family clearly hadn't thought so. Over time, their calls had dwindled away, and he couldn't now recall the last time he'd spoken to either of them, or to Daisy's brother or sisters. It felt like they'd all just forgotten him.

On the one hand he figured maybe they were trying to be sensitive, and give him space to grieve but, on the other, he felt insulted that in the midst of their *own* grief, none of them had thought that his might not be over either, and keeping a connection to other people who'd been part of Daisy's life might be important to him. He wasn't the type to push himself on anyone, and he certainly wouldn't pull anyone forward who didn't want to come, but he knew he'd done exactly that with Daisy herself, with the trip to the Spanish mountains.

For the millionth time, he asked himself what the hell he'd been thinking, railroading her into it. She'd still be here now, if he hadn't pushed it; if he'd just gone by himself, and left her to do her own thing while he was away. She'd have been there at home for him to come back to, waiting with open arms, longing to hear his stories, demanding to see every last photo taken (even the rubbish ones), and devouring the adventures with so much relish. She had such zest for life.

I robbed her of that. I robbed her of everything.

Chris' appetite was suddenly gone, as was so often the case these days. But, since he'd booked a table, he figured he may as well at least *try* to eat something. There was nothing worse than feeling hungry as well as wretched.

A quick check on Misty revealed the puppy to be extremely happy with Cassie. The two were on the floor, playing tug with a rag bone, and neither even noticed him as he poked his head around the door.

Nick showed him to his table, a quiet one set for two, by the window that looked out to the car park at the back of the pub, and the end of the walking track he'd come down, from Ravendsown Farm. He ordered a pint and a plate of fish and chips, complete with mushy peas, tartare sauce and gravy, and sat back to watch as a lovely old bottle-green Land Rover pulled in and parked up. It was an old vehicle, probably from the 1970's, but it was wonderfully restored and well-kept, and it was sign-written, advertising 'Valley Veterinary Services.'

A tall, well-built guy with short dark hair, who looked to be somewhere in his late thirties, jumped out of it and a short, slightly plump blonde woman of a similar age got out of the passenger seat. They linked hands and started walking towards the back entrance of the pub, but stopped when another vehicle pulled up and parked. This one was also a farm hack, a maroon-coloured Toyota truck, and it too was sign-written on its front doors; 'Beaconsfield Stables & Riding School.'

A man in his mid-to-late forties got out of that and walked around the side and opened the car door for a woman who levered herself out of it with a great deal of care. She was walking very slowly, as if she were afraid of falling, and the man put a hand under her arm to support her.

The couples greeted one another with hugs. Clearly, they were friends who'd decided to meet at the pub. Locals, Chris presumed. Maybe they did this every Friday night.

Soon they were all sitting down at one of the reserved tables nearby. Barman Nick came over, and the group all greeted him by name. The dark-haired man ordered a round of drinks for them all, and he knew exactly what to ask for, so it was clear to Chris that they all knew one another well.

He could hear them chattering cheerfully about their week. The stables owner was clearly a client of the vet, but they also seemed to be good friends. They were a happy, animated group. The vet took off his jacket and hung it over the back of his chair, and as he did so, his wallet fell out of it. He didn't notice. Chris immediately called him to attention.

'Excuse me! You've dropped something!' The vet looked over at him, looked on the floor beneath his jacket, then raised a hand in thanks. Chris nodded, and went back to nursing his pint and staring out into the car park. A few minutes later he looked up to find the vet standing next to him.

'Thanks for letting me know I'd dropped my wallet. We've noticed you're on your own. Would you like to join us?'

Chris' immediate response was to decline, but before he could open his mouth, the man spoke again and stuck his hand out. 'I'm Darren Davies, one of the local vets, and the incredibly beautiful blonde sitting next to me is my wife, Debby. Our friends are Stuart and Fiona. We're not nosy types, but none of us likes to see anyone dining alone unless it's by choice and that's fine of course, if it is! But, if you'd like a bit of company, please do come and join us, although I do have to warn you, we can't agree among ourselves on football, religion or politics, so the conversation's usually fairly inane and meaningless.' Darren grinned and Chris decided he liked him. He thought for a moment.

What harm can it do, to spend an hour or so with a few kind strangers? Maybe it wouldn't be such a bad thing to get out of my own head for a bit.

He cleared his throat, and shook Darren's hand. 'Well, that's a very kind offer. I should just say up front though, that I'm a bit psychotic, with a really bad case of Tourette's, but if you can put up with a load of cringe-worthy, top-level effing and blinding and name-calling, then yes, I'd love a bit of company.'

He couldn't help but grin as Darren looked slightly taken aback, but he caught the twinkle in Chris' eye, and laughed.

'Ok, mate, touché! I'm not bothered by a bit of bad language. Used to be a shocker myself, if I'm honest. Come on then, grab your pint and your chair, and come over. You'll be in good company!'

Chris obliged. 'I'm Chris Darcy, by the way. Electrician, single, recently bereaved in fact, and staying in the area for a fortnight.'

He was surprised at himself, as soon as the words were out of his mouth. *Recently bereaved?* Where the hell did that come from? It wasn't as if he made a habit of telling total strangers about his circumstances! Who'd want to know *that*, for Christ's sake? He resisted the urge to apologise since the last thing he wanted was to draw more attention to what he'd just said. He really didn't want to talk about it.

He felt a bit nervous as he sat down, but Darren introduced him to everyone and there were instant smiles all round, so he just said; 'thanks for the invite. I guess it does look a bit sad, eating alone in a pub on a Friday night.'

Debby raised her glass of white wine to him. 'Glad you could join us. I'm Debby with a 'Y.' Are you new to the area, or just passing through?'

Chris explained that he was just staying locally for two weeks, up at Teapot Cottage on Ravensdown Farm. He was astonished when all four at the table started laughing. Stuart gave him a big grin. 'Teapot Cottage! We know the place well! All of us have stayed there, at different times. We're all locals now, and believe it or not, it's largely thanks to that place, and the Raven family.'

He explained to Chris that he and his daughter had stayed there while they were in transition, and both had found the new direction they were looking for simply because of a horse in the field next to the cottage. Chris was captivated by Stuart's story. His daughter had been a troubled teen, who changed completely after meeting the horse, which had been owned at the time by a local vet – none other than Darren Davies!

Chris asked him what he did for a job, and he was surprised when Stuart readily admitted that he'd been in prison for a long time, and he described the journey he'd had, after his release, in acquiring and rebuilding a failing equine business. Chris didn't want to be rude and ask him what he'd been locked up for, but he felt humbled that a complete stranger would share such a story. He had the feeling that it probably wouldn't have come out though, if Teapot Cottage hadn't been mentioned!

'Wow!' That's quite a story! D'you miss lawyering?' He was curious to know, since he couldn't really imaging being in a position where he had to change careers himself.

Stuart shrugged, and pulled an easy-osey face. 'Sometimes, yeah, but not as much as I once thought I would. Where I am in life now is a long way from where I ever imagined I'd be, but the new life's pretty good, if I'm honest, and the business is finally threatening to start turning a profit. I don't miss the stress of corporate law, or the endless attention to detail, on which most of it turns.'

He grinned ruefully. 'It was never as glamorous in reality as it sounds, anyway. I was a bit of an arrogant twat back then too. I'm a better person these days, as well as a happier one, so on the days when I miss the legal world, I just remind myself of how far I've come in a different direction.'

Fiona, his wife, looked at him fondly, before turning her attention to Chris. 'Hello, Chris. I'm Fiona, and I ended up at Teapot Cottage myself, under some unhappy circumstances. It's a long story, but I have cancer, and I went there to stay for a few days with my oldest friend, while I worked out what to do after I found out. It's where I met Stuart.'

She was quietly spoken, and Chris could see now, the dark shadows under her eyes, that hadn't quite been fully concealed by her make-up. She looked tired, and pale, and he guessed that she was every bit as exhausted as she looked. He wasn't sure how to respond to what she'd said, other than to say he was sorry to hear it. Fiona waved his apology away.

'Well, it could be worse, and it may still get that way eventually. For now, although I haven't got any better, I also haven't got any worse. That is something, given the initial prognosis, so I'm taking it. We just try to live the best life we can and be as happy as we can under the circumstances, don't we, Stu?'

She went on to tell Chris that she used to be a Quantity Surveyor in her past career, and that she and Stuart now bought derelict houses in the Lake District and renovated them in the quieter months when the stables and riding school wasn't busy. Her health didn't allow her to undertake the stress of the work she used to do for clients, but doing things with Chris at a pace she could currently manage was working out okay for her, and she hoped she could eventually go back to her profession.

Chris was interested to learn that Fiona's speciality involved the restoration of historic buildings. He admitted it was something he enjoyed too, after doing a couple of house-wiring jobs in a row of spectacular Regency terraces that were over two hundred years old.

'They had three floors, those places, and a few also had an attic. They were amazing! The work had to be done sensitively, in keeping with the integrity of the building,' he explained, knowing that he was preaching to the already converted, but he wanted to offer his own insight, in the spirit of the conversation.

'But I *loved* that work! New-builds are easy; you can get in before the plasterboard goes up, and the wiring's usually a quick and straightforward job. The retrofit stuff can be a lot more of a challenge. It's satisfying though, at least for me. The feeling of having a hand in restoring a magnificent piece of history is something you can't describe, can you? Some of those old places were built really well, and have *so* much character.'

He laughed, then, and felt slightly embarrassed. He thought his enthusiasm might sound a bit gauche, but nobody seemed to think it was over the top. If they did, they were far too polite to say so. Stuart was scrolling through his phone, and he handed it over to Chris so he could see the photos of the two cottages Stuart and Fiona had already completed.

'We're just in the process of acquiring four more houses, two adjacent blocks of Victorian semis just on the outskirts of the market town of Keswick.'

Chris knew the town. It was less than an hour south of Carlisle, if the traffic behaved itself. Stuart explained that the houses were all owned by the same extended family.

'One pair's been derelict for a decade or more. The pair just next door have been lived in, but the dweller of one died a few months ago, and the other had tenants in it who have just bought their own place.'

Fiona chipped in at that point. 'The recently lived-in ones are habitable, but only just. They need a complete upgrade and refurbish, which won't come cheap. The derelict ones are even worse. They're pretty much a bootstrap job from the foundations up.' She went on to say how excited she and Stuart were, about them because they'd got them at a pretty fair price, at auction.

'Depending on the valuations that come in once they're all done to the standard we want, we'll either keep them to rent out, or sell them to raise capital for new ventures. It's going to be a stretch, timewise, because a lot of the work will need to be done when the stables is back in full swing, but I guess we'll manage, somehow. We have a good team, so we think we can pull it off.'

Stuart nodded. 'It'll be a challenge, for sure. I'm going to be pulled pretty thin. But we're keen to get going with the semis, because we're hoping to make them part of our investment portfolio. We had to sell the first two we did, to raise the capital to get these. We'd like to keep them, to use them as leverage to buy more, but, if the valuations suggest we should sell them instead, that's what we'll do.'

'One issue might be that they are huge,' Fiona added. 'As rentals they might not be practical unless we go down the multiple-occupancy route. HMO, as it's known.'

'That might work, but don't you have to have a whole different set of compliances for HMO? That might be a bit of a headache,' Chris ventured.

She nodded. 'Yes. It's the last thing we want, for lots of reasons. I think we will end up selling, actually, so I'm trying not to get too emotionally attached to them, which is hard, and you'd know why if you could see them. Like you said, so much character! It's like they talk to you. I know that sounds crazy…'

She tailed off, but Chris thought he understood what she meant. As he was handing Stu's phone back to him, he turned his attention to Darren and Debby.

'So, what's *your* Teapot Cottage story, if you don't mind me asking?'

He noticed that Debby blushed lightly as Darren chuckled, and started telling the story of them coming to Teapot Cottage on a month away, as a make-or-break time in their marriage. 'We were falling apart. We'd had trouble for years, trying to have a baby. We'd had seven attempts at IVF, and they all failed, in one way or another. We'd started doubting if we could even stay together, because of the stress. It was a hell you can't describe to anyone, to be honest.'

Debby gently squeezed his arm, and took up the story. 'But during our stay we managed to find the courage to decide that we *could* still have a life together without babies. Then, miraculously, they started arriving! We now have a little girl, Ruby, who's two, and our six-month-old son Thomas.'

Darren spoke again. 'It was like, the minute we gave up trying, magic took over and gave us what we'd stopped asking for! People laugh at that idea, but we conceived Ruby at the cottage, so it's hard to discount it entirely, the notion of magic, you know?'

He grinned, self-consciously. 'So then, we decided to move up here! An opening came up at the local vet surgery for a new farm vet. It was something I'd wanted to get into for ages, but there weren't many opportunities down south. When this chance came, I grabbed it with both hands. We decided we could raise the family we didn't think we'd even get to have, in a quieter, more supportive environment than Exeter, where we both grew up.'

Chris grinned. 'Sounds like it was all meant to be!'

Debby laughed. 'It definitely feels that way. Sometimes I still pinch myself at the way it all worked out, especially when I think about how close we were to giving up, and *splitting* up.'

'Darren looks after my horses,' Stuart offered, almost inanely. 'The horse my daughter Meghan fell in love with? Darren gave Astro to her, in the end. It's been the making of them both, actually, horse *and* kid.'

Chris was blown away, by his four dinner companions. They'd willingly given so much personal information! Who even *did* that anymore? In the space of ten minutes, he'd learned more about these people than he knew about some of the friends he'd had for years! He felt truly privileged to have been the recipient of so much 'realness' from strangers. In the spirit of that, and with his second pint now on the table, he felt compelled to share something too. Before doing that, he asked Nick to hold his food so it would come out with the others' so they could all eat together.

'That's a nice idea,' Debby smiled.

Nobody had asked Chris to say anything about himself. There was no air of expectation, no pregnant pauses that made him feel as if he should share his own deepest secrets, but he suddenly felt very safe with these people, in a way he couldn't define. Astonished at himself, he began to talk.

'Well, it sounds like you were all at some kind of crossroads when you ended up here, which is kinda strange, because I feel like that's where I am too. I've been here before, but under very different circumstances. Now, I'm wondering what's next for me. I mean, I have a job and a flat and everything. I'm on the last of my paid holidays, in fact. But I'm trying to figure out what I want for my life, because it's changed a lot in the last few months, and I'm still finding my feet again.'

Darren cleared his throat. 'You mentioned you've recently had a bereavement? Not that you have to talk about it, of course,' he added, quickly. Chris looked around at their faces, all of which were kind and understanding. These people all knew what suffering was, and they were kind enough not to press for information. They seemed to understand the boundaries of strangers, even though they'd demolished their own without much preamble.

Oh, what the hell. I'll probably never see them again after tonight anyway.

'Yeah, my fiancée Daisy died almost a year ago, in a climbing accident in the Spanish Sierra Nevada. I'm a fairly serious mountaineer in my spare time, and I railroaded her into coming with me to do Mulhacén. It'd been on my list for years, but it's not such a biggie, compared with some I've done, and plan to do. It's an okay climb for a first timer, with help, so I organised a guided climb, so Daisy could come with me. She was really excited for me, but she didn't exactly want to come along.' Chris swallowed the all-too familiar lump in his throat and continued.

'I mistook her encouragement and enthusiasm for something else. I dunno, I guess I hoped she'd start climbing too and could one day share such mind-blowing experiences with me. I insisted she come. I said I wouldn't go if she didn't, because I genuinely thought she'd love it, and I wanted us to have it as a shared passion.'

He swallowed hard again, and carried on with the story. 'She agreed to come, but reluctantly. I think she only said yes to shut me up. She was doing okay on the climb though, until she fell, with four others. Two other climbers and the guy that was guiding them. They all died. And now of course

I hate myself with a passion I once didn't think I was even capable of, and I'm wondering if I'll ever be able to stop.'

All four faces at the table filled with compassion. Darren spoke up first. 'I remember that accident. It was on the news, wasn't it? Didn't someone else slip, and the rope snapped, or something like that?'

Chris nodded. 'Yes, that's the one.' He didn't know what else to say. Stuart spoke up next.

'Do you feel responsible? For her death, I mean?'

Chris nodded, surprised at the bluntness of Stuart's question but strangely not offended by it. 'I *am* responsible. If I hadn't been such a selfish bastard, she wouldn't have been there, would she? By saying I wouldn't go if she didn't, I more or less blackmailed her into going.'

At that moment, the meals arrived. Grateful for the lull in conversation as everyone got stuck in, Chris forced himself to eat. He'd well and truly lost his appetite, but somewhere in the back of his mind, he heard Daisy admonishing him gently, as she often used to do, always with a smile in her voice, as if she knew he wouldn't listen, even as she was telling him.

'You have to eat! And just look at all those lovely chips! Eat them for me, if not for yourself.'

He blinked a few times and pushed her voice away.

The food was delicious, even to his disinterested palate. He managed to finish the fish, most of the chips and half the mushy peas. It wasn't a bad effort, considering he'd started off thinking he'd be lucky to eat three mouthfuls.

Nick came to clear the plates and ask if anyone wanted pudding. Fiona and Debby both giggled and made a big show of considering it before refusing, but Darren declared he'd have the apple pie and ice-cream. Debby rolled her eyes.

'You're such a piglet,' she said to her husband. She looked at Chris, her eyes twinkling. 'He'd crawl to the end of the earth for a slice of pie - any kind, it really doesn't matter.

Curry and custard pie, rice pudding and onion pie, cheese and banana, Darren would eat it.'

Stuart also declined dessert, so Chris decided to show some support for Darren. 'I'll keep you company, mate. I'll have a slice of pie.'

It was the last thing he really felt like having but somehow it felt like the right thing to do. A show of solidarity to an incredibly kind stranger. Stuart cleared his throat and pulled the conversation back. 'For what it's worth, I know about the kind of responsibility you're feeling.'

Chris turned his attention to the man, and was surprised to see how sad he looked.

'I mentioned that I'd been banged up? Yeah, I served six years of a nine-year sentence for causing death by dangerous driving. I killed a pregnant woman in the street, in Taunton. It was just over eight years ago, now. At the time, I was a cocky, arrogant prick. Until it happened, I thought I was invincible.'

There was silence at the table. It wasn't an awkward silence, since these four clearly new each other well enough to have got past any involuntary reactions. It was as if Stuart had remarked on the weather which, to be fair, would probably have elicited more of a response from his mates than what he *had* said. He sat back in his chair and looked squarely at Chris.

'Nobody can know how it feels. Nobody can tell you, with any authority, that it will get better; that you'll come to terms with it fully. I haven't, and I'm not sure I ever will. It's my personal demon – something I have to live with every day, and I sometimes wonder if I'm asking too much, in wanting to tuck it all neatly away. Maybe we're not *supposed* to do that. Maybe we're still supposed to live with the terrible things we do as ever-present, but hopefully in ways that don't torment us.'

'Are you there yet?' Chris asked quietly.

Stuart shook his head. 'Not quite,' he said baldly. 'I'm not sure it's possible for *anyone* to square something like that away, as if it never happened. I've accepted that it did, and I've acknowledged my responsibility for it, but as for forgiving myself? Well, let's just say that's still a work in progress.' Stuart took a swig of his pint before continuing.

'I went out to Bali to meet the woman's parents, after her husband wrote to me in prison telling me he'd forgiven me for what I'd done. They were a Balinese couple. I learned a lot while I was out there with their families, about forgiveness, and how the Balinese have it as a fundamental part of their culture. It helped a lot but, if I'm honest, there are still plenty of days when it's hard to feel even *close* to being at peace with it.'

Darren cleared his throat. 'I've a similar story, Chris. A while ago, in a life I had before this one, I was a criminal. Small-time stuff. Petty theft, mostly. I did time too, various stints, all short ones. A few months, here and there. But a young lad died because I abandoned him after we got sprung on a burglary. If I hadn't run off like a coward and left him, he'd probably still be alive.

'I have to live with that too. I've forgiven myself, as best I can, because the intention for him to die was never there, like it wasn't for Stuart, or for you in fact. But the truth is, you never really do let yourself off the hook, not completely. There's always something in your psyche that keeps you accountable, in all kinds of small ways.'

Chris was astonished how far this man had pulled himself up, from a life of crime, to become a respectable, highly skilled, and valued member of his local community. He was heavily tattooed, and there was a general air of world-weariness about him, as if nothing in life would ever shock or surprise him, so Chris wasn't too surprised that he'd started out on a dubious path. But what must it have taken, for Darren Davies to turn his life around so completely?

Darren was looking at him pensively, as if reading his mind. Chris wasn't surprised at that either. Daisy had always told him he had 'no face for poker.' His emotions were nearly always clearly there on his face for all to see. He was rubbish at hiding them.

Darren compressed his lips into a thin line, then spoke again. 'What happened to Tommy, my mate, it changed everything. It woke me up, and made me take a long, hard look at myself. That's when I knew things had to change. *I* had to change. I was on a path to self-destruction. I had to rewrite my own destiny, and make it count for something, for *his* sake as well as my own, so that's what I did.'

He went on to explain that he and Tom had robbed a woman called Alison Jones, who had inadvertently killed his accomplice Tom, and had then gone on to bequeath money to Darren so he could make something of his life. It had been done out of guilt, and a sense of atonement, but it had given him the chance he would never otherwise have had, to do something real and put himself on a better path.

'It was a once-in-a-lifetime opportunity, so I grabbed it with both hands. It was my one real chance, and I didn't just do it for myself. I did it for Tom, too. It became the most important thing to me, that his life wasn't lost in vain. I felt like I owed it to him, to be a better person. It was the only way I could live with myself, and the woman who killed him knew that. She had a brain tumour and she died herself not long after but, before she did, she paved the way for me with someone who offered me the chance to train as a vet.'

Fiona spoke up next, and her voice was quiet. 'I guess that's probably what it comes down to. Maybe the only truthful way you can honour the people you've wronged is to resolve to be the best person you can be. Maybe the self-forgiveness is found somewhere in that.'

She went on to explain that she'd had an affair with her best friend's husband and blown their marriage apart. 'I was a selfish bitch, helping myself to what I wanted. I knew Leo was my best friend Minty's husband, but I didn't let it stop me from getting involved with him. Then I got cancer, and it changed how I felt about everything.'

She shrugged lightly. 'I'm going to die, probably a lot sooner than I should. But at least before I do, I can be less selfish and more giving. I've split my will so that Stu and his daughter Meghan will get half of the properties we've bought together, and my friend's daughter, my God-daughter Belle, will get the other half. She's not close to me anymore – her choice, not mine. She's Minty's daughter, and she will probably never speak to me again, but I can still make sure she's financially secure, and Stuart and Meghan will be too.'

Tears pricked at Chris' eyes. Damn his emotions for getting the better of him, again! No face for poker also meant no ability to stop his eyes from leaking whenever something made him sad. But he forced back the tears. When he spoke, his voice was husky. 'Yes, you might be onto something there. I do actually feel like I have to be the best version of myself now; the best bloke I can be, for Daisy. Make her proud, as if she were still here.'

Nick came back to the table and asked them if they wanted another round of drinks. Chris decided that two pints were his limit for tonight. He suddenly suspected he may just have an unexpected night of deep self-reflection coming up, and was overwhelmed by the need to stay sober and clear-headed. He ordered a coffee, instead.

Nobody spoke for a minute, then the puddings arrived, and Chris found he was able to polish off his apple pie with more enthusiasm than he'd had for his fish and chips. Something felt like it had been ever-so gently, subtly unlocked, inside him. He wouldn't have been able to describe the feeling to anyone, even if they'd asked him to try, but he somehow felt a kind *release*, of something small but significant. He didn't know if it had been the conversation, or the revelations, the confessions at the table, or his own spoken acknowledgement of the kind of man he had to be from now on. He wore his heart on his sleeve, certainly, but he wasn't in tune with himself enough to really understand what was happening.

Nobody said anything more about his circumstances, and he was grateful. They all just seemed to know, without much consultation, when to leave a subject alone. He guessed that came from all knowing each other very well, and knowing when enough had been said on a painful topic.

Some people he'd met were like buzzards, picking away at a carcass until there was nothing new to say, then they'd just say the same stuff all over again, perpetuating the pain of it all. These four had a lot of respect for other people's boundaries, possibly because their own had been sorely and painfully challenged at various times. Their respect for him meant a lot.

Chris decided that this was an appropriate time to leave his dinner companions to their own company, and he drained his cup, and stood up. 'It was really nice to meet you all. Thank you for inviting me over and making me so welcome. I'm going to pay my bill, get my dog from the puppy crèche, and head back up the hill.'

All four stood too and gave him a quick hug. He found himself appreciating that, more than they could ever know. Darren pressed a card into his hand and told him if he fancied a pint any evening over the coming fortnight, to give him a call. Chris appreciated that too. He paid his bill at the bar and went to find Misty.

She yelped, and threw herself at him like a cannonball, with unbridled joy. It was as if he'd been gone for weeks instead of just a couple of hours. He laughed, and gave Cassie a five-pound note. She asked him to wait while she got him some change and he told her not to bother. The little dog was clearly very happy, after playing with Cassie, and a Welsh collie and a couple of French bulldogs who had all turned up while he was having dinner. He reasoned a fiver was a more appropriate payment than the measly two quid she'd asked for. She rewarded him with a huge grin, and let them out through the back door, and they set off for home.

Chapter Five

As she and Mark sat in the Feathers pub, chatting with Bob and Sheila over a few drinks, Adie was acutely aware that her daughter had things on her mind. She knew Teresa had hightailed it up here because she needed a quiet place where she could lick a fresh round of wounds inflicted by that bloody Ross Barker, the Australian guy she'd been in a relationship with. The idiot had already broken her heart once, by leaving with no warning, scuttling off into the mist without a single word at the time or since. This latest stunt, of telling the world on social media that he'd got engaged to the woman he'd been 'waiting all his life to meet' was a really cruel thing for Teresa to bear. Her anguish was profound enough for her to run home to her mother for solace, but Adie was glad to be the safe harbour her daughter sorely needed.

Of course, life went on – it had to, didn't it? But it was a terribly hurtful thing for Teresa to come to terms with, to know that the diamond her ex had apparently been saving for years was never meant for her. What the hell had that mutton-headed dolt been doing with her, then, if he'd known she wasn't 'the one'? Nothing is crueller than stringing someone along until a better option presented itself. Nobody deserved to end up feeling like they'd only been a stop-gap in someone else's life. Adie was quietly furious at how Barker had treated her daughter.

The way he'd left her was bad enough, but the fact that he'd chosen to announce his new plans so publicly was unbelievably insensitive. He must have known Teresa would hear about his engagement. He hadn't even done her the favour of 'blocking' her before he plastered himself and his new bride to be all over his social media. How could he not have known how much that would hurt?

She is worthy of more respect than that. She certainly doesn't deserve to have her face rubbed in it. It's as if she was never in his life at all! Does he not have any kind of conscience? No wonder she's in pieces again. She needs to dump him from her own social media if she hasn't already.'

But, in the midst of feeling highly indignant, Adie allowed herself to feel a sharp pang of guilt now, at how easily she'd dismissed her daughter's anguish after Ross had deserted her.

I just thought of it as an extended holiday fling, but I was wrong, and it's been pretty hard to witness how truly devastated she was – and still is – about it all. I wish I'd been more sensitive in the beginning. I must apologise to her, for being so flippant about her heartbreak, especially if it meant she's been feeling so alone with it all, like she couldn't talk to me, like I wouldn't 'get' it. I didn't, did I? Instead of being compassionate about her pain, I trivialised it. She didn't deserve that either.

But right now, Adie could sense there was something *else* on Teresa's mind that was weighing heavily, and she wanted to try and get her talk about it.

When she and Mark got home, she found Teresa in the living room, watching TV. Mark went upstairs to bed, after making a cup of tea and saying goodnight, but Adie wasn't ready, and she thought it might be an opportune moment to have a quiet chat with her daughter.

'Hello, darling. It's nice and cosy in here! D'you fancy a nightcap, in front of the fire? I'm not in the mood for more tea, and I don't feel ready for bed just yet.'

Teresa was keen, so Adie poured them each a Baileys, handed one over and sat down. She decided to grab the bull by the horns and start a conversation. 'I'm glad we have a moment alone. I want to tell you something important.'

She grinned, as Teresa immediately looked nervous.

'Don't worry, it's nothing heavy. I just want to apologise to you, that's all. I know you're having a tough time dealing with this latest development with Ross Barker. Darling, I just want to say that I know I wasn't very supportive when Ross left. I could have been of more help, but I wasn't. I think I was a bit dismissive, actually.'

She held up her hand, as Teresa shook her head and started to speak. 'It's okay, you don't have to pretend I wasn't. I didn't support you as well as I should have, over that. You yelled at me, and you told me I 'didn't get it.' That really stung, at the time but, as it turns out, you were right about that. I guess on some level I just hoped it was something you'd get over quickly. Nobody likes to see their children in pain, you know? I think I tried to kid myself that it would all blow over, for *your* sake, not for mine.' She took a deep breath, and then continued.

'I guess I kind of forgot what it's like to be young. I dismissed your love for Ross as a silly crush, and that must've hurt. I only realised how much, when I thought about it later, and I realised how hurt *I* would have been if your father had abandoned *me* without warning or a backward glance. And it would have been so much worse if someone close to me had trivialised it. I had no right to assume that your feelings weren't as valid as mine were when I was young and in love myself. I'm so sorry, darling. Please forgive me.'

She was shocked to see that Teresa had tears in her eyes. When she spoke, her voice had a tightness about it that caused Adie's heart to lurch, just a little. 'It's okay, Mum. I know you just thought it was a holiday fling. But thank you for saying that. It means a lot.'

'I think, if I'm being honest, I was actually *hoping* that was all it was! I didn't want to face the possibility of you going to live with him, on the other side of the world. It's selfish, I know, but now that I think back, I'm sure that fear was part of it. But you didn't deserve for me to hurt you like that, especially after you'd been so hurt by Ross. I should have done better; *been* better, and I wasn't. I let you down.'

'It did hurt, all of it. It still does. It's excruciating, to be honest, and I did feel that you abandoned me a bit. But I don't blame you for it, Mum. I get it, that part of you was afraid I'd take off and not come back. Aussie is a long way from here, isn't it? But this whole experience has changed me. I'm not sure how, but I feel different.'

'In what way?'

'I dunno, really. It's hard to describe. Maybe a bit less idealistic, less fanciful? More focussed on myself and what I want, anyway. Apart from having Lucy and Mark to talk to, I really feel I have been quite alone in trying to come to terms with everything.'

'I'm sorry, again. I never want you to feel that you can't talk to me about matters of the heart. I'll always help you if I can. I have had *some* experience.'

'Sorry Mum, but I think that ship has sailed.'

'Ouch!' Adie felt badly stung.

Teresa shrugged at her. 'Well, I've had to figure a few things out on my own, haven't I? I don't want you to be hurt about it, but I don't feel you're someone I can talk to about romantic stuff. Other things, yes, but not that.'

Adie tried to ignore the sharp pain she felt, at Teresa's admission.

I deserve that, I guess, but hopefully she can trust me more in the future, if the need ever arises. I'm going to try to repair that bridge.

She pulled her attention back, as Teresa was still talking.

'And if another guy comes along, he'll have to fit around whatever path I'm on. I'm not willing to change tack for anyone, not anymore.'

'Well, you might change your mind if the right man comes along. Real love can point us in unforeseen directions, but that doesn't have to mean they're not good ones.' She raised her arm, and gestured around the room. 'Look at where I ended up! I never in a million years thought I'd ever be this happy. But I met the right man, and it all fell into place.'

'Mark's the best. You did good, in finding him.'

Adiel laughed now, happy for the olive branch. 'Well, I'm not sure who found who, actually. I guess we found one another, but whichever way you analyse it, we have a very nice life, and it was one I never foresaw. Don't close yourself off to opportunities, Teresa. Follow your own dreams first, of course, but don't be dismissive of whoever might come into your orbit that gives you more than a gentle nudge. You'll find that there's room in your life for *everything* if you're with the right soulmate.'

Adie took another deep breath. 'And let me say that if you did find Mr Right in a different county, and decided to emigrate for love, I wouldn't hold you back. It would hurt of course. It would be horrible, to have you far away, but you'd have my blessing to do it. You need to know that, okay?' She cocked her head on one shoulder and narrowed her eyes.

'But there's something else, isn't there? You have something else on your mind. Is there another problem? I don't want to pry, but I'm here if you want to tell me about it. Maybe I can help?'

'Nothing else is wrong, Mum. Not with me, anyway – well, at least, nothing more than you already know, about this whole drama of Ross getting engaged to someone with a ring he didn't think I was good enough to have. That's just what it is. I have to deal with it somehow, and I will.'

She took a sip of her Baileys, before continuing. 'There's something going on with Dad, though. I wasn't going to say anything because I figured you probably wouldn't want to hear about it. You and Dad haven't been in touch for years now, and I know that what goes on in his life doesn't interest you anymore. There's no reason it should, is there? But something horrible has happened, Mum. Don't worry, he's not sick or anything, but he's got himself into a fair bit of trouble, and I don't think it's something he can easily get out of.'

'Go on, then. Tell me,' Adie prompted.

'Well, he's kind of going broke. The business is okay, that wasn't compromised, but he has to sell it anyway because Nikki has left him. She's demanding a divorce, and half of everything. It's going to break him, financially.'

'*What?* A divorce? Seriously? What the hell's happened? I thought they were happy together!'

Teresa sighed, and it sounded as if she'd hauled it up from the bottom of her boots. 'Well, I guess it's a case of leopards never changing their spots, Mum. He had another affair, and it turned out to be a complicated one. An attractive woman approached him on one of his social media accounts, saying she liked the look and sound of him, and asking if he'd send her a friend request. He took the bait, and they hooked up. Her name is Maggie Jenner.

'To cut a long story short, she wasn't really into him at all! She just let him think she was. Over the months they were seeing each other, behind Nikki's back I might add, the gold-digging slag managed to clear out his bank accounts!'

The more Teresa told her, the more horrified Adie became. Apparently, this 'Maggie Jenner' had convinced Bryan she was in love with him. When he'd realised that she she'd been more committed to draining his bank balance than she'd ever been to *him*, he'd given her the chance to return the money. He'd told her if she didn't, he was going to the police. She said if he reported her, she would contact Nikki and the rest of his family to tell them what he'd been up to, and she advised him to just let her go, with the money she'd stolen, and say no more about it.

'She intended to just fade back into the background, like nothing had happened? Or crawl back under whatever bloody rock she came out from under,' Adie added, half under her breath.

'Yeah, that's probably more like it. Anyway, he called her bluff and got the police involved. He tried to do it discreetly, so Nicki wouldn't find out, but she did and she left him. Now they're selling the house and everything, and she's as mad as hell. She's going after half of everything – including his pension, and the business. It's a mess, Mum. His life is in such a mess. Nikki won't forgive him, even though she knows it was Jenner who started the whole thing off by throwing herself at him.'

Adie was astonished and dismayed. Teresa was right, it was none of her business anymore what her ex-husband did, or how much of a ruin he made of his life. But it was still hard to hear, that Bryan had chosen to cheat on his second wife too, and he'd been stupid enough to do it with a woman who'd set out to defraud him. By the sound if it, his folly was ultimately going to cost him pretty much everything. Aside from what she'd managed to lay claim to herself, Maggie Jenner had more or less wrecked his financial security across the board. She'd certainly put paid to his marriage.

'Did Jenner know he was married?'

'I don't know. He doesn't make his marital status public. I'm not sure why, maybe to hedge his bets?'

Adie tried to ignore the bitterness in Teresa's voice. 'Or maybe because he thinks it's none of anyone's business, darling?'

Teresa shrugged. 'I have no idea. It's pretty hard right now, to give him the benefit of the doubt. I think when Jenner found out he was married it gave her even more leverage. Maybe she *did* know from the very start. Maybe it was *always* part of her plan. Bitches like that tend to do their homework before they get started on ruining someone's life. And the police already know who she is. They've had other complaints about her, some from the States, no less. She's American. She worked a fair bit of her charm stateside, before coming here, and apparently there was a guy in the south of France, who she also fleeced. I guess she preys on gullible, dick-led, easy meat like Dad, to fund her jet-setting lifestyle.'

'So how did you manage to be privy to all this? I didn't think you were on great terms with your dad. Has something changed?'

'No, not really. We're still not as easy with one another as we used to be. I'm still really angry with him, Mum, especially over how he treats Matty.'

She shook her head and sighed deeply again. 'I don't see him much anymore, and I certainly don't tell him what's going on in *my* life. But he's devastated, and I guess he doesn't have many people he can talk to, so he rang me. He was asking me questions about social media, and what's legal and all that stuff, but I couldn't really help him. I know next to nothing about what he might be able to do, in response, or how accountable someone can make a social media platform when something like this happens. I told him to get a good lawyer – someone who specialises in cyber fraud and stuff. It was all I could offer, really.'

Adie grimaced. 'I didn't know that was even a thing; women stalking men online to exploit them. I know it happens in reverse, you know, the guys who make contact and then scam vulnerable women out of their life savings. Did you know that a guy once tried to lure your aunt Miranda into that trap? Luckily, she was a lot more switched-on than he thought she was! The warning bells went off and she was able to get rid of him before she lost any real money to him.'

'God, Mum, no! I never knew that! Aunty Mand is your best friend, and yet you've never told me that, about her!'

'It was years ago, darling, back when social media first started. You were a bit too young to be bothered by such things, but it became a big issue really quickly; vulnerable lonely women being 'wooed' by guys saying they're ex-military, widowed; fine upstanding members of the community who are looking for love, offering marriage; all that nonsense.'

'It's still a thing, Mum, I watched a documentary about it recently. It's still happening to a lot of women.'

'Yeah, well, Miranda ended up getting involved in a whole new world of behind-the-scenes cyber sleuthing! She helped the authorities track the guy down to where he *really* was, which wasn't a major Airforce base in Oklahoma at all, but a backstreet call-centre in Ghana.'

Adie had been shocked when Miranda had told her what had happened. She was a successful stage actress, and financially secure, but she'd been single and a little lonely, at the time. She had never been married, and she'd always said that while half of her was intrigued by the idea of marriage, the other half of her wanted to run away screaming. While not necessarily looking for a lifetime commitment, she'd still been quietly hoping someone would come along who would cherish her romantically. She'd been a little vulnerable to someone trying to defraud her under the guise of being her 'one true soulmate.'

Miranda had had a lucky escape, according to the police. The man who'd contacted her was part of a wide ring of high-level scammers who had swindled dozens of women and left them penniless, before melting into the ether and never being seen or heard from again. They worked out of a decrepit building on the outskirts of Accra, but their modus operandi was sophisticated. Busting the ring wide open had been something of a coup for the National Crime Agency and their Ghanaian associates, but it was only one of many that existed.

Adie was saddened now, to hear that women were active predators too; preying on men they assumed to be lonely, vulnerable, or wealthy, who seemed to be 'available.' Maggie Jenner was probably only one of countless women who funded their extravagances by getting unsuspecting men to bankroll them.

I suppose it's not all that surprising, especially as guys can be just as lonely and craving of love and devotion as women. Some of those men could probably be a very soft touch. There's no reason why it wouldn't be just as big a problem, but it's not something you really think about, is it?

She shook her head, to try and clear it. 'Well, your father has to answer for his actions, Teresa. Nobody else can do that for him. It sounds like this latest indiscretion has cost him very dearly, but maybe that's what it takes, to learn the lesson that the people who love him deserve to be valued. They're not expendable commodities. *Wives* are not expendable, and sometimes when you gamble with a relationship, you lose it. He didn't learn that lesson after me, did he?'

Teresa shook her head, emphatically. 'No, he didn't, and I'm so disappointed in him – again! I was pretty disillusioned about him before, but now this? Cheating on Nikki, too? I didn't like her, Mum, but she loved him! That was worth something – or at least it should have been, to him. But he's trashed that relationship too. I know I shouldn't have much sympathy for the state he's in now, but it's hard to see him so broken. I feel really conflicted about it. He's an asshole, on lots of levels, but he's still my dad.'

Adie nodded. 'Yeah, I get that. He's not much of a role model for you, is he, in terms of what a good man should be? Ross wasn't much of one either, furtively scuttling away without a word and never looking back. Mark is a good role model though, darling. Use him as your benchmark for how a man should conduct himself. You won't go far wrong with that.'

'Mark's amazing, Mum. Like I said before, you did good, getting loved-up with him. He adores you. It's what you deserve.'

Adie nodded gently and reached across to take one of Teresa's hands in both of her own. 'Try not to worry about your father, darling. He's a big boy. Just like the rest of us, he has to be accountable for his own actions and, just like the rest of us, he has to fix his own mistakes. If he wants to keep messing up his life, you have to leave him to it. I know it's not easy, to watch someone you love making a rod for their own back, but he is who he is, and you can't change that. You have to pick your battles in this life, and he can't be one of them.'

Terea nodded, slowly, 'You're right, of course. It's hard to see him go through this but, like you say, maybe he deserves it. God knows *I've* learned the lessons from past mistakes. So have you. So has Matty. I dunno why Dad can't.'

'Does Matty know about this business with his father?'

She nodded again. 'Yeah, and he's like you. He thinks we should *all* just leave him to it. You know their relationship hasn't improved much either, since that business with Matty being wrongly arrested for murder, and the fact that he was a sex worker.'

Adie yawned, stretched, and sighed. 'Your brother made mistakes, but he's pulled his life together pretty well, all things considered. He's a long way now from where he used to be, isn't he? Being married with two kids has settled him down a lot. Marie is so good for him, and he dotes on their daughters! He's a solid and dependable man, now, and it's such a shame that Bryan can't cut him any slack. That still bothers me too, if I'm honest.'

'Well, to be fair, Matty is more okay about it than either of us. He's moved on from it all. He did try really hard with Dad, but he kept getting nowhere, and he just gave up in the end. I think he probably had to, Mum, because he *did* need to rebuild his life, but how was he supposed to do that with his father sitting on the sidelines, sneering at him and wittering on about how disappointed he was? Nobody needs that, do they? Especially not from their own parents, you know, the people who are supposed to love them unconditionally, in spite of their mistakes?'

It had been a few years now, since the events that had torn the Bostock family apart, and Adie knew that Bryan had struggled with everything. He had frozen his whole family out, even poor Teresa, who hadn't been guilty of anything! Bryan's rage at Adie had been so great that he'd lost the ability to connect on any meaningful level with his children too.

It was a terrible thing that made no real sense, and it made her sad that Bryan was still estranged from Matty. It was even sadder that he'd apparently hoisted himself once *again* with his own petard, by choosing once more to be unfaithful. He had lost another marriage in the process and was now facing the loss of his long-term financial security. A divorce from Nikki (who apparently had decided to go for the jugular) had the potential to ruin him. It wasn't a great place for a man to be, at this time of life, was it? Bryan was pushing sixty. Mark had once said that if a man didn't have his act together by that stage in his life, he probably wasn't going to at all.

Still and all, being fleeced by someone you trusted was a horrible experience. Ever the man-in-control, Bryan wouldn't have expected to have had the tables turned on him in such a way. Maggie Jenner sounded like a proper piece of work, and Adie supposed that if she was clever enough to hide her true motives from him until she'd got access to his money, she was probably clever enough to have done it in such a way that the police would have a hard time proving that he hadn't actually *given* her the cash. She wasn't in jail yet, by all accounts, so she clearly had some wits about her.

For poor Bryan, facing the prospect of losing everything must be a bitter pill to swallow. He didn't deserve Adie's pity, but she felt it for him, nonetheless.

Still and all though, as unconscionable as the Maggie Jenners of the world were, maybe they had a part to play in people learning important lessons. Maybe this time Bryan would learn his, but Adie doubted it. As Teresa had said, leopards don't change their spots. Once a cheat, probably always a cheat.

'Well, I'm off to bed. Tomorrow's Saturday, and it's always a big morning around here.'

Teresa grinned. 'Mark's already warned me, about the Market-morning chaos! I know I need to brace myself.'

'Ha! He always *thinks* its chaos, but it isn't really. I know what I'm doing, it's just that most of it tends to happen in a rush. Well, goodnight darling, and don't stay up too late.'

'Thanks, Mum, you know, for saying what you have, and for listening, about Dad. I know it's not my problem or yours, what's going on with him, but it has been a bit of a bugbear.'

'Well, I hope sharing it has helped you to put in into perspective.'

Adie found Mark still awake and reading, in bed. When she described what Teresa had told her, about what had happened to Bryan, he was incredulous.

'By 'eck, that's a tale an' 'alf! An' a tough lesson to boot, lass. 'Appen silly sod'll recover well enough, but if 'e can't keep in in 'is pants, mebbe 'e won't. Mebbe 'e'll just keep losin' everythin,' time an' time over. Some folk never learn. Mebbe the daft apeth's one o' *them*.'

'Yeah, I wonder about that. He's very much a changed man since our marriage broke, and he isn't changed for the better. He seems hell bent on a path of self-destruction, now. But the thing is, he didn't used to be! I still struggle not to feel responsible, in some way. I know that's just stupid, but...'

She didn't finish her sentence. She struggled to explain herself. But Mark understood.

'Yer still feelin' a bit guilty about the secrets you kept. It's only natural, I suppose, but y'ave to remember that 'e *were* on a path to self-destruction already, Adie! 'E were peggin' 'is mistress for a very long time before yer own misdeeds came out. Even if y'adn't 'ad owt to confess, 'e were still playin' away, weren't 'e? An' gamblin' wi' 'is family?'

She sighed, heavily. Mark was right. She could feel as guilty as she wanted, but it didn't change the fact that Bryan had already made choices that were more responsible for putting their marriage in the dustbin than anything she had (or hadn't) said or done.

Mark stared into the middle distance. 'Y'know summat? I 'ad a feeling 'is marriage to that Nikki wouldn't last. You never met 'er, but let me tell yer, she were bloody 'igh maintenance, that one. She'd 'ave kept 'im on 'is toes a'right. Maybe 'e just got sick o' dancin.' But whatever the reason 'e strayed again, it were nowt to do wi' you, lass! It were 'is choice. Where 'e is now, it's all down to 'is own daft decisions.'

Adie looked fondly across at her husband. He was contemplative, and the warm and gentle light from the bedside lamp cast shadows across his face. He was ageing, but he was doing it well, with grace and dignity. In her opinion, he looked better than ever. She still felt that gentle 'pull' of quiet wonder, when she looked at him, of how incredibly their lives had meshed.

It was odd, she thought to herself, how men seemed to age in such interesting and 'distinguished' ways, when women all-too-often looked and felt like mouldering hags, once the grey hair started to march in and the wrinkles deepened. With periods and all their associated drama for many, bodies changed forever through the physical brutality of childbirth, then the peri and the menopause that knocked so many of them around, it didn't seem like the odds were fairly stacked in favour of the 'fairer sex.' Miranda had proclaimed, many times, that there wasn't much in the way of gender justice. Women got the rawest end of the deal for the longest, in her opinion. She said that she was coming back as a man, in the next life, so she could 'get her own back.'

Miranda's opinion of men always intrigued Adie. On the one hand, she adored them, and spent most of her time with guys who were young enough to be her sons. On the other hand, she disparaged them greatly, for being unable and largely unwilling to understand women. The thought of 'ending up with some block-head who would never understand what really made her tick,' as she'd put it, was more than she could contemplate.

'I'd be homicidal in no time, darling, and no idiot man is worth going to jail for.'

But, a year and a half ago, Miranda had finally met someone; a very lovely man called Max. He had caught her attention, and gently wooed her, and they were very much in love. He was of appropriate age (for once in her life), and the two got on well.

Adie had finally met him last Christmas when they'd come for the festive break. They'd stayed in Teapot Cottage because Adie had had a full house at Ravensdown. Miranda had bowed out of doing pantomime, for once, so her Christmas and New Year were her own for the first time in years, and she'd relished the novelty of having the holidays to herself. It had been a joyous week for her, squirreled away in the 'magic cottage' with a man she adored who adored her in return, and it had been the loveliest thing for Adie too, to have her best friend around for her birthday and Christmas and New Year.

Miranda and Max had got engaged at Teapot Cottage that Christmas, one quiet night over a romantic dinner in front of the fire, and nobody could have been more delighted than Adie. Finally, her darling friend had found the courage to take that biggest leap of faith of all; making the decision to share every part of her life with someone. It had been a long time coming.

Mark poked her now, to pull her out of her thoughts, and she grinned when he gave her one of his cheeky-smirky winks. He was one of the most pragmatic men on earth, and even though that sometimes infuriated her (occasionally to the point of tears), she was grateful for it tonight. If anyone could keep her feet on the ground and stop her from drifting off for hours to a place in her own head, thinking about stuff she shouldn't be wasting her time on, it was him. He understood that Teresa's news about Bryan had unsettled her more than it probably should have. She *had* been asking herself again, if she was in some way responsible for setting her ex-husband on a path of self-destruction, but Mark had done what he always did best and told it like it was. He didn't want her ruminating on it, and she didn't blame him. She decided to put his mind at ease over it.

'I was thinking about Mand and Max actually, and how well-suited they are. I'm so thrilled about the wedding,

Mark. There was a time when I thought she'd missed the boat on settling down with someone lovely.'

'Well, why would she? *You* didn't miss it, did yer? It weren't that many year ago *you* lost yer 'eart to a dashin,' 'andsome prince wi' all't charm in the world.'

His eyes twinkled. She knew he was relieved that she wasn't thinking too much about Bryan, and the mess he'd got himself into. 'Actually, I lost my heart to a grumpy, burping, farting old codger with dirt under his fingernails and all the charm of a wet sheepdog, as it happens. And he wasn't in the least bit conceited, or prone to blowing his own trumpet, was he? But he certainly was handsome. I'll give him that.'

Mark chuckled. 'Some people find a wet sheepdog charmin,' lass, and in any case, most of em are pretty lovely when they're all dried off.'

'Granted. I suppose I can give you that too. You do tend to go a bit cute and fluffy when you've had a good towelling, it's true.' She grinned, then pulled a face.

'And, as far as Bryan goes, well; it's up to him to sort his own disasters out, isn't it? I'm not going to give him any more headroom, Mark. God knows there's enough going on in our lives already, without *that* gremlin coming back to bite me!'

'Aye, lass. Life's good, in't it? I get it, it's 'ard to square away bad news about someone yer once 'ad big feelings for, I know that. Yer were married for a long time, and it counted for summat. Y'ad a life together fer a long time, but it's in the past, Adie. Leave it there, lass, fer yer own sake.'

'I love you, so much! I can't imagine what my life would have turned out like if I hadn't met you. It seems inconceivable to me, that I could have gone off somewhere else and had a different life than the one I have with you.'

'Ay, yer've been a right soppy bugger today, an't yer? Scooch over 'ere, an' give us a kiss, woman. I might die if yer don't.'

'Ah, but I know you, Mr Raven! Within seconds you'd have your hand up my pyjama top.'

'And that is a problem *why?*'

She giggled, in spite of herself, and shuffled across to snuggle beside him. It was funny, how much sexier she felt with him than she'd ever felt with Bryan. Even in the early years, when they'd been young, and very much in love, she never really felt *sexy*, and *cherished*, in the way she did now, in her second marriage.

Maybe it's that whole child-rearing, getting the mortgage paid, getting life established, routine. Maybe the stuff we had to do, while we were still trying to prove ourselves to so many people (including ourselves) got in the way of allowing us to figure out who we really were or how we really wanted to feel. Maybe you have to be at this stage of life, or closer to it at least, to really appreciate yourself and all you're capable of feeling, rather than battling so hard to keep it out of the way while you got on with all the responsibility.

She said as much to Mark, who pulled a face and thought about it for a few minutes. When he spoke, his voice was quiet.

'All I know is that if you'd turned up any earlier in me life, we probably wouldn't be 'ere now. I weren't ready any earlier. I were still grievin' for Beth. It weren't *acute*, like, after eight year o' bein' wi'out 'er, but it were still a block I 'ad to get past on me own, in me own time. Grief's a funny thing, in't it? Yer not done wi' it until yer piggin' done wi' it, an' that's that. And I weren't, for a long time. But when you came along and 'elped me over that last little 'ump, I were ready fer it. Like Feen always says, everythin' 'appens in its own time, when its good an' ready, an' not before.'

'Timing is everything! Just like when you met Beth! Both in that remote country pub in the bowels of rural Lancashire at the same time, hearts instantly falling. If someone else had been working the bar that day, or if you'd gone in on a different day, you might never have met. But you did, and you had many great years together. You restored this amazing old farm, and you had Feen! Imagine if that hadn't happened? What would your life have been like? Have you ever wondered about it?'

Mark laughed. 'No! It were what it were, and it were grand, an' then it weren't so grand, an' now its grand again. I'm 'appy to take it all fer what it is, lass. What's point in wishin or wonderin' for summat else, when yer already as 'appy as a pig in shit?'

It was Adie's turn to laugh. 'That's what I love the most about you! Your impeccable diction and your eloquent turn of phrase.'

'What, yer don't love me willy the most? 'E's thinkin' yer don't. 'E's feelin' a bit neglected.' Mark had the usual mischievous grin on his fact that he always had when he talked about sex.

'Well, that is absolutely not true. I know for a fact that he has no cause whatsoever to be feeling neglected! So, he can stop with the 'poor me' routine, or he jolly well *will* be neglected and then he'll have something to complain *about,* won't he?'

They were both chuckling, now.

Sex was an important part of a relationship, but just before she'd started going through the menopause, Adie had experienced an abrupt and profound loss of libido. It was so complete; it had left her wondering if it was ever going to come back. A lot of women went through the same thing, when the change of life occurred, and some never recovered their sex drive. Many went through difficulties in their relationships, because of it, and some of those relationships didn't survive. Adie had been deeply grateful at how understanding Bryan had been, and how he'd never pressured her. It was only later, that she found out the *real* reason; he had a mistress who was keeping him busy enough in that department. He hadn't 'needed' Adie at all!

Some women were relieved about the permanent loss of libido, but others were distraught. Adie had feared she'd be one of those, and her fear had been intensified after she met

Mark. She'd *wanted* to marry him, and she'd said yes in a heartbeat when he'd asked her, but she'd been desperately worried. A different man, a hormonal rollercoaster to navigate, and a fear that she would never get turned on again by *any* man, had all kept her in a weird state of quiet, internal hysteria.

She had also been very nervous about sleeping with another man at all, after so many years with her ex-husband! There had never been anyone else, ever, unless she counted the 'fumble' she'd had at fifteen, that had resulted in the teenage pregnancy that had rocked her family's world when the news of it eventually came out. It had served as the one of the catalysts that had blown her first marriage apart.

So, in her fifties, wildly menopausal and dealing with all the bodily changes, concerns and self-consciousness that went with it, Adie had found the prospect of being intimate with Mark not far short of terrifying. It had been something of a revelation, when she'd worked up the courage to tell him how she felt, that he had felt the same. Beth hadn't been his 'first,' but she'd been his 'only,' until he'd found himself alone again after she died. The prospect for him, of being with a different woman, was equally daunting.

There had been a lot of reassurance for them both, in being able to admit that. Being together for the first time had been an experience of discovering one another and a rediscovery of themselves, all underpinned by a towering level of fragile but critical trust. But, as it turned out, neither of them had needed to worry. They 'fitted' together so well, in all other areas of their lives, that the intimate part of their relationship had quickly become as seamless as everything else. Now, it felt like they had always been together. *Everything* fit, and the rareness, the joy, and the preciousness of it, wasn't lost on either of them.

When they'd talked about it, before the wedding, it had been a big relief when Mark had suggested they wait until their wedding night. She'd been grateful for the offer, hoping that the extra time would allow her hormones to settle down, at least a little more.

He'd reassured her a lot, by telling her that they had all the time in the world for things to settle in whatever way they would, and they'd deal with the landscape when the time came. He'd also admitted that sex wasn't as important to him as she was afraid it might be. He'd said that he fancied her like mad, but if they didn't end up having much of a 'physical' relationship, they could still be affectionate and loving in every other way, and that would be enough for him. He explained that he'd had years on his own, after being widowed. Companionship was more at the forefront of his mind than sex. Adie knew he meant it; he wasn't capable of lying, or even dressing anything up as more than what it really was. It wasn't hard to trust him, even over something as important as that.

The fact that they had very easily overcome the barriers Adie had built in her own head was a revelation to them both. Their flirtatious banter was delightful, and funny, and sweet, and it was a constant source of wonder for Adie that she could feel the way she did about it. Mark was often cheeky about sex, and usually hilarious with it, and she'd found a confidence within *herself*, thanks to that.

She was probably past the midway point of her menopause now, and it was manageable, unlike the start of it, which had been compounded by her bewilderment about it, and by her emotional anguish over her first marriage ending, certain trusted friends turning out to be enemies in disguise, and her kids treating her like she didn't exist.

She hadn't been prepared for *any* of what had happened back then, especially the abrupt explosion of her hormonal balance. That had hit her like a ten-tonne truck, with no warning, and the chicken-and-egg question had spun around in her head for a long time; did all the other emotional upheaval make her menopause worse, or was the menopause horrific enough to have made everything *else* seem so much worse?

Bryan's affair had been unbearable, and the scorn of her children had been hard to bear too, after her long-buried secrets had come tumbling out, decimating the family, and leaving everyone reeling from the shock.

Adie had had a daughter, Ruth, when she was just fifteen and her parents had forced her to put her forward for adoption. She had eventually gone on to track Ruth down and she'd inveigled her way into her and her wife Gina's lives, by moving her own family into the house next door to them, without telling them – or anyone else – what she and Ruth really were to one another.

It was a secret she'd intended to keep but, as the saying went, the truth will out, and it did come out – hard on the heels of another terrible event that had exposed her son Matthew as a sex worker, after he'd been wrongly arrested for murder.

Everyone connected felt like they'd been unwittingly manipulated, like pieces being moved around on a chessboard, to suit Adie's whims. They'd all felt devastated that she hadn't been able to trust them enough to tell them all what had happened.

There had been a hell of a lot to deal with, back then, and a lot to overcome, and it had all cut the family to the quick. But everything had settled down a lot since, including Adie's haywire hormones, and it had somehow become less important to figure out what had been catalyst or consequence. Things just were what they were, and it was more important to navigate forward, rather than waste time looking back and wondering what could have been changed.

A lot of the stability she'd gained was thanks to Mark just being his patient, unflappable self. He was solid and strong, and underneath the gruff exterior that all-too-often had people thinking twice about approaching him, he was the kindest and most honest man she'd ever met. He had the very great gift of being able to put everything into perspective quickly, too. He was the rock of the Raven family, and Adie's one true anchor in the choppy sea of life.

She put her head on his shoulder now, and he slipped an arm around her and drew her close.

Her ex-husband Bryan had made his bed, and he now had to lie in it. Mark was right in saying that it was hard to see someone you'd once loved go through something horrible, even if they'd brought it on themselves. Bryan had allowed himself to be seduced and hoodwinked by a woman who'd actively set out to defraud him, and he'd cheated on his wife in the process. If he didn't learn anything from all that, after already going through one divorce from cheating on his *first* wife, there really was no hope for him.

In any event, Adie had to put it out of her mind. She rarely thought about her ex anymore, except in matters that related to their children. She could certainly square this latest development away without too much more thought on it. Matty and Teresa were adults, now. They could choose for themselves, how to deal with their father's new nightmare. She'd advised Teresa to pick her battles and leave her father out of them, and now she had to do the same.

Bryan's demise likely wouldn't have much effect on them. They might have a smaller final inheritance from him later down the line, if he couldn't get his finances back on an even keel but, since they'd already had a decent payout when he and Adie had downsized their house, a few years before their marriage had imploded, they weren't expecting anything more. It was just as well, she supposed, that they had no expectations in that regard. It was something they would never have to feel let down over, thank goodness. Bryan had already disappointed them enough.

Teresa had a big heart, and she'd suffered for it on lots of levels already, in her young life. Adie hoped she could be philosophical about the shambles her father's latest antics had turned into. The girl needed to focus her attention on herself, and her own future. She still had a lot of decisions to make, and she needed to make them with a clear head.

While spending time up here, away from the hustle and bustle of London life, she might just find a way to come to terms with the latest events that had rocked her world. Ross Barker was out of the picture for good, now. His engagement to someone else cut off all hope for Teresa, and that was probably a good thing. If she still hung onto even a vestige of hope for a reconciliation, it might get in the way of her meeting someone else or even making good career choices. False hope was never going to help her with anything.

She had to put Ross behind her now, and maybe that was what hurt the most. Maybe it wasn't missing out on a gorgeous pink diamond from the now-defunct Argyll mine, or the message she'd been given that she'd never been 'the right one' for Ross. Maybe it was the prospect of having to get over it for once and for all, in all the ways that mattered. Hope is the hardest thing to let go of, in a compromising situation. Accepting a final defeat was painful. But, as the saying went, whatever doesn't kill you makes you stronger, and although she'd never dare to utter such a patronising cliché to her daughter, she knew it to be true.

Teresa *would* be stronger after her experience with Ross when it was finally behind her.

Chapter Six

It was pitch dark when Chris and Misty arrived back at the cottage, and Chris berated himself for not having had the foresight to leave a light on. He'd decided to walk up the path along the side of the main road rather than go cross-country again. It was a longer trek, but safer in the dark. The little torch he'd brought with him was running low on its batteries, and its light was too feeble to be of any real help on a rocky track. The last thing he needed was to stumble and go flying. If he hit his head or hurt his back, he could lie on the track till morning, or longer still, if nobody else used it. He could even die out there in the dark. And what would happen to poor Misty if he did?

Nowadays, his own vulnerability was so much more at the forefront of his mind than it ever used to be. Daisy had done nothing wrong, that day on that mountain, but she'd still lost her life. It had left him reconsidering almost every move he made. Only now was he becoming conscious of how fragile life could be. Somewhere deep inside him, the adventurer still dreamed, of new places to go and new peaks to climb, but it wasn't the same as it used to be. The longing was still there, but the sense of needing to get going and do it, that old 'champing at the bit' he used to feel when planning a new mountaineering challenge, was gone. He wondered whether that was permanent. He hoped not. He hoped it was just a temporary aversion, after the devastating shock that had rocked his life to the core.

How *do* you come back, from seeing your beloved hurtling down a mountainside, screaming in terror, with no hope of being saved? From bellowing your lungs out long enough and loud enough to cause an avalanche and knowing, even as you were screaming yourself hoarse, that it wouldn't make a blind bit of difference? And how much more impossible does it feel to recover from something so horrific, knowing it was your own selfish fault?

How do I do it, Daisy? How do I pick through the rubble of that day, and all the days that followed, and find something strong enough to build a life on?

His dinner companions, Stuart and Darren, they'd gone through something similar. They understood where he was at, and they'd shared their own stories of anguish, devastation, and guilt. Both of them had managed to rebuild their lives, but they'd made no bones about there being no absolution. There was no silver bullet, no magic pill, to make it all go away. They offered no platitudes, no advice, about how to live with such a devastating demon, and he got it. There was no solution that anyone else could offer. Each man had to find his own path to redemption.

Chris wondered if maybe the quietly spoken Fiona had hit the nail on the head, in saying that the key to finding peace lay in resolving to be the best person you could be, going forward. Darren had taken up a vocation, fixing sick and injured animals. Stuart had done something similar, teaching worthwhile skills to others, and he was supporting Fiona through the cancer she already had when he met her. That was a monumental thing just in itself.

Maybe I need to start thinking more, about what my next move should be. I've been putting it off, Daisy, telling myself I have to go back to the mountain first, to put your ghost to rest. But the truth, is I'm just not ready. Forgive me, baby, but it's the one thing I still can't bring myself to do.

Chris wasn't in the mood for TV, or even music. It wasn't warm enough to go and lie outside in the grass and watch the stars, either; something he used to do with Daisy through the late spring and summer. He didn't fancy being outside again at all, even getting into the hot tub, but with all the lights out and the quiet glow from the fire, he could see random bits of the night sky well enough. There was a bit of a moon; not much, just enough to provide a bit of light behind the clouds. A few stars poked through here and there as the moving clouds permitted. He was content enough to just sit in the window seat with Misty on his lap, and gaze out at the night and the twinkling lights of Torley town, down in the valley below. He wondered if a shooting star might pass by, and catch his notice.

His thoughts drifted back to New Year's Eve, a couple of years ago, when he and Daisy had been ambivalent about what to do. Foolishly, they'd thought they could just wander on down to a nearby pub, close to midnight, and have a final pint for the old year, and another to see the new one in. But, of course, the landlords of all their locals had locked the doors. Unless you could produce a ticket that you'd bought in advance, there wasn't a cat in hell's chance of getting in. With literally no room at the inn, they'd stood staring at one another in the pub car park, lost for words, and not knowing whether to laugh or cry.

As the loudly shouted countdown to midnight began, inside the pub, Daisy had sprung forward and grabbed Chris and pulled him into a waltz around the cars. When midnight struck, they'd looked up to see a spectacular shooting star whizzing across the sky. They'd both gasped in wonder at the sight and speed of it. Daisy had proclaimed on the spot that *they* were the blessed ones. Everyone else was indoors, yahooing their heads off, probably pissed, and only a very few – the *chosen* few on earth, she said – would've seen that glorious gift from the universe.

That's what Daisy was like; always determined to see the best in everything.

Until around a week ago, that memory would've made Chris cry. But curiously not tonight. Tonight, it made him smile, gently and quietly, to remember one of the most amazing nights of his life; shared with the most amazing woman.

And he also remembered, with quiet joy, the nights when he'd sat high on a mountain, somewhere in the world, close enough to the stars to feel like he could reach out and touch them, and experienced the wonder of being so far above so much of the world, at night.

As Chris was getting ready for bed, Darren Davies' business card fell out of his jeans pocket and onto the carpet. He bent and picked it up. It had been a nice gesture, but he didn't think he'd be taking Darren Davies, *Farm and Domestic Veterinary Surgeon*, up on his offer of meeting for a pint.

Early the following morning, however, he was forced to reconsider. Just after he'd got up, he heard a knock at the back door. Imagining it to be Adie Raven, Chris was astonished to see none other than Darren himself, standing on the doorstep. His face must have registered his surprise, for the other man laughed self-consciously.

'Hiya. Chris. I'm not a stalker, I promise. I was called out here to take a look at one of Mark Raven's piglets. Little sod's gone lame with an infected trotter, so I've had to give him some antibiotics.' Darren checked his watch quickly. 'I'm just on my way to the surgery actually, to get everything set up for the morning's appointments, but I spoke to Debs just now and she's asked me to see if you'd like to come over for a meal tonight?'

Chris groped around in his mind for an excuse to decline but struggled to find one. '*Thanks, but I just want to be on my own*' sounded a bit pathetic and self-pitying. Even if he did want to wallow in his own misery, the last thing he wanted was for anyone else to know that.

Darren seemed to anticipate his indecision and jumped in again. 'I know it's short notice, but I was thinking you probably won't already have plans, since you just got here? Saturday nights are pretty low-key at ours. We've two babies, so we live pretty quietly these days. It'd just be a throw-together like a spag bol or a shepherd's pie or something, and a beer in front of the telly. Nothing too exciting, but if you fancy it, I can cruise over and pick you up around six, and Debs can run you home later. She's not drinking at the mo, because she's breastfeeding. So... you could have a few beers and not have to worry about driving.'

'Could I bring my dog?'

'Yeah, course you can, mate! As long as it's friendly?'

At that moment, little Misty decided to come hurtling down from her bed on the upstairs landing, through to the back door. She launched herself at Darren's legs. He bent down to pick her up and she proceeded to nibble his nose and lick his face. He closed his eyes and let her do it, and when he looked at Chris again his smile was a mile wide, and his eyes were dancing. 'Yes! Definitely friendly! Our dogs are too, so do bring her, although I have to warn you Debs might physically fight you for possession. She's even more of a sucker than I am, for a puppy.'

It was clear to Chris how much Darren loved animals. Someone who cared as much as he did had to be made of good stuff, and he did seem genuine. Chris decided to accept his kind invitation, and a big part of the reason was for Misty to have some more company. He was still socialising the puppy, and every chance of introducing her to new people and other canines was helping to shape her into a friendly and accepting dog.

'Go on, then. 'I'm heading to the Farmers Market this morning, to get some food for the week. Can I bring something? I could maybe get a nice loaf of fresh bread?'

Darren nodded decisively. 'Debs would be grateful for that, certainly. I'll swing by and get you later. About six? I have to dash. Morning surgery awaits,' he added, checking his watch again. He lifted his hand in farewell and turned and jogged back to the driveway through the exit gate in the hedge at the rear of the cottage.

As he left, Chris saw out of the corner of his eye a young woman coming through the same gate. At first, he wondered if it was Adie Raven's step-daughter, Feen, who she'd told him he might see about the place, but Feen Raven had very long, almost blue-black hair. This woman's hair was brown and slightly curly, cut in a short sassy style. She had a plastic box in her hands, and she cocked her head on one side and looked at him, smiling a little.

'Hi. I'm Adie's daughter. She's asked me to give you these chocolate cherry muffins. Home baking, and let me assure you, it's good. Mum's one of Torley's Cake Queens. She was going to put them on the kitchen windowsill for you yesterday, but she ran out of time. She was flapping about getting ready for the Farmer's Market this morning, so she asked me to drop them down to you.'

She held out the box and Chris could see that it had two chocolate muffins in it. He took the box from her and was just about to offer his thanks when the woman gave a short cry of surprise.

'Hey! Don't I know you? You look familiar to me.' Her eyes searched his face, and a small vertical frown line appeared above the bridge of her nose as she tried to remember. She looked familiar to him too, but he couldn't place her. All of a sudden, her face cleared, and she smiled broadly.

'I remember. Tasmania! Me and my friends met you and a couple of your friends in a bar in Hobart. It was a couple of years ago now. You were all buzzing. You'd just climbed Federation Peak! You were shouting drinks all night. We all got royally smashed, and I don't remember anything much at all after that. But that was you, wasn't it? I'm sorry I don't remember your name.'

Dumbstruck, Chris just stared at her.

What the ...? Here, in the back yard of a Lake District cottage, in a town most people couldn't even find on a map, in I run into a girl I met in Australia*? How bloody freaky is this?*

The woman in front of him was laughing now, and Chris started laughing too, incredulous. 'It's Chris. Chris Darcy, and my friends were Marcus and Danny. My God, how bizarre is this? I'm sorry, but I don't remember your name, either!'

'It's Teresa; Teresa Bostock, but you might remember me as Tezzie? Tezzie in Tazzie? It was a running joke among my friends.'

Chris nodded. 'Yeah, I do remember that. Tezzie in Tazzie. We thought that was pretty funny. So was the fact that you were pretty crap at karaoke. I dunno who laughed harder, us or you! What a bloody small world. So, you live *here*?'

Teresa laughed again. 'No. I live in London. Adie Raven is my mum. She got hitched a few years ago to the guy who owns the farm, so now she's lady to his lord of the manor, so to speak. I'm just visiting for a couple of weeks, between temping jobs. Just fancied a bit of a breather, really, after a pretty full-on few months in my last job. This is the ideal place for that.'

She looked around her. 'It's beautiful up here. Peaceful, quiet, not much happening. Miles and miles away from the rat-race, and assholes who want to ruin your life.'

Chris blinked at her, grinning. 'Would you like to come in for a coffee? Chat about our travels?'

Teresa looked genuinely apologetic. 'I'd love to, but maybe on a rain check? I want to go into town, and do a couple of errands before the day disappears. The time does seem to kind of weirdly melt away, up here.'

He nodded. 'Yeah, I've noticed that. But look, I want to go into town myself, at least to the Farmers Market. Why don't we go together? Maybe we could grab a coffee somewhere in the town? I know there's at least one café down there.'

'Sounds like a plan. In fact, I think Mum's friend runs a caf. Can't remember the name of it but I'm sure it can't be hard to find. Torley's not what you'd call a heaving metropolis. I think the town only has three streets.'

She grinned at Chris. 'Come with me in my car, and we can get the stuff I need, do the market, and grab a coffee…'

Her voice faltered, and she looked confused. 'Erm, unless that all feels a bit full-on, in which case you can drive yourself? Up to you.'

Chris was touched by her sensitivity. A night in a bar with a bunch of exuberant drunkards was one thing. Getting into a car with one of those erstwhile drunkards while stone cold sober and not knowing a scrap about what they were really like as a person was a different thing entirely. He was grateful she'd realised it but, to be fair, she seemed pretty 'normal.'

'No, I'd love to come with you. If either one of us turns out to be a complete weirdo, I guess the other one of us can find our own way home pretty quickly. Let me just get my jacket. I'll leave my dog Misty here, I think. We won't be too long, will we?'

Teresa bent and picked up Chris' squirming little dog and laughed and pulled away, as Misty tried to lick her face. 'Sorry, Tezzie. She's a bit of a snogger! She just wants to lick everyone to death, I'm afraid.' He reached out to take Misty from her. Teresa hander her over.

'She's adorable! I expect we'll only be gone for couple of hours, so why not bring her with us? She'll be no trouble, and everywhere in the town is dog friendly, I believe. Even the pubs and cafes.'

Chris knew that to be true, so he quickly clipped Misty onto her lead, threw on his jacket, and followed Teresa out through the back door to a slightly battered little MG sportscar parked alongside the back hedge between Teapot Cottage and Ravensdown House. Sadly, he didn't have a lot of time to appraise the lovely old house, before Teresa opened the passenger door and Misty jumped in. He lifted her into the parcel tray behind the car's two seats, where she settled straight away.

Within seconds they were buckled up and heading down the drive, onto the main road, and roaring off towards Torley town. Teresa was a confident driver, he noted.

The Farmer's Market was spectacular, and Chris was spoilt for choice. He explained to her; 'I'm not much of a kitchen hound. It's all I can do to make an omelette, if I'm honest, but what's on offer here makes me want to morph into Jamie Oliver!'

Teresa laughed. 'I'm no great shakes in a kitchen either. It's never been on my to-do list; to learn how to cook like a pro. I get by. I haven't poisoned myself or any of my flatmates yet, anyway. I do love food, but I tend to cook for survival, rather than fun.'

After they'd picked up Chris' provisions and said a quick hello to Adie, who was manning her free-range eggs, home-made preserves and kitchen-linens stand, they went for a pot of coffee and some cake at Ye Olde Torley Tea Shoppe. It was, apparently, still owned and run by Adie's friend, Peg Tripper.

'I've only met Peg a couple of times, but she seems nice, and the food in here is apparently really good.' Teresa said, as they found a table.

'Yes, it is. I was in here last year, but I'd forgotten my wallet. She very generously allowed me to leave without paying my bill. I came back and paid her later. I'm sure she'll remember me for that if nothing else.'

The food *was* amazing, and the time flew, as Chris and 'Tezzie' caught up on the last couple of years. She told him she was working in London and completing an online Master's degree in Cinematography and Film. She wanted to make documentaries.

'This is so weird! Of all *places*, and of all *people*, to meet you here, it's the craziest thing, Tezzie! I know we're both travellers, and the world is a small place when all is said and done, but I still can't believe this has happened.'

She giggled at him. 'I know, right? What are the chances? But you know, most people do have a small-world story. My flatmate Lucy, in London, once met a woman on a hiking trail in the Grand Canyon that she'd worked with years before in a small town in New Zealand, of all places! The chance of *that* happening are even more miniscule than this! And once, when I was on a train in Switzerland, I was sitting next to a woman from Canada, and her English friend in the opposite seat was from the same town where I grew up. We didn't know each other, but it turned out that we knew all the same people! It was bizarre.'

Chris laughed. 'I was once in a youth hostel in San Francisco, and the friend I was with banged into a guy in the kitchen there, who he'd been at school with here in the UK, when they were teenagers. They hadn't been mates back then, but they are now!'

'See? There you go! This is just another one of those random things we can talk about at dinner parties. Small-world stories. Now we have one we can share! Wherever we both go in life, it will always be something that connects us.'

Peg came across and took their order, for coffee and a slice of carrot cake each. To Chris' delight, she did remember him. She asked him how he was, but she didn't ask about Daisy, and Chris wasn't sure whether it was because she didn't remember, or because Chris being there with a different woman (and Peg's friend's daughter, to boot) made it inappropriate to ask. Either way, he was grateful.

'Tezzie, you mentioned something about an asshole who tried to ruin your life? Are you recovering from a broken heart, by any chance?'

She grimaced, and nodded. 'Yeah, but that's only part of why I'm here. I'm kind of at a crossroads career-wise. I have ideas about what I want to do but no clue how to make anything happen, and when I'm in London working, I don't get chance to really think about much else at all. I just needed to put some space between myself and the city to try and figure a few things out.'

'Yeah, that makes sense. London's mad. I dunno how you stand it. I hope being up here will help you pull things together the way you want to.'

Tezzie didn't ask Chris why he was at Teapot Cottage alone. He thought she was probably trying not to appear too nosy. She didn't seem like the sort of person who wouldn't care about someone else's pain. But he told her the bare bones of it, so it wouldn't start to feel like an elephant in the room.

She was horrified and dismayed, and acutely sympathetic, but she didn't ask many questions at all. Chris was grateful for that. Last night in the pub with Darren and his friends had been gentle, but excruciating, and he didn't want to strip his soul bare again to yet another stranger. He didn't have to spell it out, that it was a painful thing to talk about. Tezzie just kind of got it, and the conversation moved on.

It was clear to him too, that she had a lot of stuff on her mind. She was one of those people who almost crackled, with unspent energy. Chris could feel the restlessness coming off her in waves.

After she'd dropped him back at Teapot Cottage with his shopping he told her he hoped he would see her again. As he let himself in through the front door, he found that he really meant it. Spending time with her had been refreshing. She had a great sense of humour, and the stories they'd swapped had made him feel lighter than he'd felt in months. It was nice to laugh, and to reminisce. Neither of them could remember very much about their drunken encounter in the pub in Hobart, half a world away. But the reconnection, and the exchange of what they could remember from that night, felt nice.

He made himself a cup of tea and went to sit in the window seat, figuring there was every possible chance that he'd fall asleep in the lukewarm sunshine that flooded through the windows. As his prophecy came true, and he felt himself nodding off, the last thing that went through his mind was that he *did* hope to see Tezzie again before she went back to London.

Chapter Seven

What an interesting day it had been! Teresa sat in an armchair by the fire, but the coffee table book she'd been half-heartedly leafing through wasn't inspiring her at all. Her mind was full of the day's events instead, and the day wasn't even yet over!

Things had started out a little crazy. To be fair, Adie had warned her in advance that Saturday mornings could be a bit chaotic at Ravensdown Farm, and Mark had added his opinion about it too.

'All 'ell breaks loose around 'ere on Sat'dy mornin' so brace yerself,' he had added quietly, with a roll of his eyes, and Teresa concluded that 'a bit chaotic' hadn't a bad way of describing the start of 'Market Day.'

Her step-father was always up at 6am on a weekday, and out on the farm by 6.30. Adie was usually up with him, organising his breakfast while he got himself showered and dressed. But Saturdays were a little different; Mark would get up at half past seven instead, and Adie would make a heartier-than-usual breakfast for eight o'clock because, after that, it was officially 'fend for yourself day.' If you couldn't somehow manage to feed yourself at lunch time, a big breakfast meant that at least you wouldn't starve.

Satisfied that everyone would start the day with a jolly good meal under their belt, Adie would then be entirely focussed on getting ready for the Farmers Market down at Torley Community Hall. She'd taken it over, a couple of years before, at a time when it was a dying event with very little in the way of local enthusiasm or support.

By Mark's account, she had turned things around impressively. The market was now the pride of the region, and the highlight of most of the local people's week. It offered everything, from crafts, jewellery and practical and attractive table linens and aprons, to gardening hardware and seedling plants, and a mind-boggling assortment of produce ranging from common and exotic wild meats to home-baked cakes and pies, and jams, pickles, chutneys and cheeses to rival the best delis in the district.

People now came from far and wide to the Torley Farmers Market and many would spend time, after their shopping, having a pot of tea and a good gossip in the makeshift café tucked away in one corner.

The market had become a rip-roaring success, and it seemed to be the one thing Teresa's normally cruisy mother got tied up in knots about. According to Mark, she typically spent the first half hour of the morning on the phone, handling last-minute stall-holder cancellations, contacting waitlisted vendors to see if they were ready to take a stand at no notice, and tearing tufts of her hair out if they weren't. That didn't happen often. There was quite a long waiting list now, for regular stall-space. Any stray opportunity to come just once, even at no notice, was usually snapped up by market traders wanting to establish a toe-hold on the possibility of being offered a more regular spot.

After Adie had sorted out the list of traders, Mark would remind her that her coffee was going cold, and she would absent-mindedly bat him away while counting the eggs into the cartons that were going to be sold on her own stand, lining up the jars of lemon curd and ginger marmalade, and stacking the packets of lavender shortbread she'd baked the previous day, that would sit alongside them.

She would then load everything into crates, take a shower, reheat her cold coffee in the microwave, and have a piece of toast with heaven knows what on it. At the same time, she would answer the phone, probably another dozen times. Miraculously, she somehow managed to be out of the house with everything she needed, and on her way to the hall, right on time to get things unlocked and ready for the onslaught. Sometimes she was organised enough to have everything ready the night before but equally often, according to Mark, she wasn't.

The local youth group who used the hall on Friday nights always set it up for the Saturday market, which meant that Adie didn't have to do it herself. But there was still a lot to do, once she got there. People tended to want the same stand in the same place every week, but she liked to mix it up a little to keep a fresh 'feel,' and she usually had to handle complaints from the few who were too set in their ways to be comfortable with changing.

'It's the same few, every week, who moan about it,' she muttered to Teresa. 'I sometimes struggle to keep patience with them. People can't just set up wherever they want. There's a system, and it actually works very well, but some stallholders just don't want to be told. More than once, I've been within a hair's breadth of telling one or two of the bigger whiners to either abide by the bloody rules or stop showing up altogether.'

Teresa was impressed when her mother confessed that Mark had managed to get her to put almost everyone onto a weekly direct debit for their stand payments.

'It does take the pressure off having to collect the cash from all and sundry, but of course there's still a stubborn few who insist on not paying until the day. I've given up arguing with them over it, but I have insisted they all come to me with the cash, as soon as they arrive and before they get to set up, instead of me having to go chasing them later when they're busy, or I'm too busy myself to ask them at all.'

She said they were an honest bunch who hadn't let her down yet, so the makeshift system worked well enough. But the toilets needed to be routinely checked, with soap and paper regularly replenished, and there were always little dramas to deal with, like someone bringing a dog in that had peed on Mr Turner's carrots which had been sitting in a box on the floor, or a fuse needing to be replaced when all the lights went out without warning, plunging the entire hall into murky greyness and sending the café operator into a total tailspin.

It was clear to Teresa however, that Adie adored the Farmers Market and relished her role as its coordinator. As she'd sat at the kitchen table, quietly watching her mother work through her pre-market morning checklists, she could see that there *was* some method within the chaos. Behind Adie's charming haphazardness was a tried-and-tested formula she was sticking to. She wouldn't forget anything. She might appear to be one step removed from a hopelessly stressed and disorganised whirling dervish, but that was all part of the fun.

Nevertheless, Teresa had breathed a huge sigh of relief after Adie got everything loaded into her car and left for the morning. Mark knew the drill well. Immediately after breakfast and his dutiful reminder to Adie about drinking her half-cold coffee, he'd bolted for the relative peace and quiet of the barn.

The errand of dropping some cakes off to the new tenant at Teapot Cottage had been a complete turn up for the book! Teresa had been happy to do that small thing for Adie, on her way into town. She'd intended to just drop the muffins in and get going, but fate had other ideas. Never would she have imagined, in a million years, that the tenant in question would turn out to be someone she'd once met in a pub on the other side of the world!

People said, all the time, what a small world it really was, and she had a couple of interesting small-world stories of her own, but honestly! What were the chances *really*, of two tourists, connected only by a night in a karaoke bar ten thousand miles away two years ago, banging into one another again in the back garden of a tiny cottage in a remote Lakes District town, in such a random way?

When she'd met Chris Darcy that night in Hobart, he had just finished climbing Australia's most challenging mountain. She'd been there with a group of friends who were all travelling around together in a couple of hired campervans, after meeting in a backpackers' hostel in Melbourne and realising they were pretty much all headed to the same place. What fun they'd had on that holiday!

Ross had been with her that night. She'd been mad about him, didn't have eyes for anyone else, and the memory of being there with him was bittersweet now.

Chris Darcy and his mates were out 'on the lash' as they'd put it. They weren't looking for anything, not even a one-night stand. From what Teresa had remembered, all three had wives or girlfriends waiting for them back at home. They were climbers, systematically conquering a few of Australia's more interesting peaks, and they'd saved the best until last. Federation Peak, or 'Fedder,' as Chris had referred to it, had been their grand finale. They were high on their success and enjoying a last night in Hobart before heading back to the Aussie mainland for some sightseeing, and then catching a flight home to England. They'd been fun to hang out with, but Teresa hadn't given them another thought after that night. It was just one random night in a random bar, sharing random laughs with random strangers who were fun but hardly memorable. That sort of thing had happened all the time on her trip. She was surprised now, that she'd even remembered Chris, or that he'd remembered her.

She was even more surprised that he was a lot more interesting sober than he'd been when he was drunk although, to be fair, she'd been in love with someone at the time. But she and Chris had spent an easy morning together today, wandering around the Farmers Market and then going for a coffee at Ye Olde Torley Tea Shoppe. Peg Tripper had remembered Chris from the year before, when he'd been without his wallet. She'd been impressed that he'd gone back to her to pay, later the same day. As she'd said, some people would've 'legged it;' left town again without paying her at all.

Teresa and Chris' conversation had easily flowed this morning, and even when he told her about the death of his fiancée Daisy, it hadn't been a needle-across-a-record moment, as declarations like that so often turn out to be. Teresa had been horrified and had said so and shown it, but it hadn't left them staring at one another, wondering what to say next. She'd admitted it was hard to know *what* to say, but Chris had simply nodded at that, and remarked that most people felt that way, and it was okay.

He'd then gone on to explain his pilgrimages to Daisy, and she thought it was a wonderful tribute. 'I hope someone will love me that much one day," she'd said quietly, almost to herself, 'to honour me like that, if I died.'

From there, they had gone on to talk about their travels. Chris had also been to Bangkok, apparently, with a bunch of mates on what he termed as a 'dirty boy's stag week' but he'd shuddered as he'd said it, and then admitted he and a few others had stayed in the hotel bar while the rest of the lads all went out 'whoring.' He said he wasn't sure whether they actually did that, or whether they just said they did, so it sounded good, but he and a few other of the more sensible ones hadn't wanted to be a part of it. They had women they loved, waiting for them at home. Chris confessed that he'd been appalled too, by the levels of poverty they'd seen, in the seedier parts of the city.

It turned out they had also been to some of the same places in Australia. Even though it was a month's climbing trip, with specific goals to achieve, Chris and his two friends had found time for rest and relaxation too. They'd spent a week 'doing' the Gold and Sunshine Coast, hanging out at Burleigh Heads, Byron Bay, Coff's Harbour, and Bondi. Teresa knew all four places really well, and they chattered about the various pubs of note, the excellent seafood at one particular waterfront restaurant at Coff's Harbour, and the fact that they'd hired bikes at different times and ridden to the Byron Bay lighthouse where migrating whales could sometimes be seen off the easternmost tip of the country.

In the end, Peg Tripper had approached them and gently suggested that if they were finished their coffee and cake and didn't want any more, perhaps they'd be kind enough to give up their table for a group of other patrons who'd been standing around for a while now, waiting for one to become free. Since they'd long since finished their coffees, they readily agreed. Peg was grateful and sent them away with a free fruit scone each, wrapped in greaseproof paper, as a thank-you. Teresa and Chris understood they'd taken up one of her tables for far too long, for the price of one pot of coffee and two chunks of cake! So involved was their conversation, it had been a shock to discover they'd been sitting there 'gassing' for an hour and a half!

'Well, it's the first time I've ever been thrown out of a café!' Chris had remarked with a grin, as they made their way back to the car. Misty was wagging her tail nineteen to the dozen. She'd been the subject of attention from countless people in the street and at the market, and then spoiled rotten by Peg at the café with treats and titbits from the kitchen. Few people failed to go weak at the knees at the sight of a Cocker Spaniel puppy.

'She's going to conk out completely when you get her home,' Teresa had laughed.

'Yeah, for about five bloody minutes! Then she'll be all go, again. I dunno where she gets her energy, bless her. We're going out tonight, to have dinner with some people I've just met here, so she'll be all excited about that too, later on. It's turning into a full-on day and night for her, as well as for me.'

'She's certainly a happy little thing.'

Chris had nodded, smiling. It was obvious how much he adored his puppy. As she dropped him off at the back gate to Teapot Cottage, Teresa had thanked him for what had been a very pleasant few hours. 'It's been such fun, meeting you again! Totally random, and bizarre, but I'm so glad we got to do this.'

He'd agreed, smiling, and he'd high-fived her before getting out of her car. She'd popped the boot lid so he could get his groceries, gave Misty a final kiss on the nose, and watched wistfully as Chris and the little dog retreated to the cottage.

She'd fleetingly wondered if maybe she could get a dog, herself. It wouldn't be possible to have one in the Greenwich flat, but what if she didn't stay in London? What if she could rent a place somewhere else, maybe further up country, where she could have at least a small garden, and get a happy little dog like Misty? Someone to love, who'd love her back. London wasn't the only city in England; others offered opportunities too, didn't they? Maybe it was time to look at what might be on offer outside of the capital.

So here she was, sitting by the fire (which Mark had kindly come in and got going for her), thinking fit to burst about a *lot* of things, reflecting on a day that had thrown up more than one revelation. The best one was that her mother was ridiculously content up here in her new life in the back of beyond. The weirdest one was the random and bizarre reconnection with a bloke she'd met two years ago at the other side of the world.

But the most *interesting* one was the profound feeling that something was missing from her life. She was working towards defining her goals, and making reasonable progress, and living in the vibrant cosmopolitan city of London, but none of it was fulfilling her – at least not yet. It no longer felt like just an idle thought that maybe she *could* live somewhere other than the big smoke. And then there was the out-of-left-field desire to have a dog, with whom she could have and share some love.

All in all, quite a big day. She'd come to this 'back of beyond' bolthole, for a bit of peace and quiet and to disengage for a while from her own over-active brain. It was laughable really, how much that had backfired. For now, at least, her mind was busier than it had been for a long time.

Chapter Eight

Chris heard Darren's Land Rover before he actually saw it. It had that distinct, uniquely rattly engine that no other vehicle could lay claim to. As his new friend pulled up at the front door, Chris flung it open, waved at him, then picked up Misty and the carrier bag containing her lead and water bowl, and the promised cob loaf for the dinner table. He'd also bought some flowers at the market, to give to Debby, which he tucked under one arm, praying that the stems wouldn't crush. Darren leaned over and opened the passenger door as Chris locked the cottage.

He was absurdly excited at the idea of having dinner with Darren and Debby Davies. Hospitality had been in short supply from anywhere, after Daisy's death, and it was good to be invited out, albeit to the home of virtual strangers. It would make a change to be treated like a normal person instead of one that everyone preferred to avoid, or handle like something that would break if they said the wrong thing.

Darren and Debby didn't strike him as gushing types, but they clearly had big hearts. Salt of the earth, Chris suspected, or hoped for it at least. The evening would be excruciating if he had to spend it with someone who ladled out the sympathy and syrup. There again, if he'd thought they were like that, he wouldn't have accepted their invitation in the first place.

Darren extended a hand in greeting, and then threw the old Land Rover into gear and they set off.

''I like your wheels, mate. She's a beauty. What year is she?'

Darren grinned. '1979. Series three. Belongs to the practice. They're pretty common around here, but they do the business, so that's probably why. A four-wheel drive is a must for any vet around here. Some of the so-called 'roads' into a few of the farms are little more than pitted dirt tracks. It's a bit like driving on the surface of the moon, I'd guess.'

'I like the paint job on her, and the signwriting. Very smart.'

Darren nodded then concentrated on the road. It wasn't long before they headed down a winding, tree-lined driveway and pulled up at a small stone house. A wooden painted plaque nailed to the gate said 'Appletree Cottage.' The place couldn't be seen from the road, so unless you knew where to find it, you'd never know it was there. Chris remarked on the fact, and Darren nodded.

'Yep. It's one of the things we like about it. We got it fairly cheap because it was derelict. It needed redoing from the ground up. It was all poky, with dark little rooms, dodgy plumbing, and ancient wiring. We more or less gutted it, downstairs at least, and we've spent a lot of time and money on it, but it's pretty nice now. We love the place. The garden's a good size too, which is brilliant for the kids. My father-in-law had it landscaped for us.'

Chris took a look at the generous, square sunken front garden with its raised stone-border edges teeming with trees, plants, and flowers. It was beautiful. A picnic and barbecue area that occupied one corner looked inviting and fun.

Debby opened the front door, and Misty threw herself at her. She bent and caught the squirming dog, laughing. 'Oh, my God, she's like a cannonball!'

Chris was amazed when he stepped into Darren and Debby's lovely, open-plan cottage. Gorgeous polished wooden floorboards were the colour of rich honey. Solid load-bearing beams of a similar colour ran overhead, with a few heavy old nails hammered into them, here and there. A warming fire blazed in the wood-burner that was nestled into the rustic, wood-framed fireplace recess in one corner of the room, and two big, well-upholstered dog beds lay on the floor in front of it. A mid-sized dining table and four chairs occupied another part of the room, and behind that was a lovely, fitted kitchen, complete with a dark green Aga, just like the red one at Teapot Cottage.

The place was beautiful, and cosy. Chris had to stop admiring it however, and turn his attention to his puppy, who had already made friends with the couple's Border collie and their Springer cross. The three dogs were all rolling around the floor in growling tussle, which sounded a lot more alarming than it actually was. Darren hastened to assure him that Badger and Dolly were friendly, and their rough-house play was a sign that they got on together. The couple had another dog, a smaller one of a mixed breed, that was lying on a smaller bed under the table. Debby introduced him as Jasper.

'He's lovely and sweet, but he's a bit shy. He's a rescue, and he has issues with strange men. Once he gets to know you, he'll be fine, but he'll never shower you with kisses like Dolly or Badger will.'

'No worries. It'll be good for Misty to learn to tussle with these two, though. All part of her socialising.'

Chris took the cob loaf from his backpack and handed it to Debby, along with the flowers that had mercifully survived his rough-handling. Darren offered him a beer and gestured for him to sit down. Debby called over.

'I've just got bangers and mash, with onion gravy and veg, if that's ok? I did a handful of vegan sausages too, and some herb-based gravy, since Darren didn't bother to ask if you eat meat or not!'

Chris grinned. 'Rampant carnivore, guilty as charged.' She gave him the thumbs up, as Darren rolled his eyes.

'Shit. I never remember to ask people, do I?' Debby shook her head, grinning, and went back to her cooking.

There were a few framed photos on a sideboard in the living area. To make conversation, Chris asked Darren who they were.

'That one there in the wooden frame is my mum, Barbara, and her partner Pat. They run a chip shop in Exeter. The one next to it in the silver frame are Debby's parents, Don, and Carole. They're retired, and they live in Lytham St Annes, on the east coast, near Blackpool. The baby photos are of Ruby and Thomas, and the one in the white R.I.P. frame with the angel wings on the top of it is my friend Tommy.'

'Is that the guy you were telling me about, the one who died?' As he asked the question, Chris hoped he wouldn't offend the other man.

'Yeah. It's quite a story, actually, how he died. He was younger than me, and he looked up to me. I was quite an experienced burglar and thief back then, and he was with me on a job in a posh neighbourhood. I was teaching him the graft.' Darren snorted at himself in a kind of disbelief and shook his head.

'The owner came home unexpectedly while we were there. I ran for my life, but Tom didn't get away quick enough and she killed him. She didn't mean to. She panicked, I guess. It started off as an accident really. She hit him, to try and stop him from leaving, but he died. It was a tragic thing for everyone involved, even for her.'

Chris listened intently as Darren recounted the story of how Alison Jones, the homeowner, had then tried to conceal her crime and how she eventually killed herself after being diagnosed with an inoperable brain tumour. Badger, Darren's Border collie, had been Alison's dog. His chance to become a vet had come from her too, out of guilt, along with a big opportunity for Tom's bereaved mother to do something meaningful in his memory. It was an utterly incredible story, the kind of thing you'd expect to see on TV, and when Chris finally managed to get his head around it, he said as much. Darren grinned ruefully.

'Yeah, you couldn't have made it all up, really. And it'd certainly make a decent drama. Stuff like that doesn't happen every day in real life, does it? But I'd already screwed up Tommy's life, in a way that got him killed. So, like I said in the pub last night, when I got the chance to get out of crime and make something good of my life, I knew I had to take the opportunity for him, if not for myself.'

Chris found himself staring at the photo of Tom. The young lad was smiling, and fresh-faced, no doubt imagining that he had his whole life ahead of him. In that moment, he felt Darren's Davies' pain, so close to his own.

'Did you hate yourself? After, I mean?'

Darren nodded. His was face serious. 'Yeah, I did, totally. Even criminals have a conscience, you know, and mine almost crippled me. I found myself almost unbearable to live with, for a long time. There are days when I still do, to be honest. Odd days when I still feel haunted, when I struggle to avoid sinking, to a dark place. But there's not so many of them now. It's like Stu and Fiona said in the pub, all you can do is go on to become the best person you can possibly be, in gratitude for the second chance that allows you to.'

He looked at Tom's photo. 'There will never be a day in my life that I don't regret Tom losing his. The weight of that is something I'll probably feel forever. But I've worked my arse off to make it right in whatever way I can, and be the best person I can be, for Tommy, for my Mum, for my family, and for all the people I serve at the practice. And for the people I robbed off, too. If they could know how I'd turned my life around, maybe they'd forgive me for being such a fucking scumbag, back then. Sorry, pardon the language. I do still forget myself at times.'

They moved to the table as Debby set the dinner down in serving dishes and told Chris to help himself. She asked him what his long-term plans were. 'Now that your life's been turned on its head, I mean. Like you said in the pub, you're at a crossroads. Is anything clear about a new way forward, or is it still too soon?'

Chris shook his head. 'Nothing's clear yet, but I know I do have to figure things out. It's only been ten months, but it's still ten months, if you know what I mean. I can't sit around wailing and gnashing my teeth forever. Once this year of pilgrimage is over, I think that's when I'll feel I can draw a line under a few things and start looking to the future.'

He explained the pilgrimages to Debby and Darren who both understood. Debby smiled at him gently. 'I think that's a wonderful idea. Wherever Daisy is now, I'm sure she's grateful for you honouring her in such a beautiful way. I know I would be, if it was me.'

Chris explained that this trip to Torley, and to Teapot Cottage, was the second-to-last pilgrimage on his list for Daisy. 'There's only one more thing left to do, really, but it's the worst thing. The hardest.'

To his dismay, he heard his voice crack, and he struggled to overcome a sudden urge to cry. 'Oh God, sorry! I don't want to sit here in a blubbering heap, please forgive me! I don't have any such thing as a stiff upper lip.'

Christ, I've only been here five minutes! This wasn't how the night was meant to go!

Darren leaned forward and covered Chris' hand with his own. 'Hey, you're ok. We've got you. You're safe here.' Chris nodded and got himself under control. He wasn't sure what to say next and was acutely aware of his host watching him intently.

'You have to go back to where she lost her life, don't you? I'm guessing that's what you mean by the final thing, the hardest thing? Going back to finally say goodbye, and anything else you feel you need to be there in that place, to say to her?'

Chris nodded miserably, and sniffed hard. 'Yeah, and I just don't feel ready. I've gone through everything else, but I can't face that yet. Sorry, for snivelling. I'm still a bit of a basket case over it, sometimes.'

'Of course you are,' Darren said quietly.

A clock somewhere nearby ticked quietly, drawing out the silence that hung in the air. Chris didn't know how to fill it and neither, it seemed, did Debby. But after a minute or so, Darren cleared his throat and spoke again.

'Forgive me if I'm stepping in where I'm not wanted, and you can tell me to piss off if you like, but let me ask you something. D'you wonder if maybe there's something else you need to do first? Like maybe something that will give you the *strength* to go back, when you've rebuilt yourself a bit? Like, you know, enough for it not to be so painful?'

The question was asked in a light tone, but Chris felt the real weight of it.

He considered the question carefully. Taking the time to get into a better place before going back to the mountain wasn't something he'd thought about. He somehow just felt he had to go in anguish, for it to be meaningful, but Darren's question gave him cause to wonder now, whether that was the right way to look at it.

Darren pressed further, gently. 'Maybe that particular torture is something you don't need to go through while everything is still so raw. Would Daisy want you to do it, while you're still in such a devastated state?'

The question hung in the air. For the first time, Chris wondered if maybe he was being too hard on himself, risking what was left of his mental health, to go back to Mulhacén when his grief was still so all-consuming. Yes, he absolutely needed to go back, to make that final peace with what had happened. But would it be so wrong to postpone it, to a time when he felt more stable, and capable of handling it without it tearing him apart?

Could he make the decision to start moving on with his life, and go back at a later time, when it might feel like more of an affirming than a decimating thing to do?

'It's a good question, Darren – one I haven't asked myself. I think I've been fixated on going back because I'm not done with punishing myself. I think maybe I don't deserve to move on yet and rebuild my life, not when she can't.' Chris was surprised at how candidly he was speaking, to someone he didn't even know, about something so shockingly painful.

Darren shook his head. 'I'm not saying you're wrong for wanting to go back. I'm not. I get it, Chris, but I'm just wondering about the purpose.' He took a swig of his beer and continued.

'I guess the real questions, underneath it all, are *why* you want to go back, and what you want to get from it. Will it make you feel better, or are you just determined to punish yourself more because you feel you don't deserve to stop hurting? Is it more about you than it is about her? Would going back make it easier to live with yourself, or harder? Because if you're not sure about the answers, it could do you more harm than good to put yourself through that.'

From the corner of his eye, Chris saw Debby throwing a warning glance at Darren, suggesting that she though he'd pushed too hard. Chris was, after all, a guest in their home and a virtual stranger; one who had every right to be offended at such intrusiveness.

But, strangely, Chris wasn't. He felt, instead, like he was on the threshold of something significant; something life changing. Here in this moment, at this table with these people, he suddenly felt the ground shift beneath him. Never in his life had a conversation felt as important as the one he was having now, even though he couldn't put his finger on why it mattered so much. It just did. And *as* the ground shifted, he felt like something had a steadying hold of him. It was the weirdest feeling, that he couldn't have described if his life depended on it. But, in that moment, he felt the first glimmer of his courage, coming back.

Darren held up his hands. 'Forgive me, Chris. We don't even know each other, do we? I just want to help, I guess. But tell me to fuck off and mind my own business, if you want, and we can talk about something else.'

Chris shook his head. 'No. They're good questions, Darren, and it's just struck me as odd that nobody else, nobody closer to me, has asked them. I've been left to my own devices to deal with all this. Even my friends don't know what to say to me about it, so they say bugger all.

They don't even ask me how I'm doing, and I suppose that's just keeping me in my own head about everything. It hasn't even occurred to me to ask *myself* why it's so important that I go back,' he added, almost absently.

'I've no family support either, to speak of. I have a sister, Suzanne, who's pretty much in her own world. She lives in some far-flung, windswept corner of Southern Ireland with her husband and their two kids. We've never been particularly close. I haven't seen her in nearly fifteen years, and I haven't even met my nieces! Suze is quite a bit older than me, and we never had anything in common, apart from our biological parents. Our mother's long-dead, and our father is an asshole I don't want to associate with.'

'So, you really are alone, in dealing with this,' Debby observed. 'You know, grappling with grief alone can often put us into a really destructive way of thinking. My sister Jayne had a partner, Louise, who died in a motorcycle crash about eight years ago. Louise was a good friend to me too, so I've experienced something similar, very close to home.'

She shook her head, almost to herself, before continuing. 'Jayne said that so few of her friends knew what to say, after the crash. I was grieving too, but in a slightly different way of course. I wasn't enlightened enough to help her, and our parents were no help to either of us. I remember Jayne saying that when she was trying to accept everything, she used to think all kinds of stuff that made sense at the time, but she realised later how irrational and unhelpful it all was. She also said that the isolation just compounded her craziness.'

She laughed, gently. 'I'm not sticking up for Darren, who has a well-meaning but sometimes disastrous habit of opening his mouth and jamming both feet in pretty hard. But I do think if my poor sister had had someone sensible asking *her* to look at things differently when she was grieving, maybe she would have come out of it sooner.

'It did take her a long time. She travelled for years. She was so restless, and I think that loss was a big part of the reason why she stayed away for as long as she did; that and the general disconnection in our family, particularly with my mother, which is another story entirely.'

'I'm sorry for your loss. That must've been awful.'

Debby grimaced, and nodded. 'Yeah, it was difficult. I still miss Louise sometimes, even now. It was worse for Jayne, of course, because they were together. But yeah, it was all pretty hard, at the time. They'd had a disagreement. That's all it was, not a full-blown row or anything. Louise had just bought the bike, and she wanted Jayne to go on the back of it with her, but Jayne refused. Louise was miffed, so she stormed out, and crashed about six blocks away. She failed to give way at an intersection and someone in a van broadsided her.'

Debby's voice became pensive. 'I kept thinking, if Jayne had agreed to go on the back with Louise, I know she wouldn't have been all revved up and angry and distracted like she was. She would've ridden slower, and she'd have been in a different place on the road, and she wouldn't have been hit by that van.

'But I didn't blame my sister. She blamed herself for a long time, but the truth is, it was a complete, random, hideous, unbearable bloody accident that nobody could have foreseen! And Lou allowed her anger to push her. And she was riding a motorcycle. And we all know the risks attached to that.' Debby's tone was light and matter-of-fact, but Chris knew full well, the anguish she and her sister would have gone through at the time.

'And maybe she would still have died, on a different day, in another situation that nobody had any more control over than the choices she made that night,' he offered, as gently as he could. 'But tell me; how did you and Jayne put it all back together, Debby? How did you get to here? Chris gestured at Darren, and the house, and the baby pictures above the hearth.

'Honestly? For a while we didn't have *anything* together! Jayne was completely derailed. She went off travelling for a long time, and she couldn't stick at a job for long when she came back. I was pretty stuck. Losing Louise as a friend was hard. I couldn't imagine what it would have been like to have lost someone you were involved with romantically. But gradually, over time, I started to think less about my own grief and consider more what kind of woman Louise really was.

'She wouldn't want anyone to be unhappy. 'Do what makes you happy;' it was something she often said. I think when I decided to concentrate on that, it got me over the hump. But the truth is, nobody who hasn't gone through a close bereavement would understand how raw it makes you feel, and I saw what Jayne went through, and I can see what you're going through. It's horrible.'

Debby smiled gently at her husband and then grimaced. "And of course, when you got sepsis a couple of years ago, and *your* life was hanging in the balance, I caught a glimpse of how wretched mine would be if you *had* died. I'm glad I was spared that. I'm so sorry you weren't spared the agony, Chris. I really am.'

Debby went on to explain that when she'd first met Darren, he was still repairing his own life, battling his way through guilt and shame, and finding it hard to believe that anyone might love him. They somehow seemed to recognise and draw the best from one another, and fell in love quite quickly. As Darren said, the rest was history, and their love story was still unfolding. The rocky time they'd had with IVF, and the strain it had put on their relationship before the babies had started appearing, were all just a part of that story.

So, Chris mused, here were two people who had suffered their own adversity, both separately and together, and had overcome it and found real strength in love. They had forged a life of rewarding purpose, helping others in pain and distress. If they could overcome all that and be as happy as they seemed to be now, even with the regrets they had to live with, maybe he could too. He spoke slowly, looking up as

Debby placed a massive plate of pavlova and whipped cream on the table.

'Well, you know, I think there may be something in what you say, Darren, that maybe I could wait until I feel stronger, and in a place where I'd be sure I was going back to Sierra for the right reasons, before I went.' He was thoughtful.

'Maybe Daisy would rather that too because I know she wouldn't want me to be unhappy. I've always known that, on some level of course, but I haven't fully understood or appreciated it. Until now it's all been just words, and I haven't considered the real meaning behind them.'

He smiled gratefully at Debby. 'I believe you really might have something there, in saying that being able to focus more on the kind of woman Louise was, than on how the loss of her made you feel, made it easier.'

'Yes, but it still took me a long time, because like you I was dealing with everything by myself. My parents were useless. They didn't get it at all, and the few friends I had at the time had no idea how to help me through it either. I figured it all out for myself, in the end, but it took a lot longer than it would have if I'd had the supportive help I really needed.'

The kind that's being offered to you now!

The thought shot quickly through Chris' head. It startled him, and he wasn't sure, but he wondered if Daisy had somehow pushed it through. In some totally weird way, it felt as if she had.

Without being prompted, he found himself talking about her, describing her, how quirky and funny she was, how she always tried to see the best in people, even making excuses for the ones who treated her badly. As she 'unfolded' before them all, there at the table, he came to appreciate how important happiness had always been to her.

'She used to want to do the craziest things, like go to the beach when it was snowing. One time, I suggested going for a romantic walk in the rain, but then it stopped raining. So, she got us both in the bath, standing up in all our clothes, pouring buckets of water all over each other. We could hardly get out, at the end, for laughing.

'Another time she got it into her head to spend an entire day remodelling the collar on one of my favourite shirts. God knows why, because it was perfectly fine the way it was, but after she'd done it, it sat too high on my neck. She made such a mess of it, but I didn't have the heart to tell her I'd probably never wear it again.'

Daisy wanted to make me happy. She used to hang on every word when I talked about my climbing trips, because she cared how happy they made me. She wanted me to be happy.

Chris suddenly felt as if she were in the room with them all, sitting at the end of the table, smiling like she always did, with the left side of her mouth wobbling like she was about to burst into wild laughter, which she often actually did. Daisy had the kind of laugh that took everyone with her. You couldn't remain impartial. It simply wasn't an option, to not join in.

'She was quite a character, by the sound of it,' Darren observed. 'If you could be objective about it, what do you imagine she might want for you now, if she could tell you?'

Chris thought for a moment, feeling strangely comforted by the ticking clock.

'She'd want me to move on, and have someone special in my life again. She wouldn't want me to lock my heart away and never know love again. I think she'd tell me to pick myself up, dust myself off, stop wallowing, and go off and do and be what makes me happy. And that's not new. I guess I've always known it. The only thing is, it's easier said than done, especially when I have no idea what will make me happy again. I've no idea yet, how to get there from here.'

The baby monitor kicked into life just then, and Debby got up from the table with an apologetic smile. 'That's Thomas. He's due for his feed. Impeccable timing, as always! Excuse me, Chris. I'll be back soon.'

As she ran up the stairs, Darren turned to Chris.

'It's interesting how things come together sometimes. I dunno if you're interested, but d'you remember that my mate Stuart, from the pub last night, renovates old houses?'

Chris nodded and listened with increasing interest as Darren explained that he had talked with his friend, before he went to collect Chris from Teapot Cottage, and Stuart had asked him to 'suss Chris out.' He wanted Darren's opinion on whether Chris might be a good fit for their small team of tradesmen who were going to start work soon on the four Victorian semis he and Fiona had just acquired.

'Stu's current sparky is getting married and moving to Glasgow, of all places. His wife-to-be is from there, I think. I wouldn't have mentioned it to you if I didn't think you might slot in well with them, Chris. But Stu's looking for someone, and I do think you'd fit in. He said it was ok to run the prospect by you if I felt positive about it and, to be honest, I do. I wonder if maybe a new challenge, a change of scene for a bit, might be just the thing to help move you forward?' He sat back in his chair, with his eyebrows raised in question.

Chris stared at him. 'Are you serious? You know I already have a job, right?'

Darren laughed. 'Course I do, but I dunno how you feel about it, do I? And yes, I'm serious! Why would I yank your chain? Stu needs imminent help, and he was impressed with you. So was Fiona. I know she was interested in the work you'd done. They need a new electrician to help them fully rewire four houses. You're fully qualified and experienced in retrofitting and – if you don't mind me reminding you of your own words – you're at a crossroads.' He looked at Chris, smiling slightly, with his head cocked on one side.

'If you *were* up for a change, I just wonder whether you could do the work, throw yourself into a challenge you've already said you enjoy, then see how you felt about everything else after that.

'I dunno how long it might take to get them all done,' he added, half to himself. 'You'd have to take a look at it and talk to Stu. He mentioned something about six weeks or so, to reno each house. So that's kind of half a year, right, at best, if there weren't any complications? He has a caravan on site at the stables that you could stay in, probably rent free, and it might give you a bit of time to get your head into something else for a bit? In my experience, sometimes after I've taken my mind to a completely different place for a while, I've found myself a different frame of mind at the end of it.'

He went on to describe his vet training, and how it had demanded every ounce of his concentration. By the time he'd completed his first year, he'd stopped beating himself up constantly over Tom's death.

'It was all-consuming, Chris, the study. I just didn't have any time, to indulge in self-pity, which is what it had all turned into for me. I'm not suggesting that's where *you're* at, but I was on a road to nowhere good, until that point. It wasn't a conscious thing, or a dedicated process. I just realised one day that while I'd been busy with other things, the pain of losing Tommy had become a lot less acute.'

Darren continued to explain. 'While I hadn't been fully focussed on it, it had somehow devolved into something bearable, and I realised there was more to me than the half-arsed loser I'd been for too long.'

Chris nodded and stuck his hand across the table. Darren gratefully shook it, as both men recognised it as being a line drawn under the conversation. Enough had been said, and Darren's only further comment was to ask Chris to promise to think about Stuart and Fiona's offer, which he agreed to do. Darren fished around in his shirt pocket and gave him Stuart's business card.

The conversation then turned to Darren's work, and how he had more or less fallen into the job, after being called upon to help out in in an emergency at a nearby farm while he and Debby were up here on holiday at Teapot Cottage. The local farm vet was retiring, leaving an opening at the practice, and Darren had been so highly recommended by Mark Raven and his brother-in-law Bob Shalloe, who were two of the most influential farmers in the area, he was able to more or less walk into the job.

'It's a much nicer place to bring kids up in, and once we knew we had one on the way, the deal that we'd move here pretty much wrote itself. We didn't need much persuading, to be honest. The people are 'real' here, salt of the earth. Debs told you last night, I think, that she has part time work as a theatre nurse at Cumbria Infirmary in Carlisle. We feel more settled here than we ever did in Exeter. It's pretty easy nowadays, to keep in touch with friends and family, wherever you are in the world. We get down to the hometown a fair bit, still, and we're never short of visitors!'

Darren was explaining how much he enjoyed the fact that he knew so many of his clients – and their pets – by name, when Debby came back down the stairs.

'That's him all fed and burped and changed. He's snoring his head off again. That baby could sleep for England.' She moved into the kitchen to organise a pot of coffee.

'Any plans for more, or are you stopping at two?' The question was out of Chris' mouth before he realised how impertinent it was. 'Oh, God! Sorry! How rude was that? Forgive me, please! Its none of my bloody business, is it?'

Debby waved his comment away with a broad smile. 'It's ok. If it was up to me, I'd have a football team, but I'd have to give up work completely if we had another, and a third mouth to feed and the loss of an income just doesn't equate, financially.' She brought the pot over to the table, on a tray with some cups and condiments.

'But to be honest with you, Chris, the fact that we even managed to have one kid was a blessing and a half. Two is two more than we ever expected, so I'm grateful enough to feel okay about stopping there.'

Darren piped up, 'Yeah, I'm not sure we wouldn't feel a bit greedy, wanting any more. D'you want them? Kids?'

Chris pulled a face and shrugged lightly. 'To be honest, not especially. I'm on the fence about it. I like kids, don't get me wrong, but life can be a lot more exciting if you only have yourself to please. I know that sounds a bit selfish, but I'm an adrenaline junkie, Darren! An adventure-hound. I like to push life to the limits on the rocks; it's how I'm made. Kids don't fit so well into that framework, and I dunno if I want to give up the part of my life that has always given me the most joy. Daisy wanted a kid, and I went along with it as a future plan if it happened, but it wouldn't have mattered to me if we didn't have any.'

As he said the words, he was surprised not to feel the avalanche of grief that usually followed a revelation about his life with Daisy.

That's interesting...

They moved over to the sofa, and spent the next hour talking about all kinds of random things, before watching a thriller Debby had downloaded. Chris was relieved that the 'heavy' conversation was clearly done with, for all of them.

When he next checked his watch, he was astonished to find that it was nearly midnight. Misty, Dolly, and Badger were all completely conked out on Badger's bed by the fire. They were actually snuggled together, a sight that made his heart melt. Apologising profusely for staying so late, he was told not to be so silly, that it was Saturday night, and they'd be up anyway. Debby told him that they'd both enjoyed his company immensely, and it would certainly be nice to do it again, if the chance was available.

'I'm sorry you have to go out at this time of night, just to take me home.'

Debby shook her head, smiling. 'It's no trouble; really it isn't. It will take twenty minutes, to get there and back, so it's no drama. By the time I get back, Darren will have the washing up done and put away, the dogs abluted, and the bedcovers turned down. As trade-offs go, that's not bad.'

Chris grinned and stood up. He shook Darren's hand and gave Debby a hug. 'Thanks, guys, for the invite. It's been great, and it's given me a lot to think about. Not least of which is the chance to talk to Stu about some work.'

Darren shrugged, lightly. 'Well, you never know. It might turn out to be a win-win for all of you, but no problem if not. If it isn't this, I expect there'll be something else for you to get your teeth into soon enough, if you do fancy a change.'

Chris picked up a semi-sleepy Misty who then found a new surge of energy and decided to dedicate it all to licking his face. Darren threw Debby the keys to the Land Rover, and within seconds they were hurtling back down the drive, and onto the main road to head to Teapot Cottage, on the other side of the valley. Debby threw him a quick glance.

'Don't be offended by anything Darren said, will you, Chris? He means well. He had a shit life before he turned everything around, and he's a big believer now in everyone being able to fulfil their potential. He says the waste of talent and potential is the biggest of all the world's human tragedies.'

Chris grinned at her. 'Well, he's right about that, I think, and I'm not offended. Far from it! Tonight's done me good. It was nice to get out of my own head for a few hours. I didn't know how much I missed that. I think I'm my own worst enemy, at times.'

'Aren't we all? But for what it's worth, since you've said you were thinking about a change of scene, I think there may be an opportunity in what Stu Thomson has to offer. It would be an interesting project, and it could lead to bigger things. He's well connected, around here. Who knows what might come of it?'

'Well, you know, I actually *could* consider it. Without putting too fine a point on it, I don't have to worry financially. Daisy's travel and life insurance policies took care of that; you know, after the accident? I'm working in the same job I've had for years because I dunno what else to do with myself. Working has stopped me from losing the plot completely, and I do have a bit of loyalty to my boss because he protected my job while I was too much of a head-case to show up. But loyalty has to end somewhere, I suppose. He's well and truly getting his pound of flesh off me again now, so maybe a change *would* do me good.'

As she drew up at the front door of Teapot Cottage, Debby looked at it and laughed lightly. 'This place is kind of special. It will work a bit of magic on you if you let it. Hopefully, we'll see you again but, if we don't, good luck with everything Chris, and I do mean that.'

Chris thanked her again for a nice meal and good company, and she sped off again, leaving him standing with Misty in his arms. The little dog was quiet and still, not fidgeting at all, and as he sank his face into her warm, soft fur, he felt the tears come. This time though, they didn't feel like tears of anguish. He wasn't sure *what* they were. All he knew was that something felt different, in a way he couldn't describe. Something had changed tonight, ever so slightly and quietly, in his world.

A very subtle shift had taken place inside him. For the first time, he wondered if maybe – just maybe – he would soon find himself on the road to self-forgiveness. Maybe – just maybe – there was more out there than just the endless, brutal, daily challenge of just being able to put one foot in front of another.

It was time to start really thinking, about what Daisy would want for him now.

Chapter Nine

As they sat in the Bull with a pint each, Teresa glanced across at Chris, and grinned when he winked at her.

'It's nice getting to know you a little, Mr Darcy! Maybe we could keep in touch, you know, in case you ever come to London?'

Chris pulled a face. 'London? I can't see myself going to the big smoke for anything, unless it's to the airport for a flight to somewhere, but sure. I guess there's no harm in keeping in touch. Are you looking forward to going back?'

It was Teresa's turn to grimace. 'Not really. The agency has offered me a new post; an eight-month maternity cover gig at an insurance company. I have to interview for it, which I'm not looking forward to, and its miles from the flat, so it's a long daily commute by Sardine Express – you know, the tube? I should take it, because the money's good, but I dunno…' She trailed off, wondering what else to say about it.

'What's holding you back? Apart from the commute and the interview, I mean. If they just said, yes, the job's yours, and you can do it from home, would you want it, or is there something *else* that's stopping you from jumping in?'

They were good questions, and she'd been asking them of herself. She couldn't offer any answers though, which seemed a bit strange. She said as much, and was surprised when Chris offered to help her figure it out.

'Okay, let's look at it then. If you don't want to do it, what do you want instead? What are your options? You could go travelling again, or stay up here with your mum, or even try a different city. What are your choices, and which of them feels better than the others?'

She was pensive for a moment. 'I can't go travelling like I did. I no longer have the funds, and I'm still completing my online degree.' She shifted in her seat, sighed deeply, and shook her head.

'You know, I think I'm just ready for a change, Chris, but I really don't know what I want to do, *right now*. Eventually, I really want a career as a documentary film maker, but sometimes that seems like such a far-away dream, like I'm never going to make it happen. London is so expensive. I'm not saving as much as I need to, which is really frustrating. But the money is rubbish everywhere else.'

'Do you feel like you're caught in a bit of a trap?'

She realised that Chris' question was exactly the right one. 'Yes, that's it in a nutshell. I *do* feel trapped, like I'm in some horrible holding pattern, waiting for things to change, wanting them to, but having no idea how to make it happen! Nothing seems feasible or logical, as a move. I can do the agency job, sure, if I get it. But for some reason the enthusiasm I normally have, especially for a gig this secure, just isn't there. Eight months is a solid job, so why do I feel like I wouldn't want to do it? It's something I'd normally bite off someone's hand for.'

'Maybe you're just tired, Tez. You've been working non-stop, for a full eighteen months now. I know you said you've had the odd city-break, a few days away here and there, but it's not the same thing as a proper holiday, is it? D'you think you might be a bit burned out?'

'I actually feel more restless and impatient than burned out, but you're right. I probably am just tired, and Mum keeps telling me to slow down a bit. She thinks I'm too driven. She's worried about me working full time *and* studying part time. She's right; it's a lot. I do feel that, sometimes. But I'm already in my mid-twenties, Chris. I don't want to be dithering for too much longer about making my career change, but I can't see how to make the leap from where I am now, to having what I need to get started.'

She was almost finished her MA in Film and Television, but she still felt a long way from being able to realise her dream. The cost of the equipment she needed to start as an independent film maker was huge. She also knew that even if she did take the long-term temp job in London, she would still be short of what she needed at the end of that. And how exhausted would she be, to keep going after that?

'… get sponsored?'

She realised that Chris had asked her another question, and she'd been too distracted by her own thoughts to hear it.

'Sorry, what?'

'I said, what if you were somehow able to get an idea together for a short documentary, that might perhaps support a charity or something, is there a chance you could get sponsored somehow, to purchase the stuff you'd need, to do it?'

'What, you mean like say to someone; 'I can make this film to showcase you, if I can get donated money or equipment to do it' kind of thing?'

'Yeah. Or maybe even borrow the equipment you need from someone who has it all, covered by good insurance of course.'

She thought about it for a minute. And the more she did, the more interesting a prospect it became. A challenge, but a potentially rewarding one. She tuned back in to Chris, who was speaking again.

'I know about a woman who wanted to sail around the world. She had nothing, and she had to work her arse off to get sponsorship to do it, but she got someone to take a punt on her. She made it happen.

'I don't think what you're wanting to do is quite on that scale,' he added, 'but if a girl with nothing can get someone to bankroll a bloody yacht that's fit to sail around the entire world, for God's sake, I think you could find a creative way to get someone to fork out for a few cameras, lighting rigs and whatever else you might need to make a short film!'

'I might even be eligible for a grant, or something. I could investigate that, couldn't I? I hadn't even thought about that until now.'

Chris nodded. 'You could apply for whatever grants you might be eligible for, certainly. And, you know, the stuff you need is a lot of money, to you, but to someone else, like a corporate sponsor or something, it's probably peanuts! All you have to do is offer them something in return, like an ad, or maybe even a short film, about how great they are and then find the platform to release it that will give them the exposure they could get real benefit from.'

'Sell the benefits,' Teresa mused. 'You know, you might be onto something.' Her mind was racing, now. 'Do you know what I *really* want to do, Chris? Make a documentary about the slum kids of Bangkok. Maybe I could start a Funding page, to try and raise the money for the equipment and the flights and accommodation. If I can get enough exposure, maybe I could make it happen. It's a lot for me, on my own, but I can't let that stop me. You know, it's free to submit a film to Cannes, and not a lot of money to submit to other film festivals too. Even if I didn't get anywhere, the prestige of an actual submission is something in itself.'

'And there's your first potential stepping stone, to recognition! I think you're extremely bright, Tezzie, and you're passionate. That's a winning combination, right there. I do think you can find a way to get your equipment. I really do. And, if you did decide to go to Bangkok to do a documentary, maybe you would let a friend go with you?'

His question was light, but Teresa was intrigued. 'What, you mean *you*? No offence, but why would you want to go along with something like that?'

'Well, I wouldn't want to tag along on filming! I'd be about as much help as a chocolate teapot, on that score. I don't know one end of a camera from the other. Every photo I have of my trips was taken by the friends I went with. But there are some pretty decent peaks in Thailand, I think. It's never been on my list, as a destination, but hell, why *not?*

'We could fly out together, Tezzie, and I could leave you to it in the city, and meet you at the end of our adventures, to fly home again. I just think it might be reassuring for you to have a friend on the same land-mass, because a city-break on your own is one thing, but you'd be a long way from home, out there.'

'Can you afford to just take time out from your job, though? You said your boss was pretty glad when you went back to work, after Daisy and everything.'

Teresa was suddenly excited at the way the conversation was going. They'd had a couple of quick coffees together at Teapot Cottage, over the past couple of days, and they'd decided to come out for a pint at one of the local pubs tonight. She'd expected the conversation to be as light and superficial as usual, but this was turning into quite a plot-hatching evening! Chris' suggestions for how she could get started in her new career were causing her mind to start galloping forward.

Maybe it really *could* all be as simple as it sounded. It occurred to her, for the first time, that maybe she'd been over-thinking everything, and allowing herself to be too intimidated by what she thought were her own limitations. What if she was wrong about them? What if she could push her boundaries more, have a bit more faith in herself, and see what she could achieve?

Chris seemed to think she could achieve her dream by using leverage, to get started. That meant something. He hardly knew her, and if he could see the potential in her, so might someone who was in a position to bankroll her filming equipment!

Chris grinned at her, sheepishly. 'To tell you the truth, I might be handing in my notice at my job. I've a meeting tomorrow with someone local, who has an opening for the kind of work I do. You're not the only one who's ready for a change.'

'So, you might be moving to this area?'

He shrugged at her. 'Maybe, for a little while at least. I dunno. It's an opportunity I hadn't foreseen, but I think it's worth hearing the guy out.'

'Sometimes the unforeseen opportunities are the best ones,' Teresa observed.

Like this one. This random conversation here tonight, in this pub in a tiny town, miles from anywhere, with a guy I hardly know, has the potential to literally change my life!

'I feel like my hair is standing on end,' she admitted self-consciously.

Chris looked at her and roared with laughter. 'You look like someone's just put a bomb under you! Your eyes are all sparkly! Life's possibilities – that's the kind of thing you need to be thinking about! All the potential. Not looking for reasons to drag your arse back to bloody London, to a job you can't get excited about. If you don't mind my saying so, the reason for getting on with making your dream happen is right there, in your eyes, and in your standing-on-end hair!'

'Okay, well, I'm sure Mum would love it if I stayed here a bit longer. I do have to get Lucy's car back to her, but I could train or bus-it back here for a few weeks. I'm just about to pay my rent for the next month, and there are always temp gigs coming up if it all went tits up and I had to go back. I have a few savings to tide me over. Not much, but Mum and Mark wouldn't see me struggling, and I can probably launch a Funding Page fairly quickly, and work out how to appeal to people for money or equipment.'

She grinned at Chris. 'But there's a caveat. If I make the change, or try to at least, you have to, too. You have to take a leap, and yes, if we can make it work, I would *love* to have a mate fly to Thailand with me!'

Well, you've got the safety net of going back to your life as you know it. If I burn the bridge with my employer, it really *is* burning the bridge, Tez! I won't have the luxury of being able to go back. And money's not really an issue, but I still want to feel useful, and I like the work I do. More importantly, working's what's been keeping me sane. If I didn't have a job, I'd have lost my mind, over Daisy.'

She bit her lip, contrite. 'I know. I'm sorry. I guess I'm just excited, and wanting to not be alone in the revolution, if you know what I mean.'

'I totally get that, and I'm with you on it. It's just a timing thing really, because if I decide to take the gig I'm being offered, I would need to see it through before I went anywhere. That's only fair. But after that, I probably could take some time out.'

She felt her eyebrows drift upwards towards her hairline, as Chris explained the position he was in, thanks to Daisy's life insurance payouts.

'Wow! I know it doesn't make up for losing her, but it must feel nice to have the options that gives you.'

Chris shrugged. 'Well, it seems a bit crass, talking about how much money I have, when you're struggling to find what you need to make your dream happen. But in some ways, I envy you Tezzie, because at least you *have* a dream. My dreams are gone. Money's not much comfort, in the face of that.'

She felt a rush of compassion for him. 'Chris, I know it's probably crass too, to even be saying this, but I'm going to. You *will* pick up the pieces of all this. You *will* find a way forward. I'm guessing it's pretty hard to imagine right now, what kind of future you can have. But you *will* have one. Just hang on, okay? Hang onto the good stuff. You have your friends, you have money, you have choices, and one day you'll figure something out.'

'I have my health,' he countered, in a deadpan tone, and she laughed out loud.

'Yes, you do! And it's more than a lot of people have. You have your life, Chris. Daisy doesn't, but you do. And while I'd never presume to imagine what she would want for you; I'd wager it's something really good. From what you've told me about her, she sounds amazing, and she would want you to have something *good.*'

He closed his eyes and nodded gently. 'She would, and I am starting to realise that. I've been wallowing, but it's time to stop. One day, I'll be able to look back and love her without this crushing sadness. I know I will. I'll be able to simply be thankful, that we had what we did, together. Because that's what it was, a gift. A privilege, to have had love like that. Not everyone gets to have a love like that, but I did, even if only for a while.'

Teresa's heart went out to him. He looked so sad. But he was starting to be philosophical, about his loss and about the future. That was a good start. She was confident that he would one day have a *great* life, hopefully with someone new, and he could look back with gratitude instead of anguish, as he'd said. He was a good guy, and he deserved another shot at love and happiness.

'Well, my mum often says that life pushes us forward whether we want it to or not, and its only when we kick against the process that we start to have problems. I think she's right; you know? And, if you're going to meet this local guy who's waving an opportunity at you, and what he has to offer sounds tempting, maybe you'll be having a revolution of your own.'

Chris rolled his eyes. 'We'll see. It might be a pig in a poke, but I won't know until I hear more about it. The guy seemed genuine, and he has an interesting back story. All I can do is see what he has to offer.'

'Well, you know, I have a good feeling about that. I feel like it might just be a turning point for you. And, if it's not, there'll be another, when the time is right.'

When Chris dropped her off at Ravensdown House, Teresa wished him luck for his meeting the following morning. Apparently, it was a job doing something that interested him a lot more than what he was already doing. He might not have realised that he became a little more animated when he was talking about it, but she had noticed. She hoped it would give him what he was looking for – a fresh start.

It was funny how an innocuous conversation could create a big change, and how quickly it could happen. By the time she'd let herself in at the house, she had already decided that she wouldn't be taking the maternity cover job in London. She was going to stay here instead, and work out how to create her dream, and really make it happen.

She found her mother at the kitchen table, flicking through a magazine. Adie looked up and smiled a welcome.

'Hi, darling. How was your time with Chris? You went to The Feathers, didn't you?'

'It was good, yeah. We talked about some important stuff, you know, future stuff. Mum, I've been thinking … would it be okay if I was to stay here for a bit longer? Like, at least a month?'

She went on to describe her embryonic ideas to Adie, whose eyes were shining at the end of it.

'Darling, of course! You're welcome to stay as long as you like! You don't have to ask. We'd both be thrilled to have you for as long as you want to stay. But what about your flat in London? You're not giving that up, are you? It might be useful, you know, to keep it on if you can afford it, while you try and get things off the ground. Just in case you do need to go back.'

She pulled her bottom lip with her thumb and forefinger – something she quite often did when she was thinking. 'I could pay for two or three months' rent for you, if that would help to buy you a bit more time; take the pressure off a bit? A month isn't long, you know. The time will fly by. If you decide you need longer, I'd be happy to help with that.'

'Thanks, Mum. That's an amazing offer. I'd pay you back, of course.'

'Oh, don't worry about that! Save it till you're a rich and famous movie producer, and then you can treat me to a holiday on a beach somewhere exotic.'

'It's a deal. I have to get Lucy's car back to her, but I can come back up on the bus or the train.'

'Well, let me check with Feen first. She's heading back this weekend, but only for a short time. She and the twins are planning another week or two up here, while Gavin goes to the States on a business trip. If you can line up the dates together, maybe she could bring you back. Then you could bring a few more of your things if it would help.'

'My computer would definitely be useful, and a few more clothes, toiletries, and stuff, yeah. It would be *great* if she could do that!'

Her mother went on to remark that Teresa's father would probably happily give her the money she needed, to get her film equipment. He could probably put it through the business, if she wanted him to, before the financials all got raided because of his impending divorce. 'Might be the ideal time to do it, while he still has some money?'

But Teresa shook her head. 'I know he probably would, but I couldn't make myself ask him. We're still not really talking much, and I don't want to treat him like a cash cow.'

'He wouldn't mind, darling. I think he'd be glad of the chance to help, and he'd probably be able to write it off as some kind of tax thing, if he spoke to his accountant.'

Teresa was emphatic. 'No, Mum. I'm not asking Dad for anything. I haven't forgiven him for what he did to this family, and I wouldn't want him to end up thinking I had, if I asked him for money.'

'You know, you'll have to let him out of the doghouse eventually, Teresa. He's your father and yes, he did a terrible thing. But if *I've* managed to forgive him, I think you could at least try to do the same. He paid a price for his indiscretions too, remember, and by the sound of things he's about to pay heavily again.'

'Well, part of me thinks he *deserves* to lose everything! Besides, I want to see if I can make this work by myself. It's a challenge I want to see if I can rise to. If Chris Darcy can climb real mountains, I should be able to climb this metaphorical one.'

Her mother grinned. 'It sounds like he's really inspired you! Will you stay in touch with him after he leaves?'

'Yes, I think we probably will keep in contact. He's quite keen to come with me to Thailand, actually, if I do end up going. He said he could go off climbing while I'm shooting my documentary. He's kind of on the cusp of change too. He's looking at changing jobs, something about working for some local guy who renovates derelict cottages with his partner.'

'Ah, that might be Stuart and Fiona? They were both guests at Teapot, at different times.'

'Really? Well, he didn't tell me who they were; just that they wanted to pitch an idea to him.'

'Well, for what it's worth, I think *your* ideas are incredibly interesting, and I'm glad you're looking at ways to make this new career happen. I've felt for a while now, that living and working in London wasn't the only way you could get things to fly. Most destinations have more than one road leading to them.'

Teresa had to agree. 'Yeah, and I see that now. I think I've been a bit too obstacle-focussed, and weighed down by all this bloody Ross stuff. I have Chris to thank for giving me a nudge, to think outside the box, and now that all these ideas are pinging around in my head, I'm struggling to believe I never thought of any of it *before* now! You know, things like applying for grants, or sponsorship, and suchlike. It seems obvious now. It's what I should've been doing from the start. Leverage, Chris calls it.'

'Sometimes that's all it takes; a conversation with someone who can offer a different perspective. It can lead to all kinds of wonderful things. You have been distracted, it's true, but you have a good imagination, Teresa. Now that this different way of looking at things has come up, I'm sure you'll find a way to make it work.'

'Maybe I have to do a couple of little films initially; to at least say I have some published work. Establish credibility, and all that. I'm sure someone at one of the Cam and Video

Clubs I belong to will help me a bit if I ask them. I'm going to need a website too, I suppose.'

'Well, you can probably build your own, something modest, to start with. My friend Trudie did it, for her boutique, GladRagz. She said it was pretty easy.'

Teresa gave Adie a hug and excused herself. She wasn't ready to go to bed yet, but she did want a little time on her own, to start making sense of the jumbled ideas that were racing around in her head.

She was excited. Her mother had been right; sometimes, when you couldn't see the wood for the trees, just hearing someone else's perspective was all it took for you to change your own. Chris Darcy had nothing to gain by trying to influence her, one way or the other. He'd merely offered some ideas that she could think about, but what a difference that had made to her state of mind!

It was lovely, to be thinking positive thoughts again; to have a potential new project to get her teeth into. Her emotional wheels were no longer spinning. She had some mental traction, at last.

All of a sudden, she couldn't wait to get started.

Chapter Ten

Chris met Stuart and Fiona in the Bull and Royal for breakfast at eight o'clock. The pub was a coaching inn, and it offered a fairly decent buffet breakfast to people off the street, as well as guests. Chris was impressed that Stuart and Fiona had offered to buy him breakfast, in order to have an early meeting with him before they raced off to another commitment elsewhere. Fiona's cancer notwithstanding, they seemed like pretty busy people.

They greeted him warmly when he arrived, and they all quickly got their coffee and breakfast, and sat down to talk.

'Thanks for meeting me and Fi, Chris. I'm glad you wanted to. I know you already have a job, and a life in Derby, but Darren said you might be up for a bit of a change?'

Chris replied that it couldn't hurt to see what the offer was, and Stuart pulled an easy-osey face at him.

'Then I'll get straight to it,' Stuart said, without preamble. 'Fiona and I have a small and very good team of tradesmen, that we use to help us renovate the cottages we buy. We have a plumber, a carpenter, a brickie, a plasterer, an electrician, a couple of painter-decorators, and a landscape gardener. We employ them directly because it means they're a lot more reliable. We got messed around a lot by contractors, initially, and we don't have time for that. The team seems happy to stick with us. We pay them a basic wage, and bonuses in line with how quickly we get each project completed.'

Fiona interjected quietly; 'Our electrician is getting married and moving to Glasgow, so there's an opening.

Ideally, we need someone to start in a couple of weeks, which we know isn't much notice, to decide, and finish at your old position. We could push it out to a month, but we couldn't wait any longer than that. If that feels like pressure, I'm sorry. It's not meant to be, but the facts are what they are, I'm afraid.'

Stuart piped up again; 'We've interviewed a few candidates, but we haven't yet come across anyone we feel would be a good fit for the team. The guys all work pretty closely. They need to get on, because they rely on one another a lot, when things need doing, and everyone needs to be willing to pitch in with other stuff, as required. Say you've finished your job in a house, and there's nothing left for you to do, but the landscape gardener's behind schedule. You'd be expected to pitch in with whatever she needed help with.'

'Or lift a rafter with the carpenter if he needs it, or hold a pipe for the plumber if he can't get it in place by himself, that sort of thing?'

Fiona nodded. 'Yes, exactly that. It's moving around a bit too, and not just up here. We're in the process of acquiring a few places in Lancashire, to flick off when they're done up, so we can continue raising the capital for the ones we want to buy, renovate, and keep, here in the Lake District.'

'So, its property development, more or less,' Stuart explained. 'Buying houses at auction, doing them up, flipping them, and carrying on.'

Chris grinned. 'You haven't been on that TV program have you, Homes Under the Hammer?'

Stuart and Fiona both shook their heads. 'It's that kind of project work for sure, but we tend to keep a low profile. Neither of us is interested in that whole fifteen minutes of fame thing. We just want to build a portfolio for retirement, if I can make it that far.' Fiona spoke gently, and so quietly that Chris had to strain a little, to hear her. He remembered that her cancer wasn't an easily curable one.

Stuart pushed a document towards him. 'It's a contract,' he offered. 'Take a look at it, and let me know what you think. We're not paying bucketloads, but sometimes the bonuses are worthwhile, and Ivan has said he'd be staying if he wasn't moving away. Most of our guys seem to think we're worth sticking with. Nobody else has made any noises about moving on.'

'You're welcome to talk to any of them, if you want,' Fiona added. 'Their names and numbers are all on the back page of the document. They're all aware you might want to call, and we're not paying or bribing them to talk it up. They're honest, and they'll be straight with you.'

Chris flicked lightly through the contract, and it seemed, at first glance, to be pretty standard. The salary quoted was fair. Stuart had been right when he'd said it wasn't a shedload, but it wasn't drastically short of what he was earning now, and the money wasn't the primary driver anyway.

'It'll be bed and breakfasts for the Lancashire houses; paid for of course, with lunch supplied, and an allowance for evening meals. That's why the salary's not glittering. But for the stuff we do up here, I have a very nice self-contained caravan on site at my stables, which you're welcome to stay in at no charge, for as long as it takes you to find a place to rent more locally if you decide you want to stick with the work.'

Fiona went on to say that she and Stuart appreciated Chris would be giving up the stability he enjoyed in his current job, and that he'd be out of one completely if he took their opportunity and then decided he hated it. But Chris knew that decent sparkies always found work and it wasn't as if he had to flog his guts out earning a crust anymore, thanks to Daisy's insurance payouts. His finances were a long way from falling apart if he couldn't find a decent job. In that respect, he was probably the best bet of *anyone*, for Stuart and Fiona to take a punt on!

Stuart produced his i-pad, and showed him the current projects in a little more detail, along with the houses in Lancashire they were eyeing up to bid on at auction. There were two terraces in Clitheroe that they seemed pretty confident about getting but, as Stuart said, even if they were outbid, there would be plenty of other places to go for. He also showed Chris the caravan he'd mentioned, and the general area around Beaconsfield, his stables and riding school.

'It's ten minutes' drive from Carlisle, and of course it's not far to the motorway to go anywhere you want to, really. Quite well-connected, to coin a phrase.' He sat back in his chair.

'There's no pressure, Chris. None at all, but we wondered if this might be a good change for you. Your retrofit experience and passion for older places is exactly what we need, and we know you're considering a fresh start. We could help one another a lot, even if it's only for a while. Believe me, I know what it's like to be facing an uncertain future and wondering what's next in life.'

Fiona leaned forward and smiled, gently. 'Take some time, to mull it over, and let us know what you think. There'll be no hard feelings – none whatsoever – if you decide it's not for you.'

Chris drained his coffee and stood up. He shook Fiona's hand, then Stuart's. 'I absolutely *will* think it over, and I'll let you know by tomorrow night.'

Fiona shook her head. 'What a shame you weren't going to be here for just one more week. You could have come with us to the auctions down in Preston, and we could have shown you through the places we're about to start working on near Keswick, too. Unfortunately, we can't get the keys to those until then. It would have been great for you to see them. Maybe you could still go up from Derby and meet us there though, as an idea, but I guess that's a couple of hours each way. Up to you, whether you'd want to do that.'

As he left the pub, Chris' mind was racing. On the face of it, working for Suart and Fiona did seem like a nice opportunity. At worst, it could transition him out of his current job while he worked out what he *did* want to do with his life. At best, he could have a wonderful opportunity to do some seriously interesting retrofit work – the kind he really enjoyed. He needed to look the contract over in a lot more detail, but he knew Stuart Thomson used to be a contracts lawyer, in his past life, and he was pretty sure the guy didn't intend to stitch him up. It looked fair, at first glance, so Chris planned to get back to Teapot Cottage make a pot of tea, and go through it properly.

His mind kept going back to what Fiona had said, about him not being around the week after next. It would have been really interesting, to have gone to the auctions with them, and of course to see the houses they'd bought near Keswick. He *could* go over from Derby, but it would mean a day off work.

On an impulse he couldn't control, he quickly jogged up to Ravensdown House and knocked on the big wooden front door. When Adie opened it, her face registered surprise.

'Oh, Chris! Hi. Is everything alright?'

He nodded. 'It's all good, yeah, but I wonder if the cottage is vacant the week after next? I'd love to stay another week, if that's possible?

She looked astonished, but then she laughed at his enthusiasm, and nodded. 'As a matter of fact, it's vacant for another two, as I've had a change of arrangements for the last one. The people who were coming have moved their dates.'

Chris grinned, again. 'Another week would be fantastic! I'll say yes to just the one, if that's okay, as I'm pretty sure I wouldn't be able to get any more time off than that.'

She giggled at him. 'Am I allowed to know why you want to stay longer? Is it something to do with a job offer around here? Terasa mentioned something about it. It sounds like you two are cooking up all kinds of plans, between you.'

'It might be. I just want to take a little longer, to consider my options. Thank you, so much, Adie!'

'Well, you're welcome, and since you've evidently become a nice friend of Teresa's, maybe you'd like to come and have dinner with us one night? Just tell her which night suits, and she can let me know. The food is never too fancy around here, but it's always wholesome.'

Chris felt a small swell in his chest. Another invitation! This place was shaping up to be one of the best he'd ever spent time in!

'That would be amazing. I'll talk to her, and we can get it dialled in.'

Chris jogged back to Teapot Cottage, and immediately rang Malcom, his boss, to ask about having the next week off work, as well as the two he'd already booked. He figured it wouldn't be the easiest conversation they'd had but Malcom was usually pretty accommodating, and they weren't so busy that Chris would be sorely missed.

But he had to think twice, when Malcolm snapped at him on the phone. 'For Christ's sake, Chris! If you want a part time job, you need to look elsewhere. I'm not running a fucking temp agency here.'

Chris was taken aback. 'Sorry, I didn't think it would be too much of a problem?'

'Well, you're wrong. It *is* a problem.' Malcolm sighed into the phone before continuing.

'Look, mate, I've been as patient as I can be, with your comings and goings. You had three months off after your fiancée died, and other 'down days' besides, and that made things pretty hard around here. You were always going to come back, so I couldn't replace you. I had to get contractors to cover, and you know how much of a ball-ache that can be. And it bloody was. Even when I could get someone to show up, I had to pay over the odds for them to cover your time off, here, there, and everywhere.'

'I know, and I've appreciated that more than you'll ever know.'

Malcolm signed again. 'I know you have, otherwise I wouldn't have done it. I know how much it meant to you, to have that time. But the thing is, Chris, I can't spare you! We've just been awarded the contract for the new housing estate going up on Sunfields. It's a hundred and sixty houses! I have to have you back in time to finish off the stuff we've been taking our time over, because that's all turned into rush jobs now.'

Malcolm went on the explain that the Sunfields work was due to start in six weeks, and that left little time to finish the current jobs they were working on. It all had to be completed before they could start the new contract. Chris was needed; now more than ever.

'Malcolm, it's just one more week, then I promise I'll be there for as long as you want. You *have* been good to me, and I appreciate it, and I don't want to let you down. I'll pay for a contractor for the extra week myself, out of my own pocket, if it will help. But there's something I really want to do before I come back. It's important to me. Please? Just this one last thing. Then you'll have my full commitment.'

'Chris, I probably can't get a contractor to come in here at this short a notice, not a decent one, anyway! I haven't a cat in hell's chance of that. I'm really sorry, but I have to draw a line somewhere, mate. If you can't be here on the Monday morning when I need you back in, you'll have to find another job. Take a day; let me know what you decide. But I'm running a bloody business here, not a charity.'

Chris ended the call, stunned. As ultimatums went, that was strong. On the one hand Malcolm's lack of tolerance felt pretty insulting. What if Chris had been ill, and literally *unable* to work?

But, on the other hand, he knew it was fair enough. He *had* pushed his luck in the job, and got away with it for far longer than most people would have. Malcolm was a caring man, and a patient one, but he had his limits, and Chris had simply pushed them too far.

So, he now had to decide what to do. Should he cancel his ideas of staying at Teapot Cottage and accompanying Stuart and Fiona, and go back to work instead? Or should he let the job with Malcolm go?

He was bristling with indignation, at being called out, but the more he thought about it, the more he realised that he didn't actually *want* to go back to his current job. It wasn't a question of being resentful; he really wasn't, but he just didn't want to go back to what was now – increasingly – starting to look and feel like an obligation and a trap. Maybe it *was* time for change. Maybe he *did* need to 'get out of his own head' and do something different, to kick-start his own journey to a new life – the one he needed to make without Daisy.

Daisy. I haven't thought much about you this morning. That's new. I've been a bit distracted, with different things, and you haven't been at the forefront of my mind. Is that okay? Is it alright for me, to start thinking about different possibilities, or opportunities? I have to make a life without you, Daise, and I wasn't prepared for that, but I have to move on, don't I? It's what you'd want for me, isn't it? Maybe part of that is focussing on other things that I <u>can</u> make happen, since I can't make a life with you anymore? Maybe letting go of keeping you in the forefront of my mind is part of moving on?

Chris was suddenly gripped by the fear that he'd one day forget Daisy. Almost a year had passed now, and there were times when he struggled to remember the finer contours of her face, or the sound of her laugh. The memories of such things were still there for him, but they'd faded a little, like they'd spent too long in the sun. The edges of his life with Daisy were blurring now, as if they were dissolving. He hated it, at the same time as he recognised that part of the blurring was probably inevitable; the natural order of things; the human brain's remarkable ability to allow people to survive and transcend the worst kinds of disembowelment, and still have a semblance of a life.

Does the blurring mean I'll forget you, Daise? I never want to forget you! Please don't let that happen!

His own voice came into his head now, loud, and strong; 'you won't forget. You will *never* forget the importance of the love, or the woman you loved, but you *have* to build a new life.'

He blinked. Where had that bald, stark flash of clarity come from? It was the clearest message yet, that had flashed through his mind since Daisy's death. It was his voice, but had it come from his own psyche, or was it something else? Was it Daisy herself, trying to get through to him? As mad as that sounded, he *was* prepared to consider it.

He'd had many dreams about her, since she'd died, but nothing was ever tangible or memorable. He was always intensely frustrated, after waking, knowing he'd dreamed about her, but never being able to remember anything specific. It was like trying to hold onto disappearing smoke; the harder he tried to remember the context of the dream, the more quickly it seemed to vanish. It felt like the devil, taunting him and laughing in his face.

Now, as he sat in one of Teapot Cottage's window seats, looking out across the Torley Valley, Chris knew he had to move on. He'd known it all along, right from the start, on some superficial level. But now, for the first time, he actually *felt* the need to move forward. He didn't *want* to stay stuck in his grief anymore. It no longer felt comforting, to be wallowing. His own anguish was starting to annoy him.

As Darren Davies had said, Mulhacén could – and probably should – wait until Chris felt stronger. Nothing would be gained by going back to the mountain right now, as he'd originally planned. If he did that, he would simply feel raw and torn apart all over again. It wouldn't help him move forward at all. It would keep him in that place of eviscerating pain, and guilt, and it would only get in the way of hindering the progress he needed to make, to put himself on a new path.

In any case, he wouldn't be allowed the time off that he would need, to get out to Sierra, do the pilgrimage, and get himself over it. Malcolm had made that crystal clear. There would be no more allowances made for 'mental health days.' In that flash of recognition, Chris realised that he had to burn his bridge on that front. He didn't need a day, as Malcolm had offered, to make the decision. Instead, he resolved to answer to his own conviction, and he called Malcolm straight back.

'Hiya. Just to let you know, I've decided to stay put for a while. I appreciate I'm dumping you in it again, by not coming back, but I feel like I have to get off the treadmill.'

He ended by thanking Malcolm for all the support he'd given him, and saying that without it he probably wouldn't have recovered at all.

Malcolm wished him well, and thanked him for all his hard work over the past four years. 'I'll make up your final pay, with a month's salary in lieu of notice, and there'll be a good reference if you ever want one. Until Daisy passed away, you were the best sparky I ever had, but things have been falling apart ever since. Your heart hasn't been in it. You haven't been able to give it the full commitment, and I know it's just the way things have to be for you, Chris. I get that it's still a struggle, and I do think you're ready for a change. I hope that whatever you do, you can be happy. You deserve to be, mate. Good luck, and I'll see you around. Keep in touch, yeah? It'd be nice to hear how you're getting on.'

And there it was. Malcolm had been understanding and kind yet again, and generous to a fault. He had a business to run, and he had to play hard-ball on that, but he *cared*. Chris accepted that as the shiniest nugget from the conversation, took a good step back, and quietly allowed that bridge to burn.

It felt right, and he realised that somehow, quite a *few* things were starting to feel right, around here! It felt like gentle, subtle shifts were happening around him, unlike the cataclysmic jolt of Daisy's death that had thrown his life into a tailspin beyond his control. Here, in this quiet space, something was *reshaping* him. He couldn't describe the feeling, but he knew that things were changing, and he also knew, somewhere inside himself, that he had to go with the flow.

And there were worse situations to be pulled into, weren't there? The people here were pretty decent. They seemed genuine, and real. His 'bullshit-ometer' hadn't gone off once, in the time he'd been here, with any of the people he'd met. Normally he could sense a 'fake' pretty quickly, in any conversation, or even just listening to one between others. But all of the people he'd encountered here had been open and honest to a fault.

From Peg Tripper at the cafe in town, who'd remembered him from last year, to the Davies' who'd invited him into their home for a meal. From Adie Raven who'd done the same and lent a listening ear, to Stuart Thomson, who had offered him a job within a few short days of meeting him! And how could he exclude the surprising, random, 'small-world' encounter with Tezzie Bostock – a woman he'd met two years ago, briefly, at the other side of the world? She was part of the 'phenomena' he was experiencing here. Meeting Tezzie again had been pretty cool. She seemed like a good person too, and she was fun to hang out with. Although he didn't see himself ever spending any time in London, he did hope they'd stay in touch.

Chris quietly decided that he was prepared for whatever roads were unfolding before him, and he would stay here, at Teapot Cottage, for as long as the cottage was vacant, let each day unfold as it seemed to want to, and he'd go with Stuart and Fiona, to take a look at their Keswick semis and go to the Lancashire auctions. He was curious now, to see where he might end up at the end of his time here.

The one thing he *wasn't* prepared for was the number that popped up on his phone when it rang, just as he was nodding off on the sofa, in front of the fire.

Chapter Eleven

Teresa powered up the computer in the study upstairs. She was keen to get started on pulling her project together. She knew that already having a nice camera was a help, but she was going to need a lot more than just that for what she wanted to do. The camera she wanted was several thousand pounds, and that was just the start of what was needed. Another major purchase would be a fast-paced laptop for editing. They were just as expensive as the new camera, but there wasn't much point in trying to set up independently to produce something truly impactful and magnificent, if you didn't have the right tools for the job.

By the time she'd added lenses, SD cards at nearly two hundred pounds a pop, various different microphones, and a gimbal, the amount she needed had reached five figures. She also wanted lights, but she knew that she didn't need to spend a fortune on expensive lighting kits or equipment.

Professional-looking videos are more about your skills than your tools. Some of the techniques I've learned, especially for shooting an outdoor project, mean I can get away with spending a lot less than what it would cost if I insisted on the best of everything.

She knew that the final total would be alarming, especially when she added her airfares to Bangkok, and a fair estimate of the cost of accommodation and sustenance while she was there, based on what the booking sites showed.

The final total, as she estimated, put Teresa into a bit of a panic. She immediately texted Chris.

I've done the add-up, it's terrifying!

A text quickly pinged back.

How terrifying?

She sent him the amount, and almost immediately a laughing emoji pinged back, followed by another text.

Nah its chump-change 2 big companies. Get it in perspective. Most write off more 2 monthly expenses.

Well, it's all very well for him! He might think it's monthly chump-change, but I'd have to work my arse off and save for bloody years, to get that much money together!

But the cost was what it was, and there was no getting away from it. If Teresa wanted to go to Bangkok, and shoot the documentary she dreamed of doing, the amount sitting at the bottom of her Excel spreadsheet was the amount she was going to need, and that was that.

She shook her head and checked out a few fundraising sites. After weighing up the options, she settled on one, and got started on setting up her fundraising page. It was surprisingly easy to pull together, and write the explanation for what she wanted to do, why she needed help to get there, and how much money she was hoping to raise. She recorded a one-minute video as a heartfelt plea, and loaded it into the link-space provided.

She hesitated a little, at the end of the process, when she was invited to press the red 'Go Live Now' button on the screen, and she took the chance to go back through everything, checking all the details and making sure she hadn't left anything out or keyed in the wrong bank details. Then, after making sure her page was everything it needed to be, she took a deep breath and pressed to go 'live.'

It felt like a monumental moment; her first big step towards her new career. When she'd talked about it with Chris Darcy, and with her mum and Mark, it had all seemed a little remote, almost like a theory about what someone else might do. Now, she had her very own funding page, and it was as real as the nose on her face. She had taken the biggest leap of faith in her life and put herself out there, in the public arena.

Chris had asked her what she might do if she couldn't raise the funds. He'd talked about sponsorship, as another option, and maybe that would have been the better one than laying herself bare and more or less 'begging' for money, as some internet trolls would no doubt call it. But she had to care less about what people might think – especially people who didn't even know her! The internet was full of unhappy people who needed little excuse to tear someone down, in order to try and make themselves feel better about whatever was *really* eating them alive.

Adie had been at pains to warn her about that, and so had her aunt Miranda when she'd phoned her to ask a few questions how she managed internet trolls. Plenty had tried to attack her as an actress, but she simply reminded herself that none of them knew what hard work it was. It was no small thing at all, to learn lines, stay in shape, take whatever criticism was levelled at you from critics who might hate you, and get prepared every night of your life for putting yourself in front of the general public. There were far less gruelling ways to make a living. It wasn't all bouquets and happy fame – Miranda took her fair share of brickbats too.

It took real guts to do what she did, and none of the trolls could ever understand that. 'Good God, darling! Most of those idiots couldn't act their way out of a paper bag themselves, even if their lives depended on it. Why on earth would I let people like *that* get the better of me?'

Miranda's perspective had helped. Teresa felt ready for whatever came. Never in her life before had she gone out to the general public, to ask for something, but that took a little courage too, and if anyone was going to knock her for being brave and hopeful, they could go in the bin with Miranda's lot. She was confident that her family and good friends would help her keep it all in perspective, and if her new friend Chris Darcy thought she should do this, and *he* thought she could pull it off; well... that was good enough for her to try, at least. As he'd said himself; the worst that could happen was nothing, and she could live with that, and find another way.

She trusted Chris. It was odd, how they had met less than a week ago, but she already felt she could do a lot worse than have him as her guide and champion. She sent him another text now.

Crowdfunder page now set up, will send link.

She grinned when all she got back was a thumbs-up emoji, followed by one as a wink.

*   *   *   *   *

Just two days later, Teresa was thrilled to find that she was already over halfway to her target! Her mother had donated two hundred pounds, and Aunt Miranda had donated three hundred! A few of her friends had made good donations too, with good wishes and lots of enthusiasm. Surprisingly, the temp agency she worked for in London had contributed, after passing the hat around the office, and they had also contacted some of the companies she'd temped for, and encouraged them to donate.

By day four, she had two thirds of what she needed. Gina Giordano, her half-sister Ruth's wife, had made a big contribution on behalf of her clothing company, GinGio Designs, and her Feen and Gavin had chipped in too.

Teresa didn't know who half of the people were, on her list of donors, but there were a couple of companies, and there were at least a dozen 'anonymous' donations, three of which were for five hundred pounds each! She would have killed to know who *they* were! She suspected two would have been Mark and her father, and she wondered if Chris was the third, but she couldn't have said for sure, and she knew there was no point in asking him something he'd never admit to. But, even as donations of ten or twenty pounds were coming in, and she saw her total steadily climbing, she

163

was amazed at how quickly even the small amounts added up.

There was one donor who really warmed her heart. A lady called Eloise Fitzgerald had donated five pounds, apologising that her pension wouldn't allow her to offer more, but she was concerned enough about child poverty to want to contribute *something*.

It seemed to Teresa that the cause she was aiming to highlight was something people did care about. A number of donors had made comments on the contributions feed, that they had been to Bangkok themselves, and witnessed first-hand the polarisation of wealth that existed there. People appeared to be quite hot under the collar about the injustice suffered by so many children who had fallen by the wayside and simply been left to survive or perish while so few of the people who could do something about it (namely those in government) gave a damn.

Some donors mentioned other countries with similar problems. Child poverty was a global issue. Most people knew about it, but Teresa hadn't realised how emotive it was, for so many.

The real elevation to her campaign came when her fundraiser had been picked up by a radio station based in London. They had contacted her and wanted to interview her. She didn't have much preparation time, and when the interview went out, she'd been 'winging it,' and she'd been as nervous as a cat on a hot tin roof. But her mother had reassured her that she'd come across well on air, and by the end of that day, she had all the money she needed.

To say she was over the moon was an understatement, knowing that as soon as the funds all landed in her bank account, she could go ahead and order everything she needed, and booking her flights to Bangkok.

Chris was ecstatic. 'My God, look at you! You've pulled all this together *so* fast! It's astonishing, but I suppose it's been a combination of who you know, and who your donors know, that can help you. You're very lucky, to have people in your family like Gina Giordano, and Gavin Black. They're very well connected, I think, and it just goes to show; sometimes if you *do* ask, you *do* get!'

'I know, right? They're only family through Mum's marriage to Mark, but they've certainly come through for me, haven't they? I suppose they all made a few phone calls.'

'Well, I'm guessing Gavin Black did! You have a couple of rock stars on your donations feed! They're probably Gavin's clients, or friends of his late father's. Martin Black was a very well-known rock musician, wasn't he? Maybe the guys who donated felt they owed him one. You've had a few 'big guns' wade in, Tezzie, and it's made a really big difference. Someone even tipped off a bloody radio station! How cool was that?'

'Yeah, I'd *love* to know who *that* was!'

'Doesn't matter. What does is that someone believes in you enough to have done it. And you're there! You're really there! Congratulations!'

'And congrats to you too, for going with the new work opportunity! Look at us both, Chris! Within a few days of one another, we've each found a whole new trajectory!'

It was true. They'd both severed a critical cord, and made a choice between a safe world and a brave one. They'd both opted to take a step into the unknown, and be the ships that left the safety of their harbours. It was terrifying, but it was exciting too.

Someone had once said to Teresa, 'leap and the net will appear.' She hoped that would be right. She always had the safety net of being able to come home, and her return ticket ensured that she could retreat from the 'front-line,' as it were, if it all got to be too much. But a different kind of net was needed now. She needed to know and trust the net of self-reliance and confidence, to follow through on what she'd started.

Chris was about to do the same. He had the safety net of his insurance money from Daisy's death, so if his new plans with people he'd only just met fell through too, he could find a different way forward. He too had to trust a new net of self-belief, that he could walk forward with new resolve and purpose, instead of continuing to stumble through the wreckage of his grief, over his lost life with Daisy.

Teresa still felt devastated about the loss of her relationship with Ross, how he had chosen to handle it, and the fact that he was moving on so strongly with another woman. Her friend Helen, in Australia had texted again to tell her that Ross and Rosie had apparently announced the date for their wedding now, too. She'd wanted to warn Teresa but, strangely, the news hadn't torn her apart like it probably would have before she'd started with her new project.

Having something else to focus on, a big change that held so much promise and potential, had acted as a blunting effect. She was no longer in a screaming heap over Ross, and his plans for a future that didn't include her. Somehow, in that whole process of emotional struggle, and finding a new sense of direction that excited her, the way she felt about him had changed quite a lot.

There was a real sense now, of leaving something traumatic behind, and a movement towards being at peace with it. She realised she still had a ways to go with squaring it all away for good, but a new challenge to put her energy into had made all the difference to how she felt about *everything*, and she hoped it would be the same for Chris.

Chapter Twelve

Adie clicked off her mobile phone, with a big smile on her face. Miranda was about to descend upon Ravensdown House! This was an unexpected but very lovely thing to look forward to. Since she'd left Guildford, she didn't see her best friend as often as she wanted. They used to regularly meet for cocktails, when they lived closer to one another, and do lunch and sometimes a spa day whenever Miranda was between productions. Adie really missed those times.

Apparently, Miranda's latest West End stage play had been panned by both critics and the public, and had closed its season early. Miranda was philosophical about it, as always, and chose to see the free time as a bonus. She decided against a city break to Prague with her fiancé Max and decided to have a few days 'girl-time' with Adie instead, if there was room for her at Ravensdown.

'There's always room for you, here, you silly sausage,' Adie had laughed when Miranda had asked if she could come. 'It will be lovely, having you here, for however long you want to stay.'

She was coming in two days' time, which gave Adie time to get another guest room ready. It meant she would have a pretty full house, but that didn't matter. It would be lovely for Teresa to catch up with her aunt, too, *and* that Miranda would be here for the coffee morning.

She quickly checked her watch as Mark came wandering in for his mid-morning 'cup o' char.'

He was bang on time, as usual. It was *she* who was tardy this morning, after being on the phone for twenty minutes, so she quickly filled the kettle and set it onto the Aga hotplate, threw a couple of teabags into the bashed-up enamel teapot on the bench, and reached for the tin of date scones she'd baked the day before. They were his all-time favourite, and there were only two left in the tin, which was just as well. They tended to go dry after a day, even in an airtight container, and if they weren't demolished before tomorrow, it would be like trying to eat a lump of solid sawdust. Adie popped both scones onto a plate for him and set them on the table with a knife and the butter dish.

Teresa bounced into the kitchen. 'I've just booked my tickets, Mum! All my equipment should be arriving in a few days, by the way. I take it Amazon and other couriers can find this place, hidden in the long-lost bowels of the North?'

Mark harrumphed at her. 'We get we're deliveries 'ere just fine, thank you very much, yer cheek bugger!'

Adie laughed. 'That's great, darling, and very well done! I still can't believe how easily you've raised all that money! What an absolute triumph. I'm so proud of you. We *all* are!'

She grinned at Teresa and Mark. 'And I have a nice surprise for you both. Guess who's arriving the day after tomorrow? Miranda! She's coming to stay for a few days.'

Teresa beamed. 'Oh! That's *great* news! I haven't seen or talked to her for such a long time! I can't wait to tell her about my plans, now. Thanks for tipping her off, by the way. She made a big donation.'

'I know. She has the biggest heart. Mark and I haven't seen her either, since she and Max got engaged. I imagined her single forever, but I'm thrilled that she's getting married, and she does sound very happy, I must say. Becoming Mrs Maxwell Henry Kennedy, the Third, is a prospect that does seem to be agreeing with her.'

'She's keeping her own name though, right? Miranda Quirk?'

Adie nodded. 'Yes, that's not something she's prepared to compromise on.'

'Well, why should she? I think the days are long gone when a woman feels obliged to take her husband's name. If she wants to, fair enough, but not just because it's expected. I will always be Teresa Bostock, no matter what.'

Mark winked at Teresa as she bounced back out of the room, then he turned to Adie. 'Aye, she knows 'er own mind, that one, don't she? It's nice news, that Miranda's comin, lass. It's been a while, 'ant it?'

'Yes, it has. She's now in the throes of planning her and Max's wedding – and with me, as a medieval bridesmaid! Well, Matron of Honour, at least. Who ever saw *that* coming? What a lovely weekend it'll be, down on the Cornish Coast!'

'Tintagel, aye. Mand and Max getting' wed at King Arthur's Grand 'all, wi' all them bloody celebrities; it'll no doubt be a right fiasco, won't it, wi't film crew an' all? I'm gonna feel like a trussed-up chicken in a suit an' bloody tie!'

Adie grinned at him. 'You will look *amazing,* all dolled up. I plan to get a lot of photos of that, because I don't get to see it very often, do I? Of course, Mand plans to do things in grand style! A registry office in Clapham was never going to be her thing, was it? Not in an epically gorgeous wedding dress, at any rate, and certainly not getting hitched to one of the UK's top-earning hedge-fund managers, as Max used to be before he retired!'

Adie smiled to herself now, anticipating seeing Miranda for real, in her incredible cream satin wedding medieval-faerie dress, with its full skirt, sweetheart neckline and gold embroidered bodice and front skirt panel. She intended to top it off with a specially designed gold-set tiara, heavily encrusted with glittering Swarovski crystals. She'd sent Adie a video of her final fitting, after swearing her to utter secrecy and threatening to staple her to the nearest wall if she even *hinted* – to *anyone* – about what it was going to look like.

Adie had laughed at that. 'God, who on earth am I going to tell? I don't see any of the old crowd anymore. They are all patently ridiculous. I wouldn't give them the time of day, let alone tell them about your bloody frock! There's only Mark to tell, and he'd forget every last detail if I even stapled *him* to a wall and made him listen! Your secret is safe with me.'

But Miranda's gown had brought tears to Adie's eyes. She'd looked so beautiful. Her own Matron of Honour dress, in the same medieval style but a lot less voluminous, was being made in deep purple satin with a similar gold embroidered bodice and panels. Miranda had already sent her dressmaker up to Adie twice; once for the precise measurements, and one preliminary fitting. The dress would be ready soon, and Adie was excited. It was going to be a very high-profile wedding. The photos would be incredible; many would be taken with the ruined Tintagel Castle as a backdrop, and the rest would be taken at the medieval-banquet reception. A handful were destined to even make it into the pages of a well-known high-society magazine, who had confirmed that they would be sending a photographer, on the day.

'Aye, well, she's not 'ad a weddin,' 'as she? It's 'er first, so it 'as to be special, I suppose. But, by 'eck, I'll be right bloody glad to get that piggin' tie off me, at th'end o't day. Even now, the thought of it is makin' me queasy.'

He stretched and pulled a face, and changed the subject. 'Yer know, lass, Teresa's done well wi' all this filmin' malarkey. Yer do know I'd 'ave been 'appy to bankroll what she needed? She didn't need to go cap in 'and to people, askin' fer money.'

'I know that, of course, and so does she. I talked to her about it, before she got started on it, and I also told her that her dad would have done the same, in spite of the difficulties they're having. He wouldn't want to see her struggle either if he could do something about it. He's very short of money now, what with this fraud thing, and a costly divorce hanging over his head. But he'd have found it from somewhere. I thought that now might have been the best time in fact, to put it through the business – you know, before its finances get raided, but she was having none of it.'

'Aye, an' she's pulled a bloody blinder, 'ant she?' Mark observed.

'This fundraising project was something she felt driven to do for *herself,* Mark. I think she wanted to prove to herself that she can get out of her current rut, by pulling up her *own* bootstraps, and lo and behold, she's done it, in record time!'

Mark toyed with his teaspoon. 'She's made of stronger stuff than she thinks she is.'

Adie cleared the cups away, and Mark stood to go. She knew he had a lot to do today. He had beets to harvest, and there was heavy rain forecast from tonight for three full days. He was keen to get going, so she gave him a quick kiss on the cheek, and she expected that to be the end of things. She was surprised when he grabbed her around the waist, pulled her to him, kissed her quite passionately, and grabbed her bum.

'Good God! I wasn't expecting that! I thought you were far too busy for shenanigans!' She pushed him playfully, giggling.

'I'm never too busy for them! It's a big enough day in't fields, I'll grant yer, but if you was to raise yer eyebrows at me, all suggestive like, and give me a nudge and a wink fer a bit of 'ow's yer father, I'd 'ave no quarrel wi' a run upstairs.'

She laughed. 'You have a one-track mind! Get out, before I throw you out, you randy old sod. There will be no daytime shenanigans in this house while my daughter is wandering around, thank you very much!'

Mark looked at her, aghast. 'What, no 'anky panky? Bloody 'ell – she's 'ere for a month or more!'

Adie grinned mischievously. 'I said not in the *house.* Locationally speaking, you'll have to get a bit creative, if you want any afternoon delight.'

She turned and walked away from him, shaking with silent laughter at the look of bewilderment that crossed his face. He teased her a lot, because he loved to make her blush, but sometimes she enjoyed a chance to turn the tables on him. He wouldn't know now, whether she meant it or not, that she'd be open to a bit of daytime 'hanky-panky' somewhere else on the farm. It would give him something to think about.

*　　*　　*　　*　　*

Adie poured out the vodka martinis and handed one to Miranda. 'It's only half past two; still a little early, to be starting with the alcohol, but I think your arrival is worthy of an exception.'

'As the saying goes, darling, it's five o'clock somewhere in the world! Or half past, which means we're already late starting, and how on earth can we *possibly* put the world to rights without a decent drink in hand?'

'You're right, of course, as always. We can't get life into its true perspective without at least one, can we? I suspect we might need three or four, actually, since we have so much catching up to do. I've already made dinner. It's a lamb-shank stew that I made this morning, so all I have to do is reheat it in the Aga, and put some jacket potatoes in, to have with it. So, we can sit for a while and just chat. I'm sorry your latest show got cancelled, by the way. My gain, of course, since you're here, but annoying for you, yes?'

Miranda pulled an easy-osey face. 'To be honest, it doesn't feel like such a big deal. I'm a lot more ambivalent about it than I would have been a year or two ago.'

'But it's always been your passion! And there are a lot more decent roles for older women now than there ever used to be, surely? There must be a ton of meaty parts for you to get your teeth into!'

'Yeah, there's a fair bit on offer, but I'm just not sure whether I want to keep going for much longer. Maybe it's getting married that's got me so undecided. It's not like I need the money. I've always invested wisely, and that's going to pay off very handsomely for my retirement, whenever that starts, but I'm leaning a little more towards travelling more with Max, and for longer, after the wedding.

That's my other passion, as you know, and there's still a lot of the world that I haven't seen. My bucket list is still as big as it's ever been.'

Adie nodded, pensively. 'Well, I think that makes sense too, while you're still young and fit enough to go and see what you can. We never know what's around the corner, do we, health wise, I mean? Women younger than us are falling prey to serious illness, and some of what's happening isn't easy to recover from at all.'

'No, we can't predict the future, and life is too short to spend *any* of it living with regrets. I think I want to start spending more of my time with my new husband.'

Miranda laughed lightly. 'Get me! I'm going to have a husband, Adie! Imagine that! And, you know, theatre life is great when you only have yourself to worry about, but making a commitment to being with another person means *being* with that person, doesn't it? Not leaving them alone, night after night, while you go off and pretend to be someone else on a stage somewhere?'

'Has Max said something about wanting you to give up acting?'

'God, no! He's happy for me to carry on, if it's what I want. I'm just not sure that it is, anymore.'

'Well, maybe it's time, to consider a different direction, now that you're all loved-up, and happy in a different way. I think you've had an amazing life so far, with lots of adventure and plenty of fun, and all those awards and achievements. But I'm glad you've finally found someone lovely to settle down with. Max seems perfect for you. I'm guessing you won't let getting hitched slow you down much, since he seems pretty enthusiastic about life too?'

Miranda laughed. 'He's the last person who'd clip my wings! He's *always* up for an adventure! After he retired from hedge fund management, he found a passion for travel too, and go-kart racing, of all weird things. He insisted I go out on the track too, and he kept going on about how much fun it would be. I wasn't very keen initially, and I only said yes to shut him up, but it was tremendous fun! I've been out a couple more times since, actually.'

Adie giggled. 'You, racing a go-kart, with a crash helmet on. I'd have paid good money to see that! I hope you were wearing the right shade of lipstick on the day!'

Miranda grinned. 'Yes, of course, darling! A girl has standards to maintain. And the photos were just hilarious. I'll have to find them and show you. But go-karting? Good lord! That was something I never imagined myself even *doing*, let alone enjoying! I've never really been competitive.' She shook her head and pulled a baffled face, and Adie laughed again.

Miranda's face softened, now. 'You know, Adie, I think Max has come along at exactly the right time in my life. I've always been a free spirit, and I've made no apology for it. I've always lived life to the full, kicked my heels up, and done whatever took my fancy. I could never see myself being something 'less' than who I am, to fit some social stereotype. I was never interested in a man who would cramp my style.'

'It doesn't sound like Max is that kind of guy. Not if he's already managed to put you on a racetrack, of all places!'

'Max developed his adventurous streak after his kids left home. His two grown up sons are lovely. You'll meet them at the wedding. They're independent now, of course, so that's not something Max needs to worry about anymore. I don't want to be anyone's stepmother in the *active* sense, either,' she added, as she crunched her olive.

'I never wanted children, as you know. I could never see myself settling for a 'small' life! I always just felt that I was destined for more, somehow. I wanted the most life could give me, but I did learn early that it doesn't just happen. If you want a big life, you have to *make* it a big one! And I've always worked my arse off to make that happen.'

'You sure have! Stage actress extraordinaire, always with top reviews; I never knew you to be pinned down *anywhere*, for longer than a season's run. Even before all that, you were

never interested in any of the boys who tried to set their caps
at you when we were in our teens and early twenties, were
you? You ended up with quite a reputation for being picky
and standoffish.' Adie grinned when Miranda rolled her eyes
again.

'I know, right? But it wasn't that I didn't *like* them,
darling! Some of them were very nice; quite sweet, in fact.
But I just knew that I'd never get serious about any guy who
was going to have a small life. You know, living and dying
in the same town they were born in, having a plodder's job,
wanting little more out of life than a mortgage, a couple of
sprogs and a fortnight's holiday in bloody Benidorm every
year. That was a hell I just couldn't imagine. A man that
boring would have driven me to suicide, Adie. Or homicide,'
she added, half to herself.

'Oh, I dunno, Mand. Stamp collecting, or making model
planes, or karaoke singing sound riveting, don't they?'

'Only if by 'riveting' you mean being stapled to a wall.'

Adie burst out laughing. 'You really are fond of the
notion, aren't you, of stapling people to walls?'

Miranda grinned. 'Well, I've found that people don't
scream for long, when you do that to them. They tend to pass
out fairly quickly, and then things go mercifully quiet, at
least for a while.'

Adie giggled again, then then bit her bottom lip.

'I left home to get married, and I suppose I fit that 'small
life' mould, at least a little,' she mused. 'Bryan had his own
company, so he couldn't really be classed as a plodder, as
such, in fact he's made a real success of his business. That's
all a bit precarious now though, by the way, and just wait
until I tell you why!

'But we never moved far, and we never had many
adventures. I guess you'd say I played the safe card. I regard
my kids as my greatest achievement, and I adore my
grandkids too, of course. But did you ever think that *my* life
was small, Mand? It's okay to be honest. I won't be
offended.'

Miranda pulled a face. 'Well, you *did* play the safe card, it's true. But God, I'm not knocking you for that, darling! Not at all! Everyone needs to do what feels right for them. If they're happy with the choices they've made, that's really all that matters. We all have different dreams. *Someone* needs to have kids and raise them, you know, to perpetuate the species, and all that? But it was never going to be me. I was never going to be like your boring old Bryan, dreaming of a new *carpet*, for fuck's sake! What the hell was *that*? No! I wanted to grab life by the horns and shake it, and I was never going to compromise on that.'

Adie knew that to be true. Miranda had always been pretty unconventional. She always wanted all she could get from life, in terms of adventure, and stretching her wings. 'Sucking the marrow from the bones of life,' as the saying went.

'And just *look* at you! You've had the biggest life imaginable, and there's still a long way to go, isn't there? I think you'll have a lot more adventures, especially with Max. Go-karting is probably only the tip of the iceberg. And maybe giving up acting is the natural next step towards opening a few new doors. But we've never talked, have we, about what you may feel you missed out on? Do you have any regrets about your choices up until now?'

Miranda thought for a moment. When she answered, her voice was contemplative. 'I really don't think so, other than to state the obvious and say that I wish I'd met Max twenty years ago. But, better late than never, as they say. He's giving me a new lease of life at exactly the time of life when I need it, so I dunno, Adie. Maybe I *had* to wait this long, to really feel the benefit of that.'

'Yeah, I think people meet when they're supposed to. You've both been very career focussed, in the past. It's probably why you've both been so successful. Maybe meeting earlier might've got in the way of that, somehow. I think *I've* been at least a *little* successful, to a point. Raising my children to be independent, well-grounded, and loving; that's an achievement, I think.'

'Damn straight, it is! Look how many parents make a complete hash of that! There are so many families out there that are irreparably damaged by dysfunction, all too often because of shitty parenting.'

'Well, we did go through a fire, there's no denying that. I did screw things up, and of course my marriage to Bryan hit the deck pretty hard, didn't it? I didn't make best choices for us all, in keeping Ruth a secret and everything.'

'You could have handled the revelations better, about the baby you had and adopted out when you were fifteen, that's true. You'd never even told *me*, even when it was all happening, so I get how hard it must've been for you to tell Bryan and the kids! But you were never a shitty parent, Adie. Or a shitty wife. 'Mr Carpet' was a shitty husband, blaming you for everything even as he was being bloody unfaithful! But, even with that, you guys still did a great job of raising Matty and Teresa. It *is* a grand achievement, darling! I wouldn't have done half as good a job. I don't possess a maternal bone. I'd have been the *ultimate* shitty parent!'

'Teresa had a narrow escape with Ross. She would have settled down with him, and probably had a kid or two just to fit the mould, so to speak, but I know she wouldn't have been happy in the long run. A case of being more in love with love, than in love with the man himself, I suspect. I'm glad he bailed on her, actually, before she ended up trapped, or 'settling,' which would be a terrible waste of her passion and talent. Although, I do wish he'd done it in a kinder way.'

'Yes. That was pretty shitty behaviour too, wasn't it? But I'm inclined to agree with you, Adie. Even if she did truly adore him, and even if he adored her back, I think he'd have driven her potty, even in sunny Australia. I don't think the Northern Territories would have enough to satisfy her. It's not exactly a life on the edge, is it, unless you're a croc wrestler or something?'

Adie had just taken a hefty swig of her martini, and she spluttered with laughter.

'God forbid! There's nothing of her! She's eight stone wet through.'

'Well then, not enough meat on her for the croc to even try to eat her. She'd be safe as houses, and probably amazing at it. But that cowardly Aussie idiot was another matter entirely. He sounds like a complete tosser, and no girl needs the kind of 'handbrake' he'd have turned out to be! At best, he wouldn't have nurtured her talent, and at worst he'd have stifled it; left her alone with the kids while he went off surfing or snake-charming, or something.'

'Probably off digging holes somewhere, at least,' Adie admitted. 'He was a diamond miner, as I recall.'

She thought how ironic it was that when your kids were adults, sometimes you actually worried about them more than you'd done when they were small. When you could still have a hand in shaping them, and setting them up in life, that was one thing. But when they were grown-ups in their own right, dancing around out in the world, with the capacity to be irreparably hurt by the choices or mistakes they might make, that was sometimes a lot more to be worried about!

'I hope you're ready for tomorrow's spa day at the Beeches Hotel? Teresa is coming, and so is Trudie Sangster, from GladRagz boutique. She has organised her part-timer Kathleen to go in for the day, so she can come with us.'

'Ooh, yes! I do like the sound of Trudie. She might be great fun. It's still a big regret that I couldn't come to your and Mark's wedding, by the way. I was so looking forward to meeting *all* of your friends up here. You know I had an understudy all booked for that night and then the silly bitch came down with the flu, two days before?'

'Yeah, but don't worry. I was never upset with you for that! Work has to come first, especially with the kind of commitment you have to make, to doing a show.'

'I still think it was mean of you not to let me gatecrash your honeymoon, though! I rather fancied a fortnight or so in

Bali! And that bed did look big enough for three.' Miranda's eyes twinkled.

Adie grinned at her. 'Sorry, that particular opportunity was strictly off-limits. But maybe we could do a fortnight there sometime, just us girls. Leave the boys to it and have a ladies' jaunt?'

Miranda nodded. 'I'd be up for that, for sure!'

'You know, it's funny,' Adie mused; 'when we were young, we thought women of our age were just silly old biddies, didn't we? We never imagined that at this stage of life there would still be so much to look forward to, and so many plans still to make that didn't involve death and dying!'

'We certainly didn't imagine lovely romance and great sex to be entering our lives in our fifties! I always thought my parents were far too old for that kind of thing, even when they were forty! My God! How much we still had to learn, Adie!'

'Yeah, we thought we knew it all, didn't we? But I'm glad we've had some happy surprises, in that respect. I'm glad it's great sex, for you and Max. I'm glad you got to find out that it's not just the studs who are young enough to be your sons, who can provide a few fireworks! And love is important too, in all of it.'

And maybe, if you did have kids – especially sons – it might have felt a lot less appropriate that you 'toyed with the boys.' When I found out that my son Matty had been shagging older women, as an escort, I was really uncomfortable about it. A prejudicial stereotype, no doubt, and one I probably shouldn't have had, but I'm pretty sure I couldn't sleep with a man who was young enough to be my son.

She didn't voice those thoughts, because it wouldn't have helped. The past was what it was, and *where* it was, and it really needed to be left there. The fact that Miranda had finally found love, with a man close to her own age –

someone to grow old *with* – was something to be warmly welcomed and celebrated.

Miranda nodded, pensively. 'I do love Max, and I know he loves me, and it does make all the difference. Saying yes to his proposal, while we were here at Teapot Cottage last Christmas, was utterly terrifying. But, for the first time in my life, getting married just felt like the right thing to do.'

Miranda went on to say that she'd been proposed to before, a few times, but none of the men who asked ever made her feel that it was right, and she wasn't sure if that was just her being a 'scaredy-cat,' or whether there was more going on underneath, like some misplaced fear or something.

'I guess I was afraid, in the past, but I've no idea what *of!* I dunno… saying yes just never felt right before, but this time it did. I said to myself; 'here's a man who says he loves, me and I believe him. And I love him too, and I do deserve this.' I do deserve to take this chance at happiness.'

'Of course you do! And all those years you were afraid? I wish I'd known that. You never said, and I always knew that the way you lived your life was only ever going to work for so long. I figured that you knew that too, but it never occurred to me that you might have been *afraid* of something more permanent. Why did we never talk about that?'

Miranda shrugged. 'I'm not entirely sure, to be honest. I think I probably just never felt *worthy*, Adie. I grew up feeling like a square peg in a round hole. My parents never understood me, as you know. I was always 'too much' of one thing, and never 'enough' of something else, for them. I was always a huge disappointment to everyone who mattered to me.'

'Well, not to me. You were *never* a disappointment to me! I have always adored you, and I always will. You can talk to me about anything. Your courage and your talent, your beauty, and the fact that you've stuck by a mad old trout like me for decades, well, it all just blows me away. I'm so lucky to have you, Mand.'

Miranda looked softly at her, and Adie felt a lump form in her throat. Poor darling Miranda, needing so much more love and acceptance than she ever got, but being too afraid to take any of the chances when they came, until now.

'I adore you too, you silly bat. And you're right about me just being enamoured of the younger 'distractions,' because it *was* all fireworks, and I'd got into the groove of kidding myself that it was all I really needed, but it wasn't, was it? It's taken me a long time to realise it, but *this* is what I need, at this point in my life. Real love that lasts – well hopefully, anyway – and the kind of stability that never felt important enough to say yes to, until the right man was standing in front of me.'

'Those flings you always had, with much younger men; it was because you struggled to find or trust real love, and there had to be something that filled the gap. No woman is or should be an island. You did what felt right for the time you were doing it, and now you have something different and far more solid and worthwhile. Max is the guy! And I am so envious, by the way, of all the adventures you lovebirds are going to have! Maybe *you* should be finding beds big enough for three, on your travels!'

It was Adie's turn to be reflective now, as she sipped her second vodka tonic. There had been a time, not so long ago, when she was facing the end of her first marriage, and contemplating being alone in her old age. At the time, it had never occurred to her that she might find love again, but the fear she'd had, of being left to stumble through the rest of her life without the support and love of a partner, had been overwhelming to the point of being suffocating.

Meeting Mark had turned her entire life around, so she knew what a big thing it had been for Miranda too, to have finally found someone who cherished her, after being without true love for most of her adult life. She had got to the point of being willing to settle for whatever she could get; namely torrid flings with 'toyboys' but, on some level, she would have known that the day would come when she would no longer have the same appeal for them, and she might truly find herself alone and loveless.

She was right. Maxwell Henry Kennedy the Third had turned up at exactly the right time in her life. He'd watched her on stage for three nights in a row, before politely requesting to meet her backstage. She'd agreed, which had been quite unlike her, but on that particular night she'd been feeling a little less than happy with her own performance. Meeting an avid fan, whose praise might just allow her to feel a little better, had felt like the right thing to do. Max had been ushered in with a huge bouquet of pink roses, which she graciously accepted, along with his invitation to a late-evening diner at Covent Garden. The rest, as the saying goes, was history.

It was the kind of proof that made you think that maybe fate did have a hand in shaping your life, if you let it. On any other night, Miranda might have shrugged off a request for a fan to meet her, as she so often did.

It had all amounted to a random and curious combination of contributing factors. Her own low spirits at feeling she'd given less than her best. A man who wasn't usually much of a theatre-goer but who'd been at a loose end that first night and bought a last-minute ticket, and found himself captivated. His decision to keep returning and push for a chance to declare his admiration. Her decision to make an exception to her normal rule. An opportunity to have a lovely dinner instead of going home to a microwaved jacket potato. Conversation that had been interesting enough for them both to want to meet again.

Sometimes fate really was all over something. Max and Miranda were perfect for each other, and maybe the Universe had known it, and had engineered the variables in the way that only the Universe ever can. It probably was as simple as that.

'… getting through the menopause?'

Miranda's question burst Adie's private bubble of thought. 'Sorry, what was that you just said? I was miles away, thinking about how you two met!'

'I was just wondering how you're getting through the menopause. I know you started off having a pretty rough time. Have things settled?'

Adie nodded. 'They have, a lot. I think I'm getting there. Still having the hot flushes and the occasional night sweat, and my digestive system's still a bit haywire at times, but I'm a lot better than I was. You're on HRT, still?'

'Yeah, I kind of had to, really. My periods were so heavy at times, especially when I was in peri, I literally couldn't get out of bed. That had to stop, obviously, for me to keep working but, as you know, it was a big trial and error process, to start with. Some of the meds my doctor tried me on didn't suit me at all, but we've finally found the right pill that deals with most of the symptoms, and things have settled down a lot.'

'Well, I'm glad you're on top of it. I've steered clear of HRT, and Feen has been supporting me with homeopathic and herbal stuff, which has helped. I'm also taking marine collagen powder now, to stop my hair from thinning. It does seem to be working. Keeping it shorter definitely helps too. I couldn't go back to having it long enough to sit on, like it used to be. It would look like lank string, now, left like that.'

Miranda grinned. 'Shoulder-length suits you, and I'm glad you haven't given in yet, and joined the 'go-grey-gracefully' brigade. I'm not even *vaguely* ready for *that* yet, and I think your skin tone is still youthful enough to keep colouring your hair for a while, if you want to keep doing it. Some women suit going grey, but fewer than they think, and I'm in no rush to go stampeding towards wizened old hagdom!'

'Oh, Mand! Get real! You could *never* look like that!' Adie was confused. 'Is hagdom even a word?

'Probably not. But it's *my* word, as a state to avoid. Just wait until you see me in the morning, darling, when I wander down in my pj's with bed hair and no makeup, fangs hanging out, and snarling like a starving wolf for my coffee. I'll look about a hundred and ten. You'll get the shock of your life.'

She winked and smirked cheekily at Adie.

How utterly delightful Mand was! The best bit of her was the fact that she had no idea at all, just how funny and precious she really was, to everyone who knew and loved her.

Adie felt a huge rush of the warmest love. *Some friends are the kind you'd crawl a mile over broken glass for. She is definitely one of those.*

Chapter Thirteen

Teresa took a sip of her pint and realised that Chris had gone back into his own little bubble. It was something that had happened a few times already tonight. One minute he'd be fully engaged in their conversation, and in the next she'd have to pull him back after he'd drifted off into a different one, in his own head.

She found it both frustrating and intriguing. He'd been an open book about losing Daisy, when they'd had met up before, but as far as anything else went he was closed up tighter than a clam. He'd never said a single word about his family, even though she'd wittered on enough about her own! In most conversations, people shared at least a few details about their families, but no matter what she ever said about hers, Chris had never reciprocated by sharing any stories about his parents or any siblings. She knew very little about him, when it came to that. Her own family were a mixed bunch, with a fair few quirks and bangs that other people found interesting, such as previous family scandals that had rocked them all in the past and sent them scrambling for equilibrium. Everyone had family stories, didn't they?

Apparently not Chris, but she was determined to find out *something!* After all, if she knew nothing about him, how could she start properly getting to know him? And she did want to do that. He fascinated her, with all that he *didn't* say, as much as with what he'd been willing to share.

'What's bugging you, Darcy? You keep drifting away on me!'

He looked taken aback. The look of surprise on his face almost made her laugh. 'What are you talking about?'

'You seem a bit distracted tonight. Your mind keeps wandering off a bit, like you're thinking about something you'd rather *not* be thinking about, but you can't seem to help yourself, and I think it has to do with more than just Daisy – not that I'd ever want to try and minimise that, of course. I don't mean 'just' Daisy, as in; it's trivial. God, I know it's not! But there's something else. I can sense it.'

'Ah, Tez, I *do* have other things on my mind, but it's not something it would do you any good to hear.'

'Oh, come on, that's not fair! Don't shut me down like that. We're mates, aren't we? I just want to know more about you. I *like* you, Chris, and I don't want to be left on the wrong side of whatever wall you've put up! If you don't want us to be friends, just say that, and it's cool. I'm a big girl. I can take being told to my face, to mind my own business, but I'm not into guessing games. It shouldn't have to be this hard, to keep a conversation going. We can call it a night, if you'd rather.'

Something in her stomach quietly turned, as he looked deep into her eyes, and sighed.

'Come on Chris,' she said quietly. 'We have nowhere to take the conversation, if you can't let me in.'

'Okay, well, don't shoot the messenger. Remember that you *asked* to know, so; since you're so insistent, I'll tell you what my thoughts are. All I'll say though, before I start, is that it can't go any further. It has to stay between you and me. It's my drama, and I'm getting to grips with it the best way I can. If you want to help me with that, then fine. But no blabbing to anyone else, because its intensely private stuff, and it still really hurts, and I need you to appreciate that.'

'You have my word. I don't gossip or spill secrets, especially about the people I care about. So, shoot.'

Chris dragged out a sigh that made her think he'd pulled it from within his very soul.

'You've asked me a few times, about my family. And I've always dodged the questions.'

'Yeah. I've noticed.'

'Okay, well, it's because what there is of my family is pretty bloody awful, and I'm still trying to square away a lot of what happened, and how I've always felt about it. Recent developments have made it more of a 'thing' in my head, that needs to be resolved. I'm not sure why, but there it is. It's all blown up since Daisy died. I suppose grief makes you think about a lot of things differently.

'Anyway, I'm making good progress I think, mostly. But there are times when I still get dragged back, because you don't recover quickly from the kind of hurt that was thrown around in my family.'

He went on to tell her that he had come along late in his parent's lives. A 'menopause baby,' his mother had called him. The jury was still out, in the court of his own mind, as to whether he'd been a 'late surprise' to his parents or simply a mistake. He talked about his older sister Suzanne, who he'd never been in much contact with, and he'd been estranged from his father since Jack Darcy had married for the third time and cut Chris out of his life.

'Fancee Wilson, as she was, is Dad's third wife. She's a south-east American redneck. There's no other way to describe her. She's a religious nut too, always banging on about God, and how anyone who isn't a believer is doomed to burn in hell for all eternity.'

'Wow; that sounds like fun to be around; not! Go on.'

As Chris went on to describe his father, Tezzie found herself very quickly forming an opinion. Jack Darcy's problem seemed to be that he'd always been led by two things; a certain part of his anatomy that typically swung between his legs, and the deeply ingrained desire to have his other needs met too, whatever the cost. Jack had never had any problems expressing his adoration for his wives, but he'd never offered much in the way of tangible love to his son. Chris had been thrown to the wolves early.

He said he couldn't speak for how Jack had been with his sister, because she'd left home very abruptly when she was seventeen, and he was barely three. But Chris' mother was abusive to him, both physically and emotionally. Jack had consistently failed to intervene, in the interests of maintaining a quiet life for himself. It seemed pretty clear to Teresa that as long as Jack Darcy's boat wasn't rocking, he didn't much care who else's might be, even if it was his own vulnerable son's. The man had evidently been born without much of a conscience, and he'd clearly never gone on to build one.

It seemed that wife number one (Chris' crazy mother) somehow found enough sanity to leave. Wife number two who'd come along pretty quickly after that, had been a mean-spirited, wizened little sourpuss who'd had few good words for anyone, and she'd never given Chris the time of day. She'd also apparently driven her first husband to drink and also her own son, Chris' step-brother, who he'd never really got the chance to know. The husband had long-since died of alcoholism, and the son had flipped out after his own wife left him and he'd ended up being shot dead by armed police in his own driveway, after ranting and waving a shotgun at them late one night.

But it had taken a very long time for the 'Acid Drop' (as Chris called wife number two) to fall off her perch, and Jack had already lined up wife number three, while he waited.

'Fancee was on the scene well before the Acid Drop kicked the bucket. Dad even boasted about it to me, that he had a woman in the States that he was spending a lot of time online with. He was clearly besotted with her, or at least the *idea* of her.

'I guess he'd got bored, while the Acid Drop was sleeping her way far too slowly off the mortal coil, Tezzie. He got impatient, I guess, for intelligent female company – not that I'd ever go as far as to consider Redneck intelligent. She's cunning and clever, but that's not the same thing, is it? She sounds as thick as a plank, which probably isn't her fault, given where she comes from, and her age and everything. But when I met her, I found her about as interesting as a bucket of wet sand. She didn't seem to have a scrap of enthusiasm for *anything*. I've seen sloths that had more interest in life.'

Chris's story was riveting. It was tragic too, and hard to believe, but Tersea did believe it. By all accounts, his mother had been beautiful, intelligent and articulate; a far cry from the Acid Drop, who'd been (by Chris' account) as rough as a badger's backside. She'd chain-smoked like a train on fire, and acted and talked like she'd grown up in a slaughterhouse. Fancee, Jack's current wife, was a south-eastern 'redneck' whose monumental selfishness appeared to rival Jack's, which sounded like no small thing.

It seemed that Jack had been a raving atheist for most of his life, and at one time had kept a loaded shotgun behind the front door and used it to threaten the door-knocking 'God squad,' as he'd called them. But he ended up marrying a religious fanatic who was bordering on obsessive, who couldn't keep her trap shut for more than five minutes about the glory of the Lord. Chris had no problem with anybody having religious beliefs, but he did draw the line at having them rammed down his throat. He wasn't sure whether Fancee had succeeded in brainwashing his father, but he suspected that she had. Teresa sensed a lot of ironies in his story, and that was the biggest and saddest of them all.

Jack sure as hell knew how to pick them.

All three wives had treated Chris like he was nothing, and Jack had simply stood by and let it happen. 'Redneck' had systematically started cutting Jack off from his family and friends as soon as the ink was dry on the marriage certificate, and it hadn't taken her long to persuade him to change his will in her favour. Chris found out that he and his sister would only get to pick over what Redneck didn't want from Jack's worldly goods, after she'd casually left a copy of the will lying around for him to 'find.' Jack had changed it nineteen days after the wedding.

And what a wedding it had been. Six people, in total, including the marriage celebrant, and the organiser. When Chris had asked Redneck why she was in such a rush to tie the knot with Jack, she had declared, loud and long, that she simply couldn't live in sin.

'Ah caint live in saian! Gahd wouldn't wahnt me livin' in saian!'

Teresa erupted with laughter at Chris' falsetto attempt at a south-eastern accent. But she stopped when he went on to say that he'd wondered at the time whether that same God she professed to be such a slave to hadn't minded her spending three months in a touring caravan with Jack while she was still married to her first husband who, at the time, had been dying of cancer. She went ahead and divorced the poor man anyway, and the wedding took place on the same day he died. He wasn't even cold on the slab when Redneck dragged herself up the aisle, with a face like a well-kicked backside, to marry Jack. She even switched her phone off, so that her kids and grandkids back in the States, who were on their knees with grief and pain at the loss of their father and grandad, couldn't 'bother' her while she was getting married. Neither she nor Jack could find the decency to postpone their 'big day' out of respect for the dead and grieving.

Teresa was gobsmacked. 'Bloody hell, are you *serious?* That is literally *unbelievable!* It's the kind of thing you see on the worst kind of TV reality shows, or in trash magazines like the Enquirer, isn't it? You know, stories about people behaving so badly you can't even get your head around it. *Do* people actually behave like that?'

'Yeah, well, obviously some do, Tez. As weddings went, it was the biggest abomination I'd ever witnessed. It felt *grotesque.* My skin was literally *crawling,* as I stood there watching them say their vows to one another. I really didn't want to be there! It's always been really hard for me to respect my father, because of the way he's always treated me, and the way he let other people treat me. But that fucking wedding; that tested my respect to the limit. I was literally clinging onto the last remaining shreds of it, at that point.'

'Well, yeah. Who wouldn't be? How hard would it have been, to have postponed everything, by even just a week, out of decency?'

'Clearly, way too hard, Tezzie. They showed their true colours, and ploughed on regardless. Ruthless and selfish to a fault.' Chris laughed shortly, but there wasn't any humour in it.

'After the ceremony, Redneck didn't even kiss my father. I stepped forward to give him a hug instead, because he was just standing there, looking a bit silly while she was staring off in the other direction, like she wasn't even there at all. I felt like I had to do something. The whole fiasco was so weird, it took my breath away.'

Chris then went on to explain that Redneck had simply walked out of her house in back in the States, and left her two adult kids who lived there with her to explain everything to the bank and arrange for the house to be repossessed. One of them had two children.

Teresa stared at him. She was still struggling to believe what she was hearing. 'So, let me get this straight; she abdicated a dying husband, and their house, and made her own children homeless, and her grandkids as well, and got *them* to take responsibility at the bank? And this is a so-called Christian woman, or whatever her religion allows her to call herself? Jesus! What a piece of work!'

Chris closed his eyes and nodded. 'Yeah. She's something else.' He then went on to explain that when he'd found the latest copy of the will, and he'd seen what had happened, the last vestiges of respect he'd had for his father, fell away.

'I felt it viscerally, Tez; a complete disintegration in my chest, of something that used to be important. Something huge just *dissolved*, and I knew that was it, forever. I couldn't carry on, trying to be a part of Dad's life. Or hoping he wanted me around. It was pretty obvious that he'd *never* given a shit about me, or Suzanne.

'It wasn't even about the money, you know? He didn't have much anyway, but I wouldn't have cared if he'd left everything to the bloody Dogs' Trust charity! It was never about his assets, although he does have some pretty interesting tools, which he must have known I'd love, and he left them all to Redneck, too. Anything with a wheel, as well, apparently, which I guess includes the lawnmower, the wheelbarrow, and the outside bin. There is some irony, in her being left a trash can.'

He smirked, in spite of himself, but Tezzie just felt sad for him. *I'd be putting that bitch <u>in</u> the bloody trash can.*

'It was the message, behind what he did. That's what hurts.' She said the words quietly, and as Chris nodded, she noted that he had tears in his eyes now. She had tears in her own, because she could see, within Chris, the lost little boy inside the man; still hurting, still carrying the confusion and the hurt and disappointment of decades.

'Yep, and it pretty much killed any positive feelings I still had, towards him. Now, I just see him as someone I once knew, who I just can't face having in my life anymore.'

Jack Darcy's marriage to Fancee, and changing his will, was the trigger-point for Chris. He realised that he had to start the long and painful journey of disengaging from his father completely. Reading the will that Fancee had strategically left for him to find was the point at which he finally allowed all hope to die and begin the incredibly difficult process of accepting that he had never been important to his father, and probably never would be.

'I played right into the evil bitch's hands. I know that. She just wanted me out of the picture. It's what they do in that religion, apparently; isolate people who aren't part of the faith. I've gone a long way towards acceptance, but sometimes things happen that throw me backwards and I end up feeling like that bewildered kid again, the human sacrifice for Jack's happiness. And, as I said, there's been a new development I'm not sure how to feel about. I guess it's why I'm so preoccupied right now.'

Chris' father had dementia, now. Suzanne had phoned him, out of the blue, to give him the news.

'She didn't want or expect anything from me because she knows how I feel about Dad. She actually apologised for calling, but said she thought it was something I might want to know about. She wanted to tip me off in case Dad or Redneck did get in touch, and ask me for help of some kind. It was good of her, to try and stop me from being blindsided by either of them.

'Me and her, you know, we've never fallen out. We just don't really have anything in common, to have kept in touch. She left home when I was three. She had the measure of my parents, I think, and she hightailed it as soon as she could. I never blamed her for that, although I envied her the freedom to choose.

'So, we're not estranged, at least not in the same way I am from Dad. If there's a family crisis either of us wants the other to know about, we'd call or send an email, but that's about it. Suzanne didn't know about Daisy dying. She didn't even know I *had* a fiancée.'

Chris went on to say that Suzanne had told him she was going to be in Manchester in a few days' time, to attend the funeral of the husband of one her friends. She wanted to come and see Chris at his flat in Derby, before heading back to Ireland.

'I told her I'm not there. I explained that I was here, and she asked if she could come here instead.'

'Wow! How do you feel about that?'

'Truth? I'm not sure. Okay, I *think*, because as I said, we've never fallen out, as such. But it will be a tad strange having a virtual stranger staying the night. I haven't seen her in about sixteen years. I'm collecting her from Carlisle train station on Monday night. It's a bit much to expect her to go back the same day, or to stay in a hotel somewhere, when I have a perfectly good spare room at the cottage, with the bed made up and everything.'

He shrugged, lightly. 'She's family, and she wants to talk, probably about family *stuff*, so I don't imagine it's going to be much fun, but I'm sure it won't be terrible.'

Tezzie cocked her head on one side and looked at him.

'What will you do if she does want you to get involved?'

He shook his head. 'I don't think it's that. I get the impression its other things she wants to talk about.' He went on to say that while no call to get involved had come from Jack *or* from the colourless, wishy-washy but spectacularly manipulative Redneck, he knew exactly what his answer would be, if it did.

'I have no idea how I'd actually feel, if they wanted my support but I really don't want to be drawn back down into the snake-pit of their self-serving lives. Fancee might look and sound like an uneducated halfwit, but that old bitch is in a class of her own, when it comes to getting what she wants.'

Teresa privately thought that Fancee couldn't realistically ask *anything* of Chris, and she suspected that Jack Darcy – even in his lucid moments, however few or many he might have – would know better than to ask for help. Chris owed his father nothing. Decades of neglect and indifference, not to mention the damage done to him thanks to Jack's passivity while not just one but three 'mothers' abused him in various hurtful ways, well, that would pretty much cancel out any obligation *most* people might have felt, to step in and be of any help.

'In the back of my mind, Tezzie, I actually wonder if Fancee will go the distance with Dad. I mean, she cheerfully bailed without a backward glance on her first husband while he was on his deathbed, didn't she? Maybe the wretched woman has no appetite for sickness, no matter what she might've pledged in her marriage vows. She seemed so desperate to tie the knot, she probably would have promised *anything*, at the altar!

Teresa wondered if he was right. Maybe Fancee, or 'Redneck,' as Chris seemed to prefer to call her, would find a way to pass the buck to some other poor sap who'd pick up the runaway reins of Jack's jumbled mind.

Time would tell, but Teresa hoped it wouldn't be Chris; that they wouldn't find a way to suck him back into their selfish world. Tentatively, she said that to him, and she was relieved when he shook his head emphatically.

'No, I'm not overly anxious. Old Jack's made his choices, hasn't he? Whatever bed he's lying in now is the one he's made for himself. I'd certainly have no *pleasure* in rejecting any requests for help, but I *would* reject them. Whether it would go on to plague me or not, the decision not to get involved would be what it was.'

'I guess Daisy dying has thrown up all kinds of thoughts for you, about mortality. No wonder you're preoccupied with all this parent stuff, especially with such a messy upbringing. It can't have been much fun, trying to stay sane, in amongst all that. For what it's worth, I think you did great, to have come out of it all so well-balanced and positive about life.'

Chris laughed, shortly. 'Right now, positive is the last thing I feel. I'm getting there, but it's taken me a long time to accept that the person who was supposed to love and protect me unconditionally never valued me enough to do anything but hurt me instead.'

Tezzie smiled at him, gently. 'And, you know, even if your dad didn't or couldn't love you, it wasn't okay for him to be an asshole to you, and stand by while other people hurt you too. And it's not okay that they turn around and ask anything of you, after that. What *is* okay, is to say; 'enough is enough.' It *is* okay, to save yourself by severing the cord.'

'Exactly. And that's what I did, Tezzie. I took the power back.'

He went on to say that the biggest surprise for most people was that even after they thought they'd severed the cord that tied them to someone who'd hurt them beyond reason, time and time over, something popped up to make them question whether or not they'd done it as well as they thought they had.

She nodded, gently. 'And this news has got you asking yourself that question.'

Chris nodded. 'Yeah, I guess. It doesn't change my resolve to stay out of everything. That won't waver. But I *am* asking myself a few more questions than I thought I'd have to, ever again, about my relationship with him. I realise I haven't squared everything away as neatly and permanently as I thought I had.'

Teresa thought about what he'd said for a moment. Then she shook her head, slowly.

'I'm not sure any of us ever do square everything fully away. I still think about things that happened in my own family; stuff that hurt us a lot, when my parents split up, and I found out I had a half-sister living across the fence, that my mother had known about for *years*, and never told us about! It doesn't hurt so much anymore, what we all went through, and the family is in a much better place now, but I do still think about that time, now and again, and how difficult it was.'

She took a big gulp of her drink. 'I think there's always a few random thoughts, you know; loose ends that don't get tied up. My last relationship ending also has a lot of loose ends hanging off it, and I'm not sure whether I'll ever get to tie them off, or if I'll just have to figure out how to live with them.'

He looked at her speculatively. 'Yeah, maybe the inability to put everything neatly away is just all part of being human.'

Chris went on to explain that the sadness never left him, about his past, but the torment of hoping had, that things would change. He no longer wished things could be different. He'd long since stopped imagining how much better they could be. Moving on from his hideous family meant closing the door on them, and since he'd done that, he'd felt freer; no longer shackled to a 'maybe,' or crippled by condemnation, or insulted by indifference. He was able to stand up straight and breathe, and look forward, instead of back.

'But I think a broken heart will sometimes only heal so far. No matter how much work we could ever do, to square away the hurts of the past, some scars never fully heal,' Teresa observed. She felt such compassion, for Chris. It was hell, what he'd been through; first all the shit with his family, then with losing Daisy.

'You're right though, Tezzie. Jack deserves nothing, from me. And, in whatever part of his brain still works, if *any* of it does, he'll know that. I'm sure there won't be a request.'

'It's normal that it all still hurts though, so don't beat yourself up over that. I know he's your dad, and it's really not my place to say it, Chris, but I'm going to anyway. He's not worth your energy! You don't deserve to keep carrying any of the shit he heaped on you. You have enough to process, with Daisy being gone and everything. What you have to think about now is the future; what you want it to look and feel like. Ignore any bastard who tries to get in the way of that, especially for self-serving reasons!'

Chris smiled, ruefully. 'You're right. I have to lay Daisy to rest, and I'm on my way to doing that, and I can't let this other stuff get in the way of it. I have to let it go again. Seeing Suzanne might be a bit weird, but its only for a day and a night, and I guess the next time I hear from her after that will be another call, telling me Jack's dead. I'm not sure how I'll feel about that either.'

'I imagine it will throw up all kinds of things, just like the news of his dementia has, but I also think it's not going to help you, to be spending too much time thinking about all that.'

'Cross that bridge when I get to it?'

'Something like that, yeah. And thank you for telling me. I'm sorry if I came across as nosy, but I just want to know what's going on with you. I don't want you to think I'm just digging out of idle curiosity. I can feel us getting to know one another, and I'd like to continue with that, if you would too. Just as friends, of course.'

'Yeah, I would, Tezzie. It'd be nice, to be good friends. And of course you do need to know who I really am, for that to happen. It's just another very ugly, unhappy story in a life that feels full of them, and sharing it means revisiting it, which is never very nice. But it's helped, I think, to tell you, so thank you for listening, and understanding, and *caring* about how I feel. It means a lot.'

'Just know that you're a good man in spite of your father. With him as a role model, I really don't know how you managed to become such a good person with such a big heart, but you did, and that's a testament to your own strength of character. It's his loss, that he doesn't know that.'

'It's my loss too, Tezzie. People don't realise.'

'I get that. I really do. You lost a lot more than you ever should have, all your life, because of him, and all his terrible women that you were at the mercy of. You deserved better than that. It was horrible. But it hasn't defined you. You've had a rich, adventurous life so far, and you will keep doing that, in one way or another, when the dust settles.'

'Dad is at the end of his life having never really known me. I find that quite hard to square away. I was always there, you know? Always there, ready and waiting for him to *want* to get to know me. Waiting for the penny to drop, that I was his, and worth something for that alone. But it never dropped. He never got it, and you're right. It is his loss.'

'He didn't take the chance that was always there, to connect with the most amazing person that ever graced his life. It was his choice, to blow it, Chris. He's going to his grave knowing that. It's a hell of a thing; to be ending your time on earth knowing how much you've devastated the life of the one person who should have been able to trust you. He should be absolutely and utterly *paralysed with pride,* at what he created. *Anything* but indifferent! Jesus Christ!'

She handed Chris a tissue and he blew his nose. 'Sorry for being a bit weepy, Tezzie. For what it's worth, I'm not as bad as I was. I'm well past the worst of my screaming hysteria.' His grin was sheepish.

Teresa frowned, a little. 'I know a little, I think, about how bereft you've felt. It's not the same, because my ex didn't die, but it was as if he had, because of the way he left. I know what it's like to be left wondering how the hell you're going to find the strength to piece your life back together.'

She wasn't going to say any more than that. She only wanted Chris to know that on some level at least, she did understand his bereavement. But he asked her to tell him what had happened with Ross, so she did. At the end, he just stared at her in horror.

'What. The. Actual. Fuck? Seriously? You guys were living together, and he just *left* – no warning, a two-sentence note, and a refusal to speak to you again? What kind of bastard does something like that?'

Teresa shrugged. 'I dunno, Chris. It's a question I've asked a thousand times, but there's no real answer. I'll probably never figure it out.'

Chris shook his head in disbelief. 'Sorry, Tezzie, but a guy who doesn't have the balls to end it properly, who has to run off like a coward instead and leave so much unfinished business behind him, is not the kind of man you'd *ever* need! I know you loved him, and probably still do, but if you don't mind me saying so, he sounds like an irresponsible, immature wanker that you're better off without! The new bint he's planning to marry is welcome to him, isn't she? You deserve so much better than that, mate, and I hope one day you find it.'

'I hope so too, although right now I can't imagine being in love again. I'm certainly not looking for anything right now. My stepdad Mark told me to focus my energy on building my career instead, and I now think he's right, especially with my trip to Bangkok coming up. I'm so excited about it, and what it might eventually lead to, and it *is* taking my mind off the whole thing with Ross getting engaged and planning his wedding, and everything. We do need *something* to focus on, don't we, so we don't go bloody mad trying to deal with all the shit that hits us?'

Chris pulled a face. 'Yeah, having something to aim for definitely puts the mind in a better place than wallowing. God, in so many ways, we are what we always were, aren't we, Tezzie? Little kids, trying to figure out what we did wrong all that time ago that still has us feeling the way we do now.'

'I don't know what I did wrong, and I'll probably *never* know, because good old chicken-shit Ross won't tell me. But you did nothing wrong, Chris. Fundamentally, your father has something really important missing, in his psyche. He wasn't capable of grasping the importance of what it really *meant*, to be a father, a good example, a decent role model, a loving protector at any cost, to his child. That was never your fault.'

Privately, Teresa thought that part of Chris' grief over losing Daisy was tied up in his feelings about his parents, and his childhood experiences, and the grief that was still unresolved. Daisy had been the love of Chris' life. She'd loved him completely, and maybe that was a first for him. Maybe he'd waited all his life for someone to come along who finally 'got' him, who loved him completely for everything he was *and* wasn't, who he never had to battle to get attention from, or be in fear of disappointing. After finding the kind of unconditional love he'd been needing all his life, to then have it so cruelly and randomly ripped away, no wonder losing Daisy had hit him like a thirty-tonne truck. It was desperately hard for *anyone*, to lose the person they were in love with, but this loss had so many layers beneath it, that made it so much more complicated for Chris.

'Well, I'm glad you're going to be sticking around for a while.

Chris laughed. 'Me too! And I have a feeling you're going places, Tezzie Bostock, with Bangkok being just the first place on the list. Have you got your plan together, for what you need to do out there?'

'Yep. The idea is to grab as much footage as I can, then edit it later. I'll probably just roll the camera for a straight week, then spend the last couple of days lounging around by the hotel pool, and come home, which is when the *real* work will start!'

She was already excited about running around the Bangkok slums with a videocam. She couldn't contain her sense of thrill, at the prospect of doing it.

Come hell or high water, I am going to make my new career happen. If Chris can take a leap of faith, so can I. We only get one life, and we have to make the most of it. I am going to give this my everything, and failure is not an option.

'I hope it all goes okay with Suzanne, Chris. Get a takeaway in, and make sure you've got plenty of wine, and you never know what might come of it all. You might end up in a really good place with her, after this.'

Chris pulled an easy-osey face. 'I'm not expecting anything. We hardly know each other. At best we'll have a clearer line of communication. At worst, things will just go back to being what they always were. No expectation, no disappointment, right?'

'Right.'

But she lifted her glass in a toast, anyway. 'To new beginnings,' she announced; 'Whatever they may be.'

'To new beginnings,' Cris echoed, and smiled at her gently. Something in her stomach did a quiet, unexpected flip, but she forced herself to ignore it.

Chapter Fourteen

Chris recognised Suzanne immediately. She hadn't changed much at all in the last decade and a half since he'd last seen her. Her curly dark hair was greying a little at the temples now, but she otherwise looked the same. She was dressed fairly conservatively, in dark grey leggings, black suede slouch boots and a well-fitting violet jumper that looked home-crocheted, beneath her smart grey trench-coat. Chris really had no idea how 'fortyish' women dressed these days, but he thought his sister looked pretty damn good.

He raised a hand and waved as she came down the platform. She had a heavy-looking holdall with her, and he sprang forward to grab it as she approached him.

'Hi, Chris. Thanks. I'm headed straight for the airport tomorrow night, so I have everything with me.'

'It's good to see you,' he mumbled as she drew him into an unexpected hug. 'I hope you'll be comfortable at the cottage for the night. It's a nice little place. Quiet, at least.'

She nodded. 'I'm sure it'll be great, after a noisy airport hotel. The triple glazing doesn't *really* filter all the noise out at night! My train back to Manchester goes at two tomorrow afternoon, and then I'm on a flight to Dublin at nine o'clock, so it's a flying visit in every sense of the word.' She gave Chris a slightly apologetic smile.

'I hope you don't mind me just inviting myself to stay with you, but I don't often get back to England. It's been a long time, for you and me, and I thought me being here was an ideal opportunity to touch base again.'

'Sure, no problem. Shall we pick up some fish and chips or something, on the way back? There's a nice chippy in the town where I'm staying.'

Suzanne nodded. 'Sounds good.'

Chris phoned ahead to Cat's Fish, Torley's local chip shop, and ordered their food for collection on the way home. He'd already bought a bottle of wine, and there was another at the cottage, as one of Adie Raven's welcome gifts.

'You drink wine, I take it? I hope you do – it's all I've got.'

Suzanne grinned and nodded. 'Wine is fine, and I've got a bottle too, in the holdall.'

They made small talk in the car, on the way back to Torley town. Suzanne said that her friend had lost her husband to an incredibly fast-acting cancer, and the funeral had been hard.

'He was only forty-seven, with hardly any symptoms, for God's sake. It's no age these days, is it? He was fit and healthy, otherwise. Nobody had a bloody clue, until it was literally too late!'

Chris privately thought that at least the man had had almost twice Daisy's 'innings' but it wouldn't have helped the conversation at all, to have said that, so he kept quiet while Suzanne carried on talking about how difficult the funeral had been.

'The family were so distraught. He had three teenage kids. My heart went out to them, Chris, they looked so bewildered.'

'I know what that feels like,' he said quietly, and Suzanne quickly turned to him.

'Oh God! I'm so sorry! How bloody insensitive of me! I wasn't thinking just now, about what's happened to you, or to your fiancée. Daisy, was it? I'm so sorry for your loss, Chris. Its unimaginable.' She turned towards the window, clearly uncomfortable. Chris felt compelled to put her out of her misery.

'It's okay, you don't have to be sorry for what you've said. It is a horrible thing at *any* age, to lose a life that shouldn't have been at risk in the first place. Cancer's meant to be a lot more curable now, isn't it? We expect that now, which makes it harder when the so-called 'life-saving' treatments still don't work in so many cases.'

She turned back in her seat to face him. 'Do you want to talk about what happened to Daisy, Chris? Maybe later, with a wine or two under our belts? No problem if not, but I'd like to understand, and maybe offer some comfort, if I can. I know we're not close, but that doesn't mean I don't care about what happens in your life. I would like to support you, if it would help.'

They collected their fish and chips, and when Chris opened the door to Teapot Cottage, Suzane gave a small cry of pleasure. 'Oh, this is lovely, Chris! Such a warm and gentle space!'

He showed her up the stairs to her room and placed her holdall on the bed.

'We should eat now, before the food goes cold. But I can put it in the Aga to stay warm for a few minutes, if you want to have a shower or something first.'

Suzanne nodded. 'I would, if you don't mind.' She dug into her bag and pulled out a bottle of what looked to be a good French Sauvignon Blanc. 'Here. Sling this in the icebox for ten minutes, and I'll be right with you.'

By the time Chris had finished tidying the kitchen and laid plates and cutlery out at the little dining, Suzanne was back. He was astonished.

'That was quick! Most women take forever in the shower.'

Suzanne grinned at him. 'I'm used to being quick. With two teenage daughters constantly clamouring for bathroom time, I've had to learn to move fast. We've recently installed a second bathroom, which has restored my sanity, but I guess old habits die hard.'

Chris doled out the fish and chips and poured two glasses of red wine. The white needed a little longer in the icebox, to be chilled enough to enjoy. The red was a decent Argentinian Malbec, and it would certainly be a little strange with fish and chips, but he didn't care, and he was fairly sure Suzanne wouldn't either. She seemed to be pretty laid-back. He was no wine afficionado, in fact Daisy always called him a 'vino peasant,' since he'd drink pretty much anything that came out of a wine bottle, with no idea of how cheap or expensive it was. But he did know there was nothing worse than a lukewarm white, no matter who made it, or what it was put with.

'I'm starving!' Suzanne laughed lightly and tucked straight in. Neither of them spoke while they ate. Chris was hungry too, and it wasn't long before they'd both demolished their platefuls of food.

'I love chips. Daisy and I used to get them at the seaside. We used to go to Scarborough on the train once a month. It took hours to get there, and we had to book it weeks in advance to get the tickets cheap enough, but we'd leave early, to be there in time for lunch, and we'd get the latest train back we could manage. It was always a mission of a day, but we always looked forward to the fish and chips on the seafront.'

Suzanne reached over and covered one of his hands with her own. 'I'm so sorry. I had no idea what you've been through, and I can't imagine what it's been like for you, trying to come to terms with it. Have you had some good support?'

He inclined his head a little. 'Yes and no. People don't know what to say, you know? My boss was good, letting me have a lot of time off, and my friends all said they were there for me. They really were, I think, but losing Daise the way I did wasn't really something anyone else could relate to. I mean, it wasn't just like she died, in a car crash, or from an illness, or something. This was the kind of freak accident that I blame *myself* for, and people have no idea how to respond to that.'

'Must feel pretty lonely,' Suzanne observed quietly.

'Yeah. I've had times when I've felt pretty disconnected from everything. Grief is quite a process. You can't prepare for it, not under those circumstances. It never even occurred to me, when we went to Sierra, that anything was going to happen to *either* of us. You take out the high-level life insurance for extreme sports but even as you're doing it, and giving them your card details, it never resonates, that it might actually be *needed.*'

'You thought you were invincible.' It was a statement, rather than a question, and it surprised him. He thought about it for a moment, then nodded slowly.

'You know, I'm sure I *did* think that. Not consciously, you know, but I guess on some level I did believe I was untouchable. I've done so many peaks, and never had a single second where I ever felt in danger. I always had the confidence to just get on and do it. Combination of arrogance and adrenalin. It's a powerful mix'

'Yeah. And, by default, you assumed Daisy was invincible too?'

'No. I think the problem was that I didn't think about her safety at *all*. If I'd thought more about how it might feel, to a novice, to be climbing a fucking mountain, it might have been enough to stop me from insisting that she do it.'

'But it was her choice to go and do it, Chris. I know you feel responsible for 'railroading' her, as you've described it, and I can only imagine how unbearable it must be, to carry that. But you were engaged to be married! She knew you as well as anyone ever could. Would she *really* not have had the confidence in the relationship to have properly put her foot down if she didn't want to go?'

'Of course she would have. But she didn't want to disappoint me, Suzanne.'

'I get that, but I have to say, if I really didn't want to do something, I mean *really* didn't; if ever fibre of my being was screaming against doing it, it wouldn't matter how much I loved someone. I would put my foot down and refuse to go. And there's nothing special about me. I'm just a normal, average woman. On some level, maybe Daisy *did* want to give it a try, because if she liked it, she *could* share your passion, and it *could* have been something you'd have gone on to do together.'

'Even if she did, she didn't deserve to die screaming in terror, plummeting down a mountainside.'

Suzanne shook her head. 'No, of course she didn't. But let me ask you something. Bear with me. I'm trying to get it straight in my head. Before that stage of the trip, had you talked? Had she said anything about how she was feeling about the earlier parts of it?'

Chris thought for a minute. When they'd all stopped for a breather, Daisy *had* expressed a sense of wonder at what she'd already seen. She *had* been enjoying it. The smile on her face had been huge. He admitted as much to Suzanne, who just nodded.

'Okay, so let me ask you something else. If nothing had gone wrong, if you'd all got safely to the other side of the ridge, what do you think Daisy would have said to you, at that point?'

'I dunno. She might have been terrified, but I think she'd have been buzzing about the climb. She'd have understood why it matters so much to me, to do it.'

'So, if that rope hadn't snapped, if the climb had gone the way it was supposed to, she would have been happy?'

Chris closed his eyes. 'I think so. Yeah, I think she would have seen it, and felt it, you know – the wonder? The rush?'

'But the rope snapped. A freak accident happened that neither of you could have *ever* foreseen, and she lost her life because of it.' Suzanne's voice was soft now, as Chris' tears started to fall.

'She wanted to be there, on some level at least, and she was enjoying herself. And then a terrible accident happened.

So, tell me, what was it about any of that, that made it your fault?'

'If she hadn't gone, she'd still be alive.'

'That's true, Chris. It's an inescapable fact. But so is the fact that she *chose* to go, love. No matter how much leverage and coercion you think you exerted; no matter how much you think you 'forced' her to go, at the end of the day it was still her choice. She made the choice, for whatever reason, to do it. Nobody expected her to lose her life. She didn't, you didn't, hell, even the *guides* didn't! What happened to Daisy was the worst kind of nightmare, the worst kind of 'freakish accident,' to quote your own words.

'You didn't kill her, Chris, and you didn't *let* her die. The truth is that the situation had gone bad before that trip even started. A faulty rope. There was nothing you could have done, to either foresee that, or prevent it. It could just as easily have been *you* that lost your footing that day and been on the wrong bloody rope. It could have been *you* that plunged to your death.'

'I know. And what really upsets me is that I didn't need guidance myself. I got it for her. Mulhacén is one of the easiest ascents in Europe, on the face we took! I could have done it blindfolded. I trusted those guides, that company, that process. I picked that trip *because* it was meant to be safe for her.'

'You couldn't have known it wasn't.'

'The powerlessness I felt, Suzanne, as she hurtled down that mountain. The horror. I can't describe it. It haunts me. It probably always will. I think I'll hear her screaming for the rest of my own life.' Chris' voice broke as he gave into the sobs that racked his body.

'There was nothing you could have done. Not a damn thing. I'm so sorry, my darling.'

Chris felt Suzanne's arms go around him. He buried his face in her hair, and cried for what felt like a long time, and his big sister simply held him, without saying another word.

Eventually he pulled back, and Suzanne refilled his wine glass. She looked at him, pensively.

'So, what does this mean for you, as far as your passion for climbing goes? Will you carry on, do you think?'

Chris nodded. 'I definitely *want* to carry on, but not for a while. I still have a lot to square away, you know, in my head? Daisy would want me to keep it up, I'm sure about that. But I don't know what it means for ever getting involved with someone again. I guess with extreme sports it's hard to have it all. A wife and kids don't sit comfortably alongside the thrill of mountaineering, and all the risks that come with it.

'It's not that I ever really put my life on the line, you know, because there's a proper technique to climbing, tried and tested principles. There's a lot of judgement involved too, about what's feasible, safe and realistic. I'm not so much of an adrenaline junkie that I ever take risks with my safety, so it's straightforward process for me.'

Suzanne picked up on what he was trying to explain. 'But it's how *they* feel about it, right, a wife and family? Their anxiety, or fear, that you have to manage? I can see how hard that might be. And I can see how being with someone who's afraid for you might stop you from doing what you really love.'

'Yeah. It didn't seem to faze Daisy, but she was one in a million.'

'But she can't be the only woman on the planet who'd be cool about you running off and climbing mountains from time to time. A lot of mountaineers have families, I'm sure. Relationships are all about compromise, aren't they? Someone once told me that if you're with the right person, you don't *have* to give up anything, but you'd *want* to if it made sense. And believe me, I know all about that.'

Chris frowned at her. 'Are you okay? Your marriage, and the kids and everything?'

'Yeah. There's nothing wrong on the home front, but I did give up dancing when I married Ian. He just wasn't into it. You probably don't remember how involved I was, with ballet and tap and everything. But Ian just never got excited about dancing. He never suggested I stop, or anything like that, but he wasn't interested in it, so it was always going to be a solo thing for me. I decided I didn't want to have a big interest that he didn't share, so I let it go.'

'Shit! I'm sorry, Suze! Do you miss it?'

She shook her head. 'Nah. Not so much now. I do get a bit wistful, from time to time, but the girls are doing dance lessons, so I watch them. I also do a weekly dance class at my local gym, to keep fit. That's quite nice, and it's enough for me. The point is, you should only ever give something up because you want to – because it feels *right* to – never just to suit someone else, even if you love them, because resentment can rear its ugly head in all kinds of ways, if a relationship goes through a bad patch.'

'I'm sorry you gave up dancing, even if you're not. I do remember you bouncing around in a leotard. But then you left home, and that seemed really sudden, to me. One minute you were there, the next you were gone. I did miss you, for a long time. I think it was worse because I didn't know *why* you left. I figured it out, of course, when I started realising what kind of man Dad was.'

'You weren't even four years old, Chris, when I left. You might not remember, but I did talk to you before I went. I didn't explain much, because you wouldn't have understood, at that age, and I didn't want you to start feeling unsettled about being with Mum and Dad. But they weren't nice to me. Mum drank a lot, and she was very abusive to me, and Dad ignored her behaviour, so he more or less condoned it. She attacked me one night, and hurt me quite badly, and I knew I just couldn't keep living under that roof. I had to get out. I managed to convince myself that I wasn't abandoning you, because you seemed okay there. They weren't nasty to you; the way they were to me.'

'It didn't take long, for Mum to start on me, Suze, after you left.'

'I should have checked on you. It probably feels like I abandoned you, and I understand that. In many ways, I really did, didn't I? I left you with them, knowing how dysfunctional they were. I know I used to phone you, but that wasn't enough. I appreciate that now. For what it's worth, I don't like myself much, for leaving, and not doing enough to make sure you were okay.'

'Mum never hit me, but she yelled at me a lot, when she wasn't completely ignoring me, and Dad ignored me too. He was never interested in anything I tried to tell him. He always brushed me off. It was kind of like being in a vacuum, then Mum left and divorced him, and more or less the minute she did, Dad took up with 'The Acid Drop,' as I called her. Did you ever meet her?'

'No, I didn't. Dad invited me to the wedding, but I didn't go. I do know someone who knew her, though. They'd worked together, years before, and from what I understand it seems that The Acid Drop is actually a perfect name for her. Was she horrible to you?'

'Yeah, she was. I never understood what Dad saw in her. She really was a nasty piece of work. She accused me of stealing a jade ring from her, which was bloody outrageous. What would I have wanted with something like that, for God's sake? She also accused me of bringing someone home in the middle of the night, once. That was also untrue, aside from being completely ridiculous, and it really pissed me off, but Dad was on her side about everything. It was like he never believed a word I said to him.'

'That doesn't surprise me, Chris. He always had his head up his arse. I needed him to stop Mum from abusing me, but he never did. I'm sorry he let his second wife treat you that way. I don't know what's wrong with him. I've never been able to figure out why we meant so little to him.'

'Well, the third wife, the one he already had lined up before the second one died, she is a *real* piece of work!'

Suzanne laughed, but without a trace of humour. 'Fancee Wilson! Yeah, I know. I did meet *her*. She is an abomination in human form, and the worst kind of hypocrite with it, spouting her religion to all and bloody sundry, and never living by a single one of her so-called 'principles.' She's greedy, manipulative, self-serving, and totally lacking in morals or empathy. That woman doesn't give a flying fuck about anyone, if you'll excuse my language.' Suzanne grimaced.

'I once made the mistake of asking her about her religion, you know, to try and be polite and interested, since she'd joined the family and all. She sent me a huge A4 document, screeds and *screeds* of absolute bloody nonsense. I took one look at it and ran screaming for the hills.'

'It's so ironic though, isn't it, Suze? Do you remember how Dad used to hate religious door-knockers, when we were kids?'

This time Suzanne's laughter was heartfelt. 'Yes! That's right! He kept a shotgun behind the front door, didn't he, that he used to threaten them with? I remember seeing a pair of Mormons running hell for leather down the drive after he brandished it at them once.'

'What happened to him, Suzanne?'

She shook her head. 'I dunno, Chris. I think he's just a weak man, fundamentally. He's always needed someone to take care of him, and Fancee was in the right place at the right time, for him. In some respects, I think he's a hopeless romantic, but he's lacking in good judgement. That's aside from having no clue whatsoever about how to be an appropriately functioning parent. That gene never graced him.'

'I sometimes wonder if that's the reason why I don't want kids myself, Suze. Maybe I haven't got the Decent Parent gene either.'

Suzanne looked at him, surprised. 'Really? You don't want children? Admittedly, it would be hard for you to do a worse job with him as a role model, but maybe you'd turn the tables and be an *amazing* parent?'

Chris shrugged. 'Dunno. I don't trust myself. And of course, there's my rather precarious hobby to consider, when thinking about whether to contribute to world-overpopulation. As we've already said, it doesn't seem fair to have vulnerable kids waiting at home, even if it *was* what I wanted. But I really don't think it is – and that's okay, isn't it? Not everyone has to be a parent, do they? We're not *all* obsessed with the continuance of our gene pool! Consider ing ours is pretty rubbish. No offence,' he added, half to himself.'

'None taken, little brother! And your choice is just that – a *choice*. And I totally get it, that you've got a different life in mind. I'm glad we're alive, but when you think about it, our parents should never have been parents, should they? What a mess they made of everything. I was in therapy for bloody years, actually. I'd got to the point where I didn't think I'd ever have a relationship, because I hadn't a clue what love really looked or felt like.'

'Then Ian came along.'

'Yes. Ian came along, and I finally felt like I was worth something. We have a pretty good life, and I *did* want to have kids, in spite of the emotional desert you and I grew up in. I've made something of my life, but for a very long time I didn't think I would. I had no self-esteem, no self-belief, no sense of being lovable. Ian changed *everything*. Meeting the right person – it does change everything.'

'You know, Suze, you had the strength to leave, at seventeen. You had guts, to do that. You were brave and amazing, even before you knew it.'

Chris was surprised to see Suzanne fighting back her own tears now. 'Thank you, for saying that. I actually felt like a coward, at the time, for leaving *you*, and it was something else to hate myself for.'

'You had nothing to hate yourself for, Suzanne. You *saved* yourself! Someone had to do it, and nobody else was putting their hand up. Dad certainly wasn't.'

'But I didn't save *you*, Chris. I should have saved you too, but I didn't. I left you with those mad bastards.'

'How could you have saved me? I was three! They'd never have let you take me away.'

'No, but I should have stayed more *connected* to you, in some way at least. The phone calls were pathetic – nowhere near enough. I'm so sorry, love. I left, and I just couldn't bring myself to look back, except for those stupid calls. It's all I have to offer, as a reason, but I know it was selfish and cruel.'

'You weren't much more than a kid yourself, Suzanne. Seventeen is no age, and you still had so much to try and figure out, all by yourself. You did what felt right for you. I get that, and I don't feel bad towards you for it. I'm *glad* you got out. God knows what you'd be like, if you hadn't. You did the right thing. And the phone calls were great. They helped me, Suze. More than you know.'

Suzanne reached over and put her arms around him again, in a warm, tight hug.

'I'm glad you got out too. How old were you, when you left? Eighteen? Not much older than I was?'

She closed her eyes and smiled at him. 'You're a good man, Chris. And I want to tell you that whatever happens with Dad, you won't be expected to get involved. I won't let them suck you under, if they try to wade into your life or pull you back into theirs. Fancee might want or need support to manage Dad, but she'll have to get it from somewhere else.'

'Will *you* step in, you know, if his dementia gets worse and more help is needed?'

Suzanne sighed, heavily. 'It depends on what they ask for. I don't really want to help him, but as the dutiful daughter I suppose I probably should. Put it this way; if there's anything I can do, without it causing any anguish to me or my own family, I'll probably pitch in.'

''You're a better person than I am, if that's the case.'

'Nope. Don't even think like that! Dad let mum abuse me, and he didn't give a toss, but he let *three* mother-figures kick the *shit* out of you, in different ways! That gives you an unequivocal pass. They don't deserve you. They never did, and they never will. Don't get me started on what I think Fancee deserves,' Suzanne added, half to herself.

'I don't call her Fancee.' Chris admitted with a grin. 'I call her 'Redneck,' because that's what she is.'

Suzanne barked a laugh. 'Ha! That's perfect! Let's drink a toast.' She lifted her glass and Chris did the same.

'To 'Redneck,' as she either sticks around or not, to wipe Jack's arse and chin. And to a fitting end for *her*, as whatever karma serves to her! I might be a horrible person for saying it, but here goes… I don't hope Dad burns in hell for all eternity, but I really, *really* hope that she does!'

Chris raised his own glass.

'That's something I'm happy to drink to. I guess I'm a horrible person for thinking it too but, there again, we react to what we're faced with, don't we? There's no logic in someone thinking that they can treat you like you're worthless, and expecting to get anything positive back.'

'Those two deserve one another, little brother. Let's agree to leave them to it. We're doing just fine without them.'

Chapter Fifteen

The coffee morning was about to start. For Adie, it was always the happiest day of her month. For three weeks in every four, she had Friday morning coffee at a reserved table in Peg's café in town, usually just with her close friends Peg and Trudie, and her sister-in law Sheila. But once a month she hosted it herself at Ravensdown House, and it was more of an open-door event. Other friends would come, and it was always a real delight to catch up with people she didn't see as often as she'd have liked. Most of her friends were businesswomen or farmers wives, and they were all busy, but when they got together, it was always a lot of fun. The conversation was always unexpected and interesting, usually pretty funny, and everyone always left feeling like they'd managed to put the world to rights, in some respects at least. It was especially lovely that Miranda would be here this time.

She put the finishing touches to the table now; pretty plates, little cake forks with their gorgeous rose-patterned bone china handles, a matching cake stand, water glasses, and all the various accoutrements that were needed for the coffee, which was about to be brewed in two huge cafetieres. She'd put a vase of flowers in the centre of the table, too. You could never go wrong with a pristine white tablecloth either, could you?

Feen, Miranda, and Teresa were the first ones into the kitchen, followed closely by Peg Tripper, who was carrying a tray of delicious double-chocolate brownies. Adie knew, from long experience, how good they were. Peg said they were usually the first 'bake' to sell out in Ye Olde Torley Tea Shoppe. She couldn't bake them fast enough to meet demand, sometimes. The people of Torley loved their cakes, pastries, and pies, which meant that Peg's café always did a great trade. More than a handful of people had said they wouldn't know what to do if she decided to retire. Fortunately, she wasn't ready to hang up her apron just yet.

Miranda looked at the brownies, with an expression of mock dread on her face! 'Oh, get thee hence, wicked woman with all that godforsaken chocolate! Those look insanely delicious, but also like the one true symbol of a lifetime on the hips, thighs, bum, *and* tummy! All in one brutal hit, with a double-chin thrown in.'

Peg laughed at her when she rolled her eyes and smirked. 'Yeah, I know! But they're easy, and I literally ran out of time to make much else. Sorry for giving you all so much of what you love, ladies! Here's some milk too, for the coffee.' She handed Adie a generous two-litre bottle of semi-skimmed.

She set the tray on the bench and pulled a large serving plate from the cupboard. She knew her way around Adie's kitchen well enough to know where everything was. Adie thought it was nice, that her friend could come in and make herself so at home.

She introduced Peg to Miranda, and reintroduced her to Teresa. 'You guys have met already, haven't you?'

Peg beamed. 'Yes, we met at your and Mark's wedding, and then again, last weekend, at the café. It's nice to see you again. I know Adie's been looking forward to having you here for a bit. She plans to spoil you, I think.'

Teresa nodded and laughed. 'She is doing exactly that, but she needs to be careful because if it carries on, I might not want to leave!'

Peg gave her a wink. 'Well, that may be no bad thing, love.'

The kitchen door opened, and Debby Davies came in with her little toddler Ruby. Her infant son Thomas was being held and cuddled by Meghan Thomson, her good young friend and babysitter. Debby smiled gratefully as Adie pulled a highchair down from its hook at one end of the kitchen.

'Hi, Adie! I've a chocolate-iced banana cake in that bag over there, and Meghan's brought an apricot and custard flan, if you'd be kind enough to get it all out?'

She got her little son settled into the highchair and then turned to greet everyone. She had a special smile each for Teresa and Miranda.

'Hi. I don't know you, do I? I'm Debby, with a 'y.' My husband is Darren Davies, one of the local vets, and these two tykes are our terrors: Ruby and Thomas. This is Meghan; my friend, babysitter, and right-hand-I-can't-do-without. Adie told me you'd both be here. She's been really excited about you coming. It's nice to finally meet you.'

The doorbell chimed, and Adie went to answer it. Her sister-in-law Sheila Shalloe was standing on the doorstep with Gavin's mother, Carla Walton-Holloway. Carla had a recycled furniture shop and workshop with a flat above it, right in the heart of Torley town, but she'd recently got married to a local farmer, whose land was next to Sheila and Bob's, and she'd moved in at his farm. It was always nice to see her, and of course it did make sense for her and Sheila to travel together, since they lived next door to one another.

It was great that they could do it. A few years ago, they hadn't got along very well at all. Carla's attitude had been a bone of contention for *many* people in the town in fact, until she'd had a few epiphanies and learned how to deal with her demons. She was a much nicer person these days; still bitingly sarcastic, but no longer mean with it, and she was often surprisingly funny. Nobody could poke fun at themselves quite like Carla could, and it was refreshing, and sometimes hilarious, to be in the company of someone who was under no illusions about themselves.

Sheila called a spade a spade, too. Mark's sister was one of the kindest people you could ever hope to meet but, like her brother, she didn't suffer fools, and she shot straight from the hip. As the saying went, 'if you don't want the truth about something, don't ask Sheila Shalloe.' Like Mark, she spoke with a Lancashire accent, but it was considerably more refined than his unusually broad one. Sometimes, the words that came out of Mark's mouth were virtually incomprehensible, but Sheila's worst linguistic crime was dropping her 'aitches when she talked.

Carla handed Adie a covered plate of beautifully prepared mango, pineapple, and watermelon slices, laced with thin curls of lime.

'God, Carla! This looks *amazing!*'

Carla grinned. 'Never let it be said that I've added an inch to anyone's hips. Not this time, anyway. It's not as good as my usual generous contribution of unspeakably delicious shop-bought digestives, but I'm sure you'll all survive.'

She seemed to be as 'on-form' as usual, this morning. She never failed to make Adie laugh.

Sheila's offering was a dozen mini chocolate eclairs. 'I know I probably should've made more. These are a bit of a tease, aren't they? One mouthful and they're gone, but I know there's always plenty of cake, one way or another. Good God! Who made that amazing custard and apricot flan? I could eat that whole thing by myself!'

Adie giggled. 'I think we all could! We can thank Meghan, for that one. By the way, I'm not even going to ask why you're not at college, young lady...'

It was Meghan's turn to giggle. 'Study day. They don't always fall on a Friday, but this term they do, so you might see me at the next coffee morning too.'

'Well, I think I speak for all of us in saying how thrilled and humbled we are, that you actively choose to spend your precious off-time with a bunch of old fuddy-duddies like us. I guess we must be doing something right, to have you joining in.'

'Are you kidding? I still remember the first coffee morning I ever came to here, back when Dad and I were staying at Teapot Cottage! You were all telling jokes and comparing stories, about the menopause, and I've never laughed so hard in my life! I'll take a morning of that *anytime!*'

Adie gave her a quick hug, and looked up as a heavily pregnant Josie Valley came in, carrying a tray of oat and raisin cookies. 'Here you go, freshy baked last night. I hope you don't mind me just wandering in? The door was off the latch. My mother-in-law said she'd have my daughter Nelle this morning, so I thought it was good chance to catch up with Feen, and you too of course, Adie. It's so nice to see you, and to actually have a bit of girl-time!'

Josie was Feen's best friend. The two women had been close since their school days, and both had young children. Josie was the local postmistress, but was currently on maternity leave, expecting her second baby. She rubbed her belly a little and smiled, a little self-consciously.

'I'm not due until next week, but this little girl has suddenly started to act up more than I'd like her to right now, so please forgive me if I suddenly lose my water all over your floor. Let's all keep our fingers crossed that I make it home without that!'

Feen looked at her, and quietly said; 'you'll be fine today, Josie, but don't go far tomorrow night, okay?'

Josie rolled her eyes in response. 'God, I hope you're as right as you usually are, Feen. I am so tired of looking and feeling like a beached whale. I want this baby out, now. I'm totally over the two-ton-Tessie act. Why can't I be a slim, elegant, yummy mummy-in-waiting? I was the same fat blimp with Nelle, wasn't I?'

The women all sat down. Adie reintroduced everyone to Teresa and then set about brewing the coffee and putting her own contribution – a batch of her famous lavender shortbread – onto the table.

Inevitably, with Debby's two kids in the room, Feen's twins upstairs with Gavin, and Josie being pregnant, the talk quickly turned to babies. Josie's new arrival would be another girl, and she said that her husband Tony was making a great show of not being 'gutted that they weren't having their first football player.'

'He's only teasing. He isn't bothered at all, really. He's like me; excited, and grateful for a happy, healthy baby. But I think, on some primeval level, he would love for us to be having a boy.'

'Show me a man who wouldn't be! Feen muttered. 'It *is* very much a thimal pring. Gavin and I are so grateful to have one of each. Neither of us would've have cared either, if they'd both been girls, but Alder gives Gavin the chance to be a bit of a boy again himself. I don't know which of the two gets more delight from laying with the plego, the tip-truck and the train set.'

Debby nodded in agreement. 'Well, after struggling so hard to even have one child, I was never going to be less than over-the-moon with *any* baby. Having Ruby was an absolute miracle, and then to get Thomas as well; I have to say I still don't have the words for how blessed I feel. We're stopping at two, though. Economics, and the fact that I have to work, at least part time. That's a big enough juggle with two kids. I simply couldn't do it with three.'

'We're the same,' Feen admitted. 'If there was to be a third, we'd be fine of course, because we do have the luxury of being able to work from home ninety percent of the time. But I don't want to be one of those exhausted mothers who end up feeling guilty that they don't give their kids enough time.

'When we're in London I do have some hart time pelp, but we agreed from the start that we didn't want our kids to be nought up by brannies. I have a woman who comes in three mornings a week, to clean up the breakfast stuff, run a vacuum cleaner around, and entertain the kids a bit. It gives me and Gavin time to get some decent work done, and that means I can give Willow and Alder the best of myself, for the rest of the time. I once never thought I'd be as busy as I am. But I am, so...' She trailed off with a shrug.

'Well, you have to do what you have to do, love,' Peg said. 'It's a tricky balance, I know. Andy and I didn't have kids. He was my first husband, and he died young, as you know.'

'Did you want to have them? I mean, if he hadn't died, would you have had them, do you think?' Teresa leaned forward with interest.

Peg shook her head. 'No, I don't think we would have. And that would've been a brave decision, back then. In my day, you were regarded as something of an oddity if you hadn't managed to pop out a baby or two. There were women who couldn't, for different reasons, and they were always viewed with sympathy. But if I was ever to have told anyone I wasn't having any because I didn't *want* to, that would have been a tricky thing. People judge. They shouldn't, but they do. I'm not sure if it's still a big deal. I hope it's not. It used to be pretty hard for women to make choices that went against what society expected.'

'It's still a thing,' Teresa blurted out, and blushed violently. 'I mean, I've had this conversation with my friends, quite a few times in fact, and even now there's still an assumption that we'll all just get on and do it. But for those of us who don't want to, it's still hard to make that choice, because whenever it comes up, people always want to know *why* a woman doesn't want to have children! It's like, nobody demands to know why you *do* want to, but they don't seem to have any such sensitivities when it comes to demanding to know why you *don't*.'

Debby nodded. 'Yeah, you end up feeling like you have to justify yourself, and that's just wrong, on every level, but no one gets it, do they? People don't know when to back off. Even when I kept failing at IVF, a lot still judged me for not getting pregnant. It was like they thought it was my own fault or something. I *did* want to have kids. I can't imagine *not* wanting them, but I'd never condemn a woman who doesn't. Whether you procreate or not, it's none of anyone else's business, is it?'

'No,' Teresa said quietly. 'But somehow, they think it is. They think they have the right to tell you what to do.'

Miranda looked at her kindly. 'I never wanted children, as you know, just like you don't. I understand your choice completely, by the way, and believe me I know what you're up against, with the social expectations! People can be monsters, with their opinions, and their self-entitled penchant for being so insistent with them.' She rolled her eyes dramatically.

'There's always some opinionated idiot who seems to think they're the expert on a younger person's life and can't shut up about it, even when it's someone they don't know! It's outrageous, when you think about it. But, if this wonderful project of yours is anything to judge by, young lady, you are destined for a *very* big life. I think we can all safely assume that and I, for one, choose to celebrate it!'

Adie was suddenly pensive. *I never knew she'd decided against having children. I'm a little sad about it, but I understand it, I think, and I certainly don't want her to feel pressurised to do something she doesn't want to do. That's a really big thing to be railroaded about. It's a life-changing decision. Some people have a lot to answer for, in meddling with their judgements!*

She chose her words carefully. 'I think it's every woman's choice, about whether or not to have a baby. It's something she has to do – or not – for the reasons that are right for *her*. It can't be about what anyone else expects! When I had you and Matty, it was the expected thing, but for those of us that wanted kids, it wasn't an issue. That's a different thing entirely from feeling as if you 'should' have them because you'll be harshly judged if you don't. I'm so sorry it's still a pressure, and I'm even sorrier that you're feeling it, because it shouldn't be that way at all. Not in modern society.'

Teresa shrugged. 'You know, oddly enough, it's some of my male friends that have the biggest issue with it. It's like; '*what?* so you *don't* want to be a *mother?*' And they're kind scandalized, like mortally offended by it! I've been treated like I have two heads or something, and that's from people who actually say they like me! God knows what the people who don't would say.'

Peg bit her bottom lip. 'That sounds like a reaction to not being able to control you. Ego-centred. A lot of men don't want you to have the ability to make big decisions like that on your own, without their input.'

'Maybe it's hard for some men to love a woman for who she really is, not just for what she can give them,' Adie ventured.

Carla piped up, then. 'Oh, no. Make no mistake; the men who hate childless women for being childless are the same ignorant bastards who hate women who have kids too! It's misogyny in its purest form. Men behaving badly, for want of a better term. Some guys just hate women, full stop. Especially the independent-thinking ones who don't want to be pregnant and chained to the kitchen sink.'

Sheila added her two penneth, and her voice was quiet. 'Peg's right, and so's Carla. Your choice to be childless gives you a freedom they don't want you to 'ave, love. They 'ate that you 'ave it, so they 'ate you *for* it.'

Adie felt sorry that her own daughter was facing hostility simply for considering being childless. She felt compelled to say something more about it.

'Darling, your choices are yours to make. Nobody who loves you will condemn you for them, and the people who do are the kind you don't need in your life. Believe me, I know what it's like to be judged by so-called 'friends.' But the fact is that people who judge you are *not* your friends. They actually don't care much about you, if they can't respect your choices – even the ones that make them feel uncomfortable. That's their 'stuff,' not yours. The only people you need in your life are the ones who do respect and support you.'

'So, you wouldn't judge me if I told you I wasn't likely to produce any grandchildren?'

Adie shook her head. 'God, no! I'd be upset if you *did* have them just to please *me!* I'm never going to be one of those terrible people who put pressure on their kids in their own self-interest! You can trust me on that!'

She shook her head. 'No, darling. Being a grandparent is a privilege and a blessing if it happens, not a *right* that people feel entitled to get all upset and start moaning about if it doesn't happen! All I want is for you to be happy, and nothing more! There are a few grandchildren in the mix already, remember? I'd only be disappointed for *you*, if you changed your mind later, when it was too late. But, for what it's worth, I don't think you'd make that mistake. I do think that if you find yourself getting to the place when your fertility starts to wane, you'll know, one way or the other if you want to catch that train before it leaves the station without you on it.'

Debby nodded, in agreement. 'All I would say is ignore other people and their unwanted opinions. Listen to what your body clock tells you, and if it *never* hits you over the head about time running out for getting pregnant, that's fine. Just don't ignore it if it does, because that might mean you end up living with regrets. At the risk of sounding patronising, you never know what the future will bring. It's perfectly okay to be a childless woman, but it's also okay to change your mind later if you want to, before time runs out.'

'What about you, Meghan? You're the next generation of brave new women! What are *your* thoughts on having children, and a woman's right to choose?'

Adie was interested to hear Meghan's perspective. The teenager was preparing for university and had a big career path planned. It would be interesting to hear her thoughts, as the youngest in their group, and Adie was also very keen to include her in the conversation, because she hadn't had much chance to contribute yet, although she had been avidly listening.

'Well, I think the same as you, I guess. I do see kids in my future, but not for a long time yet. And it's interesting, your perspective on men's frustration at the inability to control a woman's choices. I feel like most guys my age have gone past that way of thinking, but maybe that's just because I hang out with more liberal people. I suppose a lot of guys my age may still be old-fashioned; you know, thinking like their fathers have taught them to think. But modern women are educating their male peers, so hopefully that old way of thinking will just fade out. And if I want to have a baby, I don't want to think I need a man to make it happen – apart from the obvious initial input of course!'

Carla nodded. 'You're right, but it *is* a lot easier with two people! Raising a child alone is tough work. I did it for nearly sixteen years, with Gavin, and sometimes it was bloody hard, making every decision alone, and trying to provide more than just the basics. Just because we *can* do something, it doesn't mean we always should.' She stopped for a second, and her voice became reflective.

'I guess it depends on your emotional and physical resources, and what you can realistically give a child, as a prepared single parent. I didn't choose to be one. I ended up that way, after my partner came out, and then went to live with man he'd fallen in love with. I gave Gavin as much as I could, on my own, but it was a struggle. I didn't cope very well mentally, through it all, and we both suffered for that. He missed out on a lot, for not having a father figure in his life through his formative years. And people do judge you for trying to do it alone, even if you're successful. There's no getting away from that.'

Teresa commented quietly on how surprised she was, that she was negatively judged by other women about her choice to be childless.

'I always thought we'd all be in each other's corner, you know? It was a shock, to learn that some of the women I know, of all ages actually – not just my peers – are very quick to condemn me for having my own mind, and wanting to do something more with my life than get married and have a couple of kids. The idea that I can be more than that, that I want to be successful without that massive juggle as part of it all, seems to create real hostility. I don't know whether it's envy, or what, but I saw a lot of it while I was travelling, in different countries, and it's absolutely rampant in London. It seems to be a generic attitude.'

Carla nodded. 'Yeah. Envy is huge, between women. Did you know that over in New Zealand they actually have a name for it? They call it Tall Poppy Syndrome, where women can't stand the thought of other women being more successful, so they do whatever they can to tear them down to size, and 'level the field' so nobody stands taller than anyone else. That's why I've called my Women in Business Networking Group 'Tall Poppies.'

She shook her head in frustration. 'It amazes me too, Teresa, how some women hate others for shining a little brighter. There's no room for that sort of shit in my group. There's no place for *any* woman if all she can do is bleat about support but not put her money where her mouth is. Talk is cheap. Actions are what count. If you ever want to go into business, you'd be welcome to join, by the way. All women get to stand tall, in there.'

Adie smiled gently at Carla. Her group was doing very well, in Torley. There were a lot of women in business in the town, and not all of them were 'visible.' Many worked from home, or commuted to Carlisle or other towns. As such, they were often quite isolated. Carla's Tall Poppies group filled a gap in the lives of many women who otherwise had little support, and Adie knew how hard some of them struggled. The group had proved to be a godsend for them and, as their network had grown thanks to that once-a-month meet-up and the social media community the group also offered, so had the women's confidence to keep being those tall, beautiful poppies in fields full of averageness and mediocrity. It seemed that the average and the mediocre were by far the most vicious, in business. It probably did all come down to envy.

Miranda had been sitting quietly, listening to the conversation. She hadn't contributed much, and had in fact seemed a little shy of joining in, which wasn't really like her at all, but then Adie realised that apart from Teresa, Mand hadn't met any of her new friends, and it probably was a little intimidating, coming into an established group.

But Miranda spoke now, quietly, to Teresa. 'Darling, closed-minded attitudes come from the age-old patriarchal rule that still prevails. When I was at university, I studied a lot of sociology stuff, including women's issues, and I got to understand a fair bit about how these outdated opinions originated. It's a deeply entrenched internalisation of the way we were all educated, with all kinds of unconsciously delivered messages of bias that we've been encouraged or even expected to accept, even from so-called liberal women teachers. And, because they were taught to teach *within* that system, the bias was inescapable.'

Teresa nodded; 'Yeah, I understand that too, I think. And even though you're very successful, I guess you've still had to deal with the same prejudices as every other single, childless woman. But you've had to do it in the spotlight. That must have been uncomfortable, at times?'

Mirand a inclined her head, gently. 'Yes, it's had its moments, but I made a conscious choice, right from the start, to never let myself be too affected by it. As a doctrine, patriarchy is still alive and well, even unconsciously. It dismays me greatly that it's still something we have to deal with, all these years on. Prejudice from other women is particularly hard to accept, even when you know where it comes from.'

'I agree, and I think it's sad, and its actually quite scary,' Sheila observed. 'I suppose we 'ave to challenge ourselves too, to be sure we really *are* in each other's corners, and work out why we might not be, and fix that. It should be a simple, primeval thing to support one another, as women. It's a shame so many of us don't.'

'It's not a conscious bias, in most cases,' Miranda offered. 'If you ask a woman why she hates another successful woman, even one she doesn't know, she probably can't explain it. It's just there.'

'Yeah, but it does have to be challenged, if we're ever going to make real progress,' Sheila insisted, and everybody agreed.

The conversation then drifted towards more mundane things, and it didn't seem like very long at all before the clock struck midday.

Everyone started to get up, and Adie grinned widely at them all. 'Thanks for coming. Gosh, I've missed Trudie today though, and where was Hazel? Is she okay, Carla?'

Hazel Walton was Carla's mother. The elegant old lady usually came to the Ravensdown coffee morning, and she had been noticeable by her absence today.

'Yeah, she and Dad have gone over to Lancaster to see my brother Tristan. He's giving a guest lecture at the university's medical faculty, and they wanted to attend. They're all coming back here later for dinner at our place. Dave's cooking, which should be interesting. We may yet be sending out to Cat's Fish for a chippy tea, once we've stopped the house from burning down. Or we could turn up back here for what's left of the cake.'

'Oh, ye of little faith! Dave might surprise you. But do give Tris my warmest wishes, won't you? I do like him, Carla. He's a lot of fun. And please tell Hazel that we've missed her today. Fiona Frost couldn't make it, either. She has a huge order of wedding flowers for tomorrow, so she can't leave the shop, and Trudie is in Hamburg on a buying trip for the boutique. She won't be back until Sunday, but I can't wait to see what she's bringing in for summer stock at GladRagz. Lots of Lagen-look stuff, I think, which always flatters us all.'

Carla did her trademark smirk and eyebrow-lift. 'Ah, yes; Lagen-look, the world's most forgiving clothes! Rescuing middle-aged women from bumpy frump-hood for the rest of their days. I'll be the first one through the door with my svelte, lean, Lagen-transformed figure, putting you all to shame.'

Adie laughed at her. 'Well, you might be a bit lumpy and bumpy in places, but that makes you one of us. You're a part of the sisterhood now, whether you like it or not.'

Carla gave her a small, grateful smile, and one of her trademark winks. 'As long as by 'sisterhood' you don't mean nuns. I'm way too far gone to be saved by the Lord, and if you don't mind my saying so, I think we probably *all* are.'

As they reached the front door, she turned and said, 'I do like your friend Miranda, by the way. She's one woman I'd love to spend more time talking to.'

'She's here for a few days, so if you have time, pop back. I'm sure we can get some cocktails on the go. If we do, you might have to get Dave to drop you off and pick you up! Call me if you want to do that.'

As Adie hugged her friends and waved them all off, she felt a warm sense of contentment. They were a fabulous group, and although a few faces had been missing today, she knew it wouldn't be long before she'd see Fiona Frost, down at the florist shop, and catch up with Trudie and Hazel. As ever, it had been a lovely morning of light-hearted chatter. But there were undertones today, and Adie felt them connecting with some of the other conversations she'd had over the past few days, especially related to her daughter.

Teresa was dealing with a lot. Her relationship had ended, then the unpleasant reminder had popped up, of how doomed it had probably always been. Her father had selfishly roped her in to help him deal with a disaster he had wrought upon himself, when her relationship with him was already under some strain. Then, on top of all that, it seemed that while she was struggling to answer a few critical questions, like what she really wanted to do with her life and how she wanted it to be (and manage her emotions around all that), she was also being judged and criticized for not wanting children! That last nugget had been a bolt from the blue, although it hadn't surprised Adie entirely.

It wasn't so much that Teresa had ever expressed an actual *dislike* of children. As far as Adie was aware, she had no problem interacting with them. But there had never been a time when she'd expressed any real maternal instinct. Even as a little girl, she was only superficially interested in playing with her dolls or teddies. She always preferred to draw pictures, or read. She had always immersed herself in music too, and it meant a lot to her. It still did. She would sometimes lose herself in the lyrics of a song she liked, or one that resonated with her, and where she was at that moment in her life. She often said that certain tracks 'defined her life journey,' and although Adie didn't fully understand what that meant, she knew her daughter found a lot of meaning (and also at times a lot of comfort) in music.

She also had never been overly enthusiastic about the traditional 'homebody' skills. She could cook a basic meal, and she kept her flat clean and tidy, but she wasn't what Adie would describe as a 'nester.' She wasn't the sort of woman who'd ever spend time worrying whether her curtains matched the cushions on her sofa.

Now that she thought about it properly, Adie actually couldn't readily imagine Teresa as a mother. If she ever was, she'd be the kind who would teach her kids how to pack a perfect suitcase, read a map or an atlas, camp out in the woods, and think about the plight of the poor. The stories she would read them would more likely be adventure ones than fairytales, and she'd encourage them to be as independent as possible from an early age. Those were all good things to know, and do, and be, but as for being 'mumsy' and maternal, no – she didn't appear to be very solidly built that way. Not that it mattered; not everyone wanted to be a parent. A lot of mothers didn't make a very good job of it, as living proof that just because you *could* do something, that didn't mean you *should* do it – as Carla had rightly said.

Some women were simply destined for other things. Her best friend Miranda hadn't wanted kids, and it had been the right decision for her, too. She'd determinedly followed her dream of acting. Before she'd met and got engaged to Max, she had also been very happy jetting off for exotic holidays with lovely (and usually much younger) men. She'd recognised early that the way she wanted to live her life wouldn't happen if she'd made a different choice about children.

A great many women did manage to have kids *and* careers, and many did a great job of balancing lives that included both, and keeping it all together. But Adie took her hat off just a little bit faster, to the ones who recognised that the way they wanted to live their lives involved more compromise than they felt willing or capable to make, if they put kids into the equation.

As far as I'm concerned, a woman who knows her own mind, and sticks to it, regardless of how much criticism she has to endure, is someone to be applauded for her strength – not feared as someone who won't conform!

Peg had been right when she'd said that it took guts to stand against the tide. Adie wondered now how many women could have been braver, and made different choices, if they'd felt less pressure to fit in. She wondered if it had occurred to any of them, that they even *had* different choices.

She had a sneaky feeling that Teresa had a big destiny. She had no idea what it might be, because Teresa didn't quite know, herself! But Adie suspected that her daughter was going to have quite an impact on the world, in one way or another, and maybe children just weren't part of the equation. Maybe her path was being shaped in such a way that the desire to have a family was taken off the table early, in preparation for what was coming.

That's what Feen would think, and maybe there was something to it. As the old saying went; 'what's for you won't pass you by.' And maybe what *wasn't* for you wouldn't rock up and cause anxiety or dilemmas you could do without. Maybe the choices you made, without really knowing why, were all part of a 'divine' preparation for a clear run to where destiny wanted to take you.

It was all a bit 'woo-woo,' in one respect, but if Adie had learned anything over the past few years, it was the fact that sometimes a decision was made at a time when it couldn't readily be explained, but the reasons always made sense later.

She might surprise herself, somewhere down the track, and opt to have a 'conventional' life with a partner and the two-point-four, but I'm not going to hold my breath for it. It is annoying though, that if being childless turns out to be her forever choice, she's going to keep having a tough time from people who think they're entitled to challenge her about it or ask her to justify herself.

It was sad and frustrating that such unfair expectations were still rampant in society, and that you sometimes had to fight really hard to stand against them, even when your choices were the right ones for yourself. The age-old expectation, that a woman 'should' procreate and be happy to do it, was still such a strong one – even in a world where so many standards had shifted, and so many stereotypes had been busted. It was also sad, as Sheila had described it, that so many other *women* would judge her daughter badly for wanting to be successful in a different way. It was so ironic, that the things that never changed were the ones that needed to the most.

Adie thought about Bryan again too. A different vulnerability had exposed *his* flank and, even though he'd brought it on himself, it still reinforced the fact that no matter what stage of your life you were at, you could be susceptible to having your resolve severely weakened by outside influence. Bryan's life was being decimated by his inability to say no to a certain ruthless villain; a, 'ordinary' woman who had a hidden agenda that was anything *but* ordinary. It was sad and living proof, that you could end up making a life-altering and potentially damaging decision by ignoring your inner voice of integrity and going with the flow instead, because it was easier than trying to stand against the tide.

Teresa was helping her to clear away the dishes. 'I'm sorry about landing the kid thing on you without warning, Mum. I meant to talk to you about it, but somehow the time never felt right.'

Adie smiled at her, as gently as she could. 'That *was* a bit of a bolt from the blue, I must admit, but it's your life, darling! Your choices are all your own, and I meant it when I said that I never want you to feel unfairly influenced, from *anywhere*, and I certainly wouldn't do it to you myself! That would be monstrous! All I want is for you to be happy, whatever that means for you.'

'Thanks. I like your mates, by the way. They're a nice bunch, aren't they? Straight-talking, and wise, but kind with it. I like that. Even Carla is a good laugh, in her own way, isn't she? Sarcastic, but funny. She cheered me up today. And good on her, for championing women in business. It takes some guts to do that and fly in the face of the haters.'

Adie nodded. 'Yeah, Carla is one out of the box. She's been through some shit in her life, and she's had her fair share of demons. Because of the way she let them drive her, she attracted her fair share of haters, but she has learned some painful lessons. She's much nicer than she used to be, and the rest of the crew have budged up and made room for her. Most people around here have their feet on the ground, and they usually know when a second chance is deserved, especially to someone who wants to help *them* succeed. This lot are pretty genuine. I think it has something to do with living in a country town.'

'How do you mean?'

'Well, most people around here are either farmers, or businesspeople who connect with them in some way. Most folks tend to be busy getting on with the practicalities of living in and serving a rural community. There isn't a lot of room for preciousness, or whatever you want to call it. A fair few of my other friends here have been through some tough times too, not just Carla. It makes them real. The town has a few prima donnas and gossips, and other idiots you'd choose to avoid. It's just like anywhere else, in that respect, but what you see is what you get with most of the people around here.'

'They're such great women, full of wisdom and insight! Proper matriarchs! I'd love to talk to them again, Mum. I kind of felt *safe* with them, like I could really talk about stuff that matters, and get the real lowdown on how to handle it. Aunty Mand is a fantastic source of wisdom. I adore her! But it's nice to hear some other sensible perspectives too. They're all a far cry from the crowd you used to hang out with, when you were married to Dad, that's for sure!'

'Yeah, you're right about that. It took me a long time to realise that I never knew what most of those women were ever thinking, about *anything!* They were always so terribly careful, never to talk about anything meaningful.'

'So many masks, and no glimpse of what was behind them.'

'Yes, right again! That's a good way of putting it, actually. Some of the women I knew before I moved up here were lovely, but others were a bit strange; kind of superficial and two-faced, and always moaning about something. They had very comfortable lives, but they never seemed satisfied, about anything at all. I think most of them were pretty unhappy, in one way or another.'

'Well, they must've been, to behave like they had to hide so much of themselves. It's hard to live a guarded life with people you should be able to trust. Did you never try to find out more about them?'

'I think I did, in my own way, but I'm not much good at small talk, which I suppose might have been a way in. I didn't have the patience for that, and whenever I asked a direct question, I was made to feel like I was being nosy or something. I felt a bit like a square peg in a round hole with them, most of the time. If it hadn't been for Miranda, I don't think I'd have had any close friends down there at all. I don't think many of them liked me much, looking back; probably because we never had anything in common.'

'Yeah, and I know some of them hurt you a lot, Mum. One or two were absolute bitches, weren't they? That crazy Pickitt woman who threatened to have you arrested; she was the worst. I dunno how bitches like that live with themselves. And there were a few examples of really bad marriages too, as I recall.'

Adie stared at her. 'Really? Like whom? I'm surprised you remember anything like that! You weren't around much, to have any real contact with any of them, especially after you started at uni.'

'No, but I still noticed a fair bit of stuff that was going on, and different things you said. You had friends called the Benthams. They often came to our house. I remember you saying she was always cheating on him, and quite openly, but he never left her or kicked her out, even after she gave him an STD. It used to frustrate you, that he didn't seem to have much pride or self-respect. I remember you and Dad were friends for a while with another weird couple too, but it wasn't for very long. Some fat-bellied guy with glasses, I can't remember his name, but he had a wife called Jo.'

Adie thought for a moment, then she remembered. 'Oh, you mean Jo and Callan Blackfoot? Gosh, I'm surprised you remember them! You only met them once or twice, didn't you?'

Teresa nodded. 'Yeah, but you used to talk about them. They seemed to piss you off a lot. The guy did, anyway, and it didn't take me long to work out why. I was invited with you to their house for dinner one night, if you remember, when I was home between uni terms? It was a horrible night. Callan – is that his name? Yeah, he just bulldozed everyone's conversation all night, cutting people off at the pass. You were telling us all a funny story about something that had happened when you were a child, and he interrupted you, mid-stream, and started with a similar story of his own. It was like he needed to trump you, before you got to your own punchline. You just blinked and shut your mouth, because I guess you were too polite to do anything else, but it was like he put you in a box and slammed the lid on you. It made me furious.'

'I don't remember that, but I'm not saying you're wrong.'

'I'm not, Mum. And when Jo corrected him on something he'd got wrong, he turned around and f-bombed her, in front of us all! Surely you must remember that?'

Adie pulled her bottom lip out with her forefinger and thumb, and frowned slightly, as she always did when she was thinking.

'Actually, I think I do remember that a little bit.'

'It was so disrespectful. I just froze, when he did that. It literally took my breath away, and I've never forgotten it. He was *so* nasty to her, and the worst of it was that she just rolled her eyes and let it go, like it was something he did all the time! Like she was so used to being abused, it didn't affect her anymore. That was outrageous. It did teach me something valuable, though. I promised myself, right there and then, that I'll *never* let a man speak to *me* like that.'

Teresa went on to confess that she'd thought about that night a lot, over the years. She also said that if any man ever treated her like that in front of friends she'd probably get up and punch him in the mouth, and walk out of the room. Tolerating that level of disrespect, especially shown in front of other people, was never going to be a choice for her in a million years.

'Any man who did that to me would only ever do it once. I wouldn't stick around to suffer a second slur, no matter how much I loved him.'

Adie blinked, astonished. 'Wow! That was certainly a big impression to be left with! But you're right. Callan Blackfoot wasn't a respectful man at all, and he was horrible to Jo quite often, actually. I remember a time when your dad and I were out with them one day, having a coffee after we'd all been to a flea market. Out of the blue – literally from out of nowhere – he said that he was pissed off with her because she kept saying no to sex. He wasn't joking, either. I was *beyond* horrified, as you can imagine, and so was your father!'

'What an asshole, Mum.'

'Honestly, me and your dad didn't know where to put ourselves! We didn't know them that well, really, for him to say something like that to us about Jo – especially while she was sitting there, and he said it as if she *wasn't* there! I remember wondering how we were supposed to react to that. I think I just took the easy way out and changed the subject. It didn't even occur to him, that it made us uncomfortable.'

'Or it did, Mum, and the manipulative prick didn't give a monkey's, what you thought.' Teresa's voice was quiet.

Adie grinned, and bit her lip. 'Yeah, that was probably more like it. Manipulative, like you say, and no respect for his so-called friends either. You know, he grumbled once to your dad that he'd 'married a whore and ended up with a nun,' or some such thing, and how was poor Bryan supposed to respond to that? Jo was his friend too! I never knew what the point was, of the terrible things he used to say. The man had no respect for women, certainly, but he didn't really seem to like *anyone*, to be honest. He even called his own daughter and her husband freeloaders, and I'm not sure that was strictly true.'

'Well, even if it was, why would he badmouth his own kid to people? No decent father does that. As much of a dickhead as *our* dad is, he wouldn't do that, would he? I also remember the way Blackfoot yelled at his dogs all night when we were there. I wanted to give them a cuddle, but he made it really obvious that he didn't want me to, and he yelled at *them* for trying to respond to me! He never stopped shouting at them all night, for one thing or another. I wanted to scoop them up and run away with them, and never let the bastard have them back.

'My heart broke for them, Mum. It was the shittiest behaviour ever. He wouldn't let me give them any love. They looked so sad. He didn't deserve them, *or* a nice wife. And I thought she was nice. He was fucking horrible, if you'll pardon my French.'

Adie had to agree. Any man who openly disrespected and belittled his wife in front of others, and yelled at his poor innocent dogs all the time, was definitely a few cookies short of a full tin of niceness, wasn't he?

She started to recall a few more of her and Bryan's conversations with the couple, now, and chuckled.

'You know, Callan didn't have any respect for his mother, either. I remember they had a big row and stopped talking, because she was convinced that he was cheating on Jo with a family friend. Quite a few members of his family believed it, in fact. He hotly denied it, of course, and accused his mother of trying to ruin his marriage. She became the devil incarnate, as far as he was concerned. The things he said about her were unbelievable.'

If Matty ever talked about me like that, it would break my heart.

'Urgh, Mum! I'd like to say that there's usually no smoke without fire but seriously – who in her right mind would have an affair with *that*? He wasn't even slightly attractive! All that fat, and hot air!'

The look of shock and disgust on Teresa's face, and her turn of phrase, made Adie burst out laughing.

'God, you are so funny sometimes, do you know that? You could never pretend *not* to be outraged, could you? Well, Jo was Callan's third wife, believe it or not, so he had to be good at *something*, at least initially, didn't he? But you're right, darling. Jo did put up with a lot of shit from him. I do remember that, and I don't know why she did, but believe you me, she wasn't as nice as she seemed. She was as bad as he was. In fact, she was worse, because she would *pretend* to be nice. Quite a few people warned me that she was two-faced, and nobody seemed to like him much.'

'Well, it had to be reassuring that you weren't the only ones who were uncomfortable around them, Mum. I suppose most intelligent people will only take so much bullshit, right?'

'Yeah, I guess that's about the size of it. It's funny how you can do your best for someone, and be as generous as you can to them, and they'll still only remember or gossip about the things they didn't like about you.'

'I've had friends like that too. I got rid of them. Life's too bloody short.'

Adie giggled. 'Good for you! I love how you so quickly get the measure of people You're a good judge of character, darling. It's a good skill to have.'

I didn't get the measure of Ross as quickly as I should have though, did I?

Adie shook her head, adamantly. 'No, but that wasn't your fault. He pulled a blinder, Teresa, and you were in love with him. You can't beat yourself up over his choice to hide that ruthless part of himself from you. Don't ever blame yourself for loving the man he let you think he was. He's the one who should feel ashamed, not you!'

'Feen says that everyone gets what they deserve in life. She told me that Ross leaving was inevitable; to clear the path for something better that's still on its way to me.'

'Then hold onto that, because it makes sound sense. Feen is never wrong about these things. She also believes that things happen, not just *because* they are supposed to, but *when* they are supposed to. If you can find some faith in that, it's the first step towards acceptance.'

'Yeah, I'm working on it but, going back to the original conversation, I'm really glad you don't see the Blackfoots anymore. They were bloody awful. What was their deal really, do you think? Why were they so horrible to you?'

'Oh, it wasn't just me. I think they hated almost everyone. Your father said he thought they were just waiting for a reason to fall out with us. He also said he wasn't sure which of them had the biggest chip on their shoulder, and I think he was right on both counts. I didn't realise until much later that neither of them really had many friends, and the ones they had seemed to be just as dysfunctional. Gosh, how bizarre!

The Blackfoots, of all people! I haven't thought about them in years!'

Or the Benthams, come to that. I wonder if Mick ever did throw Olivia out? They stepped out of our social circle, quite suddenly as I recall, and none of us ever heard from them again, I wonder what ever happened to them? Conversely, we had to actually turn our backs on the Blackfoots! Callan was just too much, in the end.

Adie cast her mind back now, and recalled her decision to step back from Callan and Jo, after a series of meet-ups where Callan had consistently put her down, whenever she tried to talk about anything. His attitude was condescending, when he let her speak at all. He almost never let her finish her sentences or stories before hijacking the conversation with something – *anything* – to try and put her, and her opinions and experiences, firmly in the shade where he clearly thought they belonged. It was interesting that Teresa had noticed it, even before Adie had become fully conscious of it herself!

But I've never been the most observant person, have I? Wherever she gets her ability from, to sum others up in a flash, it certainly isn't from me, or her father. I give people the benefit of the doubt for far too long, and Bryan needs to be hit over the head before he'll detect an undertone.

As Adie, recalled, it hadn't been long after the three of them had been at the Blackfoots for dinner that Bryan had begun to notice the nuances that always hurt her. It had started to wind him up too, and she wondered now if maybe Teresa had talked to him about it, and triggered his awareness.

In any event, they started to see less and less of the other couple. Whenever they did get together, Adie had largely stayed quiet, after reaching the conclusion that it was better to say very little, to avoid being shot down, patronised, belittled or ignored.

She'd grown weary of the man's mean-spirited back-biting about other people in his and Jo's circle too, especially when he gossiped about a mutual friend's broken marriage, and when he described in graphic detail how big a 'slob' he thought his best friend's wife was. She'd been a functioning alcoholic at the time, with a fair few problems to grapple with, but she'd been a good person, and worthy of respect. Callan's attack on her had been spiteful and pointless and, of course, it had been made when she hadn't been around to defend herself. Adie knew, from bitter personal experience, how hurt and mortified the poor woman would have been, if she'd known what was being said about her by someone who she thought was a friend!

She mentioned that to Teresa, just to 'poke the bear,' and was rewarded with a fresh wave of outrage that made her laugh out loud again.

'What? He talked about *her* being a slob? He had guests in his house for dinner, and he couldn't even put on a decent shirt, Mum! He sat at the table in a stained old t-shirt with a gaping hole in the belly. Yuck! Who was the *real* slob?'

'You're right, again. And of course, since anyone who will gossip to you about others will happily talk to others *about* you, I could only imagine what he'd been saying to his other friends about me, and probably your dad too!'

'He didn't deserve to have you and Dad as friends. You're well shut of him.'

Adie shrugged. 'Well, we weren't perfect ourselves, you know. We probably said or did things they didn't like or agree with, but we're only human, aren't we? We were kind to them, and generous with our time and our resources, and I don't think we deserved to be treated like that. And you're right; an older man who sits at a dinner table with a gaping hole in the belly of his shirt in front of guests – especially a young woman like you were – is pretty short on respect, even for himself!'

Adie had been more than happy to step back from Callan and Jo, and she hadn't thought too much about it, until they whined to Bryan that she had 'insulted them' by doing it. That had been a truly baffling outcome. The Blackfoots didn't give a toss about her, and they'd made that very obvious for a long time, so why would they have got bent out of shape about her disengaging from them? It hadn't made any sense to her *or* to Bryan.

She'd very quickly let it go, after deciding that trying to figure it out wasn't worth the mental energy, but Bryan was more furious than she'd ever seen him. As far as he was concerned, talking nastily behind someone's back was disrespectful enough, like Callan had done with his other friend's alcoholic wife and a host of other people, but actually belittling and denigrating a woman to her partner's face was simply unacceptable. No decent man would ever have so little respect for another. Bryan quickly pulled the pin on the friendship, as the more dignified alternative to what he *really* wanted to do, namely going over to Callan's house and beating the shit out of him.

It wasn't an apology for Adie in the real sense, but at least it was some kind of validation, that Bryan also finally understood how futile it was to keep trying to have a friendship with a self-opinionated and condescending man who knew everything about everything (even when he didn't), insisted on being *right* about everything (even when he wasn't), and didn't want to listen to anything – especially if it came out of a woman's mouth.

No woman can be friends with a rampant misogynist, no matter how hard she might try, and no decent guy would allow his wife to be treated like something on the bottom of another man's shoe. Blackfoot simply wasn't intelligent or respectful enough to appreciate that he might have anything to apologise for, so it wasn't a difficult decision for Adie and Bryan to break their connection with the couple altogether, and life moved on.

Adie did recall now how openly abusive Callan had been towards Jo in front of them. It *had* been shocking, but she was surprised at how the incident had left such an impression on Teresa, who would have been about nineteen or so, at the time. The fact that Jo Blackfoot had simply rolled her eyes and let it go was probably because it *did* happen all the time, but it was her own choice, wasn't it, to accept it? She wasn't a weak woman, or a particularly nice one, as it had turned out. If she was prepared to tolerate her husband's horrible behaviour towards her and other people, and believe or pretend it didn't matter, then bloody good luck to her. Neither of them spoiled another pair.

It's funny how the ghosts of the past come back, from time to time. I haven't thought about the Benthams <u>or</u> the Blackfoots for such a long time now, but here they are, in my mind, like I only saw them yesterday. And I have to give my daughter some serious credit. That incident with Callan – like so many others lately, with how her cowardly ex-boyfriend and her own philandering father have behaved – has given her so much clarity, about how a real man should conduct himself.

I really don't think I have to worry about my girl, and how the world will affect her. She knows her own mind better than anyone else I know.

There was no denying the fact that Teresa had dealt with some difficult stuff. A few of the lessons she'd learned were hard, but they were helping to make her strong. She *needed* to be strong, in the modern world, if she wanted to stick to her guns about wanting 'a more exciting life' than what marriage and motherhood would offer. Those things were important to most women but not to her and, sadly, she was facing a lot of backlash for her choices. It was wrong, but it was real, and she needed to stand strong against it, if she was going to succeed.

But Adie was quietly confident that her daughter would rise above it all. She had a pretty good measure of most people now, and while she still wasn't entirely sure of exactly what she wanted, she knew what she *didn't* want, and that was a pretty good start.

Like Miranda said, Teresa was destined for a very big life. One day, she would shine bright enough to blind the people who doubted or judged her, and *they* would be the ones with something to answer for.

Every day, she makes me proud. I can't wait to see what she goes on to do in the world. She's a rare bird, and I hope she gets to fly as high and as far as she can.

Chapter Sixteen

It had been remarkable, how quickly Tezzie Bostock had pulled her dream together. Chris was in awe of her, and inspired, too.

His own future also felt a little more solid now, after a time of deep uncertainty. Pulling the pin with his old boss Malcolm had felt like the most illogical thing he'd ever done in his life, especially because he hadn't even seen the project being offered by Stuart and his partner Fiona, when he'd made his decision. But cutting that cord had felt like the right thing to do, because the security that his job had once represented, when he and Daisy were planning their wedding and working towards buying a house, didn't feel important anymore. The need for new direction did.

Reconnecting with Suzanne had been a massive step forward for him too. Her visit to Teapot Cottage had been a significant turning point in his life; much bigger than he'd anticipated. The things they had shared on the night she'd stayed over, had brought them a lot closer. Chris now felt that he could have a relationship with his sister and her family that hadn't seemed possible before. They were his family too, and he *felt* that now, in a way he hadn't imagined he ever would.

Whether he liked it or not, his life had irrevocably changed, and he'd come to realise that he had to make brave decisions now, to avoid staying stuck in the past. Happily, those decisions were proving to be a lot less painful than he'd dreaded, in the aftermath of Daisy's death.

He was looking forward to starting his new job. Fiona chatting about her passion for restoring old buildings had woken up his own desire to do something more meaningful than wire-up a thousand identical 'ticky-tacky' boxes on housing estates that always looked the same, no matter where they were. They were the kind of places where, if you didn't have your house number on your front door, you could easily walk into the wrong house. The endlessly repetitive work on those places had bored him silly, and he hadn't even realised it.

Fiona and Stuart's work offer was a good one, and after Chris had seen the cottages in Keswick, he had been immediately convinced that it was a project he wanted to be involved with. The 'couple of blocks of semis,' as Fiona had casually described them were anything but ordinary. Chris had been expecting four fairly run-of-the-mill houses that needed renovation, but 'run-of-the-mill' could not have been further from the truth.

The houses were seriously impressive; three-storey Victorian homes, solidly built of stone, with high-pitched apex-roofs, and the ability to extend into their existing loft spaces. They all had big basements too, all of which needed refurbishing. To call them substantial was an understatement. They were spectacular – or at least they would be once they'd been renovated. They had amazing views of Derwentwater.

'God, I can't wait to get my sleeves rolled up here! These places are amazing! How the hell did you get them? There must have been a shit-fight and a *half*, for these!'

Fiona had laughed out loud. 'Is that a yes, then? To taking the job? Maybe you should wait until you see inside!'

Chris had shaken his head. 'I'm in love. Sorry, but I have just lost my heart to these. I'm in. No question!'

Stuart explained that they'd got the houses at auction, and he admitted that it really had been a battle to secure them. 'There was a lot of interest, although some people only wanted a pair, and another couple only wanted one. The family wanted to sell them as an entire lot, though. There was only us and one other guy who did want all four, and it really went to the wire.'

Fiona shook her head. 'I was sitting there with the biggest lump in my throat, because the bidding was going really high, and I was convinced they'd go out of our reach. I was devastated because I'd lost *my* heart to them too!'

Stuart grinned. 'I took one look at her sad and almost-resigned face, and it damn-near broke my heart. I told myself that even if I had to take a mortgage out on the stables, I was going to get these for her. I immediately raised the stakes by twenty thousand, after they'd been going up in increments of two. I wanted the other guy to know I meant business.'

'It must've been hard to hold your mettle *and* your face, even as you were wondering how you'd pull it off!'

'Yep, it really was. But I wanted the other guy to get the impression I would go as high as it took. I was tapped out at the extra twenty and even at that I felt like I was dancing on the edge of a cliff. But luckily, he caved, and the gavel came down in our favour.'

Fiona's eyes sparkled. 'It was a pretty audacious bluff-call, but it worked. And here they are... our four sweet sisters. Levers House, Lowes House, Rydal House and Elter House,' She gazed up at the houses, with real pride in her smile. 'Stu and I are more or less teetotal, but we drank a very nice bottle of champagne, that night!'

'And who could blame you for that? If the chance to save these old beauties isn't worth celebrating, I don't know what is.' Chris gazed up at the houses too. All of a sudden, he couldn't wait to get inside, to take a real look at the scope of the project.

The houses were all in something of a state. The two derelict ones were particularly sad but, as Fiona said, they just had to look past what was in front of them, and concentrate on how they would look at the end of the job. And there was no denying how gorgeous they *would* all be, with their glorious high ceilings, solid floors, and big rooms.

Every house had five bedrooms – six if you converted the loft spaces. They were massive; homes for families, destined to be filled with kids and dogs, and love and laughter.

'We can start as early as two weeks from now, if that suits? I need to wait for our crew to get reassembled down here.' Stuart's question permeated Chris' little bubble of imagination. He shook himself a little and nodded.

'Yeah, that does. It suits perfectly, actually, and since one of them has just been vacated, I presume the power's still connected, and could be switched back on? What would you think about me moving in here, in the short term? I could keep an eye on everything, since vandals love to target empty properties, and it might help keep them safe if someone's here?'

Chris knew he would have to stay in the area. There was no realistic way of commuting from Derby, and all of them knew it.

'We talked about that,' Fiona said, quietly. 'You could stay in Stu's caravan, over at the Stables, if you like. It's lovely, actually. He set it up when his carpenter came to work on the barn conversion. Its fully self-contained, and it's very comfortable and cosy.'

Stuart nodded. 'You'd be most welcome to do that, but staying here is a good idea too, if you'd rather. I do take the point about security. I'm sure we could make it work, for you to be here. The best house is still pretty scruffy, and a bit draughty I think, but the central heating still works, and there's still a cooker in the kitchen, that the tenants didn't want to take with them.'

'Well, I have to leave Teapot Cottage next Friday morning, so I could go back to Derby, load up my van with my stuff, and be back in plenty of time for a Monday morning start?'

Chris knew he had to give a month's notice on his flat, but he could certainly get a couple of friends to help him clear everything out and put it into storage over the weekend. That would mean he wouldn't have to go back there. He could simply hand the keys back to the agent and close the book on that chapter of his life. He wasn't attached to the place at all. He'd moved there after finding it unbearable to keep living in the flat he'd shared with Daisy. It had simply been somewhere to live while he figured everything out. He wouldn't miss it at all.

It was amazing, how well everything was coming together here. Even the timings were working. It was as if the hand of fate were gently but determinedly shaping Chris' pathway. It was amazing – and almost scary – to think that if he hadn't put Teapot Cottage on his list of pilgrimages for Daisy, he would never have met these amazing people, and this new life would never have unfolded. He'd simply have gone back to work, at his old job, and heaven alone knew what might happen after that.

The thought of going back to his old life no longer held even a scrap of appeal. Just as things were working out for Tezzie Bostock, the way she had expressed the desire for, his need for a new direction had unfolded for him too. He laughed a little, to himself.

Fiona looked quizzically at him. 'Are you okay, Chris?'

'Yeah. I know it sounds mad, but I'm starting to think there's a bit of magic at Teapot Cottage, just like you said.'

He went on to explain the conversations he'd had there with Adie's daughter, after having already met her at the other side of the world, and how they had got to talking about recovering from trauma and needing to find a new way forward. He also told her about how he'd reconnected with his sister there, in a way that he believed would take them both forward as reunited family.

'And let me guess – things are falling into place in ways you all could never have imagined!' Fiona was laughing too, now. 'Believe me, that is *not* a new thing. Teapot Cottage has a way of bringing people together and showing them what's important. Believe me, I've had my own experience with that lovely little house!'

She carried on and explained a bit more about how she had come to be there herself, and how she had met Stuart, purely by accident.

'I had no idea, when I arrived there, that within the first *minute* I'd be meeting the one real, true love of my life! Especially since I wasn't meant to be arriving there until hours later, when I would have missed him entirely. Something just compelled me to get on a train from Bath late in the afternoon, instead of the following morning as originally planned, and everything happened from there.' She shook her head, as if she still couldn't believe it on some level, herself.

'I even made up with my friend there; the one I'd hurt so badly. We found a way forward, and I'm not sure we would have if we hadn't been there in that cottage together. Things aren't what they used to be, but we are friends again.'

Chris was delighted. 'I know you said, when we first met, that you'd met Stuart there, but I didn't know the whole story. And what a story it is, Fiona! That's fantastic, and so romantic too!'

'Well, there's more. Remember that Stuart told you he was staying there himself, the year before, with his daughter Meghan? They were trying to reconnect after he'd been in prison, and Meghan fell in love with a horse in the field next to the cottage? Well, that's how they eventually ended up buying Beaconsfield Stables and moving to the area.'

'God, you weren't kidding in the pub that night, were you, when you said that you all had a Teapot Cottage story! I know Darren and Debby's too, with eventually getting pregnant there, and everything. But what *is* it, about that place?'

'Exactly what you said – a little bit of magic,' Stuart grinned. 'Believe me, I was the biggest sceptic on earth, of 'ethereal forces,' or whatever you want to call them, before I stayed there. Suffice to say, though, that the place has left me no choice but to believe in everything working for our greater good. Sometimes you really shouldn't question things too hard. Just go with them and accept them with grace and gratitude. That's the biggest lesson I took from it all.'

After they had finished looking around, and Chris had almost filled his little notebook with measurements and scribbled ideas, and taken dozens of photographs, they went for lunch. He texted Tezzie.

Project looks interesting. I've said a big yes. Dinner @ the Bull & Royal, so I can tell u all about it?

It was a few minutes before a text pinged back, and he started to wonder if he'd been too enthusiastic about suggesting they meet later. The'd been catching up a few times, mostly at Teapot Cottage when they would share a pot of coffee and talk about their plans. But maybe he was asking too much of her, to keep expecting her to share her time with him. He wasn't expecting anything from her. It was just nice to have female company again, especially with someone who had big, exciting plans. It made him feel less hopeless, somehow, as if there really was a way to move forward in a positive and meaningful way. If Tezzie Bostock could pick up the pieces of her devastated relationship, and find a way to be happy again, it made Chris believe that maybe he could too. And just now, in saying yes to this fascinating project, it felt like he'd made a solid start.

Happily, a reply text came through.

Sounds good. I'll come to the cottage half six?

He sent a thumbs-up emoji, and he tried not to dwell on the little spark of warmth that had flared in his chest, at the thought of seeing her later. He simply put it down to another positive thing that had happened in his life – meeting a new friend that shared his zest for life, who had helped him just a little, to find it again.

*   *   *   *   *

Chapter Seventeen

Teresa was exhausted. After five solid days of filming, and a couple more to relax at the end of it, she was ready for home. Her flight to London from Suvarnabhumi Airport was due to leave at nine o'clock in the morning, and she was already packed and ready to go. It was time to grab a shower and head downstairs for some food before hitting the hay. She needed to be on the train well before six thirty, for the half hour journey to the airport. She'd already managed to check in online, but the last thing she wanted to do was miss her flight.

The hotel was lovely, and very central, which was what she'd been looking for. It felt safe too, and the staff were friendly, welcoming, and helpful. When she'd arrived and told them what she was there to do, they were very enthusiastic, telling her the best places to go to get the footage and information she was looking for. They shared stories too, of what they knew, and how they felt, about the state of the nation.

They told her that Bangkok's displaced children needed all the profile they could get, in the world. More than twenty thousand were living on the streets, and more than a million had fallen out of education. The government wasn't interested in helping them stay at school or go to degree level, and their parents couldn't afford to bankroll that. It meant that their prospects for getting out of poverty were slim. Some of the people who talked to Teresa were genuinely afraid for the future of the country.

She saw it for herself; the filth and squalor, especially in the 'communities' built in ramshackle form along canals that were full of raw sewage and household rubbish and infested with monitor lizards. She tried not to cry, as she saw barefoot children in grubby clothes that didn't fit them properly, playing in the dirt as they breathed the air around the heavily polluted water. The fact that they knew nothing better was tragic. The way they were forced to live was 'just their lot,' and they had little idea of what life-chances they were being denied by a government who simply kept saying there wasn't enough money to improve their lives or prospects.

She decided to phone Chris Darcy, now. He was staying in Keswick, in one of the houses that he was helping to renovate. They'd texted a few times while she'd been away, but not much; just basically check-ins for her, and funny memes from him, just to let her know he was thinking of her. That was nice. She wasn't sure whether he'd pick up her call, with the seven-hour time difference, but she figured it was just past noon in the UK, so he may be having lunch, or getting close to it at least. At worst, she could leave a message to say hi.

She was in luck. He'd just downed tools for a sandwich and a cup of coffee. He sounded pleased to hear from her, and she was happy to hear *his* voice.

'Hey, you! How's Bangkok treating you?'

'It's hot and humid. Being on the streets makes me feel like I need six showers a day, but I've got what I came for, I think. I'm on a flight home tomorrow. I was going to wait until you'd finished work to call but that would be midnight here, and I have to be up at half past five in the morning. I'm completely knackered, so I'll probably be dead to the world by ten, and I'd miss my chance. How are things going in Keswick?'

'Great, thanks. We're making good progress with everything, so the timeframe of six months to get all the work done is realistic. I did wonder about that, back in the beginning. It seemed a bit optimistic, but Stu's team are really onto it. They're a bunch of powerhouses, when they get going, so it's all ticking along according to plan. I think we'll make our target of six weeks per house, unless we find something major to address, like dry rot or termites, or major issues with getting stuff supplied, or something. So far, we've had no major drama. We might be finished earlier on the second pair too, because they're not as bad.'

Chris went on to say that the team was doing one house at a time, and the one he was staying in was the last one on the list. It was liveable, so it was the lowest priority of the four, and that meant that by the time the team got around to renovating it, Chris might be able to move into one of the completed ones.

Tezzie giggled. 'Sounds like it's a big project. I saw the photos you sent, but I'm sorry I never got to come down and see the houses myself before I left. Once the funding came through, and I was able to order and get delivered what I needed, everything kind of happened at really short notice. I was more or less here before my feet even touched the ground.'

'That's okay, I get it. You had the momentum, so you had to keep going with it. I didn't have a hope of getting on a plane with you, as the timing's turned out. How's it been?'

She sighed, heavily. 'Oh, Chris. Honestly? It's been wretched, seeing all this in such stark detail! When I was here before, as a tourist, we kind of 'did' the slums, almost as part of a tour, and that was upsetting enough. But seeing the real guts of it, especially the parts the tourists *don't* go to, is so much worse. I dunno how they live like this.'

She went on to say that the children themselves were lovely. 'They're a cheerful, smiley bunch, even though they have nothing. But they deserve a decent life, a much better one than this! I know so many of them could really thrive in the right environment, but the government just keeps them living in the dirt. There's a lot of corruption here. It's outrageous, especially when you see other places like Sala

Daeng, Chidlom, and Langsuan, where the billionaires live in their fancy penthouses.

'Some have *mansions*, for God's sake! And fucking *castles*, if you believe that? Just crazy. A lot of have multiple investment properties in those areas too, and I really struggle to get my head around how that can be allowed to happen; how people can get away with flaunting such affluence, while so many people in the same city are leading such desperate lives.'

'Money talks, Tezzie.'

'But not where it should, right? Don't these rich, entitled bastards have any kind of moral conscience? It's like rubbing these poor people's already dirty faces in it. Everyone leaves it to everyone else to solve the bloody problem, and no one fucking does.'

'Yeah. It's insane, I know. But everywhere you go, it's always the same. Like the multi-million-dollar mansions of Beverly Hills being less than ten miles away from poor old cash-strapped Santa Monica, where countless homeless people live, and Santa Monica itself has a big wealthy population. It's so stupidly ironic, it's hard to get your head around it, that's for sure.'

'I know that even in the UK some rich folks can see the homeless living in cardboard boxes at the edge of their road. But what does anyone with money ever do about it? Nothing. They all see it as someone else's problem to find a solution for. Not enough people really care.'

'I think a lot of people do – just not the ones who have the power to do anything about it, Tez.'

Chris asked her whether she'd had any time for sightseeing, and she recognised it as his gentle way of getting her to focus on something good again, before she got too hot under the collar. She often found herself acting like a dog with a bone over an issue that bugged her, and she was grateful to him, for understanding that, and being so subtly adept at getting her to switch her attention.

'Not a lot. I did it all before when I was here with my friends. This trip has been mostly focussed on just getting enough footage to try and make a film from. I have been out to restaurants most evenings though, and had some really nice food, and I've had my two days by the pool. Last night I took a bus tour, which I didn't do last time I was here. That was pretty cool, actually. The city looks completely different at night, kind of magical, especially with the lights reflected in the water. I got some *stunning* photos last night. They're beautiful. I hope I get the chance to show you, sometime.'

'I'd be excited to see them. I'm glad you've had a little fun, at least. D'you think you really have got what you need for your doco?'

'I hope so! I've worked my arse off to run as much as I possibly can, so there has to be enough worthwhile footage to do something with. I've edited some of it here in the hotel and it looks okay so far. It needs to be – it's no easy thing to come back here! I've tried hard to make sure I haven't left anything out.'

Teresa added that the people in the hotel were really helpful too. They'd given her some good nuggets of information she could learn more about and extrapolate on, and they'd introduced her to a couple of people who had kindly acted as tour guides, taking her to the worst places so she didn't have to go there alone.

'Most people in the tourism industry here speak good English so I've been able to interview a few, sort of, who were willing to share their knowledge of how things are here, with the class divide and everything. A few have even been happy to be on camera, talking about how they feel about it.'

'That sounds valuable, and quite enterprising,' Chris commended. 'It sounds like you'll have something really worthwhile at the end of the process. Narrative from local people is always interesting.'

'Yeah. I had to shield the faces of a couple of people because they wanted to talk quite scathingly about the government's attitude to the poor here. They have relatives in extreme poverty, and they do what they can to help them, but they're frustrated at the lack of support from higher up. They took a chance to vent their spleen, but…'

'But they had to be anonymous so there wouldn't be a back lash,' Chris finished her sentence for her after she trailed off.

'Yes, exactly. I think more people would say a lot more if they didn't have concerns about their safety. But some do, Chris. There are people here who would want to shut them up, as much as we'd all like to think that's not the case.'

'I'm not very politically inclined, I have to say, but I do know it's a complicated government structure out there. I've also heard that it's become a little more authoritarian than it used to be. I guess nobody really wants to rock the boat.'

'No, they don't, but they still have opinions, and they still want to be heard. I guess if I can help in some small way, who knows where it might lead? Not that I have much experience with interviewing! That might come across as a bit amateurish, I don't know.'

'Well, you're a young starter, remember, and I don't think it would hurt to remind the viewer of that,' Chris pointed out. 'Might actually get you a few brownie points, you know, for not being all slick and polished to the nines?'

He had a point, she supposed, and it was nice of him, to put such a positive spin on something she was more than a little anxious about.

'I'm sorry again, Tezzie, that I wasn't able to come out to Thailand with you, as we talked about. Believe me, I did really want to.'

'I know, but as I've said before; I really don't mind. You couldn't put off that opportunity with Stuart and Fiona. It didn't make sense to do that, just to honour a conversation you'd had with me! We've both done what we needed to do, and its fine. It's only been a week. I'd have come for longer if you were going to be around too, but in all honesty I'm not sure staying longer and filming more would contribute much more to what I already have. I think it's worked out the way it was supposed to, Chris.'

Teresa meant it. She would have been happy for Chris to have flown out and back with her, and to go off climbing somewhere else in Thailand, while she shot footage around the capital, but it hadn't felt scary, being here alone. A lot of people thought Bangkok was dangerous, but it was no worse than anywhere else, as long as you were sensible about your own safety. Nonetheless, she was glad she was heading home, and it made her smile when Chris told her he was looking forward to catching up with her again, whenever that might be.

She was going straight back to her Greenwich flat, until she had finished editing her footage. She had friends in London who would help her put the documentary together. One friend who had taught media studies at the university of Bristol would be a big help. He had all the necessary 'big-gun' equipment that would help her put everything together, and he was happy to help her as a mentor, which she knew would be valuable training for self-production later.

With any luck, she would be ready to submit her film in time for the next Cannes Film Festival. She'd just have to keep her fingers crossed that it would be accepted. She wasn't sure what she'd do if it wasn't.

I'll cross that bridge when I get to it.

She decided she would head back to Ravensdown after she'd finished getting the film ready. It would be nice to be with her mum and Mark again for a while. They were easy company, and she somehow never worried quite as much about everything, when she was there. London was great, for all the contacts, and the ability to connect with a lot of other people who shared her growing passion for filming but, day to day, it was a serious drain on mental and physical energy.

I guess it's okay to admit that. Maybe I'm just not the kind of person who can live without buttoning off. Feen's like that, isn't she? She lives in the city for a lot of her time, but it eventually gets the better of her, and she flees to the sanctuary of the Lake District for a 'recharge,' as she calls it. I know why Mum is so happy up there. It seems like a world away from anything that can hurt you.

She grinned to herself now. *Maybe I'm more of a chip off the old block than I thought I was. Bangkok is certainly frenetic. I didn't notice that as much, last time, but I guess I'm seeing more of the reality this time.*

Teresa loved adventure, and travel, but she was starting to realise that she also had a penchant for closing the door, drawing the curtains, and 'nesting' in a quiet space, away from the fray. Who ever knew that she would be the sort of woman who'd ever crave a home fire? It made her giggle.

What's got you laughing?' Chris asked.

'I think I'm experiencing something of an epiphany, and it feels a tad strange, to be honest. I think I'm finally understanding the concept of work-life balance. I want to be flying high, but I'm realising I can't do it twenty-four-seven, three-six-five. What does it all mean?'

Chris laughed too, lightly. 'I think it means that you're a proper grown-up now. You've got past that point; you know, where someone asks you if you're tired and you furiously deny it, even as you're dying to crawl into bed and pull the duvet over your head.'

'Oh God! I used to do that all the time! But I don't mind admitting now that the duvet idea is very appealing. It's exactly what I'd do, right this very minute, if I didn't have to undertake the tiresome task of having to eat something!'

'Are you jetlagged?'

'No, not really. I have some melatonin, that I take at bedtime so I shouldn't feel too knocked around at the end of it all. For now, anyway, I seem to be okay.'

She'd been incredibly jetlagged after she and Ross had got back from Australia, until her flatmate Lucy had offered her a handful of melatonin tablets. They had been an absolute sanity-saver, especially since she went straight back to work, literally a day after landing. The tablets weren't available to buy in England, but she'd managed to pick up a few packs on a recent city break to Barcelona, and she was grateful now for the fact that she had a good supply.

'And speaking of tiredness and all that, I'm going to get some scoff and get my head down. It's a twelve-hour flight, tomorrow.'

'Okay, Tezzie. Have a safe trip home. Ping me a text when you land in London, and I hope I'll see you soon.'

Chris seemed pleased when she told him she was planning to head back to Ravensdown, after her edits were complete.

She decided it would be nice, to see him again. She felt keen to see the houses in Keswick, too. They sounded gorgeous, and he seemed very enthusiastic about the work being done. He'd taken a lot of 'before' shots, and she was looking forward to seeing the 'after' ones, when the work was all finished.

Chapter Eighteen

Stuart and Fiona had been adamant, from the very start, that everything they did in the Victorian semis was done from the ground up. It would all be done as 'bootstrap' fitting, especially when it came to the plumbing and wiring. There would be no compromise. They wouldn't risk trying to salvage or reuse anything original. Everything had to be new and done as if the places had never had water pipes or electrics in them at all.

They wanted the peace of mind of knowing that no shortcuts had been taken, and Chris couldn't blame them for that. He knew how destructive water and electrical systems could be to a house if they went wrong. It wasn't worth the gamble of using anything recycled, but it meant a lot of work for the team. In some instances, it was possible to 'thread' wires through existing walls and ceilings, which allowed Chris to utilize access points like outlets and light fixtures, to replace wiring, but mostly it meant opening walls and ceilings, and lifting floorboards too, to access and rip everything out, before installing new wiring, cables, electrical circuits, mounting boxes, and other equipment, with live, neutral and earth wires forming loops of cable operating on brand new ring circuits.

He was enjoying the work, especially as he could see how much of a difference the updated electrical circuitry would be to the houses. Antiquated wiring was a nightmare, and he was pleased that his employers didn't want to try and 'maintain the integrity of the dwellings' that far! He was pleased that everything would be brand spanking new. Fiona had gone to a lot of trouble to find retro-*style* socket and switch panels, in keeping with the age of the houses, so the finished product would all look beautiful, and appropriate for their age and style. Few people would guess at the intricacy behind the walls, and above the ceilings. The new wiring would be state-of-the-art.

Chris felt proud of the work the Winterson-Thomson team was doing. Everyone was skilled and enthusiastic, committed to seeing the project through, and excited about how the finished product would look and feel. It was wonderful to be working with such a visionary bunch who all took pride in their work. It was a far cry from some of the guys he often used to find himself working with in Malcolm's 'teams.' Sometimes they didn't pull their weight at all, and even the ones who did often managed to treat the job as something they had no choice but to show up for, with as little commitment as they could get away with. 'Jobsworth' was good name for a few of them too; guys who wouldn't do a scrap more than what they'd been contacted for. Teamwork was more or less non-existent, sometimes.

This was a different experience altogether. Chris was also happy about his new friendship with Tezzie Bostock. She was on her way back from Bangkok, and he hoped he would be around when she finally made it back to the Lake District. She was a friend, and nothing more, but he'd enjoyed her company in Torley, and there was a lot to be said for having a platonic female friendship. It meant he had someone to share things with, bounce ideas around with, and gain a woman's perspective, without any romantic pressure.

He wasn't sure when (or if) he would ever want to get involved with another woman again. Daisy was still very much to the forefront of his mind, and he often found himself talking to her in his head, while he was working.

What do you think of this, Daise? Would you put a plug socket here? Would you want more lights in the kitchen? I know you'd love the double-ended Victorian style bathtubs we're putting in, but you probably wouldn't like those tiles much...

It was probably a bit silly, he knew, chattering away to her in his mind. But it was *comforting*. Having a project to run with was good, in fact it was exactly the kind of distraction he needed, but he wasn't ready yet to close the door completely on his imagined line of communication with Daisy. It still felt important to 'include' her, as best he could, as he slowly moved on with his life.

Some days were still rocky. Some mornings, he still woke up knowing he'd cried in his sleep. Some nights it was hard to will sleep to come, without her there in the bed beside him. He could only ever pretend so much, that she was still a part of his life.

He knew the day would come when he would be able to let go of his monologue, at least a little. Eventually his link to Daisy would fade to something less intense; more casual, and less emotional. It *needed* to, so that he could properly move on with his life. But he was determined never to forget his sweet, sunny, beautiful fiancée.

Chris understood that moving on meant letting go, and he was already starting to feel that time and 'busyness' would help him do it. He didn't have to go rushing through the process of putting his life with Daisy behind him, but he'd already made up his mind that it would serve no good purpose to drag his feet and resist it either. He simply needed to do what he needed to, day by day, and week by week, and allow the healing process to weave its way through his life. He needed to do what Adie Raven suggested, and let life gently push him forward.

It's funny how you end up knowing you've got more courage than you ever thought you had. Getting past the bit where it even hurt to breathe, and I felt guilty for sleeping even an hour, in the aftermath. I didn't think I'd survive Daisy dying, but I did. Maybe we're all a lot stronger than we give ourselves credit for. I don't imagine Stuart or Fiona ever knew how strong they'd have to be, before they were *forced to endure the worst life could throw at them, and they are <u>still</u> being brave, aren't they, in the face of Fiona's cancer, and her uncertain future? They just roll up their sleeves and get on with living. It's all you can do, isn't it, if you don't want to be completely steamrolled and flattened by life?*

The human spirit was remarkable. Tezzie Bostock had managed to battle her way through what she'd described as the 'wreckage' of her failed relationship - and look where she was now! In bloody Bangkok, of all places, recording human misery, determined and committed to bring it to public attention. That was an act of bravery. He admired her a lot for it, and he had the feeling that this was just the start of what would turn out to be a remarkable career for her. She had a certain quiet fire, within her, a determination, and a faith, that she could make a difference.

He really hoped she could. The world needed more people like her, who were willing to stand up for the underdog. Too many people cared only about themselves. They weren't interested in making much of an effort to help the dispossessed. It was a big part of the reason people felt the world was going to hell in a handbasket. They all complained about it, but nobody tried to do much to stop it. Like Tezzie had said, everyone wanted it to be someone else's problem. Nobody wanted to feel even slightly uncomfortable about anything they *felt* they couldn't change so they didn't even bother trying.

Tezzie was a different kind of woman, and he thought that was pretty cool. Maybe there was hope for the world after all, with people like her in it.

Chapter Nineteen

Adie was looking forward to having Teresa back at Ravensdown again. She'd been a breath of fresh air around the place, and it helped a lot that Mark had such a soft spot for her too. Blended families could be a tricky thing, and the more people you added to the mix, the more of a challenge you sometimes had, to ensure that everyone got along, at least to some degree.

She'd been vastly relieved when Teresa had phoned from her flat in Greenwich, to say that she was safely home from Bangkok. The Thai capital was pulsing with life and culture. It was vibrant and exciting on lots of levels, but it also had a very seedy underbelly that couldn't be ignored, and the city was rife with scam artists, and others who saw westerners as cash cows to be ripped off, right, left and centre. Adie had been of the opinion that if Teresa wanted to go there, it shouldn't be for very long, and the sooner she got what she needed and got back out again, the better.

But her daughter was excited at what she'd filmed, and who she'd managed to talk to, while she'd been out there. She'd stayed at a good hotel, where the staff had helped her a lot to connect with people who had happily showed her around, and allowed themselves to be interviewed. Teresa felt she had enough footage and interview material to put together a compelling film. The spark in her voice had warmed Adie's heart. She and Mark were looking forward to seeing the finished product.

Teresa had worked hard at her MA degree in Film and Television, and she was almost at the end of it. She had also shot a short film, as her final submission project, interviewing temps in London, and getting perspectives on the positive and negative aspects of continual transient work. She'd interviewed agencies, clients, and workers. That little film was never going to set the world on fire, as a piece of work, but it was solid and relevant. Teresa expected to get a decent grade for it, and it would probably set her direction as a documentary film maker.

The Bangkok film would be her first foray into independent filming, and Adie was proud of how she was pulling things together. While she'd been floating around the world on her travels, falling in love with a wholly unsuitable man, and dithering about coming home and getting down to business, Adie had been worried that she might not settle. As it turned out, she still *wasn't* settled, but she did have a plan, and Adie suspected it would be one that combined her passion for travel with her emerging career as a film-maker. Maybe she would never 'settle' in the true sense of the world, but maybe she was never supposed to! Maybe resigning herself to a 'normal' life would simply smother her creativity and spirit.

It was a perfect choice for the restless, itchy-footed girl who never felt comfortable being in one place for long. Adie had no idea where that restlessness came from, because both she and Bryan had been 'settled' sorts, who never felt the need to keep upping sticks and relocating. They'd only moved house once and, even then, it had only been to suit Adie's ulterior motive that she'd quietly kept to herself. That hadn't happened until after Matty and Teresa had started at university, so it hadn't been a catalyst for ongoing disruption. There had never been any familial patterns before that, that could have instilled Teresa's chronic inability to sit at home for long.

But that was the magic of your children, wasn't it? They grew up and went off in different, often unforeseen directions, and did all kinds of things that either dismayed or enthralled you, and sometimes their behaviour was so far out of the box you'd brought them up in, there was simply no explaining it. Teresa was a free spirit, and Adie was coming to realise (with a little help from the endlessly pragmatic Mark) that instead of worrying about it, she should take a leaf out of her daughter's own book and embrace, celebrate, and encourage that spirit.

She knew she would never be free of concern, about what Teresa would be doing, and where, but that was all part of the 'good-parent' deal. Good parents weren't just in it for the time it took for their kids to become independent. Good parents *never* stopped worrying about their kids, even when they were old enough to have kids of their own! It simply went with the territory.

But it's important to rejoice in them too, in all their imperfections, and acknowledge their achievements, spectacular and small. I can still be proud of them, even as they make mistakes and figure out how to pick themselves up, dust themselves off, and carry on walking forward. There's nothing about any of that, not to love!

When she'd learned that her son Matty had been moonlighting as a sex-worker, 'servicing' wealthy old women as a sideline to his poorly-paid graduate job, she'd been upset, embarrassed and, yes – even disgusted – at his behaviour. But she'd almost exploded with pride in the aftermath, over what he'd learned about himself in the process of being wrongly arrested for the murder of one of his clients. It had been a terrifying time for the entire family, but once he'd been exonerated Matty had rebuilt his life beautifully.

Ruth, her first-born daughter, was a gem. Adie had given birth to her at fifteen and been forced to give her away. She'd kept the fact from her family for all of their lives, even after she'd found Ruth again and moved in next door to her and Gina, to try and be close to her in whatever ways she could. It had still been a big secret, even from Ruth herself, and the truth had come out could only be described as a freakish set of circumstances that nobody could have foreseen. Matty's murdered client had been Ruth's adoptive sister, and the fallout from revelations all coming to light had been seismic.

It had taken a long time for the family to recover. Everyone had felt torn apart, for a long time, until most of them started to realise that they all mattered to one another, and what could be salvaged *should* be. Adie and Bryan's marriage hadn't survived, but it hadn't been for want of Adie trying, and it hadn't just been because of her mistakes. He had just as much to answer for, and their marriage couldn't withstand it.

But, despite her failed marriage, Adie had discovered that her family was solid, and closely tethered by indestructible cords that could survive a lot of upheaval. She had put her kids through a fire, when the secrets she'd had for all their lives finally came out, but the cords had been strong enough to withstand that fire. There had been a bit of fraying and melting, to be sure, but time, love and new honesty allowed them to weave back together in a way that seemed to be working. Nobody was anywhere near as upset as they had been in the beginning.

They were all in a much better place now. Things would probably never go back to the easy-going way they'd always been before the events that had rocked the family boat, but with Adie's remarriage, two families had 'blended' well, with new dynamics emerging. It was inevitable, of course, that it would grow and change as a result, but Adie and Mark both believed that everyone was better for it.

Bryan was still bitter, but he was gone. His current circumstances had shown that he hadn't learned the lessons of the past. As sad as that was, it wasn't Adie's problem anymore. It wasn't Teresa's either, and Adie hoped that her daughter's new direction, careerwise, would take her mind off what was going on with her father. It had been wrong of him to involve her, and she had to concentrate on getting to where she wanted to go, instead of worrying about him. Kids shouldn't have to bear the burden of their parents' mistakes, should they?

It was inevitable, that life rumbled on, taking you in directions you maybe wouldn't have anticipated. Miranda was another case in point. She'd finally met the man of her dreams, but she'd had to wait fifty-odd years to do it. At one time, Adie would never have predicted that her outgoing, flirtatious friend would settle down. It was something she always *hoped* for; that Miranda would find true love, but she was a free spirit too, and it was clear to Adie that most men wouldn't be able to catch or 'tame' her.

But Max Kennedy had managed to do both! He was wealthy in his own right, so Miranda would never have to worry that he wanted to marry her for the wrong reasons, and he was happy to share all that he had, instead of expecting her to bankroll everything, like her young bucks had always done. Miranda had never minded, but it had always felt to Adie that she was paying for company, and her friend deserved so much more than that. She deserved a man who would cherish her, and fly high with her, and encourage her to *stretch* her wings, instead of trying to clip them. Max was that man, and the change in Miranda had been profound. Knowing that she wouldn't being alone in her old age, after fearing for so long that she would be, had made her feel secure in a way she'd never been before.

Love was everything. Nothing made any sense without it, and Adie was profoundly glad that she and the people she cared about had so much of it around them.

Chapter Twenty

'Mum; I've been offered a job by a national newspaper, as a war camera correspondent, and I've accepted it.'

Teresa's words came out in a rush. It wasn't the way she'd *planned* to tell her mother about her new job offer, but somehow there didn't really seem to be a 'right' way of doing it. Her momentous news just sort of wanted to come out, over a cup of tea in Ravensdown's big kitchen, so she let it, and the reaction didn't surprise her at all.

'What? Good Christ, Teresa! Are you serious? What on earth has made you want to do *that*, of all bloody things? Isn't it incredibly stressful and dangerous? And don't you need to train for *years,* for that sort of thing?'

The anguished look on Adie's face was almost unbearable, but Teresa ploughed forward.

'It is stressful and dangerous, yes. And there is training involved, but it's what I want. I want to shoot at the frontline – with a camera, I mean, not with a gun.'

Her attempt at humour bypassed her mother completely. Adie simply looked horrified, and unsure of what to say next. Teresa felt compelled to try and explain.

'The true horror of war escapes most people, Mum. The real cost of it, to humanity, isn't properly portrayed enough. I want to change that. I want to bring the plight of the victimized to the attention of the public, and to policy makers, in a way that they can't forget. I suppose I want to kick a world full of complacent assholes out of their collective bubble of ignorance, for want of a better phrase.'

'But why do you have to do it *that* way? Why does it have to mean going to war zones and risking your life, just to take pictures?'

'Don't do that.'

'Don't do *what?*'

'Don't trivialise what it means to make a visual record of people and places that have been devastated by some insane political despot or inhumane regime who thinks that blowing people and their homes up, or forcibly denying them their human rights is the best way to use or gain power. This kind of work has the ability to bring war criminals to justice, Mum, and save countless lives that might otherwise be lost if nobody intervened. Please don't make it less than what it is, just to try and make yourself feel better about it.'

'I'm not... I wasn't!'

'Yes, you were. '*Just* to take pictures?' Do you know how bloody patronising and ignorant that sounds?'

Her mother sighed, and shook her head in frustration. 'For God's sake, Teresa! I wasn't trying to minimise, *or* patronise! But you need to appreciate how much of a shock it is, for a mother to be told that her daughter intends to go to places where she might get shot or blown up, in her quest for the greater good! What am I expected to do? Not worry? Not express my concern? This is a huge thing to throw at me. You have to allow me my reactions to it, even if you don't agree with them.'

'Okay. That's fair enough. But *you* have to appreciate how important this feels, for me. I've only just qualified with my Masters, and off the back of my Bangkok documentary alone, I've been offered this incredible job. Few people get this big a break, so early in their careers. It's the opportunity of a lifetime!'

And turning it down was never going to be an option.

She didn't say the last sentence out loud, but she knew her mother would know her stance on it; that she would run as fast and as far as she could, with a chance this big, to do something so important.

She felt the need to try and reassure Adie. 'Look, Mum, I'll be classed as a journalist. They will train me fully, in all aspects of self-protection in a war zone, and we're protected under the Geneva Convention too! Journos working professionally in areas of armed conflict have to be treated as civilians. I'll be trained in battlefield first aid, and dangerous environment awareness, among other things. I'll be fully protected, to the best of everyone's ability, as long as I don't take any actions that conflict with my status as a civilian. And I don't intend to do that, obviously!'

She sighed, and tried to elaborate. 'All parties involved in a conflict are legally bound to protect journalist-civilians, and avoid deliberately targeting us. Our rights have to be upheld in every scenario, even as prisoners of war! The Rome Statute of the International Criminal Court establishes that intentional attacks against journalists and photographers and suchlike, are officially classed as war crimes.'

'Well, I'm sorry, but that's not much bloody comfort!' Adie returned, hotly. 'How the hell am I supposed to feel reassured, that if someone kills you, they'll be punished for it, supposing they're even found? A lot of them never are! And let's not forget that sometimes foreign civilians and journalists are shot dead or taken as hostages and tortured, and sometimes even beheaded, by renegade groups who don't give a fuck about being punished for that. Some of them actually *want* to be seen as martyrs, Teresa.'

'Mum!' Teresa was shocked at her mother's vehemence. The fact that she had 'f-bombed' the conversation was proof of how upset she was. But, she supposed, it wasn't realistic to have expected much less, was it? Adie was never going to roll over and simply say, 'oh well, alright then, have fun, tickle my tummy before you go.'

'You know I can't give you my blessing, to do this,' Adie stormed. 'I will support you, of course, because that's what parents are supposed to do, but I won't do it happily. You need to know that if you don't wake up and see sense; if you *do* go ahead with this job, without any real experience behind you, you will be doing it without my approval. Not that I suppose that matters much to you.'

'Look, Mum, I know I'm a rookie, but everyone has to start somewhere, and I will get top level training, not just for physical safety, but for the preservation of my mental health too! They won't send me *anywhere*, if they don't think I'm ready, but I really want to do this. Someone has to do it, for the good of the world!'

'I get that. Really, I do. I just don't want it to be *you* who risks everything to do it. Why can't someone *else* be the frontline hero with the camera?'

'Because *I* want it to be me! I can't honestly explain what it is that drives me to do it. It's not about heroism, Mum! The real heroes are the people of war – like the women who will do anything and *everything* to protect their children. Helping raise awareness of what they are continually suffering and dealing with is part of it. I want to be there, to experience what some of these people experience, because only then can I really understand it! And unless I understand it, I can't really show it the way I want to; the way I think the world should see it.'

'It's so hard to explain,' she wailed, in frustration. 'But I need you to trust me Mum, when I say this is something I just can't imagine *not* doing, now that I have the chance! I know you don't want me to do it, but doesn't what *I* want matter, too?'

'Not when it involves risking your life. Not when it involves me lying awake every night wondering if someone has captured you, and raped you, or tortured and murdered you and left your body in the middle of the street somewhere, in God knows how many pieces, as a statement of ruthlessness. Because that shit happens out there in a war-torn world, Teresa. You're naïve if you think it doesn't. Why couldn't they have chosen someone else?' she muttered half to herself. 'Please don't tell me you were the only one crazy enough to apply?'

Teresa was horrified to see her mother fighting back tears. She did everything she could to keep her voice even and quiet, as she continued to try and help her make sense of it.

'Three hundred applied Mum, and I was on a shortlist of six. Two of us got the job, and I actually feel pretty good about that. To be in the top two, from three hundred, is not a bad achievement. I applied thinking I didn't have a cat in hell's chance, actually. But they were so impressed with me, and with my Bangkok documentary, they told me I was a stand-out candidate.'

'Well, I'm sorry, but I wish you weren't,' Adie muttered. 'As impressive an achievement as it is, to have been chosen from so many, I just can't feel good about it. If something terrible happens to you, how do I ever live with that? How does this *family* live with that?'

'I'm not worried about anything happening, Mum.'

'Well, you should be. If you're not, it's simply reckless. There's no other word for it.'

'It's not reckless! I keep telling you! We will never be sent to places where the danger is too extreme. And if we're somewhere where it does become too dangerous, they'll get us out. I'll be trained to minimise the risks to myself and my colleagues. We *all* will! There's a lot of safety – more than you think – in that collective ethic of us all watching one another's backs. And I have the older journos to learn from. Their experience will be invaluable.'

Teresa knew her mother would be a 'hard sell.' She suspected that *everyone* would be. Nobody who cared about her would want her to put herself in danger. But she simply had to keep trying to explain. The desire to take this opportunity was almost visceral. War photography was something she now felt driven to do. She had to try and make them understand. If she couldn't, if they all continued to refuse to get on board with it, and just sit around howling at the 'folly' of her actions instead, it would be a lot harder to get on the plane, but she knew she would still do it.

I don't want to be ruthless! I hope I don't end up that way, but I have to do this, no matter what people think. Eventually, people will have to accept my choices, won't they? What's the alternative? They all give up on me? If that's the case, so be it. People might be uncomfortable, but that's for them to deal with. I can't be responsible for other people's fear, and I can't <u>not</u> live my life because of it!

When she'd talked to Chris about it, he hadn't been massively enthusiastic either, but he hadn't poured cold water all over her. He'd been deeply concerned, but he did recognise the scale of the opportunity, and her passion for making it happen. He understood how much it meant to her. His response had been more cautious; less immediately reactive, but that was who he was. Chris was very measured, and not at all impulsive.

He also understood that there was a process involved in getting officially employed war correspondents and photographers out to the front lines and back again safely, and a very solid infrastructure, around ensuring emotional and physical safety in an incredibly risky environment. Teresa wasn't going to be freelance. That meant she had more protection. It was something, at least.

He'd been at pains to point out that there was only ever so much a person could do, to stay safe, and that forces outside of their control could compromise or even kill them if they happened to be in the wrong place at the wrong time with no chance of escape. He'd used the analogy of climbing, and avalanches and other forces of nature that could rock up unannounced and cause havoc. He also, very quietly, mentioned ropes that snapped without warning, because not enough attention had been paid to the details of making sure they were safe.

'You get the idea, Tezzie, don't you? I'm not going to spell out every worry I have, around this. I'm sure your mum and other members of your family have already laid enough of that on you. It's a very conflicting thing for me, to be honest. I know how important it is that you go; believe me, I do, but I don't want to see you come to any harm. Just know that as a friend who cares about you, I will worry as much as they will, and for all the same reasons.'

He'd paused for a beat or two, as if the words he wanted were difficult to find.

'But I do wish you well, of course! I know you'll be great at this, and I'll be looking forward to seeing you get back off that plane with limbs and mind intact. I'll be interested to see your footage. It's exciting for you, to be going, and I'm excited *for* you! Just don't draw any undue attention to yourself. Keep your head down. Don't put yourself in a situation where you can make a mistake that get you captured, or shot, or anything.'

Chris had told her to embrace the challenge, but not to the point where she took any reckless chances. He spoke from his own experiences, of extreme climbing, in regions where many people thought it was 'silly' to go. He still wanted to do those peaks and, in spite of what people thought and said about it, he *did* still go and do them, and he had a lot more on his list. He knew how big a thing it was, to feel driven to follow your heart, even when it came at great potential risk. He got it, totally. But he never took more than a calculated well-managed risk, and he made Teresa promise to do the same.

It was a lot, to trust someone else with your life, and it was something every person who went to report on war, in whatever shape or form, had to do. Trusting the powers that be, to make sure she wouldn't be any more at risk than she needed to be, observing all protocols, and trusting her colleagues to 'have her back,' was something she had to do. They *all* had to; everyone who went. No civilian or journo had the space or entitlement to be a hero out on the front line. Everyone had to look after themselves and everyone else on their team, to the best of their human ability. It was a different scale of trust from any other Teresa had known or felt the need for in the past.

Yes, it was daunting. Yes, it was risky, and yes; it was scary. It was worrying for the people back at home, who also had to trust the safety nets that were put around her to ensure she stayed in one piece. But she trusted the process, and it was up to her loved ones to try and do the same. She could say and do whatever she could to reassure them but, in the end, how they chose to feel about it was entirely up to them. She couldn't let other people's fears stop her from doing something she wanted with all her heart to do.

I only get one shot at life, don't I? So why should I settle for less than I deserve? What does it matter, what Mum or anyone else thinks? I have to do what feels right for me.

She was grateful to Chris, for his pragmatism, and for his encouragement. That meant something big to her; that a kindred spirit, with a penchant for living life on the edge at times too, understood where she was coming from.

She wondered now, how he was doing. He was down in Keswick for another few months, and she wondered if it might be time to pay him a visit. They'd talked on the phone a bit, after she'd come back from Bangkok, and their friendship felt quite solid. She figured he wouldn't mind showing her around if she invited herself down to see the houses. She checked her watch and decided to give him a quick ring now, as he was finishing work for the day, just to touch base.

He was chatty, and he sounded pleased to hear from her. He chuckled when she asked him how he was.

'Ah, I'm still working through my demons, Tezzie, and laying them to rest, but you'll be pleased to know that I'm making a bit of progress with that.'

She commented at how more upbeat he sounded, and how enthusiastic about his work.

'Well, I signed up for an important project, so I have to focus on it, don't I? I'm part of a dedicated work team, and people are depending on me, so I can't let them down. It means my days are all pretty much gobbled up by the work we're doing on these houses, but that's no bad thing. I'm enjoying it, actually, even more than I thought I would. It's a fun job, and it's true what people say, that having something to get your teeth into takes away a lot of the opportunity to dwell on stuff you're better off not thinking about.'

He'd gone on to admit that by the time the team finished at night, and he'd got cleaned up and cooked himself a meal, he was too knackered to think about much at all. He'd started off feeling like that was a bad thing. He wasn't thinking so much about Daisy, anymore – at least, not in the way he used to.

'I felt really guilty about that, to begin with. It felt like I was betraying her, somehow, by not keeping her in the forefront of my mind. I talked to Fiona about it, a bit, and she said the same thing you did, right at the beginning; that Daisy wouldn't want me to stay stuck in the past. She'd want me to get on with my life. And life does have to go on, doesn't it?

'I have to let myself have a future, Tezzie. What's the alternative – to sit in a paralysed heap of grief and anguish, and achieve nothing for the rest of my life? I might as well be dead if I'm going to do that.'

It sounded to Teresa like Chris had turned a corner, and although he was clearly still feeling a little wobbly about it, he had come to understand the inevitability of it. Daisy would always be in his heart, and he still missed her like he'd lost her just yesterday, but now there was a glimmer of a pathway forward, out of the fog. It was a path he had to take without her, and he knew that there would still be times when his grief would feel as raw and visceral as it had on day one, but he was trying to prepare himself for the peaks and troughs of letting go, as best he could.

'You're doing great. Like you said yourself, there's no roadmap or blueprint, or timetable for grieving. It just takes you where you need to go. But you're sounding better; more positive, and I do think you're finding your feet again.'

'I'm not confident at all though, Tezzie, that I can ever fully put what happened behind me. Maybe the guilt and horror of Daisy's death will always be a part of my life. Maybe I'll never fully be able to square it away, and leave it all behind, but do I have to try, don't I?'

'Yeah, you do, mate. And for what it's worth, I'm in a slightly different place too, about Ross. Don't get me wrong. I know it's not the same. I'm not trying to compare it, at all. Daisy didn't make a choice to leave you. Ross did, so it's a different kind of grief, but after having my head in different place too, with the fundraising and the trip, and the documentary and everything, I understand what you mean. It's like Mum said, its life pushing us forward. Taking us to a different headspace that allows for a change of perspective.'

'What's important has changed, I guess, Tez. We've both taken big steps towards making new lives, and I suppose by definition that means leaving the old ones behind, along with the people we can't take with us because they can't or don't want to come. Do you still miss Ross? It's probably a stupid question, but I wonder how you feel about him now?'

Tezzie had thought for a moment. How *did* she feel about Ross Barker now? The pain of loss was still there, but it wasn't acute anymore. Now, she just felt sad about the past.

'You know, it's occurred to me that if I'd stayed with him, I'd be on a different trajectory, and probably a far less interesting one. He would have held me back. Not intentionally, I don't think, but he was pretty keen on settling in small-town Australia, so the compromises would all have been mine. By all accounts he didn't enjoy England much.'

'Well, he didn't give it much of a bloody chance, did he, if you don't mind my saying so? Were there any trips out of the capital at all? Did he even *want* to see past London? I reckon anyone who'd judge their England experience simply by living in that one crazy city is a bit of a shortsighted twat, to be honest.'

She laughed at that because he was right – as he was about most things.

'It's true. Clearly, there were more issues going on in his head than just the location. I don't know what they were, and

I probably never will. But that doesn't seem so important anymore, and what I *do* know is that he wouldn't have been happy at me being away taking photos or making films about war. He'd have kicked a lot of shit up, over that.'

I probably would have made the decision not to do it, if it had even come up as an option at all. I'm pretty sure the Bangkok documentary wouldn't have happened if we'd stayed together. I'd still be in bloody London, temping, and gnashing my teeth over what I was going to do with my life. Settling in the Northern Territories and popping out a couple of kids while Ross was away in the mines... that was never going to spin my wheels, was it?

She thought back to her and Ross' time in North Australia. That was where she would have ended up, for sure, and with what, as a career prospect? Sure, there were opportunities in Darwin; it was a fair-sized city, after all, but she and Ross had never talked about the possibility of her moving to Australia anyway. She'd made it clear that she wanted a career of *some* sort, and he'd more or less agreed to everything she said she did and didn't want, but he'd never actually invited her to make a home in Australia with him. Since she was being more honest with herself now, about their relationship, she had to admit that with so much left undecided about what their future would look and feel like, she'd wondered – even at the time – if he might change his mind about having one with her at all. He'd made the choice to come to London, though, and she'd taken that as a sign of real commitment. But even if it *had* been real commitment, it hadn't lasted, had it?

As it turned out, Ross hadn't been honest about very much at all, in the end. He hadn't been happy, but he'd kept his true feelings under wraps about a lot of things, and he'd chosen to run out rather than admit them.

What if they had gone further together, and made a real commitment? What if he changed his mind further down the track, about being part of the life *she* wanted to have? Where would that have left them, as a couple? If they'd stayed together, and Ross decided to do a big U-turn, she would probably have left him anyway, as the slightly less miserable alternative to ending up feeling trapped in a life she didn't want.

'All signs are pointing to the fact that it was never meant to be, Chris. Ross turned out to be a man I couldn't trust, and I'm sad, but I'm starting to feel a little more resigned now, to the fact that we want different things out of life. It took him splitting up with me to make me realise that. Maybe he knew more than I did.'

'Maybe he just got in first, Tezzie, before you realised your life was too big to have him in it. Maybe he knew he'd never be a match for you.'

'I've wondered about that, and maybe you're right. Maybe, when he boiled it all down, he just wanted a regular life, you know, something a lot less intense that what I want.'

'You are pretty driven, I do have to say. Not that that's a bad thing, but it can be a bit intimidating to someone who's not.'

'Maybe that's the key to understanding all this.'

'Possibly. But he still should've stepped up and been honest, instead of taking off without a word. No good bloke does that, Tezzie, but he *has* done you a favour.'

'I'm starting to see that. But what about you? It sounds like you're coming to terms with losing Daisy, but how are you feeling now about all that shitty stuff with your dad?'

She was conscious that Chris hadn't mentioned his father, or the truly terrible Fancee, since his sister Suzanne had visited him at Teapot Cottage. She genuinely hoped he was in a better place in his own mind, about everything concerning them.

Chris Darcy was a really good guy. He was honest, and caring, and he didn't deserve to be tormented by the worry that people who had treated him so badly all his life would expect something big of him, that they couldn't even hope to deserve in a million years. You had to have your limits with people who walked all over you and treated you with contempt, didn't you, even they were family?

'I'm doing better thanks, Tezzie, I guess. I'm kind of back to where I was, with it all. I've managed to put Jack and Fancee back in the mental box I put them in, all those years ago, and I'm not thinking much about them anymore, to be honest. I'm back to being prepared with the big firm 'no,' if they do rear their heads to ask for anything.

'It did help, that Suzanne gave me her perspective. They were horrible to her too, so it wasn't just me. I kind of knew that, but it was nice to have my own thoughts about it validated, especially by her. Nice to have her blessing, if you will, to step back and stay in the background. She thinks I have the right.'

'And I agree with her completely! So where are you with *her,* now? D'you think you'll keep in touch more, now that you've reconnected?'

'Yeah, I'd like to. She said she would too, so we'll see what happens. She's in the bowels of Southern Ireland, but she mentioned that the girls would like to meet their uncle. She's invited me to visit.'

'Maybe you should,' Teresa observed. 'It might be nice to finally meet your nieces? In essence, they're the only family you have. No man should be an island, Chris. Not when there are nice people who do want to have you in their world.'

Chris sighed into the phone. 'You're right, Tezzie. There really isn't anyone else. I never thought about it much when I was with Daisy. She was to be my family, wasn't she? But yeah, I think it might be nice to be a little more connected; you know, to have a sister and a brother-in-law, and a couple of nieces that I'm in touch with. To feel part of something bigger than just myself. It's starting to feel a little lonely, with nobody to love.'

Teresa tried to ignore the little pang she felt in her chest. She didn't want to be alone, without love, either. Just because she was planning to work in war zones, that didn't mean she had to forego love and romance, did it? It might be a tough call though, finding someone who would accept her chosen way of life. Kids weren't on the radar and – given her career choice – that was probably as sensible and practical as it was emotional. You couldn't risk leaving your children motherless, could you? The alternative was to do a different job, and that felt out of the question.

The future seemed clear, at least in part. But didn't war reporters and camera crew have partners waiting for them at home? Was it selfish to want that too? Was it too much to ask of a man, to allow her to routinely work in situations of extreme danger, and still be waiting when she got home? Would any man take that risk, to be with her? Would she be fair, in expecting that?

If the boot were on the other foot, if she was the one waiting at home for a partner in a risky job that might mean he didn't come home at all, how would *she* feel about it? Army wives and husbands did it, and many of them had kids. They accepted the risk and, as ever, the primary feeling that sat alongside love was hope. Hope for a safe return, even as they also accepted that there may not be a long future. The understanding and honouring of what it meant to that person, to go and do and be what they felt driven for.

It takes a special sort of person to accept a reality like that. Surely, at some point in her life, she would find the right guy. But she knew that compromise went both ways. She would have to be prepared for what a partner might choose to do that she might not be thrilled about, herself.

Chris Darcy was a case in point. He wanted love in his life too, yet he didn't want to give up extreme climbing. But that was fair enough, wasn't it? Mountaineering was his passion. Any woman he ended up with would have to understand and accept that. Daisy had been that woman, but she was gone. Chris deserved to have love again, but it would have to be with someone who was prepared to make that compromise.

'Tezzie? Are you still there? You've gone all quiet on me!'

She shook herself, and turned her attention back to the conversation. 'Sorry! Was just drifting off there, for a second. Anyway, I wondered if you'd like a visitor tomorrow night? I thought I might come down to Keswick for a few hours. It's less than an hour's drive. I haven't a car now, but I can borrow Mums old Mazda, and pop down.' She suddenly felt a little shy.

'I was thinking, you could show me the houses, and maybe we could go for a pub dinner or something? I presume there are some nice places to eat, down there? It's just a thought. It doesn't matter if it's not convenient. I know it's Friday night; maybe you already have plans.'

She felt a little foolish, like she was babbling and trying to correct herself, and she cringed inwardly, hoping that Chris wouldn't think she was being too forward, or barking up the wrong tree.

'It would just be nice to see you, have a pint and a quick bite, and a proper catch up,' she clarified, and quietly waited, with a peculiar feeling of dread in the pit of her stomach.

But Chris' voice was warm when he answered. 'That'd be *great,* Tezzie! I'd love to see you! I do get sick of chomping on brick dust and washing it all down with TV dinners and a lukewarm can or two, on my tod. We do go out sometimes, as a team, but most nights everyone goes straight home after work, especially on a Friday night. A pub dinner would be great. And some intelligent company!'

'Don't tell me the team are all knobheads?'

Chris laughed, and she decided she really liked the sound of it.

'No, they're a decent bunch actually, but the conversations are usually about the work we're doing, or football, or the woeful state of the nation. It gets a bit boring, after a bit. And they never hang around for longer than it takes to down a pint. They've all got partners, kids, and other commitments. I'm the only one who doesn't, so they kind of leave me to it. It's a good job I don't have abandonment issues. I'd be continually traumatised!'

Teresa laughed too. 'Well, I promise not to talk about politics or Everton's match against Hotspurs, and I know not one thing about wiring! We can talk about religion instead.'

They arranged to meet the following night at five thirty at a pub called The Dog and Gun, in the town, where he and the team sometimes went for a pint after work. It was a historic inn, and Chris said the food was good there. There was parking nearby, and he would pick her up there and take her back out to see the houses, which were a little out of town on the south side, along the Borrowdale Road, then they could drive back in for dinner at the pub.

She was a little excited at the thought of seeing him again. She was excited to see the houses too, because he'd told her a lot about them, and had sent different photos of the work in progress. They looked interesting, full of character, and she found herself inexplicably wanting to *feel* that, as well as see it.

It would be nice to have a little male company again, even if it was only with a friend.

Chapter Twenty-one

They were working on the second house, now. The first had been completed bang on schedule, and this one was a mirror image of the first, so it would simply be a case of replicating the work. If that went according to plan, they'd be starting on house number three in just a few more weeks. The target was completion of all four houses by Christmas, with a bit of extra time built in to cover any unforeseen issues that might take longer to resolve. So far, they hadn't been caught out by anything, and Chris was cautiously optimistic that they'd reach their proposed deadline with plenty of time to spare.

Spring was about to give way to summer, and he was looking forward to some *slightly* warmer weather (they were in the Lake District, after all) and the chance to sit outside in a beer garden after work. The evenings were drawing out nicely now, and he already had a sense of summer – that inexplicable feeling you get when you know the season is changing but you can't really say how you know – you just do.

Tezzie was arriving in less than an hour. She'd texted him to tell him she was on her way, and he decided to down tools early and get cleaned up *before* he went to meet her, rather than expecting her to wait while he did that, after he showed her around. Fiona had let him have the keys to the finished house, so he could show off a bit, about the team's work. The place really did look amazing, and he couldn't wait for Tezzie to see it. Somehow – he wasn't sure quite how – it seemed important that she liked the finished house, although he wasn't sure why it mattered so much.

He grinned to himself, as he took a shower. He was getting used to living in this funny big old semi-decaying house, and he thought he might just miss it a little, when the work was all completed.

The houses were far too big for one person, but maybe he wouldn't always be on his own. Maybe one day there might be a woman to share it with. This would still be a ridiculously large house just for two people, with its five bedrooms, massive reception rooms, and cavernous kitchen. But it didn't hurt to daydream a little, did it?

He set up the ironing board; after pulling a clean shirt from the wardrobe and deciding it could probably do with a press, to freshen it up a bit.

When he'd given up the flat in Derby, Fiona had insisted that he bring all of his belongings with him. She thought it was ridiculous for him to pay for storage, and more or less ordered him to have everything brought to Keswick, instead. Although the house was liveable enough, it only the most basic of amenities. Having his bed, his sofa, and a few other things around him helped a lot, to make it feel a little cosier.

He felt kind of 'at home' here now. He wasn't ready yet, to contemplate where he would go after this. He was content to just be in the moment, for the time being, and he did like Keswick. It was a lovely town and, outside of the main tourist season, it was a fairly quiet place. It was well connected too. Getting to bigger towns or cities wasn't a major mission, from here.

Things were going okay – better than expected, in fact – and without really making a conscious thing of it, he realised that for now, at least, he was content to simply let the days and weeks take care of themselves, in the same way they already doing.

Tezzie laughed when she saw him, and she ran towards him and gave him a big bear hug. He couldn't keep the smile off his face, at the warmth of her greeting. She looked great, and he told her so.

'Wow! I love this new confident woman! Your eyes have a very big sparkle, Miss Bostock! Living proof that life is taking a good turn for you! It's great to see you, Tezzie.'

'Well, it's *Ms* Bostock thanks, and it's good to see you too, and *you* look happier! I guess life is heading in the right direction for us both. I can't wait to see what you've been working on.'

'It's still very much a work in progress. Don't expect too much, and you won't be disappointed. I booked at table at the pub for six thirty, by the way, which gives us an hour to get down and back.'

Tezzie climbed happily into Chris' van, and Misty immediately launched herself at her, licking her face and making little yip-yip noises. Tezzie laughed, 'Oh, little love! She's really pleased to see me, isn't she?'

As they pulled up at the houses, Chris gestured at them. 'Meet the four sisters, as Fiona calls them.' He grinned to himself at the hint of pride in his voice. 'These are Lowes House, Levers House, Rydal House and Elter House.'

Tezzie was enthralled. 'Oh, wow, Chris! You weren't wrong! They're really something. I saw the photos you sent, but they're a lot more imposing when you actually stand in front of them, aren't they, with three storeys and the high-pitched roofs? Two pairs of two, side by side, I can already imagine how wonderful they'll be when they're finished. Let's get inside, to take a proper look!'

'The ones on the right, Lowes, and Levers, were in the worst shape, but Levers is finished, and we're working on Lowes. Mine's Rydal, and that will be done last. But Fi gave me the keys to Levers, so I can show it to you. We'll see that one last, so you can get a true sense of before and after.'

Chris unlocked the door to Lowes house; the one the team had recently started. It was still stunning, but the amount of work it needed was clear to see. This pair of houses hadn't been lived in for more than twenty years. The smell of damp, and old wood filled his nose, but Tezzie seemed to have no trouble imagining the house finished, and she talked enthusiastically about its different features. She liked the staircase, the high ceilings, and the sash windows,

Next, he showed her Rydal House, where he was staying. Again, her eyes sparkled. 'Well, it's certainly in need of mega modernisation, but its liveable enough, right? That old bathroom is a bit of a cringe, especially the loo, but I guess everything works. Are you comfortable enough in here?'

Chris laughed. 'Yeah! I sometimes think I'm *too* comfortable, actually! It's pretty scruffy and in dire need of renovation, like you say, but I'm starting to think I might not want to move out, when the time comes! Especially with all my own furniture and stuff in here. It kind of feels like home now, and I'm not sure if that's a good thing or a nightmare waiting to happen!'

The final flourish in Chris's demonstration was Levers House – the one they'd just completed. Teresa was gobsmacked, just as he thought she might be.

'Oh, my God! I *love* this, Chris! Are they all going to look this good, when they're finished?'

He nodded. 'That's the plan. This is the prototype, if you will.'

'I like that Fiona and Stuart have decorated it in neutral colours, for the best impact, you know, to maximise the sense of space, but people would want to put their own stamp on them, I guess. They're actually crying out for a few audacious colours, in my humble opinion.'

Chris laughed. 'Yeah, it's funny you should say that. If this was my place I'd do a few things differently, certainly with colour schemes. This is all a bit bland for my taste, but there's nothing wrong in here that a lick of paint wouldn't fix.'

'God, look at these gorgeous parquet floors! All restored and gleaming. And those sash windows have been so beautifully renovated! Haven't you all done an amazing job?'

Tezzie's eyes were shining. 'I love that most of the bedrooms have fireplaces, and I especially like the high ceilings. Not terribly practical, when you think about the cost of heating these days, but hell, these places have *so* much character, Chris! That loft conversion is amazing! And I think this incredible reception room is *begging* for a proper chandelier!'

Chris was more pleased than he wanted to admit, that Tezzie loved the houses so much. He wasn't sure why it mattered so much that she did, but he found himself laughing at her enthusiasm, which seemed completely genuine, and more or less matched his own. She was a bit like a kid in a sweet shop and, as she wandered around muttering to herself about what colour she might paint the dining room's back wall, and how the right curtains would matter a *lot*, to frame the spectacular street-facing windows, he felt something slowly move, in his chest.

He checked his watch. 'Have you seen enough, for now? Sorry, I don't mean to jog you along. We can stay longer if you want to, but time's lurching along and I'm starving. I need to eat something soon before I get the wobbles.'

To his relief, she nodded. 'I'm starving too. I didn't get lunch today. By the time I'd worked through the last online training module for the job I'm about to start, it was half past two. It didn't seem worth making anything to eat at that stage, when I knew I'd be out for dinner. Mum usually reminds me to eat, but she went over to the city today with Sheila, after her morning coffee meeting at Peg's. She wasn't around, to throw me a sandwich like she normally would.'

'I think you'll like the pub. The food's good, and it's cosy at night. I've booked a table in a little nook, where it's a bit quieter, and we can have a proper catchup. I know it's only a few weeks since I last saw you, but it feels like longer.'

After they ordered their food, and a pint, and got Misty settled under the table, Chris felt a little awkward. Suddenly, he wasn't quite sure what to say.

Tezzie grinned, and he wondered if she might feel the same way. They were friends, and recent ones at that, but they'd greeted one another like they'd known one another for a lot longer than just a few weeks. She was easy company, and fun to be around, and she seemed to find him the same way. Almost without thinking, he blurted out what he was thinking.

'Thanks for coming. I was really pleased when you said you wanted to.'

She looked a little taken aback, then smirked at him, cheekily. 'Why wouldn't I want to? You'd hyped the houses up so much, I had to come, didn't I, to see what all the bloody fuss was about?'

He responded with a bit of banter of his own. 'I didn't hype them up! You hyped them up yourself, in your own mind, but I'm glad it gave you an excuse to come down. I hope the old shacks lived up to your wild expectations!'

She laughed, a proper belly laugh, and he thought that was just wonderful.

'Are you kidding? God, yes! They totally did, and I'm in love with all four of them – even the sad old place you've just made a start on. I think I like that one the best, actually. It will be the most dramatic in my own mind, once it's done up, because I will have seen the full reno on the same house. Not that it should matter, but I dunno – somehow, it might… Oh, and I didn't, by the way.'

'Didn't what?'

'Need an excuse to come down. I wanted to. It felt important, you know; to reconnect. Oh God, what did I just say? Ignore that, or at least any implication that I can't live without you, or something silly like that.'

She laughed to herself, even as she blushed, violently, and he could see that she was self-conscious. He decided to put her out of her misery.

'Tez, it's fine. I know what you mean. I've been really excited to see you too, and I have no idea what it means either. But I am not going to sit here and put it under a microscope, and nor should you. We're two consenting adults. We like each other, and we enjoy spending time together and having a laugh, and there's nothing wrong with that, is there?'

His voice was light and soft, but he was aware of the weight of his words and, even as he said them, he felt a short, sharp stab of regret, that it wasn't Daisy sitting here at a pub table with him. She would have tucked into a steak pie and chips, ended up with most of the gravy all over her face, and she'd have laughed it off without feeling in the least bit self-conscious. Nothing much had *ever* made her feel self-conscious. He couldn't bear Tezzie's embarrassment. The last thing he wanted was for her to feel uncomfortable.

And what he said was true. They were two adults, free to have dinner or do anything else, with someone. Whether they chose to let their baggage get in the way of enjoying one another's company was something else altogether, but neither of them had to make excuses for spending time with someone who cheered them up.

'I guess I feel safe with you,' she said, unexpectedly. 'That's all anyone wants, isn't it – to feel safe? I don't think it's ever so much a question about whether or not we actually like or dislike someone, unless of course we feel we know them well enough to properly decide. I think how we feel about someone is related to whether or not we feel *safe* with them. Safe, to say things, be yourself, share parts of yourself, you know, that sort of thing. I don't think you can be anything, with another person – not even friends – if you don't feel at least some level of security.'

It made perfect sense. Safety. That was the fundamental cornerstone of *everything* wasn't it? Whether or not you felt safe.

'Oh, God. You know, I think that's the best way I've ever heard it described. *Safe.* And not just in the physical sense. Feeling emotionally safe is everything, isn't it?'

Teresa simply nodded, as Chris found himself processing what she'd said. It resonated with him, profoundly. He cleared his throat. She turned to face him, as he rubbed his eyes with his knuckles and looked wearily at her.

'You know, I'd never thought of it that way before, but you're absolutely right. I never really felt safe with anyone, before Daisy. I didn't feel safe with my parents. I mean, I did in the physical sense, in terms of having a roof over my head, and food on the table. But emotionally? No way. Never, not for any stretch of time that I can remember.'

'They never gave you anything good, emotionally, Chris. Jack hung you out to dry, in fact. You grew up vulnerable. I wonder how he lives with himself.'

She said the last sentence almost under her breath, but Chris responded in a way that surprised even himself.

'He lives with himself very successfully, Tezzie, because he's so emotionally stunted, he hasn't the faintest *idea* of the damage he's caused. He exists in a bubble of ignorance. He's a selfish bastard who never gave a damn about anything other than getting his own needs met. But, after talking to Suzanne, I no longer think that was wilful. He just didn't – and still doesn't – know how to be a decent dad! And I have to forgive him for that, don't I? I mean, who's the loser, if I don't? He doesn't give a toss, Tez! I'm the one who'll be eaten alive by all the shit he put me through, if I don't let it go.'

Teresa was thoughtful. He could see the cogs turning, as she chose her words with care.

'Maybe you're right, you know, about Jack not being wilfully terrible. I've been wondering if he had some biological weirdness going on, like gaps in his mental framework, or something. Deficits, that wouldn't enable him to do or be certain things to someone. Parts missing, you know? Something like that.'

'What, you mean like synapses falling, failing to connect? I suppose that makes sense, in a way. We don't know as much as we should, do we, about how the human brain works? It could be biological, I suppose; a chemical deficit that manifests as a lack of capability.'

He tried to rationalise that. 'Knowing right from wrong on some abstract level isn't the same as actually *feeling* it, that your kid is in pain because of you. Maybe it's the synaptic leap to empathy that Jack could never pull off, or maybe it's a critical biological tie that's missing; the one that parents are supposed to feel, where they'll fight to the death to protect their children.' He shook his head and sighed, heavily.

'That might explain why he's never been able to love his own son or daughter, but it doesn't exactly explain why he's been able to give so much love to his batshit-crazy wives.'

Teresa shrugged, helplessly. 'I dunno, Chris. Different kinds of love? Maybe he's capable of some but not others? Personally, I think it's all tied up somehow with knowing what he needed from other people, but not being capable of giving what others expected from *him*.'

'You might be right about that too, Tezzie. Kids don't give much to their parents, do they? And even when they become adults, it's probably a bit wrong for their parents to expect a lot from them.'

'And nobody knows what goes on behind the doors of someone else's relationship, do they? Maybe it wasn't as rosy as it looked, with him and his wives. Perhaps he was harder work than you know, for them.'

'Maybe. Who knows? And honestly, I really don't care how difficult he might have been, for any of them. What I do know is that nobody should have a kid if they're not prepared to protect it and put it first. I have to forgive Dad, for the sake of my own sanity, but I'll never forgive any of those bitches, for the way they treated me. They all knew right from wrong, and it's too much of a coincidence to say all three of *them* had failing synapses too!'

'Your dad *allowed* them to be horrible. That was a conscious, active choice – to do nothing to protect you. It's a tall order, to forgive any parent for that, but fair play to you if you can. Its more than I could do, I think.'

'Fancee is the worst. She's selfish and ruthless to a fault.'

Chris was surprised, when Tezzie remarked on how little emotion he had in his voice now, when he talked about his father and stepmother.

'The first time you talked about everything, when you were staying at Teapot Cottage, your voice and your face were full of anguish. Now, you're talking a lot more objectively, and matter-of-factly, about it all. It's a significant step forward, Chris. Maybe you haven't realised how far you've come, in laying that demon to rest. It seems to me that Suzanne's visit was a big turning point for you, over that.'

He closed his eyes and nodded. 'You're right, about all of it. And, going back to talking about safe, I think Daisy was the one woman I ever had a relationship with, who never expected more from me than what I was able to give. Previous girlfriends, well, let's just say that I was always the one that got dumped, even though with a few I did feel relieved, that they'd got in first. I've never been comfortable with letting people down. But I wasn't what a lot of women wanted.'

'Daisy knew your limits and she accepted them, and never judged you for them. She took you for who you are.'

Teresa's statement was simple, yet profound.

'Yeah, it was different with her. I just knew we were for keeps; you know? It's hard to explain…'

'You felt safe.'

'Yeah. I did. Tez, has anyone ever told you how good you are, with the nutshell comments? You have a terrific way of putting everything in context. You don't take three hundred words to say what you can in three or thirty. That's a good skill, and I appreciate it.'

It occurred to him that she had just done in a handful of sentences what he suspected a high-charging counsellor wouldn't manage to do in a year of therapy.

'I guess I've never really understood how hard it might be for a woman to feel really safe with *me*, either, as an extreme climber. But Daisy seemed to. Well, at least, she never said she didn't.'

'Don't doubt that, Chris. Don't *ever* doubt it. You'd have known if she had any big qualms. Clearly, she didn't. She was one in a million. I wish I could have met her.'

Chris bit his bottom lip. 'She was pretty special, I'll give you that, but hopefully not one in a million. That significantly reduces the odds of me ever meeting another woman I could one day feel the same way about. And I'm only twenty-eight. I'd like to think I could one day meet someone else who would enable me to feel safe, and loved. More importantly though, I'd want her to know *she* could feel safe with *me*. That might be something of a taller order.'

'Given your penchant for scuttling up mountain faces and placing all your trust in a piece of rope, you mean?'

'Precisely.'

Tezzie shrugged.

Well, for what it's worth, *I* feel safe with you. I feel safe enough to explain how I feel about a lot of things, and there's few people in my life I can say that about. I told Ross everything I could, about myself, and it turns out I shouldn't have. But, looking back, I think I told him so much because I thought he should know, not because I wanted to feel understood. They were two different things. I told him stuff in *hope*, but not in real *confidence*, I don't think.'

'And the hope was misplaced, because on some level, even subconsciously, you knew it wouldn't work, because you had to actually try, to get him to understand you.'

She nodded, slowly, as she considered his words. 'You're so right. It shouldn't be about trying, should it? At least, not that hard, with someone you think is your everything.'

She turned to face him instead, and it felt to him like something small but significant had changed for her too. She looked less bothered by the recent events of the past. Maybe she'd moved on a little, too. She put her head on one side, now, and smiled at him gently.

'You mentioned kids, before. You said that people shouldn't have them if they weren't going to put them first, above everything. Did you and Daisy plan to have them? Is that something else you're trying to come to terms with? The loss of another dream you had with her?'

Chris shook his head. 'We had a really big talk about that. She wanted us to have children. I didn't, but we agreed to compromise if one turned up. To be honest, Tezzie, kids aren't something I've ever wanted or planned for. Complicated reasons, as you can probably imagine, but children are definitely not on my must-have list.'

He explained that he and Daisy had regarded being together as more important than anything else but, now that she was gone, he'd returned to thinking mostly about himself and his own needs. His plans for the future were still being reformed, but they didn't include raising a family.

'I don't talk about it much, because a lot of people think I'm a bit weird if I admit to not wanting to walk down that road. I mean, most guys want to procreate, don't they? I'm a bit of an oddity, in bucking the trend. Some guys definitely see me as a social pariah, but keeping the family gene pool going just isn't big on my list, like it is for most men. Whenever it comes up, it's one of those conversations that ends up like the proverbial needle scratching across a record, so I never really talk about it.'

He went on to add that he had to deal with people asking him if he didn't want to have kids because he was afraid to be around them. 'Like maybe I don't trust myself, like I might be some kind of paedo or something. Its fucking outrageous, but that's what some crass bastards somehow feel entitled to ask me.'

'That's awful. I can see why you don't bring it up in conversation. I don't want to have children either, and it's something I'm always being called upon to justify myself over, like its anyone else's bloody business! I've had my fair share of hostile comments from men *and* women, about the fact that I don't want to be a mother. I think that says a lot more about them than it does about me, but I've never considered the male perspective on childless choice. A man experiencing censure from his peers: I didn't even know that was a thing!'

'It is, believe me, and I can understand why so many people go on to comply with social expectations and have kids, because the pressure is just so great.'

'I suppose you love them when they come. You adjust, I guess, don't you? Life goes in a completely different direction, and you go where it takes you. But it's one of those things that everyone thinks is their business. That's what irritates me the most – the fact that people can't respect my choice. Don't get me wrong; a lot do, but it changes everything when your friends all start having babies and you don't. You're left on the outside of everything. You suddenly have nothing to contribute, so they stop seeing you as a critical part of their social circle. They can't just come out and get pissed on cocktails at the drop of a hat anymore, so they avoid you because it's easier than letting you down.'

'Yeah, the spontaneity goes, and you don't fit into the changing landscape of their lives so easily anymore. I get it. It's a lonely place to be, unless you hook in with other people who feel the same way you do.'

Tezzie sighed, through her teeth. 'What gets me is all the assumptions. Because I don't want my own children, none of my child-endowed friends even want to talk about *their* kids with me! They just assume I don't want to know. They certainly never ask me to babysit – and I would, you know? I do want to know about their kids! I have no problem with being an aunt, but very few of them seem to get that. They avoid even talking about what's changed for them. They've forgotten that they've been my friends for ever, and that I do still care what's going on in their lives. My brother isn't like that; he knows I love my nieces and enjoy spending time with them, but far too many people just assume I don't care. It's awful.'

'Well, maybe they don't know how to act around you anymore. Have the conversations with them, Tez. Let them know you're still there, and interested, and willing to engage. Assumptions can drown good friendships. It feels like somehow, over the time, we've lost the art of really talking to one another, haven't we? I think we need to fight to keep that, before we all become so fragmented we end up in bubbles so thick, there's no way for anyone else to get in.'

'I worry about what will happen when I start working at front lines. Will people know how to talk to me then? My life will be as different as night and day, from what my friends are all doing.'

'I think it's important that you keep the communication lines open, whichever way you can, and have the conversations about that too, with people who matter. Let them know you need them. Out there, in Syria, Ukraine, or wherever else war will eventually pop up and you get sent to, having strong connections to people back home who care about you will be critical to you feeling like you're not in an isolated bubble. Like you said to me once – no man is an island? No woman should be one either, Tezzie.'

I don't want you to be an island I can't get to.

He was surprised at that thought, that had whizzed through his head, and he was relieved that he hadn't spoken the words aloud!

What was going on, here? He looked at Tezzie, and she looked at him, and she held his gaze for more than just a moment.

In that moment, something happened. Something moved, in his stomach. He suspected it did for her, too, because something changed in her eyes. She smiled, just slightly, and reached over and took his hand. He grasped it and squeezed it, ever so slightly. When she spoke, he had to strain to hear it. It was almost as if she only half wanted him to hear what she needed to say.

'I'm an ordinary woman, and there's nothing special about me. I would feel safe with you, without question, no matter what you wanted to do. So, please don't think you'll never find another woman like Daisy. I don't think you'll have much trouble at all, in finding love again, when you decide you're ready for it. There'll be a ton of lovelies, lining up.'

He felt the lump in his throat, and realised how hard it was to breathe properly, all of a sudden. He looked at the floor, and mumbled words that fell over one another, but he knew he had to get them out. All of a sudden, it was the only thing that mattered; that he let them come out.

'What if I've already found it? What if love is sitting right here in front of me, Tezzie? I'm sorry. Maybe it's not what you want to hear, and maybe I'm barking up the wrong tree, but let me say that you are anything *but* ordinary, and there is nothing about you that *isn't* special! Ever since you phoned yesterday, and I knew you were coming tonight, I haven't been able to stop thinking about how well we could fit together. I would like to see where this could go, if you would?'

His heart was in his mouth. What if he'd read the signs wrong? What if his gut-driven instinct, to take this leap of faith, had been wrong? What if she wasn't ready, or didn't see him that way at all?

He couldn't meet her gaze. He couldn't find the courage to look at her face. He was so afraid that what he'd just said had shattered a perfectly lovely friendship.

'I can't believe I just said all that, and I can't believe how shit-scared I am, right at this very moment.' He spoke in a rush, to the floor, and he wasn't prepared at all when Tezzie reached across the table and lifted his chin with her forefinger.

'Look at me, please. Chris? Please, look at me.'

He dragged his eyes towards her face, and was humbled to see that her eyes, just like his, were swimming with tears.

He let his fall, as he bit his lip.

For fuck's sake! Look at me! Sitting here, crying in the pub. What a bloody sap!

Tezzie let her tears fall too. When she spoke, her voice was husky.

'I didn't know what this was, even tonight as I was driving down here. All I knew was that *not* coming down was unthinkable, and the minute I saw you and Misty, something clicked into place, in my head. I think something clicked in my heart too. My feeling is that we *need* to see where this goes. I think we'd be doing ourselves great harm if we *didn't,* and I think we've both had enough of that already, don't you?'

She scraped back her chair and stood up, and came around to Chris' side of the table. He stood up too, and she stepped into his arms, and he held her close. The feel of her was wonderful. The smell of her was intoxicating. Her hair smelled of sweet almonds and he inhaled, deeply.

He whispered in her ear; 'I am not going to kiss you for the first time in here, in this pub, in front of everyone, but please be sure that I plan to kiss you very thoroughly indeed, as soon as we get out of here.'

She giggled, and he felt it through her whole body.

'I'll have to make a quick decision then, about whether a strawberry sundae is going to be worth putting off a kiss with my very own Mr Darcy.'

Chris laughed, with relief. 'I'd suggest that it isn't, but it's entirely up to you.'

'Oh, get you! Mr Full-of-himself! Just for that, you can wait until after I've had my pudding.'

'If you don't eat your pudding, you can't have any kisses. How can you have any kisses if you don't eat your pudding?'

Teresa collapsed in his arms, shaking with laughter.

'Nice take, on Pink Floyd! Very clever. Okay, pudding, then kisses. In that order.'

The tension had been broken. They were back to being in banter-mode, and for that he was grateful. Their direction was clear now, and certainly he could wait until she'd had her ice cream before he kissed what might be left of it from her lips. He decided to have a strawberry sundae too.

If you can't tempt them with kisses, join them with food.

As they ate their desserts, they kept grinning and winking at each other, and bursting into random fits of giggles. Tezzie kept shaking her head and closing her eyes. She was like a fourteen-year-old, all self-conscious and smirky, and Chris felt fifteen; gawky and slightly overwhelmed.

What the hell have we just done?

He wasn't sure. But what he *was* sure of, was the fact that it didn't feel wrong. Even as his thoughts touched on Daisy, he still saw her smiling, in his mind's eye. He had the absurd but comforting notion that she would approve of this aspect of him moving on. Whether he and Tezzie would make a go of things, it was still unclear. But they had so much in common, and they felt the same way about so many things – including each other. What better starting point could there possibly be? They had to give it a shot, didn't they? What was the alternative? Always wondering, possible for years to come, if they should have?

Time would tell, where it went, where *they* went, as a couple but, after leaving the pub, Chris found himself unable to make it as far as the van before the urge to kiss Tezzie finally overwhelmed him. He pushed her gently against a lamppost and held her face in his hands. She put her arms around his neck and, as their lips met for the first time in a sugary, strawberry-ice-cream-flavoured kiss that made him turn to jelly inside, the first feeling that warmed him was a sense of coming home.

Chapter Twenty-two

'My God, Darcy! If you kiss me like that again, you're going to have to hold me up! My knees have completely gone!'

Teresa was beside herself. Nothing in her life had ever felt like that. It was like an electric shock. All of a sudden, the chemistry was there, in a rush, and virtually overwhelming. Did she want to stop kissing him? Hell no. It was the best feeling she'd ever had in her life. Her first kisses with Ross hadn't felt like this. They had been lovely, yes, but the chemistry had been a lot less of a wow-factor. If she was honest with herself, it had been more hopeful than actual. Yes, there had been a spark, and it had been rather delicious, but it hadn't been *anything* like this.

Chris was blinking, as if he'd been in a dark room, and someone had just switched on the lights. He started to laugh, and she wasn't quite sure why, until she realised that he was in a state of disbelief, too.

'Well, I think that answers the question about whether or not this is the right thing to be doing. Now, I can't imagine never doing it again.'

She grinned at him. 'Then you'd *better* do it again, hadn't you? You know, just to make *sure* it's the right thing?'

'It's not the kind of thing I'd normally make a mistake about, Tezzie.' Chris' voice was serious, but his eyes were dancing. Teresa stepped forward and put her arms around him again. This time, *she* kissed *him*, and it felt as good as it had when he'd done the 'first favour.' And then he kissed her again. And again, after that.

'Mm… yummy,' she whispered. 'I could get very used to this, very quickly. And let me just say; now that you've started, I really hope there's no danger of you stopping.'

It was only after a teenage youth wandered by and muttered; 'urgh, get a room,' that they broke apart fully, and started walking back to her car. Chris pulled her close again.

'Wow! Just for the record, this was *not* what I had planned! I hope you don't think I've lured you down here just so I could pull a charm offensive and have my wicked way with you.'

'What, you mean you *don't* want to do that? Oh, God, I'm gutted!'

Teresa kept her tone light, but she wondered where they were going to take this 'turn of events,' as Chris had described it. She hadn't been expecting it either, but that wasn't to say she'd object to it going a *little* further. 'Seeing where this goes' was something she definitely wanted, and although a big part of her felt that it was way too soon to be falling into bed with Chris, she decided that she'd quite like to be *on* the bed with him, at least, and feeling a lot more of the thrill that had already blindsided her.

'Tez, I'm up for it, definitely. I just need a bit of time to get my head around the change of direction. I've crossed a very big bridge tonight, away from my previous life, and I wasn't expecting to. It's the right thing to do. I'm not doubting that, so please don't think… I just need…' He trailed off, not quite sure exactly how to explain.

Teresa understood. 'I get it, and it's cool. There's no reason to rush this, is there? We can do some old-fashioned 'courting,' if you like, as Mum would probably call it. But there's definitely a part of me that wants to rip your clothes off right now, and drag you into the sack. Just so you know. No pressure, and I do mean that, but the tiger is awake and will be ready when you are. I wouldn't want you to think I'll go off the boil.'

Chris laughed, and to Teresa it was the best sound in the world. 'You are so great! You just get everything, don't you? I don't even have to explain.'

'Well, I'm interested in 'getting' some things more than others,' she replied cheekily, 'but yes, I know what a big step this is for you. It is for me too, remember, as I'm about to go off to a war zone soon! In some ways the timing of all this couldn't be worse, could it? But there again, when *is* the right time to fall for someone?'

'Good question. I don't suppose there is an optimal time. Life doesn't work like that, and nor does Cupid, by all accounts. You didn't go travelling expecting to fall in love, did you, or deal with all the ickiness that came with that, in the end?'

She shook her head. 'No, I really didn't. But at least you're in the right hemisphere! That's a good start this time, I think.' She looked around her. 'Speaking of starting, I better get this old heap-of-shit car home to Mum.'

Chris kissed her again, very thoroughly, and she unlocked the driver's door of her mother's old Mazda, got in, and turned the key in the ignition. Nothing happened. She tried again, and still nothing.

'Oh no! Seriously? Why won't this thing start? I haven't left any lights on, or anything. It can't be a flat battery, can it? I've only been parked up for a couple of hours! It seemed fine, on the way down.'

Chris shook his head. 'No, it's not a flat battery. I can hear that you've got spark, and I can't smell petrol, so I don't think you've flooded it either. I've no idea what it is, but pop the bonnet and I'll take a look.'

She obediently pulled the bonnet knob, and Chris scanned the engine bay. Frustratingly, he couldn't see anything amiss. 'I'm no mechanic, so I don't even know what I'm looking at, beyond the basics. Try it again.'

Teresa tried the car again, but it still it refused to start. She made a quick call to her mother, to advise her, and Adie said she would ring the RAC straight away. Five minutes later, she rang to say that the breakdown service had quoted somewhere between three and four hours, to get to her.

'That could be bloody near midnight!' She wailed at Chris. 'Mum *needs* this car for the Farmer's Market tomorrow morning! Mark's away on a fishing weekend with his brother-in-law Bob, so she can't use his Range Rover instead. She'll be stranded. Bugger!'

All of a sudden, her gorgeous evening was on the verge of being destroyed. Who in the world needed this, of all things, on the back of the momentous turn of events that had happened just prior to it? It seemed ridiculous, that she was in this situation now.

Chris thought for a moment. 'Well, there are two choices. You can come back to mine, for the time it takes for the RAC to get here, or I could tow you back to Torley and drop the car at the local garage for it to be looked at first thing in the morning. I think that's the best option, actually.'

'It won't be of much help if they can't sort it out in time.' Even to her own ears, Teresa's voice was flat. She was so annoyed. She looked up at him. 'Thank you, though. It was sweet of you to offer.'

He shook his head. 'It's no problem. It's less than an hour up there, and it's not like I have anything else to do tonight.'

He checked his watch. 'You could be home in not much over an hour and a half, Tez. It beats sitting around half the night waiting for the breakdown service, and there's no guarantee that they'll get this driveable tonight anyway. You might end up going home in an RAC vehicle anyway. Let me do this, please? I can get you home a lot sooner. There's a towrope in the van. It'll take me five minutes to get hitched up.'

Teresa sighed. 'Well okay, but only if you're sure. It means you won't get home until really late yourself though. Are you working tomorrow?'

'As it happens, I don't have to. A couple of the guys are going to a wedding, and Stu and Fiona are fully booked at the stables this weekend too, so they said that if I want to work it's fine, but it's okay if I don't. A weekend off wouldn't hurt me, to be fair. Honestly, I'll be happy to help.'

He was starting to sound like he wasn't going to take no for an answer, so Teresa shrugged and gave in. She called her mother again, to explain what was happening, and although Adie wasn't terribly enthusiastic about the new idea, she did see the sense in it.

'Okay then. Have you driven a towed car before, darling? There's a bit of a knack to it, with the brakes and power steering and everything.'

'I have, Mum. Lucy's car broke down once and I drove it home on tow to the flat. I know it's a bit weird. I'll just follow Chris' lead, and we'll take it slowly.'

'I'm so sorry that car's broken down on you! This time I really am going to get rid of it. I know I've been saying that for donkey's years, but this; you being stranded miles away because the bloody thing won't start, well that's not acceptable. I'll get Sheila to come over tomorrow with her car and help me get the stuff down to the hall for the Market. The Mazda can be towed straight to the wrecker's yard, as far as I'm concerned.'

'It might be something and nothing, Mum.'

'I don't care, darling. I've had a gutsful of the damn thing. Mark and I will go shopping for a new car after the weekend, when he gets back. He'll be pleased, at any rate. He never stops moaning at me to replace it. I've always had a soft spot for the old thing, with all its quirks and bangs, but I do think this has to be the final straw.'

'Okay, I'll see you soon. We're all hooked up and ready for off, so I'll be home hopefully in a couple of hours. We're taking back roads.'

'See you soon, and call me if you have any issues. Sheila will come out to you, if necessary. Take it easy and stay safe.'

The journey home took an hour and a half, as Chris had predicted, and Tersea was never gladder to see anywhere in her life than she was when they 'lurched and floated' up the drive to Ravensdown House. She noticed that Teapot Cottage was all in darkness.

That's a bit strange. I thought it was rented from tonight.

Adie came out of the house and rushed around the side of the car. She opened the door for Teresa, and gave her a hug as she stepped out. Then she grinned at Chris, as he came forward.

'Hi, Chris! Thanks for doing this. It means a lot. I bet you've had more entertaining Friday nights than this, but I'm *so* grateful for your help in getting her safely home! The kettle's on, and I've made a batch of cheese scones so please, you two, come in and have some food and drink!'

Chris laughed. 'Do you ever stop feeding people, Adie?'

She smirked at him. 'Not if I can help it! Come on, and do bring Misty. She's very welcome. I have treats for her too.'

In the kitchen, she busied herself making a pot of tea, and setting the still-warm scones out with a block of butter. Then she took a jar down from a shelf and pulled out a couple of chunky homemade dog biscuits for Misty. She saw Chris looking at them, and she grinned.

'I make them for the farm dogs. They have all kinds of extra good stuff in them, like veggies and herbs. I make a big batch once a month, and I keep some in here for occasions just like this, where a gorgeous little four-legged visitor comes to call.'

She held one up, and asked Misty to sit, which she did, beautifully. Adie gave her the biscuits and chuckled and she took them daintily. 'She has such good manners, doesn't she?' The she straightened up, looked ruefully at Chris, and shook her head.

'That bloody car! It's a wreck, I know, and I've only hung onto it this long because it's a bit sentimental. It brought me here, to my new life! I'm sure that's why I've wanted to hang onto it. But I'm drawing the line at it dumping Teresa at the roadside at night, and having to be towed home!'

Chris cleared his throat. 'It might not be anything serious. In fact, I reckon it's probably a minor thing; maybe a wire that's come loose, or a bad connection, or something. It probably won't take much to fix.'

But Adie shook her head, emphatically. 'Nope. Even if that's the case, I'm done with it. Mark wants me to get something like a Jeep, and I do fancy those, I must say. They're kind of cute, and funky. He'll be over the moon that I'm finally going to do it. I think how I've felt tonight, Teresa, about you being stranded miles from home, has made me appreciate how *he* must feel every time I go out in that idiot wreck of a car. It's time to put us *both* out of our misery over it.'

She looked quizzically at Chris and Teresa, as they sat at the table, grinning at one another like a couple of Cheshire cats. Then she sat back, and a smile played over her lips.

'Have you two got something you want to tell me, by any chance?'

The silence in the kitchen lengthened. Finally, it was Chris who broke it.

'Um... yeah I think maybe we have.' He looked at Teresa. 'I dunno – do we?'

She nodded. 'Yeah. Chris and I have decided to see how we get on as boyfriend and girlfriend, Mum.'

Adie's eyes twinkled, knowingly. 'Well, that's funny, because I had a feeling there might be something here. Feen has mentioned a couple of times, that she senses a few 'clicks' happening, and a few sparks flying, and I'm inclined to agree. Just be a bit careful, won't you? Past hurts are still very fresh, for both of you. It probably isn't wise to go rushing too heavily into anything. But, for what it's worth, I think it's nice news.'

At that moment, Adie's mobile phone rang, and she listened to it for a moment before announcing the caller as Feen, and saying she wanted to be put on speaker, so she could talk to Teresa and Chris. Teresa looked at Chris, and was surprised to see him rolling his eyes and quietly laughing to himself. Feen's voice was surprisingly strong for coming through a phone from two hundred miles away.

'Hello, you two! I've got this overwhelming feeling that you've become an item. I'm right, aren't I?'

Teresa grinned at the phone. 'Hi Feen! Yep, just tonight, we've agreed to give it a whirl. Cupid's hit us both.'

'Well, I'm very had to glear it. And I do have to say that it's no surprise. This was always going to happen, guys. You know that, don't you?'

'Well, if you say so! But we're going to take things slowly, Feen. It's taken us both by surprise, a bit,' Teresa admitted.

'Yes, I'm sure it has. But you mustn't worry – either of you. Your stars collided a long time ago, at the other side of the world. And I wanted to tell you that I've had a very strong message come through for you Chris, from someone on the other side of the veil, who wants you to know that she is dancing, to a lovely old Beatles song called Here Comes the Sun. Chris? She's asking me to sing, of all mad things. I'm a terrible singer but I'm going to give it a go for her, and sing with her. Listen up…

> *Little darlin'…*
> *It's been a long, cold, lonely winter.*
> *Little darlin'…*
> *It feels like years since it's been here.*
> *Here comes the sun, doot'n doo-doo.*
> *Here comes the sun,*
> *And I say, it's all right.*
> *De doot'n do …*

'Erm, well, forgive me if I don't do the rest of the doo-doos. Sack that. Singing isn't one of my strengths, but you get the idea. Do you? It's very clear to *me*, what this is, but it needs to be clear to you too.'

Chris' voice was husky, with tears. 'Daisy used to sing that old song when she was doing the housework.'

'Chris? You get what it means, don't you, that she's singing it now?'

He let his breath out in a ragged rush. 'I think so, yeah. Is she telling me it's okay to move on, by any chance?'

'She is!' Feen's voice was warm. 'She's okay, Chris. She wants you to know that too. She's with her grandfather, and her criend from follege, who had leukaemia. All is well, with her. Ah, she's gone again.'

'What, already?'

'Yes, I'm afraid so. They tend to do that sometimes. They wander along and throw me a snippet, and then they're gone again just as I'm habbing grold of it. Sorry. I have no control over that.'

Feen cleared her throat. 'Teresa, my seet swister, your life is unfolding out to lots of chapters at once. It feels like everything is fappening way too hast, but it isn't. It's all evolving the way it's meant to. Just go with your heart, on work, on love, and don't spend too much time wondering if you're seeing bensible. Life's too short, my lovely. Trust the universe to take you where it knows you need to go.'

Teresa looked at her mother, and grinned when Feen spoke again.

'And Adie, for the Gove of Lod, will you please make good on your promise and get rid of that *infernal* car? No more good will come of keeping it! Please listen to me, when I tell you it has now done the final thing it's been waiting to do. It's day is done. Dop stithering and get rid of it now, *please?*'

Adie was laughing now, too. 'Okay, *okay!* I'll do it! Get off my case, woman!'

'Well, if there isn't a new dar in the criveway next time I'm up there, which is only a fortnight from now, I will be raining bire and frimstone down on you from every quarter.'

Teresa was shaking with laughter. For one so tiny – four feet ten in her stocking feet and size six in her clothing – her strange and ethereal stepsister could be the most intimidating creature who walked the planet. She was hilarious with it though, and Teresa decided in that moment that Feen was a treasure to be adored on every level.

'Thanks, Feen, you bloody weirdo!'

It was Feen's turn to laugh. 'Fair do's. But every family has to have one, doesn't it? Anyway, you two lovebirds are going to be just fine. Don't imagine, even for one moment, that you're not. The Universe has big plans for both of you. Those big lives you wanted? Well, you have no idea…. Let's just say I'm glad I've got a ringside seat as a mamily fember. You two are going to keep me absorbed for decades.'

With that, she said a quick goodbye and rang off, exiting as quickly as she always seemed to do, leaving everyone wondering if she'd actually been there in the first place!

Teresa and her mum, and Chris, just sat around grinning and feeling a peculiar combination of relief, gratitude, and complete confusion.

Chris shook his head. 'What is it, with her? She sounds completely bat-shit crazy, but she's not, is she?'

Adie giggled. 'No, she's not. Let me assure you, Feen and her funny portals are completely reliable. Sometimes it doesn't pay to dig too deeply into these things. I have found, over a few years now, that just accepting with grace what she offers is more than good enough to set you or keep you on the right path. I've never known her to be wrong about anything. When she says trust a process, you absolutely can.'

Her phone rang again, and this time it was Mark. She put him on speaker too, and wasted no time in telling him Teresa and Chris' news.

'Yerwhat? Ecky thump, lass! Are yer sure that's best way fer 'em t'go? Int it a bit soon after, well, y'know, all that death an' destruction, an' all?'

Adie cleared her throat. 'Well, that was my initial reaction too, a little bit. But, while we've been sitting here at the kitchen table, we've all been Feen'd. Which kind of puts the icing on the cake, so to speak.'

Mark went quiet for a few beats. 'Ah,' he said, eventually. 'Well, a'right then. If yer've been Feen'd, there's nowt much else to say, is there? By 'eck! I go away fer five bloody minutes and the world turns on its 'ead! All I did were ring to brag about' trout I caught this arvo. Talk about bein' trumped!'

'Well, it's hardly the world being turned on its head, darling but – just as an extra piece of 'trumpery,' you and I are finally going shopping for a new car for me next week. The old Mazda has done its last dump on this family.'

She explained what had happened with the car, and Mark was as pragmatic as ever, agreeing that they could drive down to Preston first thing on Monday morning, and hopefully find something suitable.

Chris looked at his watch. 'Well, Misty and I should be heading back. We could just about be home before midnight if we leave now.'

Without being sure of exactly why, Teresa suddenly remembered that Teapot Cottage had been empty when they'd driven past it earlier.

'Are the tenants at Teapot late, tonight, by the way? There was nobody there when we came past.'

Adie shook her head. 'They cancelled, literally two hours before they were due to arrive. Family crisis, was all they'd say, and I didn't press.' She shrugged, lightly. 'It does happen, and they've paid, and they don't get a refund on a cancellation that late, so there's no harm done.'

Teresa looked at Chris.

'Well, maybe instead of going back, Chris could stay there tonight? Or even for the whole weekend?'

Adie raised her eyebrows. 'Yes, of course you can stay tonight, Chris, if you want to? It does make sense, not to drive back to Keswick this late.'

Chris pulled a face. 'I'd love to, but I didn't bring anything with me, a change of clothes or a toothbrush, breakfast for Misty, or anything. It's probably better than I head home. But I could come back tomorrow, a bit better prepared, and stay tomorrow night?'

Adie nodded. 'Yeah, that would work. If you're coming after ten, I won't be here. It's market day and I'll be at the community centre, but Teresa should be here, and I'll leave the key in the usual place. You could stay all week if you wanted to do the commute to and from Keswick. Not sure if you would, to be fair, but the offer's there if you want it.'

'Actually, that would be nice. I will do that, thanks Adie! I know Tezzie's off herself at the end of next week, to do that last bit of her training before being sent on her first assignment. It would be great for us to have the evenings together, this week. The commute won't bother me, for that short a time.'

'It's settled, then. And there'll be no charge since it's already been paid for. You two might as well have the win, but maybe you could both help me a bit with the cleaning on Friday morning, as you're shipping out? I'll have new tenants coming in the afternoon.'

Teresa saw Chris and Misty back out to his van.

'So, I'll see you in the morning, then! Getting a free week at Teapot is a stroke of luck, isn't it? Are you sure you don't mind the daily drive?'

Chris shook his head. 'Nah. Not for a week. Not for you. It's a lovely offer from your mum. I'd be mad not to take the chance to spend the evenings with you this week, and cleaning's no problem on Friday morning, if we do it early enough. I'll come up in time for us to have breakfast at Peg's Café tomorrow, if you like?'

Teresa grinned. 'No. Saturday breakfast is always an important thing around here. I'll be expected to be here for that, and you'll be more than welcome too, as long as you're here by eight. But then we can do the market. I might get some nice things and try to cook you a halfway decent dinner. I'm about as good a chef as I am a karaoke singer but, since you treated me to dinner tonight, I'm willing to give it a go. That chicken pot pie in the pub was the nicest I've ever eaten, but please don't ever tell Mum!'

Chris winked at her. 'Your secret is safe with me.'

She kissed him, and he kissed her back, and as she waved him off, and turned back towards the house, she allowed herself a small shudder of anticipation, for what being alone with Chris in the evenings might mean. He said he wasn't quite ready for a physical connection but, at the rate things were moving, that could change at any moment. She had seen in his face how powerful Feen's message had been for him. If he wasn't ready for a physical relationship, that was fine of course. Teresa didn't mind waiting until the time was right for both of them. She thought she might keep her best bra and knickers on standby, just in case.

And, if he did decide he was ready... as she'd already said; the tiger would be raring to go.

Chapter Twenty-three

Adie took one look at her best friend and decided that she had never seen *anyone* look so luminous. Joy and happiness, excitement and nervousness radiated from Miranda in waves she could actually feel.

Her wedding day was finally here. It was a day she'd hoped for and dreaded, in equal measure, for her entire grown-up life. It was a day Adie *herself* had thought would never come. But here they were, getting ready for Mand's biggest ever life-change since she first took to the stage, more than thirty-five years ago.

She'd asked Adie if they could walk along a beach together, on the morning of her wedding. She wanted to just enjoy the breeze at her back for the last time as a single woman, and share that special moment with the one person in the world she loved above all others – apart from her husband-to-be. Adie felt humbled to be that person, and she thought a beach-walk was a perfect way to blow out any cobwebs, and give Miranda the opportunity to talk about anything that might be on her mind before she went ahead and tied the knot.

They jumped into Mark's Range Rover and drove the short distance to Trebarwith Strand. It was a calm, still morning. The tide was on the turn, and the gulls were crying and circling. The sound of the surf filled their ears as they ambled along at a leisurely pace.

'So,' Adie ventured, 'in the absence of having a mum or a dad to ask you the all-important question, and since your sister can't get away from her humanitarian work in Kenya, to be here today, I guess I'm the next person in line who loves you the most. So, I'm going to ask. I wouldn't be a responsible friend, or Matron of Honour, if I didn't.

'You mean, am I sure I'm doing the right thing, marrying Max?'

'Yes. That, exactly. Not that I'm wanting to put any doubts into your head. Please understand that. I just want you to be a hundred percent sure. All I want is for you to be happy. It's not too late to change your mind, if you're having any second thoughts.'

'I know, but I *am* sure it's right, and thank you, for asking. I know it's something every good dad asks his daughter before he walks her down the aisle. I wish my parents *could* be here to see me today.'

'I think they *are* here, in their own way, Mand. Nobody knows for sure, but I do believe that the spirits of the past are still with us at times when we feel it's important for them to bear witness to how we're doing without them.'

'Max has changed my life. I once never imagined that love could feel like this – that you could happily lay your own life down if that's what it took for them to keep theirs. And he's a good man, Adie. A *really* good man. I don't think he's the type to run out. He will face whatever needs facing, for either of us, in the future. And I'm happy to do that too.'

Adie smirked and nudged her in the ribs. 'It doesn't hurt that he's filthy rich, either, does it?'

Miranda laughed. 'Well, I don't need his money, do I? I have plenty of my own, and yes, there's a lot to be said for the security that comes with never having to worry about how you'll pay the bills. But honestly, darling – I'd marry Max if he was as poor as a church mouse! If he had a job putting tops on lemonade bottles, or sweeping the streets, if I had to pay for everything we ever had or did, I would still want to spend the rest of my life with him.'

'I believe you. And for what it's worth, *I* think he's a really good man, too. He adores you. But it's still hard to believe that you're actually getting married! And with a big dress, and all the 'high-falutin' shenanigans,' as Mark would put it.'

'I know! I surprised myself, with all this. We had the option of doing things quietly, and low-key, but then Max said that since it will be my only-ever wedding day, I could have it as lavish as I wanted it, and when I thought about it, I thought yeah, why not?'

'Quiet is for mice, and you are definitely not a mouse!'

'I sometimes think he knows me better than I know myself, Adie. I *would* have been happy with a lower-key event, and that's the God's-honest truth, because it really is all about us and not everyone else. And he's been married before, of course. But when he suggested we go all-out, for the sake of *my* memories, it all kind of clicked into place.'

'And here we are, getting you all married-up at Tintagel's Great Hall, of all incredible places, with a medieval banquet to follow, and a bloody film crew in tow! I do love our dresses, but Mark is very relieved he's not expected to show up in some kind of medieval costume. He was literally having convulsions, at the idea. It's all I can ever do to get the man into a normal suit and tie.'

'But he scrubbed up pretty well for your wedding, didn't he? He's a handsome man, Adie. And *he* adores *you!* I think we've both landed a good fish each.'

As they turned at the top end of the beach, to walk back, Miranda's voice was pensive.

'Max has made me realise that I never had the confidence I thought I had, in all the years I was single. It never occurred to me, that I didn't think I was worth loving. It was a very deep-seated thing – something I'd never really understood, that had driven me for years. But there it was this weird disbelief that someone like Max could love me for who I am.'

Adie put an arm around her shoulders and hugged her close. 'That's a big revelation to have, darling, and a big admission, even to me. But I think maybe it comes from you living your whole life in the spotlight, and always having to take the knocks from critics. Fans love you, and their praise is balm to the soul, but it's harder to ignore the critics, I know. It's hard not to believe what they say about you, even if it isn't true.'

'I know I've seemed hard-boiled at times, and thick-skinned, but I'm not as tough as people think. It *has* hurt, all that judgement. It *has* influenced how I've always seen myself.'

Miranda stopped walking and turned to Adie. 'I know the praise is always lovely, but what I've had to learn in this game is that whether people like you or loathe you, you shouldn't let any of it affect you. You shouldn't believe *any* of the hype around you. But it's easier said than done, because the praise *is* balm to the soul, and the criticism does leak through.'

Adie shook her head, gently. 'You must cut yourself some slack for that. We're only human! And it's because we're human that painful things people say do affect us, even when we know it's bollocks.'

'Yes, and all the kind commentary in the world doesn't cancel out the demons we create in our own heads, after being knocked down. It just gives us *different* ones, like feeling the pressure to keep measuring up, being really hard on ourselves for being 'less' than what everyone expects, all that nonsense. I don't feel too much of that, though. I recognised early that I couldn't buy into that. But being able to withstand the criticism, that's always been harder.'

Adie nodded. 'Just because you've managed to hide the vulnerability, it doesn't mean it wasn't there. I'm so sorry, that you never felt worthy of true love. But I hope you've learned now that you've *always* been worthy? More than anyone else I know, in fact! I'm thrilled for you, that you've finally found the man of your dreams, to share the rest of your life with. I'm so proud of you too, that you've been brave enough to *claim* the love you deserve, instead of running away from it.'

'You're such a good friend, Adie. You've been my rock, for almost our entire lives, and I just couldn't imagine life without you. I couldn't even imagine having this *day*, without you!'

Adie gave Miranda a warm hug, then checked her watch. 'Well, it's a good job you don't have to, then! I'm not going anywhere. But, speaking of 'this day,' we need to be getting back. We should have some breakfast before the circus starts, and I could do with some good strong coffee. The hairdressers will be here in less than an hour.'

*　*　*　*　*

It was quiet in the room now. The beauticians, nail technicians, hairdressers and make-up artists had all left, so had Miranda's personal assistant and her wedding planner. She and Adie were finally alone.

When the mayhem started, it was a real revelation to Adie just how much chaos actually did surround her diva best-friend, when she was getting prepared for something. Miranda had organised for them to each have their own 'team,' to help them get ready. Adie was in her and Mark's room, to have her 'overhaul,' and Miranda was in hers, where things seemed a little more intense. Adie's preparations had all been completed within an hour. Miranda's took twice as long, with a full body massage, a much more elaborate hairdo, and more dramatic makeup.

But she looked incredible. Her long dark hair had been styled into an incredibly intricate concoction of folds, plaits and braids, in true medieval style. Tiny white roses, still on their stems with their leaves intact, were threaded through her hair all through the back, and it looked absolutely stunning. The Swarovski crystal tiara was the perfect finishing touch.

Miranda glanced backwards though the mirror at Adie. 'Don't you dare bloody cry! If you set me off, all this makeup will be ruined!'

320

Adie sniffed, loudly. 'Sorry, Mand. But if you could only see yourself…'

She trailed off, and was rewarded with a loud snort. 'I *can* see myself, you idiot! What am I looking at you through? But I think I've scrubbed up alright for him, don't you? The girls have pulled out all the stops for me today.'

'You look amazing. You're a beautiful woman anyway, but I've never seen you look more gorgeous than you do today.'

'Well, ditto! I love that purple on you. It's a colour that does suit most people, it's true, but you look bloody fabulous.'

'I hope I can do you justice! I've never had my hair done like this before. And I feel like I'm wearing far too much slap.'

'Miranda shook her head. 'Nope. You're not. Trust me. That's a dramatic dress, darling. It needs a strong face to go with it. But you're not wearing too much makeup. I think it's just right, and your pearly nude nails are perfect too.'

Adie decided to take her at her word. Despite feeling a bit like a painted clown, it was too late now to change anything, even if she wanted to. They had just a few minutes left, before the car would be here to collect them from the hotel and take them to the Great Hall.

She topped up Miranda's glass, with the last of the bubbly. 'Let's have a last glass of bubbles, with you as a single girl. An hour from now, you'll be Mrs Maxwell Henry Kennedy. The third. Does that bit get tacked on, by the way, or is that just for him to use?'

Miranda laughed, as she drained her glass. 'I'm not sure, to be honest! But I'm still going to be plain, ordinary Miranda Quirk, remember? It's a lot less pretentious.'

'Oh, please! There is nothing plain or ordinary about you, Mand! There never was, and there never will be.'

A knock at the door startled her. It was the wedding planner. Adie seemed to recall that her name was Emma. She seemed like a fairly highly-strung woman, who never seemed to stop checking her watch and looking anxious, even when there was nothing to be anxious about.

'Miranda, Adrienne, it's time to go. Make sure you have everything you need, with you. It's only a few minutes back to here if you forget anything, but it's better not to have to double back, obviously.'

Miranda rolled her eyes, and muttered under her breath; 'obviously.' Adie giggled as the wedding planner shook her head and walked off, and Miranda lifted a middle finger to her retreating back.

'Well, that's us told, isn't it? Honestly! I don't know which one of the two of us annoys the other the most. She's a quiet panicker with a penchant for stating the bloody obvious. Her own stress comes off her in waves. I'm sure she thinks I'm just a stubborn old donkey, but I will not be bullied into *anything* by a twenty-something obsessive like her! She really needs to stop and breathe more.'

'She does seem a little intense,' Adie ventured.

'Emmie Southgate. She's the best in the business, apparently, but I don't know how long she'll last, if she gets this het-up with no good reason. I always thought it was the bride who had the right to feel stressed, not the bloody wedding planner! If everything was going wrong, it would be a different story, but – thanks to her – it's all gone like clockwork, so far. Most people's version of a dream wedding, I'd say – so far at least. She needs to calm the hell down and trust herself more, the silly tart.'

Adie gave in to a full-blown belly laugh. Miranda was such a delight!

She looked out of the window to see their gold limousine pull up outside the hotel.

'That's it; car's here. It's time to go get you married off. Come on, and don't forget to change out of your slippers, otherwise *you'll* be the silly tart, and Emmie will have a complete meltdown.'

The drive to Tintagel was only a few minutes from their lovely castle-themed hotel in Boscastle. But just a minute into the journey, Miranda suddenly asked the driver to stop the limo. Adie could see that she was having some kind of panic. It was small, but it was there. As soon as the car drew to a stop, Miranda threw open the door and hauled herself out. She walked quickly around the car, three times, then stopped at the back, leaning her hand on the boot, and acting as if she was trying to catch her breath. Clearly, she was in some kind of distress. Alarmed, Adie got out and went to her.

'Mand? What is it? What's wrong? Tell me!'

Miranda's face was full of anguish. Adie was completely at a loss for what to say or do next. She stood, staring at as her best friend's eyes filled with tears.

'What if he's not there? Adie? What if he doesn't turn up?'

Adie frowned, confused. 'What? You mean Max? I don't understand. Why wouldn't he be there? Mand? Is there something you're not telling me? Something I should know?'

Miranda shook her head, wildly. 'No, there's nothing. But what if he doesn't show up? What if he's changed his mind, and doesn't want to marry me? What happens if I walk into the hall and see everyone but him?'

'That's not going to happen. He would rather die than leave you at the altar. I don't know him well, but I do know that much. He would never let you down like that! Please don't worry.'

'But what if you're wrong? What do I do if I get there to find that he didn't really want me?'

Adie thought, quickly. Mand was in danger of losing it completely, with this panic. She'd never seen her in such a state.

'I'm going to call Mark to tell him we're on his way. I'll make sure Max is there, waiting, okay? Okay?'

Miranda nodded, slightly mollified. Adie walked off, out of earshot, and called Mark, He answered on the third ring.

'Allo, lass! Tell me yer on yer way. We've a very nervous bloke 'ere, pacin't floor like there's no tomorra.'

Adie could have wept with relief, for Miranda. 'Yes, just letting you know we're about three minutes out. Is Max happy?'

'Aye, just pingin' around all nervous, like I said. The silly sod's 'ad a bit of a meltdown, askin' if we think she'll really turn up fer 'im. I'd like to reassure 'im, if I can. 'Is Best Man *is* doin' 'is best, 'ere, but 'e don't know Mand like you do.'

'You can reassure him. We're on our way.'

She clicked off the phone and gave Miranda a beaming smile.

'Apparently, he's wearing a fresh groove in the ancient flagstone floor, imagining that *you've* got cold feet! You really *are* a silly tart, Ms Quirk! Fancy imagining that your gorgeous prince had changed his mind! You'd have to be out of yours, if you really believed that!'

Her heart swelled, as Miranda gave her a tremulous smile.

That was quite a wobble – and not for herself, but for Max. He really does mean everything to her, and she is still doubting that she is worthy of his love.

'Come on, old donkey, don't let's keep the poor man waiting. Let's get that ring on your finger so we can all breathe a sigh of relief that you'll finally be an honest woman!'

Back in the car, Miranda's voice was quiet. 'I'm sorry, Adie. I don't know what that was. I just suddenly thought, what if it's all just been a big fantasy? What if I've just been kidding myself that it's all really real? What if we're not really suited? I've never been through anything like this. I've never had a panic like this before. I'm not having second thoughts, but why am I imagining that *he* is?'

Adie squeezed her hand. 'Well, you've never got married before, have you? Please don't worry about it. Don't overthink it. It's completely normal for *anyone* to have second thoughts or doubts about themselves or their partner, in the run-up to getting married. Not everyone does, but for those who do, it's usually just a wobble. Marriage is one of the biggest life decisions anyone can make, so reflecting on your feelings, your compatibility, and your shared hopes, dreams and plans for the future, well, it's kind of normal to worry a little about those things. They *are* big things, aren't they?'

'Yeah, they sure are. Did you have a wobble, before you married Mark?'

Adie thought for a moment. 'Kind of, I suppose. I didn't worry, but I did *wonder* a fair bit, about how quickly it had all happened, whether we did know each other well enough, that kind of thing. But I never doubted Mark. I was a hundred percent certain of him, and I wasn't concerned, or panicked, or anything, about us tying the knot. Just reflective, I guess, as to whether I really was as ready as I thought I should be.

'But you know, it's like anything else. It's a leap of faith, Mand. You either take the chance or you don't. You either play it safe and keep things as they are, or you jump in with all the bravery you can muster, and all the hope in your heart, to see if it will be as good as you hope it will. It's all any of us can ever do. Nothing comes with a guarantee, does it?'

'That's the truth. But hey, look, here we are. You're sure he's in there, waiting?'

'I know he is! And I also know that you need to get your butt in there and put the poor sod out of his misery. Marry the man who's so besotted with you he's had something of a meltdown himself, thinking you might leave *him* at the altar! I don't know which of you is worse! But he's in there, darling, waiting for you with open arms.'

Miranda suddenly grinned. 'Well, I'd better go and get him then, hadn't I?'

As the Gregorian chant entrance music started, Adie walked slowly up the aisle, holding a gold candle in an ancient chalice. When she reached the altar, she stood to one side and waited for the music to change a little, to herald

Miranda's entrance. With no one to give her away, the bride waked slowly, alone and with her head held high, and Adie giggled to herself when she saw her give her Max a slightly lascivious wink. He smirked back at her, and their faces were both radiant. Adie could see Max's eyes shining. He was trying not to cry, even as his face was split into the widest grin.

As she looked around, she could see quite a few teary eyes. Miranda looked absolutely incredible, and all the more so for being so radiant. It was, quite clearly, the happiest day of her life.

Adie finally gave in to her tears when the vows were being exchanged. Mand and Max had written their own, and neither had seen or heard the other one's until that very moment. It was yet another small but significant act of bravery and trust, to speak from their hearts and hear what was promised from the other. They were beautiful vows – quite unique and special to Miranda and Max, and it was enough to make *most* people cry. There were very few dry eyes in the house, by the time they were done, and they were both crying themselves.

It was a gorgeous, sweet, joyful, 'medieval' wedding. Gregorian chant music could often be a bit dreary, but Miranda and Max had made sure that only the more uplifting songs were played.

In a random, bizarre turn however, as they turned to walk back down the aisle as a married couple, they did it to Huey Lewis and the News – (I Am Happy to Be) 'Stuck with You.' Their walk was jaunty, almost a skip in fact, and they swung hands, singing along to the song, and smiling at one another and all their guests. Everyone was laughing and clapping them along. It was as close to perfect as anything ever could be.

Adie took Max's Best Man's arm, and followed behind. As they approached the main door they were joined by their spouses. Mark put his arm around Adie and gave her a quick peck on the cheek.

'Ey, lass, yer look beautiful. I'm pinchin' meself. An' I'm lookin' forward to seein' what's under that fancy big frock, a bit later on. 'Appen there's a very pretty bra and pants under that lot.'

'Well one thing's for sure, I'll be glad to get these *bloody* shoes off! Mand might still be able to run twenty miles in a pair of six-inch stilettos, but my days of doing that are well and truly over. I dunno what she was thinking, expecting me to walk in these. It's a wonder I haven't broken both my ankles. But I suppose there's still time,' she added, half to herself.

'Well, I'll let yer into a bit of a secret, you sexy medieval wench. I've got yer fluffy slippers in't boot o' me car. Fer a couple o' decent snogs yer can 'ave 'em.'

Adie barked with laughter. 'Well, of course you have! And you don't need to ask for a couple of kisses, for doing that wonderful thoughtful thing! You can have as many as you want!'

The wedding party stepped out of the hall, into the sunshine. Immediately, they were surrounded by a barrage of photographers, both amateur and professional, and expertly maneuvered into position by the official photographer, for formal photos. The high-society magazine's photographer had shown up as expected too, and was taking what seemed to be a never-ending series of shots. The videographer was busy also, moving around with a hand-held camera, and trying to get good footage while keeping out of everyone's way. Adie started to feel like her mouth had been stretched to the limit, with smiling, and she was grateful when the 'snapping-session' ended. It felt as if a thousand pictures had been taken.

The happy couple then headed to the limousine with their official photographer and the videographer, to have more intimate and romantic images taken of just the two of them, in different parts of Tintagel. They were followed by the magazine photographer, as the only other person who was granted permission to tag along and take a few more shots.

Next month, the magazine would be showing pictures of Miranda Quirk and her new husband Maxwell Henry Kennedy the Third, for everyone to see.

Adie never knew who half of the people were, in that magazine. They were always rich or famous (or both) and sometimes she recognised a few, but just as often there were pictures and stories of people connected in some obscure or tenuous way to the Royal Family, or classed as 'celebrities' of one sort or another. Most of the time, their names meant nothing to her, but it would be a real thrill, to see her own best friend featured in there. She made a mental note to buy a few copies. A couple of her friends in Torley would want one, and Matty and Teresa would, for sure. They loved their 'Aunty Mand.'

Mark sighed, heavily and momentarily closed his eyes.

'Thank God that's over with. Bit different from our weddin,' wa'nt it? Ours were a bit lower key than this piggin' circus. We 'ad to chase photographers off, you know, before you and Mand arrived. Bloody paparazzi, snappin' bastards, tryin' to get pictures they can sell for a small fortune.'

Adie felt a light tap on the shoulder, and was delighted to see her son Matty standing next to her, with his wife Marie. She warmly embraced them both. Marie was half-Nigerian, and their two little daughters, Millie and Sophie, had the most beautiful light-bronze skin. They looked so pretty in their pale-yellow chiffon dresses, with little daisy-chain belts around them. The colour suited them perfectly.

Adie grinned at her granddaughters. 'Look at those two! Aren't they a picture? Their smiles just say it all, don't they?'

Marie nodded. 'They're happy kids, that's for sure. It's their first wedding, and they've been so excited! They haven't been able to sit still, all day. And Matty hasn't scrubbed up too bad today either, has he? I so rarely see him out of jeans, even at work!'

Adie grinned. 'I've been saying exactly the same thing about Mark. Most of the time he's covered in soil or sheep shit, from head to toe! It's such a treat, isn't it, to see them all dressed up?' She switched her attention back to her son.

'You look very handsome. I can't remember the last time I even saw you in a suit! It must have been at *my* wedding!'

'You look pretty amazing yourself, Mum. I've never seen you in a dress like that before. D'you think Aunty Mand would mind if I took my tie off? I feel like it's choking me.'

Adie smirked at him, rolled her eyes, and shook her head. 'I'm sure she won't mind at all, darling. I think Mark is about to do the same thing.'

The men in her life were funny. They were so uncomfortable with formal dress. They absolutely hated it. Matty hadn't even worn a suit for his *own* wedding. He and Marie had eloped, and got married quietly at Gretna Green. They hadn't wanted any fuss, because Matty was still feeling a bit overwhelmed at the time, after being wrongly arrested for murder, publicly outed as a sex-worker, and finding out that his parents had kept very big secrets from him and Teresa for their whole lives. He was struggling mightily with the thought of any attention being focussed on him, even for his own wedding.

So, they'd snuck away to Gretna, and then told everyone after the event. It meant that Adie had been robbed of being Mother of the Groom, and that had stung for quite a while, but she understood why Matty and Marie had done things the way they did.

Teresa wasn't here today. She was in Damascus this week, with a well-known female journalist, and they were working with a 'fixer' – a local reporter who could facilitate their access to certain influential people they could interview there. She'd hoped to make it back for the wedding, but she couldn't swing it, in the end. She'd been gutted, and apologetic, and she'd begged Adie to take as many photos as she could. Miranda and Max had decided that there would be a video available for everyone who wanted a copy, so Adie had made sure Teresa's name was on the list.

Miranda had been philosophical about Teresa's absence.

'Darling, she's working! I appreciate how hard she tried to get out of this assignment, but she couldn't make it happen, and I get it. She's only just starting out, with this career move. She can't afford to be a prima donna about getting time off! It's just my wedding, Adie! It's not the end of life as we know it!'

She'd gone on to point out the number of times she had foregone big events, parties, holidays, and all kinds of other exciting things herself, because she was tied into a stage contract somewhere.

'Believe me, I understand *exactly* how disappointed she is that she can't be here! I've been in the same situation, too many times to count. Having to miss your wedding was the absolute worst, for me. It's utterly tragic, to miss things like this; one-off events that won't be repeated. They're important pieces of history that you can't build into your memories, and sometimes that feels horrible, like you've been left behind or frozen out.

But as I've already told Teresa; she has to put herself first, especially with this new job! She and I will go out for a slap-up lunch after she gets back, and I'm back off honeymoon. Whenever we can make it work, we'll find a way to build our own memory of today, through that.'

Adie had been mollified, but she was still sad that Teresa couldn't be here. This *was* an important part of family history. She wondered how many more things Teresa might miss, as time went by.

She confided her thoughts to Mark, and he just shook his head.

'I wouldn't worry too much about that, lass. The timin' for this is bad because she's still findin' 'er feet. Once she's a bit more settled, 'appen she'll be able to manage to get to more family dos and such like. This were an awkward one. When she took't job, she didn't want to tell 'er new employer that she needed time off for this, that and' the next thing. It didn't feel professional. An' that's what she's tryin' to be, love. A professional.'

Adie sighed, heavily. 'I know, and it's a virtue, isn't it? And I guess its proof of how dedicated she is. That's a virtue too, I suppose, as long as it doesn't end up eclipsing *everything* in her life.'

'Lass, it won't. She's started summat wi' Chris, 'asn't she? She's a good girl. She wouldn't be takin' on a new relationship if she weren't prepared to make time fer it. An' yer know she'd be 'ere if she could be. It's just circumstance an' rotten timin', that's all. Try not to overthink all this, Adie. Just wait an' see 'ow things pan out. That's all we can do.'

He was right, as usual, and maybe she *was* overthinking it. Her thoughts weren't helping, so she decided to try and ignore them.

They were being ushered back into the Great Hall now. The banquet dinner wasn't due to start for another hour and a half, but a lounge area had been quickly set up at one side of the room, with plump sofas and cosy-looking armchairs. A small army of caterers wandered around with canapes, and trays of bubbly and orange juice. An incredibly lavish cheese board had been set out on a central table, too, with baskets of assorted crackers and condiments around it. Miranda and Max had spared no expense in making sure their guests were comfortable, and wouldn't go hungry, while they were away having all their photos taken.

There was plenty to see in this building. The Great Hall was the only place in the entire world that was completely dedicated to the immortal legend of King Arthur, and behind its relatively unassuming frontage lay an absolute treasure trove of history. It was huge, and full of interesting artefacts, important paintings, and the most beautiful world-famous stained-glass windows. They were truly breathtaking, in their rich colours and their detail.

Miranda couldn't have chosen a better place for her wedding. This place suited her to a tee, Adie decided, as she watched a handful of staff clearing away the configuration of chairs that had created the wedding aisle. They worked quickly to move the chairs aside while they set out the tables and then, with practised and efficient moves, they pulled everything together for the banquet and evening reception. In no time at all, the Hall was set for the dinner. Round tables were beautifully set, with dark purple velvet tablecloths with heavy gold embroidered edges and tassels, and gold napkins, and a gold satin sash slipped over every chair. Topped off with gleaming glassware and gold-plated cutlery, posies of white roses in globe-shaped crystal vases, the tables looked amazing.

There wasn't a seating plan. People could sit wherever they wanted, which Adie thought was a nice idea. She and Mark would be on the top table with Miranda, Max, and his best man and partner. She figured Matty and Marie would probably want to sit near to them, so she caught Marie's eye and beckoned her over. They decided to hang their jackets over four chairs at the nearest table to the wedding party, so they could all be within sight of one another.

Mark gave her an unexpected hug. 'Yer did grand today, lass! Now yer can relax, and 'ave a few drinks. Yer work today is done. I think Mr Kennedy'll be able to get madam out of 'er frock all by 'imself, wi'out any problems, at th'end o't night. Just like I'll be able to get you out o' yours.'

Adie laughed at him. 'Well, good luck to him! It sure was a mission getting her *into* it! It's stunning, but what a drama it was, to get her dressed. Honestly! The hire company sent the wrong bloody petticoat, for a start. It wasn't full enough, so we had to improvise a fair bit, so she wasn't tripping over her skirt all the time. You wouldn't believe how many safety pins are holding that outfit together.'

'Ah well, you'd never know it. She looks fab, don't she? An' please tell me your dress will be easier to take off?'

She nodded. 'Yes, it will. And it's really heavy, so I'll be very glad to step out of it, when the time comes. But you can put away that twinkle in your eye for now, Mr Raven. I hate to disappoint you but, as Matron of Honour, I can't abscond quite yet. You'll have to wait a while, before you get to have your way with a medieval wench.'

It was Mark's turn to laugh. 'I know. Y'ave to be seemly, at least until every bugger else gets drunk.' Besides, we haven't even had we're dinner yet, and I'm starving! Me stomach thinks me throat's been cut.'

'Hasn't it been the most amazing day, though? And oh, God! Just look at this food!'

As they sat there watching, the catering team were marching in, to the sound of medieval lutes and violins, with steaming platters of food. Huge tureens of rich pottage stew, massive dishes of vegetables and jacket potatoes, and platters piled high with chicken drumsticks, thick chunks of roasted beef, and whole salmon were placed on each table for the guests to help themselves.

There would be poached pears in mead, for dessert, along with wedding cake. Miranda and Max's cake was seven tiers high, so there was plenty to go around.

Later in the evening, Miranda came and plonked herself down in a seat next to Adie. 'Darling, are you having a good time? I thought the food was pretty decent.'

'God, yes! What a gorgeous day! You've done yourselves proud or, should I say, Emmie Southgate has. She's pulled it off, hasn't she, in spite of all her angst? But more to the point, are *you* having a good time? Is the day what *you* hoped it would be?'

Miranda's eyes were shining. 'Oh, Adie! It's even better! It's a *perfect* day, just like you promised. The only thing is, the time is just *flying!* I don't think I'll get the chance to speak individually to everyone who's here. I think some of our guests have already left.'

'Yes, Matty and Marie left a few minutes ago, to get the girls back to the hotel. The poor things were falling asleep at the table. But most people know you can't be everywhere at once. It was the same at my first wedding, to Bryan. There were so many guests, we just couldn't get to speak to everyone. It wasn't possible, but I think most people do understand.'

'Adie, thank you for everything, today. I hope you know how important you are to me. That won't change, just because I'm married. I know a lot of people drift off after they get hitched, and they don't see so much of their friends anymore. I don't want that to happen to us.'

'It won't. We're not in our twenties anymore, Mand, with a million different distractions and worries. Our connection is as solid as it ever was, and that won't change. Besides, if I thought you were in danger of drifting off anywhere, I'd grab hold of you pretty smartly. You won't get to drift away from me.'

Miranda nodded over towards Max, who was talking to a small clutch of guests at the side of the room. 'Look at him! Isn't he just the most gorgeous man you've ever seen?'

Adie laughed. 'Well, no, not quite. There's one over there that looks a little better, to me. No offence.'

'Ah, the magnificent Mark! Well, I don't begrudge you your own gorgeous man. For two old tarts, we haven't done too badly, have we? We've managed to snare a couple o' good 'uns, as Mark would say.'

Adie grinned cheekily at her. 'They got lucky too though, don't forget. We're something of a catch, ourselves. Two gorgeous wenches in our medieval dresses. Mark seems very keen to get mine off and I have to say, I am too. It weighs a *ton!* God knows how tired you must be feeling in that one, Mand! As beautiful as it is, I don't know how you can keep wandering around in it. You must be exhausted.'

'I'm kind of used to wearing heavy costumes, but yes, the day is starting to take its toll. I'm no spring chicken anymore, am I? I'll see the night through, but I'll be glad to get to bed, at the end of it.'

'I think we all will. It's been quite a day. Magical, and fabulous, and probably one of the best days of our lives, in fact. But it's been long, and I'm wiped out. I see you've taken your own towering shoes off now! Mine came off two hours ago. I've got my slippers on, would you believe?'

She and Mark would be heading away themselves in another hour or so. It was a long drive back to the Lake District tomorrow, and she knew he wanted to get an earlyish start, straight after breakfast.

When they got back to the hotel just over an hour later, she was surprised to find a beautifully gift-wrapped package on her pillow. When she unwrapped it, she found the most exquisite gold chain, with a small, solid gold heart-shaped pendant, with a diamond embedded in one corner, hanging from it. The back of it had been engraved.

Love, friendship and fortune favour the brave.

The little card inside the box had a heart on the front of it too. Inside, the handwritten message was simple.

With love and thanks, M.

Adie showed it to Mark, and he smiled, softly. 'That's lovely in't it? It's pretty special, this friendship. Means a lot to 'er, just as it does to you, lass.'

And it does. It means everything. True friendship, the kind that lasts a lifetime, is a rare and special kind of love. It deserves to be cherished and protected. I am blessed, a thousand times over, to have such an amazing woman as my best friend. Watching her take the biggest leap of faith of her life today was something I'll never forget.

All of a sudden, a mental picture popped into Adie's head. It was a vision of Miranda, in her glorious wedding dress, sitting behind the wheel of a go-kart, wearing a gold crash helmet with a crystal-studded tiara perched jauntily on top of it. Crazy, and unexpected, it made her giggle to herself.

Yes, indeed; Miranda Quirk had bravely embraced, with open arms, what was surely going to be a very interesting life with Maxwell James Kennedy the Third.

I can't wait to see where life takes her, now. It seems that two of my most treasured 'girls' Mand and Teresa, are going on some pretty wild rides.

If love, friendship, and fortune did indeed favour the brave, both 'girls' seemed destined to have plenty of all three.

One Year Later

The alarm went off, next to Chris' head. It told him it was ten to four in the morning, and he grunted and turned over. It took some effort, but he sat up, rubbed his eyes, and reached for his phone, in the forlorn hope that he'd got it wrong, and had a few more hours of kip to come, before Tezzie's phone call crashed through his morning like a freight train.

Of course, it wasn't the case. His phone clock told him that he had precisely eight and a half minutes left, to get up, let Misty out for a wee and have one himself, make a quick cup of coffee, get the dog back in, and head back to bed before she rang him.

It was nearly seven in the morning in Syria. Tezzie always wanted to talk to Chris before she left the hotel where she and her press colleagues were staying. They had breakfast at seven-fifteen, and they were on the road by half past, with their packed lunches made by the kitchen staff, headed for the front lines and battle zones. The ten-minute call she made to Chris was a brutal shock to the system every morning, but it was always a welcome relief to hear her voice, and he understood how important it was for her too, to touch base before she left the relative safety of the hotel.

He struggled a little, most days, with the notion that when they said goodbye there was no way of knowing if it might be for the last time. But he was getting better at managing that. Tezzie was pretty good at reassuring him that she was okay, and she always sounded positive and upbeat, in spite of every awful thing she faced out there, every single day.

He was usually more worried about her safety than she was but, as time went by and she gradually found her feet 'at the coal face,' she'd started sounding more confident and that made him feel a lot better. She admitted to sometimes feeling intimidated by her surroundings but, as she said, that was no bad thing. It encouraged vigilance, and that was a critical survival skill in the world's most humanly hostile environments.

She always said that she wasn't the brave one, in going out to a war zone. The brave ones were the people who lived daily, cheek by jowl, with the war that raged around them. They were the courageous ones; the women who protected their kids at any cost, even if it meant picking up guns or fighting with their bare hands. The people who were willing to act as covert reporters to help get news out. The ones who refused to be silenced. Ordinary people who scrabbled for hours through the rubble of a freshly bombed building, sometimes moving one brick at a time, to try and find survivors. Resource-deprived doctors, nurses and medics in overcrowded hospitals and makeshift clinics who tried, every hour of every day, to save lives with what little they had.

They were the *real* heroes of war. Everyone impacted was fighting it, in their own way. Tezzie described herself as just one small piece in a very large puzzle, but she knew how important it was, to highlight as many facets of a war-torn nation as she could.

Chris managed to get his and Misty's ablutions sorted, and get back into bed with his coffee before the phone rang. He had this morning routine down to a fine art, now, and as horrific as that 4am start always was, their 'coffee and convo' connection was still the best part of his day. He usually did manage to go back to sleep for a couple of hours, until the alarm went off again.

His phone rang and he pounced on it.

'To of the morning to you, Darcy! I'm dressed and ready to rock and roll, as usual.' Tezzie's voice was upbeat, and warm.

'Hey, Tez! Please come home. I'm almost ready to do a hands-and-knees beg-job, now. I'm starting to really miss you. Like, *majorly.* I'll be so glad when you get back next week. It will be a very lovely experience to sleep through the night again, for one thing, supposing my poor old brain and body remember how to do it.'

'Hang in there, babe. Four more sleeps, and I'll be there, even though it's only for a week.'

'Four sleeps? I was counting six …'

'No, we're coming back a couple of days early. Logistics. Don't ask; the details are as complicated as everything else around here, but I'm not asking any questions. I'm just taking it.'

'Well, that *is* good news so yeah, me too! Four sleeps it is, then, but that does mean I've got two less days to get this place cleaned up! You should see it, Tezzie; it's like twenty fat sweaty blokes have been living here, burping, and farting, vomiting in corners, and leaving their pizza crusts and beer cans everywhere. This place stinks so bad, even Misty has left home.'

Tezzie laughed down the phone. 'Yeah, you slob. Get the bloody cleaners in, and tell them to gird their loins. I know what you can get like, after two weeks on your tod.'

'What's it like, where you are?'

'It's raining this morning, but its set to clear. Oh, I wish you could see this place, Chris! I'll show you on the map, when I get back, and I have some nice photos to show you, as well as the usual rough ones. But let's just say that when the dawn breaks here, the gorgeousness of this place brings tears to my eyes. This is such a beautiful country! I know warmongers don't give a toss about the backdrop or the stage for their battles, but I do struggle to see how somewhere as beautiful as this can end up in such a mess of human destruction.'

'Yeah. A bombed-out city isn't much of a monument for someone to be well remembered by, is it?'

'Ah, they don't care about how they're remembered, Chris. Giving something positive to the world is not on the radar for the twisted-thinking bastards we're dealing with out here.'

Well, stay safe, as ever. I love you, and I'll be at Manchester airport to pick you up, just send me the details.'

After she clicked off, Chris decided he could use a second coffee. This didn't feel like one of those mornings where he would go back to sleep. He toyed with the idea of waiting until a respectable hour, and calling Stuart to see if he could have the morning off. He did sometimes have that luxury, and this might a good day to choose, because a pair of semi-detached cottages they were working on in Cockermouth was going pretty slowly, thanks to some problems with the roof.

He decided he could spend some time on the phone, arranging to get the cleaners in early, have a nice bouquet of flowers delivered in time for Tezzie's arrival, and book a decent restaurant and take her out to dinner. He wanted to make a real effort for her, and spend the most time he could with her, in the precious week they'd have together before he went off on a pretty amazing adventure of his own!

Chris would be shipping out to Antarctica in just over a week. Finally, he was going to realise his long-cherished dream of climbing Vinson Massif. He and Marcus were flying to Chile, and then on to Antarctica's Union Glacier, where they'd take the short flight from there to Vinson Base Camp at the foot of the Branscomb Glacier in the Ellsworth Mountains. They would only be six hundred miles or so from the South Pole. The plan was to be out there for three weeks, doing Vinson, the dormant volcano Sidley, and any other peaks in the area that there may be time for, after that. It was, to many mountaineers, the trip of a lifetime.

It was going to be Chris' first climb, after Daisy's death, and he had very mixed feelings about it. On the one hand, he was super-excited. This particular dream had been a long time coming together, and being down on the ice with Marcus, and their guides, and exploring at least a little of the vast Antarctic region, was probably one of the most thrilling things he'd ever planned. It was certainly the most expensive, by a country mile, and not something he could ever realistically have done for a very long time – if ever – without Daisy's insurance money.

But he was nervous too; far more so than he'd ever been in his life before. Vinson wasn't a technically difficult mountain to climb, but the conditions for scaling that and Sidley, and any other peaks they might have chance to do could be challenging. Whatever they could achieve would depend on the weather and other conditions, and it would also depend on their level of fitness. It had been two years since his last climb, and he hadn't been in the best physical shape of his life when Marcus had floated the idea, and they'd made the decision to go.

He'd started preparing straight away; doing some long work-out sessions in the gym, to strengthen his leg, arm, back and shoulder muscles, and get himself as fit as he could possibly be before the trip started. Initially, he'd worked with a personal trainer for a few weeks; to get him back into stride, but he was now managing his fitness regime on his own. Physical strength was a major factor in feeling *emotionally* prepared too, for something like this. If you weren't in the best shape, and you knew it, it became something to worry about on the rock; especially if you met difficult conditions. Self-doubt could harm a climber's confidence, which needed to be at top level, every step of the way. Physical capability notwithstanding, Chris knew there was no way he could do a trip to Antarctica if he wasn't a hundred percent confident of his mental strength too.

Emotionally, he was preparing himself. He'd stared meditating, and working on mindfulness; being in the present, and focussing on what was around him and what he was doing. That was a learned skill he'd used well, throughout his climbing career, but Chris knew he needed to master it to a greater level now, to be able to experience the joyful moments that came with mountaineering and the all-important focus on staying safe.

He needed to complete his climbs without being plagued by the vision of Daisy in freefall down Mulhacén, and the terror and disbelief he'd felt as he'd watched it happen. If he couldn't keep that vision out of his head, and the emotions that went with it, he'd be wasting his time even going. Being scared or mentally focussed on the wrong things, even just mildly, could put a climber in real danger. He'd never had a problem being fully focussed before, but he knew that what had happened with Daisy had put him in a very different head space, and he couldn't let himself stay there. The meditation and mindfulness training were vital now, to his success. He didn't want to feel again, even for a moment, that horrible lurch in his gut when Marcus had called him and suggested going to Antarctica.

Saying yes had been terrifying. Even as he was agreeing to go, Chris felt a trembling, a fear he'd never experienced before. For two full nights, he'd paced the floor, trying to decide whether to call Marcus back and pull out. But something inside him knew, on a very deep level, that if he didn't follow through with this, it was highly likely that his mountaineering days would be over.

He needed to get back on the horse. It was as simple as that. Daisy would have wanted him to, and he wanted to for himself. He just hadn't been prepared for how the reality of it had made him feel.

Talking to Tezzie had settled him down a lot. She'd been excited for him. When he'd confessed that he was balking at the idea, she'd gently reminded him of how long he'd dreamed of doing Vinson Massif. She'd also pointed out that someone with his level of skill was simply wasting it if he *didn't* get back on the horse, and she'd asked him if he really wanted to hate himself forever, because she known as well as he did, that he would beat himself up for the rest of his life, if he didn't take the opportunity.

'The longer you leave it, the harder it will be to get back to your passion. Bite the bullet. Get mentally and physically fit, get your gear together, get whatever else you need that you don't already have, and get on the bloody plane.'

He hadn't asked her if she wanted to go with him, and experience the ice. It wasn't that he didn't want her to have that chance, but it felt a bit like deja'vu, planting a seed that might mean she felt some obligation. She said was happy to stay at home with Misty and their two rescued 'Flintstone' cats, Barney and Fred, and he was happy to accept that. She was ready for a break, and she told him the same thing he always told her; 'go and follow your dream, just come back in one piece, and your little family will be waiting when you do.'

Chris also knew that the time for going back to Mulhacén was finally coming, too. He planned to go as soon as he got back from Antarctica. It felt like the right time, to go back and 'talk' to Daisy from a place of new grounding and personal clarity. He was actually looking forward to that; the chance to tell her what was in his heart, knowing that he could do it in a good way for them both.

He looked around the bedroom, and smiled gently to himself. Buying Rydal House had been an unexpected opportunity, and he had Tezzie to thank for it. When the four houses were all finished, the estate agent valuations had come in as predicted. It did make more sense for Stuart and Fiona to sell them than try and rent them out.

They'd all been sitting in the pub; Fi, Stu, and the team, when Fi had announced the news, and tried not to cry in the process.

'I'm a bit sentimental about the 'sisters,' she'd sniffed. 'I know I shouldn't be, but it will be such a shame to let them go.'

Stuart had drawn her close and tenderly kissed the top of her head. 'But think of the magic you'll be able to make with the next lot we buy! We're creators and passers-off, with these. A means to an end. Chin up, sweetheart. I'm sure they will go to people who will cherish them.'

Tezzie had been there too, that night, and she'd audaciously asked Fi what the valuations were. Then she'd pushed a little more.

'Speaking of cherishing then, to quote Stuart's phrase, what's the lowest you'd let Rydal House go for, to a friend who's slaved his arse off getting it to Grade 'A' Gorgeous?' Her question had been light, and her smile had been warm, but Chris had known it was a weighted question. In spite of never having thought seriously about it, he'd suddenly very much wanted to know the answer himself!

He and Tezzie had sometimes joked (dreamed?) about what they'd ever do with four spare bedrooms, and kitchen, dining and reception rooms that were big enough to seat and feed the five thousand. It had only ever been a semi-humorous chat; he'd never expected buying one of the houses to ever be a *real* idea.

But then; 'along came Tezzie,' and she'd pushed Fi and Stu to say what they might be prepared to sell Rydal House for, at the lowest end of their range. They went outside to talk about it, and when they came back in, they told Chris that if he really wanted the house, he could have it at 15% off the agents' quoted price. It seemed like a *very* decent offer.

The size of the discount was so astonishing, it was almost laughable. It wasn't far shy of the entire budget for a house he once imagined being able to afford with Daisy, with a mortgage that would have been barely comfortable! But he was in the 'big leagues' now; collaborating with people who were talking and dealing in millions. Fi and Stu were set to triple their money at least, on the 'sisters,' and they said that taking the hit they'd proposed on Rydal House was something they were prepared to do – but only if Chris was prepared to extend his contract by another three years.

He couldn't stop grinning, and pinching himself, as he'd begged for the pen. He'd been more than happy to sign away the next three years of his life, and he'd waved aside the contract's clause that he'd need to buy his way out, to the tune of half of the discount, if he changed his mind before that time was up.

He knew it wouldn't happen. Fi was the honey of the century, and Stu was kind, considerate and insightful. The entire team was an absolute dream to work with. As jobs went, Chris was pretty sure it would be pretty hard to top what he was doing now. He had no plans to go anywhere else.

A few months after that, when the sale had officially gone through, Fi and Stuart had met him and Tezzie in the pub, ordered a bottle of bubbly, and handed over the keys. They'd asked what the plan was for living in such a cavernous house, as a childless couple. Chris and Tezzie had looked at one another and laughed.

'Lots of cats and dogs! Well, a few, anyway,' Tezzie proclaimed. 'And a proper library. And a sound-proof music and film room, where I can set up a bunch of screens and sound stuff and edit my work, and we can also relax and watch movies, or headbang without pissing off the neighbours.' She grinned cheekily, as she looked around the table at everyone.

'That still leaves two spare bedrooms, doesn't it? But that basically takes the place to an average three-bedroom house, and if someone comes to stay, like Chris's sister Suzanne and her family, or my brother Matty and his lot, both guest rooms will be needed.'

Chris had jumped in, then, explaining what they wanted to do with the kitchen. 'We've decided we need a central island, and we also want a full wall of custom-made shelves.'

Tezzie was determined to have an Aga, like her mother's. 'I have no idea how to work one, but Mum will set me straight on that. I'm going for one the same size as hers, but in red, as a nod to Teapot Cottage. That place is so amazing, I just have to have a piece of it here, even if it's only a replica.'

Chris had agreed with that too. 'That little cottage actually pulled us together. I'm convinced of it. Random coincidences like us meeting there, after first meeting at the other side of the world, are just too freaky to ignore. Adie says there's no such thing as coincidence, and I have to say I'm starting to believe her, as mad as that sounds.'

Fiona had laughed at him, then. 'It doesn't sound the slightest bit mad! Don't forget that Stu and I met there too, in another random moment of weirdness! That sweet little cottage has a lot to answer for, doesn't it?'

Furnishing the big house was still something of a work in progress for Chris and Tezzie. They'd needed a lot of stuff. The furniture Chris had taken there from his flat in Derby had seen better days, and there hadn't been much of it. Tezzie had lived in a furnished flat, so she had nothing of note to contribute. They'd started picking up random things at antique markets, second hand shops, and outlets, that they felt to be at least a *little* in keeping with the age of the place.

It hadn't taken them long to learn that not all Victorian furniture was nice. They wanted stuff that looked more 'funky' than just hopelessly ugly or outdated, but that meant they had to be patient. It would still be some time yet before they had everything they really wanted.

On a weekend when Tezzie had been in Torley, she and Chris had gone into Carla Walton-Holloway's restored furniture shop in the town, to see if she might have anything suitable for their new home.

Carla had been working on a huge, twelve-foot mahogany dining table, at the time. It hadn't been finished, when they'd seen it in her workshop, through the open door. It had very simple but beautiful turned legs, with little wheels on the bottom. It had four leaves in total, and extended to seat at least ten people.

Tezzie had been beside herself. 'It's an absolute stonker, Chris, but it would look *so* cool in the house! It's old, but it's gorgeous!'

The table had been ridiculously expensive, in the end, but once they'd seen it, they'd decided that they simply had to have it. Carla finished it for them and Chris collected it in his van. He'd commissioned a local cabinetmaker to make ten gorgeous chairs to match it, but with a slightly modern twist. Even with all that, it hadn't looked too big in the dining room.

Chris and Tezzie had picked up a couple of other nice pieces of period furniture from Carla's, too. She regularly acquired old sideboards, chairs, and other items that were in dire need of renovation, and she lovingly worked on them to turn them into extraordinary pieces. Chris had been thrilled with a huge, mirrored wardrobe and a matching chest of drawers and bedside cabinets. They'd also been quite expensive, but they were perfect for one of the guest rooms. Carla had done an amazing job of restoring them, with a lovely patinaed finish in charcoal grey and gold, with funky gold matching door and drawer handles. They were old, but not 'old-fashioned.' They looked stunning.

When Chris had gone to pay for and collect them, he'd been astonished to find that the bill had already been settled. As Carla's husband Dave was loading them into his van, Carla had silently handed Chris a card, with a smirk and what he'd come to learn was a 'trademark' raise of her eyebrows.

It had been a housewarming card, from Adie and Mark, saying they hoped Chris and Tezzie would enjoy their gift of the wardrobe, drawers, and cabinets. Adie had written a P.S. saying 'I wanted these! Trust Teresa to get in first!' and she'd followed it with a smiley face. Chris hadn't know whether to laugh or cry. Such generosity, it had left him speechless.

'Clearly they don't like you much,' Carla had smirked, as he'd left the shop.

Chris couldn't stop pinching himself about being a bona fide homeowner! Not only that, he and Tezzie had bought the kind of house that would be a 'forever' home. They wouldn't need to climb the property ladder, to try and improve their lot. They already had an incredible house, for a smaller mortgage that most people their age had for something far less spectacular. And there was no doubt about it; Rydal House and her 'sisters' *were* spectacular! They'd been built in 1868, so they were more than a hundred and fifty years old.

Chris had put down a hefty deposit, and Tezzie had contributed a chunk too from recent savings, bolstered by an interest free loan from her father, which he'd managed to swing, before he'd tied up what he could in a family trust, before his company had had its assets frozen when his divorce got underway. There was no rush to pay the money back, in fact Bryan Bostock had said he was prepared to wait until Rydal House had attained enough equity to cover the repayment. He'd hastened to add that Tezzie wasn't to worry about it for a long time, if ever.

That had gone some way to restoring their relationship. Bryan still had a ways to go in regaining Tezzie's trust, but the fact that he was willing to help her out counted for a lot. He'd given her brother Matty a similar amount, which meant that he could be mortgage free. As he'd said, at the time, if he was going down in flames financially, he could at least ensure that his kids got the best of what he could get for them before he hit the ground. His wife couldn't take what wasn't there.

The shameful fraudster Maggie Jenner had apparently been apprehended in Portugal. She had made a couple of silly mistakes in the process of defrauding a wealthy Englishman who had a house out there, and her history of fleecing a whole string of unsuspecting men had all come tumbling out. Boxed in by her own errors, she had decided to come clean, and was now preparing for a stint in prison. Most people were more than happy that she'd be broke when she eventually got out. There was still a substantial amount of money in her accounts when her 'assets' had been seized.

She hadn't shown a scrap of remorse towards any of the men she had targeted and lied to, and the transactions on her accounts showed that she did enjoy a very lavish lifestyle, courtesy of their money. By court order, she would have to pay back what she could to her victims. Bryan stood to get a little of his money back from her, but not much, and of course it wasn't going to stop his divorce. Sadly, that was inevitable, but there was some solace to be had in Jenner being apprehended, and at least a little justice meted out.

Chris had met Bryan Bostock a couple of times now. He seemed a decent enough bloke on the surface, and although his moral code left a lot to be desired, he did want to do what was right and fair for his kids. That mitigated some of his behaviour, in Chris' book. Tezzie was still quite ambivalent about her father, but she was grateful for his financial support, and she did make sure he knew it. A true reconciliation and a state of 'open-armed forgiveness' was probably never going to happen but, slowly but surely, the fence between dad and daughter was mending, at least to the point where they could both sit on it and have a conversation.

Everything had come together with surprising ease, in the end. After Chris and Tezzie had realised how much they meant to each other, they'd had a long conversation about what being together would mean. It hadn't taken long for them both to realise that they had something deep and meaningful – all the more so for having been built on a solid foundation of friendship, a mutual understanding of grief and how it felt to have your world torn apart, and the need for living life on the edge, for at least part of the time.

Tezzie was an interesting mix of practicality and sensitivity. Chris was often impressed by her pragmatic approach to things, but equally so by her capacity to understand the pain someone else might be feeling, and the level of compassion she felt towards the struggling. Her feelings for Ross Barker had run very deep, and even though it wasn't to be a lasting love, and she'd felt the loss of it keenly.

She and Chris had fallen in love with one another at roughly the same time and it had happened fast. Their response had been swift, too. Knowing how precious real love was, and how fragile life could be, they'd decided that they didn't want to waste a moment longer, dithering about how practical or sensible it might be, to start building a life with someone who could either fall off a mountain at the drop of a hat, or be bombed to oblivion in the course of doing their job.

None of that mattered, in the face of real love. Tezzie had cried when she'd admitted to Chris how she really felt about him. She'd come back from her first assignment in Ukraine, and the importance of confessing her true feelings had started to overshadow everything. It had been terrifying for her, to tell him how she felt, but she knew she absolutely had to. She explained that she couldn't have gone back to a war zone with something so distracting on her mind. But she said that it was better to be brave and lose, than to be safe and say nothing, and maybe lose anyway what you could have had if you *were* brave enough to declare yourself.

'I need to know exactly where I stand with you, Chris. I can't go back to work without knowing. But you have to be really honest, even if it's not what I want to hear. You understand, don't you?'

Chris had understood perfectly, and he'd explained his own feelings the best way he could.

'I want us to be together Tezzie. You've changed so much in me, just in this short time we've been together. I'm getting my mojo back. I'm not in a dark place anymore. I'm actually thinking about the future again, and whenever I think about it, it has *you* in it. In fact, if I'm honest, I can't see a future *without* you in it.

'So maybe we were meant to be, after running into one another in Tasmania, and then meeting again at Teapot Cottage. I mean, what are the chances? If that's not something that's meant to be, I dunno what is, Tez.'

He'd had tears in his own eyes, then. It had felt, at the time, like one of the bravest thing he'd ever done. Coming to terms with Daisy's death had been the biggest challenge of his life, but declaring his feelings for Tezzie hadn't fallen far short of it.

In that moment, he realised exactly how brave they had both been, in saying how they felt. It would have been so easy to have said nothing, for Tezzie to have gone away to the front lines again, and maybe never returned – to his life, or even at all – and he'd never have known how she really felt about him. And for her, too, to have gone back without saying anything, and always wondering if she should have. They had come so close to 'missing' having a true and lasting love with one another, through playing the 'safe' card. Instead, they'd both chosen to be brave, and now here they were, in love, planning a life together, and they'd even bought a house.

Again, Chris sent a silent thanks to Daisy, whose life insurance payouts had made it possible for him and Tezzie to buy their beautiful house. Without that money, he'd still be what he always was – a dreamer. The fact that he had set up home with a new woman sometimes felt a little strange, within the framework of his life, but not in an acute way. Deep in his heart, he knew that Daisy would have wanted him to be happy, and settled too, without financial pressure. Even if she couldn't have it for herself, she would never have begrudged someone else a chance at happiness. And she'd loved him, right up to the last breath. She'd loved him like fire. Of *course* she would want him to be happy!

Tezzie was a very different person from Daisy. She was more strong-minded, more focussed on getting what she wanted out of life, and she always spoke her mind. But she was kind too, and generous with what she had. She always made a real effort to help other people, just like Daisy had.

In their lovely music and film room, on the second floor, a very special item hung on the wall. Tezzie had commissioned a gold-plated disc of the old Beatles song, 'Here Comes the Sun.' She'd had it mounted into a specially designed frame, next to a picture of Daisy, looking at the camera and laughing her head off, like she always used to do. She'd presented it to Chris on the day she 'officially' moved in with him. She said it was a tangible reminder of

Daisy and her ethereal blessing, delivered through the incredibly wise and witchy Feen, that would always be with him.

It had been such a sensitive and kind thing for Tezzie to do, and it had brought a lump to Chris' throat. Daisy would always have a piece of his heart, and Tezzie knew that. She told him she though it would be a bit strange if he *hadn't* lost a piece of it forever, to someone he'd loved so much.

Daisy had been an extraordinary woman but, in her own way, Tezzie Bostock was too. She was strong, fearless, and adventurous. She understood what it felt like, to be taking a big new direction, and learning to trust yourself to go with it. She was brave, and she made Chris feel brave again too.

He'd had courage before, but it felt different now. He knew how it felt now, to worry about someone *else* out in the word taking chances. It made him realise that his passion for extreme climbing came at a cost to the people who loved him, just like Tezzie's new job of taking front-line pictures of war came at a cost to *him*.

Diasy had never once confided her worries about Chris' safety, but she'd had them. She had said, many times, that mountaineering wasn't her cup of tea. Chris realised now that it was her subtle way of admitting that it scared her. But she'd never actually *said* she was scared, because she knew that if she had, Chris would have started to question his own passion, and the impact it was having on her. She hadn't wanted to stop him from doing what he loved, so she kept quiet about how afraid she always was, when he walked out the door. The half-hysterical glee she always felt, on his return, was partly her expression of relief.

Tezzie was more open, and more accepting of the risks, because she was taking similar ones herself. But they were both very mindful of the impact on one another, of the things they'd chosen to do.

Chris liked the fact that Tezzie never held anything back – she always said what was on her mind. It encouraged him to do the same, and they had become very much in tune with one another, beyond the usual level of most cohabiting couples. Elements of their lives involved living on a razor's edge, and that made it all the more important to have a more profound resonance, and a deeper level of trust.

Chris' final week at Teapot Cottage last year, when he'd stayed and commuted to and from Keswick, had been the biggest turning point for him and Tezzie. They'd spent every evening together, sharing more of their past, their experiences, and their hopes and dreams. They'd finally slept together, but in the spare room, because Chris said he still felt the need to honour Daisy by not sleeping with another woman in the same bed as the one he'd slept in with her. Tezzie had understood completely, and he'd been grateful for that.

That night had been Chris' last at Teapot Cottage, and it had also been Tezzie's last at Ravensdown. She was heading back to London the following morning, to complete her final week of training before being sent immediately to Ukraine. Chris had dropped her off at the train station in Carlisle, and he'd felt a peculiar mix of fear, sadness, relief, and hope. It was a poignant moment, and he'd endorsed her sentiment, that heading off to war was a hell of a time to be falling in love. He'd laughed a little, and said that squaddies did it all the time, and a fairly high percentage did make it home. Tezzie just needed to make damn sure she was one of them.

He hadn't managed to see her again before she left for Ukraine, on that first assignment. That had been upsetting because he'd already known he was falling in love with her. He was desperate to hold her, and tightly, before she left. Frustratingly, schedules meant they couldn't make it work but once again she had touched him profoundly through music.

As she'd been getting on the plane she'd texted him a simple heart emoji, and a link to a Foo Fighters song about wheels. When he played it, and listened to lyrics that described second chances, finding faith again, and there being another chance for him to be happy, Chris understood what Tezzie was trying to say. One line talked about reaching the end of their beginning, and he suddenly felt very safe, in assuming what that meant; that she could see a future for them too. And they *had* been sinking – 'going down' – in their own separate ways before they met, caught in downward spirals of grief, with no real clue how to pull themselves up again. But they'd pulled one another out of those spirals, and they'd landed safely on terra firma again.

The song was so poignant, and he wasn't sure whether she knew (although he suspected she might) that it also talked about wheels touching ground. He took that as another message; that when they did, he could stop worrying, because she would be back.

When the full power of her message finally hit him, the tears poured down his face. He listened to the song, a dozen more times, until it became his favourite song in the world. And his tears were happy ones this time, that he had landed safely, after the unspeakable storm that had rocked his world. *His* wheels had touched ground, and there *was* another 'round' for him.

Again, so sensitive and caring of Tezzie, and he was learning that about her. Certain songs in life meant everything to her. She'd talked about 'growing up with' a handful of really significant ones from musicians who'd come to feel like friends who knew her, and were writing to or about her. Music was a powerful thing for her, as a way to express herself, and she was sharing that with Chris. He saw that as a beautiful, trusting thing.

It was taking him a while to get into her genre, though! Commercial rock-type music wasn't really his thing, but he knew how important it was to her. He spent a lot of time, while she was away, listening to bands like Pearl Jam, Foo-Fighters, Creed, Greta Van Fleet, and others she'd recommended. He was already familiar with a lot of the early stuff she listened to, 'classic' and timeless rock songs from before either of them were even born, but it was good stuff, some of it.

Chris had always enjoyed music, but only superficially. Tezzie was opening his mind to what he'd now started to appreciate as the formidable *power* of music, for expression and inspiration.

She talked often, about how much music resonated with her. He remembered her telling him about the first time she realised how powerful it could be to the world. She'd been listening to Boby Dylan's song about a black heavyweight boxer who'd been wrongly convicted of murder. The injustice of Reuben Carter's story, told through music, moved her to tears. 'I was just a teenager, when I heard that old song 'The Hurricane' for the first time. That was when I realised just what music can do, Chris. Carter was eventually acquitted, after Dylan released that song. It was instrumental in getting his case re-examined.'

She had also talked about an old protest anti-war song from the 1960's, by an artist called Barry McGuire, and said how it should be played more again, because it was as relevant today as it was decades ago. 'We should all be listening to that again, Chris. I wish they would re-release it. Sometimes if feels as if we *are* on the very eve of world annihilation!'

Chris loved Tezzie's passion for highlighting and railing against injustice. He wondered what she might go on to do later, if and when her days of photographing war-torn places and people ever drew to a close. Many war correspondents made it their lifelong career, but he wondered if she might one day hang up her video camera, and do something a little less risky. But, even if she did, he suspected that the kind of passion she had for righting social wrongs would never be put on the back burner, now that it was cooking. She might one day go into politics, or do something else that meant she was home a little more.

If she wanted to be in the field for her whole life, he knew he would support it. He did just quietly hope, however, that he'd one day have a lot less to worry about than whether she would come home intact or in a body bag. He knew she had the same feelings about him, and his recreational penchant for scaling the world's most famous and challenging mountains. They both understood that in order to have a life together, they each had to accept and manage a unique combination of emotional and practical risks. Being together meant being fully committed to making it work. They were, and things were going amazingly well, so far.

The choice between living a safe life or a brave life was a big one, especially when it involved someone else. On some levels, Chris thought it was probably *easier* when it involved two risk-takers, rather than just one who danced on the razor's edge while the other always stayed at home, fighting off the paralysis of fear. His and Tezzie's commitments to doing what they loved was a behaviour that most people thought was insane. Only those who really *understood* that kind of passion, and the risks that came with it, could live with it in any degree of comfort or acceptance. And, of course, understanding one another's profound need to have someone to come home to was critical too. No matter who you were, where you went, or what you did in life, anchors were important.

Tezzie had admitted that she was a little envious of Chris having the Antarctic experience. She suggested that maybe they could go together another time, on a cruise or something, and he was happy with that idea. He did want to see the world with her. There were places they both wanted or needed to go on their own, and that was fine. But there were plenty of places on both their lists that they'd happily visit together. Mexico, Alaska, Canada, to name a few. There were mountains in those places too, some of which he could possibly do while they visited together. Tezzie had already joked about having spa and health retreat days, or days when she ran around with her videocam, capturing no end of interesting things, while he was off clambering up a rock face somewhere. They were both confident of a happy, rich life of travelling, where they could share a lot but still enjoy themselves alone from time to time.

'I'd have no trouble sitting quietly in front of a roaring fire with a good book and a bottle of wine, in some fancy lodge, while you're scuttling up a mountain in Alaska. I'd happily do that for days.'

She'd said it more than once. It made Chris realise that with her blessing and understanding, he could do a lot more international climbing, and possible to places he'd never considered before. Being with Tezzie was opening up a whole new world of possibilities for feeding his passion. She suggested he use a go-pro camera on his Vinson Massif and Sidley climbs, and maybe she could interview him and Marcus after the event, for a short docufilm about mountaineering in Antarctica. He was considering it.

Another happy outcome for Chris, over the previous year, was his relationship with his sister Suzanne. It had become more important to them both, to strengthen their connection. He and Tezzie had recently travelled to Ireland to visit Suzanne and her family, and Chris was now a properly recognised and much-included Uncle to his nieces, Orla, and Bridget. They were due to come to the Lake District for the next Easter break, and Chris and Tezzie were looking forward to showing them around. Tezzie's time off was always hit and miss, especially if there were multiple hotspots that needed covering out in the hostile world, but she was hopeful that she'd be able to take a break.

Mercifully, Chris' father Jack and his horrible wife Fancee had stayed quiet. No requests for support had popped up but, as usual, there were never any birthday or Christmas greetings either. Chris and Suzanne had both worried needlessly, about being roped back into Jack's world. Nothing had changed one iota. The old man still wasn't even remotely interested in either of his children. They both figured that maybe Jack and Fancee had decided there wasn't much point in seeking support from them, since Jack would no doubt remember (in his lucid moments, at least) that he was the last person on earth that either of them really wanted to hear from. That ship had long-since sailed, with any obligation they might once have felt sitting squarely in the bottom of its hold.

On a perfectly ordinary, everyday morning, Chris had quietly experienced a random revelation about his father. He'd been out at the local playing fields, throwing a ball around for Misty, when a weird sensation, that he couldn't have explained if he'd tried, came over him. As he'd stood there on the grass, with the sun on his face and a light breeze blowing around him, he'd simply looked up at the surrounding fells and suddenly felt something *lift*, and gently leave him. In that moment, the emotional shackles that had bound him to the loveless Jack and the ruthless Fancee were gone. The demons had dissolved.

It was interesting, he thought now, how warmly he'd been welcomed into Tezzie's family. Daisy's parents, and her brother and sisters, hadn't been a close family at all. They'd been friendly enough, and there had never been any issues that made being around them awkward, but they'd never been welcoming, or *warm*, like Tezzie's lot.

Adie Raven was 'mumsy' and treated everyone she met with warmth and kindness. She and Mark were open and generous to a fault, with their time and other resources. They happily welcomed Chris into their family, and within just a few weeks, it was like he'd *always* been a part of it.

That was something he'd never had with Daisy, and probably never would have had. That would have been absolutely fine, of course, because you just got on with what you knew, and you couldn't really miss what you'd never had. But after reconnecting with his sister and her family, and becoming part of Tezzie's, there was so much more love around him now. He'd gone from having pretty much no one in his life, except Daisy, to being part of a big, boisterous bunch that accepted him – warts and all – in a way that even his own parents had never managed to do. Tezzie's family was a blended one, but they all seemed to get on pretty well. Chris hadn't met Ruth and Gina yet, but he'd heard enough about them to feel that when he did, they'd be as open and welcoming as everyone else had been.

Christmas promised to be a big and jolly affair. Adie's birthday was on Christmas Eve, and the whole family were going to Ravensdown for Christmas this year. It only happened every second year, so that her children could spend the 'off' year with their spouse's families, but this time Chris was going to have a proper 'happy-family' Christmas for the first time in his whole life. He and Tezzie would be staying at Ravensdown House for Christmas Eve and Christmas night. He'd been a bit disappointed about that because Teapot Cottage was so special, for so many reasons. He would have loved the chance to stay there again. But the cottage was booked for a full fortnight over Christmas and New Year, and unavailable to the family. Ravensdown would be chock-full for Christmas, with Adie's best friend Miranda and her husband Max joining in, and taking up the last guest room. Adie's very comfortable caravan, parked behind the main house, would serve as overflow accommodation for Matty, Marie and their kids.

As Tezzie had reminded him, however, Teapot Cottage was always going to be there, and they could go and stay in it any time it was free. It seemed a little bonkers, since they lived less than an hour away, but Tezzie felt the same way about the place. There would be plenty of chances for them to stay there again, and they would seize the first one that came. Nostalgia was a powerful thing that you sometimes just had to give in to.

Chris' phone pinged now, and he expected a message from Stuart, agreeing to his request for the morning off. Instead, it was a two-sentence message from Tezzie, with six heart emojis at either side of a link to a well-known Mark Knopfler song, about going home.

"Playing this one and counting the days till I come home to my hero. That's you, by the way."

He played the song, closed his eyes, and smiled softly, as something quietly wonderful swelled in his chest.

He figured Tezzie already knew that she was his hero too. And she probably also knew that while she would be counting the days to coming home, he would be counting the hours.

If you have enjoyed this book, or any of my others, I would
love it if you'd leave a review for me on Amazon or other
literary platforms.

Good reviews are the lifeblood of every author.

Thank you.

The Power of Notes and Spells
A Teapot Cottage Tale (#2)

Every woman dreams of finding the love of her life. But what do you do when yours brings baggage that can hurt you and your family?

Feen Raven is often described as more than just a little bit barmy. The young 'white witch' has finally found her soulmate, but old family wounds are opened again when she finds out who he's involved with.

Gavin Black is on an unhappy errand that forces him to reconnect with his estranged mother. All he wants is to claim what's his and go home again, without any complications.

Carla Walton can't let go of a grudge. After a lifetime of pushing everyone away, she is isolated, bitter, and blaming everyone else for her problems. She wants to be left alone so she can keep ignoring her demons.

But Teapot Cottage, with its mysterious ability to heal the broken-hearted, always has a more complicated agenda for people who don't want to rake up the past. Pretty soon, Gavin, Feen and Carla come to question everything they think they do and don't want in life.

Will love and a little bit of magic help them find a way forward? Or will old family fractures be too hard to heal?

Come to the Lake District, to a gentle place where a beautiful blend of music and magic can heal the hardest hearts.

A MORAL SWERVE

Nobody comes home expecting to find intruders -
But what would you do if you did?

Alison Jones is single, lives alone, and doesn't have a lot of self-awareness. But, after coming home to find burglars in her house, she does a terrible thing without thinking, and is forced to confront some ugly truths about herself.

Darren Davies is a petty thief, stuck in the revolving door between small-time crime and prison. After he makes the biggest mistake of his life, he is compelled to re-evaluate the path his life is taking, and deal with the demons that drive him.

When Darren and Alison's lives intersect, they each find themselves on a soul-searing journey, as they struggle to come to terms with the catastrophic impact of their acts and omissions. After stumbling through the wreckage, the future for them both becomes crystal clear, but it's not what either of them expected.

As one door opens and another slams shut, choices expand and diminish.

At the crossroads of Beginnings and Endings,
who decides to go where?

When It's Meant To Happen
A Teapot Cottage Tale (#3)

**Having a baby is something most women
dream of and plan for. But what does it mean if you can't
make it happen, no matter how hard you try?**

Debby Davies longs for a family of her own. She is desperate to have a baby with the husband she adores, but fruitless years of trying to conceive have left her feeling like a failure. It's starting to make her crazy, that she can't seem to achieve the one thing she always felt destined to do.

Darren Davies is at his wits' end with his wife. Her simmering resentment is changing her in ways that really scare him, and the horrible way her parents treat him is starting to take its toll. He's beginning to question whether their marriage can survive what feels like a never-ending series of storms.

As their doubts take hold, that their love can survive, they know they're in the last chance saloon. But Teapot Cottage, with its mystical ability to pour balm on battered souls, has plans for Debby and Darren that show them what's possible in ways they could never have imagined.

Can they stay together and face a very different future from the one they had planned, or will they find the challenges too great, and go their separate ways?

*Run away from home for a while! Come to the Lake District,
to a place where miracles can happen, with the help of
a little bit of magic!*

Ruin, Reins and Redemption
A Teapot Cottage Tale (#4)

Everyone makes mistakes, and some of them are hard to come back from. When you've taken someone else's life, and destroyed your family in the process, where do you begin, to pull things back together?

Stuart Thomson is a disgraced lawyer whose catastrophic error of judgement has all but ruined his life. By the time he leaves prison, after six years, he no longer has a career, a home or a marriage, and his troubled teenage daughter is barely speaking to him.

Meghan Thomson is almost fifteen. She's a mixed-up mess of anger and confusion, and she has no idea how she feels about anything at all, especially her father. When he books a holiday to the Lake District together, to reconnect, it's the last thing she really wants to do with a man she doesn't trust.

On holiday, father and daughter both struggle to understand each other. But Teapot Cottage, with its enigmatic way of turning troubled lives around, reveals an amazing opportunity they once could never have imagined. The future on offer means a whole new level of faith and commitment from them both, to make it happen.

Stuart and Meghan desperately need a new start. Can they trust themselves and each other enough to make it happen? Or does the heartbreak of the past make the leap of faith too tough?

In Torley town, in a very special cottage, lives are often transformed with the help of 'a little bit of love and magic.'

THICKER THAN WATER

Earth-shattering secrets will always come out, and the truth doesn't care about the cost.

Adie Bostock has finally found the baby she was forced to give up at fifteen – the one her husband and grown-up children don't know about – and she intends to keep her secrets. But, in the wake of a shocking crime, her tightly-woven web of deceit starts unravelling and she doesn't have a clue how to stop it.

Matty Bostock boosts his graduate income with sex work. Everything ticks along nicely in his smug, self-satisfied world, until one of his clients is murdered. With another refusing to give him the alibi he needs, he can't prove his innocence, and he faces going down for a crime he didn't commit.

Ruth Stenton has a happy, settled life with her wife Gina Giordano, and she is blissfully unaware of just how big a lie she's been living. When she discovers who has been hiding a terrible truth from her, and for how long, the impact is profound and far-reaching.

Ruth is forced to face demons she didn't know she had, and Gina has to find a way to help her. Adie can't protect one of her children without destroying another, and Matty must confront the consequences of the way he has chosen to live.

As moral dilemmas start to crush a family that's been buckled by betrayal, everyone has to decide; how much does 'blood' really matter, and what can or can't be forgiven?

THE STUFF YOU FAIL TO NOTICE
A Teapot Cottage Tale (#5)

You can live your whole life without knowing what's happening around you. But how can you stop the things you haven't even seen from blowing your world apart?

Minty Cartwright is peri-menopausal, and reeling from the discovery that her husband has been having an affair with her closest friend from childhood. She takes refuge at Teapot Cottage, a quiet holiday house in the Lake District, while she considers her next move.

Fiona Winterson hates herself with a passion she once never knew she could feel. Her selfishness has shattered the heart of the 'soulmate' she's known and loved all her life. But faced with the worst of circumstances, she discovers that she needs that woman's help.

With decades of love and trust destroyed, Minty and Fiona are thrown back together in a sea of shame, fury and fear. Both women are forced to reconsider the value of a friendship that has influenced their entire lives.

Will the mysterious, healing energy of Teapot Cottage help them rediscover what's important to them both? Or is it all to painful – and too late – to even try?

Come and join new friends in the Lake District, where shattered lives can be gently pulled back together, with the help of a little bit of magic!

www.ingramcontent.com/pod-product-compliance
Lightning Source LLC
Chambersburg PA
CBHW070738190726
48292CB00002B/322